TWISTED DARES

A.R. BRECK

No part of this book may be reproduced in any form or by any electronic or mechanical means, including information storage and retrieval systems, without permission in writing from the publisher, except by reviewers, who may quote brief passages in a review. The characters and events in this book are fictitious. Any similarity to real persons, living or dead, is coincidental and not intended by the author.

Copyright © 2022 by A.R. Breck. All rights reserved.
Cover design by TRC Designs
Editing by Nice Girl Naughty Edits
Proofreading by Rumi Khan

Twisted Dares contains mature themes that might make some readers uncomfortable. Foul language, criminal activity, drug use, physical and sexual abuse are included in this book. People with triggers should read with caution.

PLAYLIST

Creep by carolesdaughter
Cradles by Sub Urban
Outrun Myself by Jack Kays, Travis Barker
The Quiet Things That No One Ever Knows by Brand New
Black Dresses by The Spill Canvas
First Day of My Life by Bright Eyes
A Walk Through Hell by Say Anything
When The Party's Over by Billie Eilish
Copycat by Billie Eilish
Transatlanticism by Death Cab for Cutie
Strange Love by Halsey
Bad Guy by Billie Eilish
Gasoline by Halsey
Nothing Better by The Postal Service
Sign of the Times by Harry Styles
Ocean Eyes by Billie Eilish
Still Waiting by Sum 41
Helena by My Chemical Romance
Moments Passed by Dermot Kennedy
Hostage by Billie Eilish

"Sanity is a small box. Insanity is everything."
– **Charles Manson**

PROLOGUE

Have you ever felt the burning flame beneath your skin? The rush of heat that rolls through your veins, the thick, dark blood swirling and pumping from one part of your body to the next?

Dragging you into the darkness. Suffocating your very existence with just one spark, one simple flicker of madness.

How do you hold yourself in the light?

Your fingertips can grip the edge of sanity for dear life, but all it takes is one slip of a finger to drop over the edge, and you'll succumb to what you were always meant to become.

Manic.

I don't hear voices. I don't feel people around me that aren't really there. I'm not *lock me up in a straitjacket psycho*. No, I'm *come within a foot of me, and I'll rip your throat open with my bare hands.*

It's not something learned.

It's what I was born into. It runs in my blood. It beats in my heart.

The hate, the rage, the need to cause pain burns behind my eyes and aches in my fingertips to the point where I shut myself down because I know, without a doubt, if I don't, that there will be bloodshed around me.

TWISTED DARES

I can feel a piece of myself falling into the darkness every single day. I'm losing this battle of good versus evil. I'm beginning to find myself slipping away, and I try so damn hard to keep ahold of myself, but bit by bit, I'm crumbling, a shred of my humanity falling off the precipice to never be found.

I can never gain back an ounce of what I am losing.

What is gone, is lost.

I fear that in no time at all, I will no longer be Raven Abbott.

I'll only be what I am, and that is my fate.

Unfortunately, if fate is true, that means I'm soon to be my worst nightmare.

A killer.

chapter one
RAVEN

Wrapping the white tape around my knuckles, I pull tight, making sure it's not enough to cut off circulation, but enough that I have the support and protection I need. I clench my fingers into taut fists, my shortened nails jagged against my palms. Adrenaline hums through my veins. I'm ready.

I'm so damn ready.

I can hear the cheers down the hall as I sit in the makeshift locker room, the bench and metal lockers bolted to the floors and walls. Besides that, there's an open shower with no walls surrounding it, no curtain. This is it. This is the best I get. Fortunately, I'm the only girl down here. Which means I'm the only one that uses this locker room.

I've walked into the men's locker room next door only once. Shockingly and unshockingly, this is a retreat compared to that shithole.

This place is part of the unknown. Underground, but when people say *underground*, do they even know what it means? This place, *the Inferno*, is literally underneath the streets of Portland. It's unknown to almost everyone except the small group of the chosen. Those who know, *know*.

Those who don't, never will.

TWISTED DARES

The Inferno is a place where people come to die. Sometimes figuratively, sometimes literally. The fighters are much more than MMA fighters, boxers, martial arts weirdos, and the like. The chosen are those who take the ring of the Inferno with the understanding that death may be a consequence, or a reward. Whichever you choose it to be.

I've never killed, though that's from my own choosing, not because I don't have the ability. When I get between those frayed ropes and onto the mat stained with blood, I bring out the fighter, but hide the killer.

My friend slash trainer, Corgan, is the one that introduced me to the Inferno. For about a year now, I've been working out at a local gym. Corgan saw me exercising. I'm guessing he saw me fighting the demons that rage beneath my chest. Though I try to hide my darkness, I know my emotions are transparent. I'm shit at hiding the true me, and Corgan was able to see me for who I truly am. Someone who battles the devil inside her chest on a daily basis. He was instantly nice to me, giving me pointers and tips during my gym sessions. The tips turned into him training me. It's unconventional, but he's always stuck in my corner. He's always wanted to help, even though I always believed he could sense the toxic blood in my veins, it never once deterred him. He could see that I had a need beneath the surface. A need to inflict more than just a punch, but to spill blood.

He knew what I needed, and that was the Inferno. He introduced me to the owner, Reggie. A big, grizzly man standing at about six-seven with a beard and shaved head. He has tattoos along his skull that stretch ear to ear, flames and bones and so much death I wonder if it signifies the lives he has taken himself. I don't know. I don't ask.

Reggie is nice enough to me, though that wasn't the case at first. In the beginning, he was cold, didn't really care for me or the fact that I wanted to fight in his ring. Reggie fought with Corgan about my ability to fight, saying he was just giving me a death wish. He didn't realize my small, thin stature isn't a weakness. It's an agility, a quickness on my feet. It's a power that resides in my muscles and eagerly pumps a killer's blood. People underestimate me. I'm not a girl with beefy arms and a six-pack. Maybe I should be. I'm toned, just not overtly so.

I think during my first fight, Reggie said a prayer for me. In his mind, I'm sure he coordinated with the cleaners to carry my beaten corpse from the ring. He didn't believe in my ability or my darkness, finding the weakest, dumbest fucker to fight against me. I laid him on his back within minutes, blood running from his nose into his eye sockets while I stood behind him with barely a labored breath.

Every fight since, Reggie has given me fighters who I can fight without much effort. Granted, they are stronger than the first guy. I have sweat trailing down my temples by the time I'm finished, but I can still fight them much too easily.

Reggie doesn't believe I have it in me. That, or he's grown fond of me and wants to see me live another day. He picks my battles with precision. I'm only able to come here during the weekend, and I know Reggie uses those fights to pick the weakest fighters that come to the Inferno. He doesn't allow me to choose. He's particular, and there's no bending his rules.

Tonight, is another night where I'll be fighting someone who'll be flat on their ass. I'm the only girl that fights, and it infuriates the men who I knock down. But it doesn't mean they're weak, because they aren't. They're beefy, corded men who can kill with a snap of their wrists.

They just all underestimate me. The small girl with hair the color of dark chocolate, and eyes as blue as the Pacific Ocean. It enrages them that I can make them bleed and cause them pain.

They also don't know that I'm only seventeen.

No one does. Not Reggie, not Corgan. They all think I'm eighteen, and I'll keep it under wraps until I'm legally an adult, because on the chance they kick me out, I'll lose my shit.

The Inferno is the only thing that keeps my sanity. Walking in here is like shedding a pair of wet, itchy clothes. And that unbearable feeling immediately returns the moment I head home. I need the Inferno.

TWISTED DARES

I need it like air.

They allow minors in here. I've seen gangly, seventeen-year-old boys who are homeless and have beef to pick with everything that breathes. But I know the moment I say I'm a young, broken female, I'll be sent back home with a pat on the ass.

I'm startled from my thoughts when a knock sounds on the heavy door, and it slides open as Corgan pops his head through. He's an attractive man, always dressed in sweats and a hoodie. But he's in his forties and treats me more like a surrogate daughter than an attractive woman.

"You're up, Rave." He glances at me up and down, checking to make sure I'm ready before shutting the door without another word.

I set the tape down on the bench beside me, letting out a deep breath as I glance in the floor-to-ceiling mirror beside me. My black sports bra and tight spandex shorts mold to my body. My hair sits in a tightened ponytail on the top of my head, and the white tape is wrapped securely around my hands.

Nothing else.

No shoes for me, though it's not a requirement. Some wear shoes, some wear gripped socks. Others go barefoot like me. I need to be barefoot, because it's just an added weight on my body that I don't need.

Then there's the fact that some people can bring weapons. Some bring brass knuckles, some billy clubs. No guns, that's the only restriction of the Inferno. All other bets are off.

Win or lose, kill or be killed. Survival of the fittest. If you aren't checking any of those boxes, you don't belong here.

My hands go to my hair, and I tighten my ponytail once more before spinning around and opening the heavy door. It's dark down here, damp and cold. The tunnels beneath Portland have been reconstructed and maneuvered to become this crazy pit that people fight and fuck in.

It has an air to it that is both claustrophobic and euphoric.

The soles of my feet rub against damp gravel as I walk toward the noise, the thin, shallow tunnel growing wider as I get to the main area. There are no tables or bars or even fucking chairs. You stand, that's your only option.

I make my way through the darkened hall and into the light, the crowd going wild as they see me. My popularity has only grown in the last few months. I keep my eyes averted as I walk through the back of the room, feeling Corgan slap his hand on my shoulder. "Any questions?" he asks, already knowing I have none.

My body tenses as his hand hits my skin. Touch is something I cringe at. He knows this, but he's normal and touch to him is second nature. Touch to me is taboo, forbidden. It's akin to spiders crawling on my skin.

I detest it.

He's not bothered by it. He knows my inability to care about anyone except my cousin. She's the only person who can tear even an inch of emotion from me. Everyone else, even Corgan, don't matter. It doesn't mean I dislike him. I'd slit someone's throat if they were threatening him. I have this odd… fondness when it comes to Corgan, but it never goes further than that.

He's him, and I'm me.

I shake my head and step out of his hold. I don't want to know about my opponent. I don't care about his life story or whether or not he has a family or is homeless. I don't care. I'd rather go into it blind. Me against him. Let's keep the humanity outside of the Inferno. I know some people want to know every detail. Height, weight, stats, where the fuck he was born and what time. I don't want to know. Not one detail.

Ducking underneath the rope, I push the top row up a bit so it doesn't snag on my hair. The rough mat of the ring is stained brown from attempting to clean the blood off so many times. It's just a discolored light gray and brown mat at this point.

I can hear my heart in my ears as exhilaration hits me. I've been waiting days for the next fight. Leaving my house is always a battle. Things are… rough. But I'm here, and I can finally be me again.

I pop my neck from side to side, listening to the never-ending crack. I hear my name shouted over and over again. Chanting. Cheering. They want to pump me up, but I drown out the voices and focus on the here and now.

I'm at the place I don't have to hide who I am. I can be me and not have to worry about judgment or fear of snapping. Blowing up and going wild on your opponent is welcomed here. They thrive on that shit. Out of here, though, I have to tuck my crazy in and pretend to be the sweet, shy Raven that my aunt and uncle want me to be.

My name echoes through the underground and I close my eyes, wanting to block it all out. I don't have a fighting name. No one does here. It's just a constant, *Raven, Raven,* shouted from the pit of their lungs.

The thump echoing beneath my feet alerts me of my opponent. I barely spare him a glance as I clench and unclench my knuckles. I can tell he's a big guy, just from his feet. I'm experienced and probably considered psychotic enough to tell his weight from his steps. I'm guessing he's somewhere around two hundred pounds, give or take a few burgers. He doesn't seem too tall, maybe around five-ten or something. I've had shorter. I've had taller.

There is no announcer. No bell. Nothing to alert us to the start of the fight. There are no rules, really. When the person's down, you can show humanity enough to quit, or you can keep going until your opponent takes their last breath.

I know the stakes. I know my risks by entering this ring time and time again. I might go against someone who is even more psychotic than me. But I've yet to lose a fight, so I'm counting my fucking stars.

As the screaming settles, I finally glance up, seeing a man with short hair and a five o'clock shadow. He has a snarly face and a ripped stomach. Tattoos line his left arm and his right leg, tribal lines and swirls that look so chaotic they make me dizzy.

He clenches his jaw, and I know he isn't happy to be fighting a girl. He can't be bothered, because if he is he'll be a shitty fight. I've had enough of those. They refuse to throw a punch, which only makes me angrier. Just fucking fight. That's why you're here.

People are such damn pussies.

He lifts his hands, his own fingers wrapped and ready for battle. I lift mine too, and that's the silent go-ahead. The imaginary bell rings in my ears, and we're off.

He bounces to his feet, sliding to the left of the ring. I walk to the right, my legs crossing over the other as I step back and forth. I'm less acting and more ready to just hit him in the face. He doesn't want to step forward, though, from the way he bounces from foot to foot.

We do this dance, until he finally steps forward. One shuffle of his left leg and his weakness shows. His right arm bows a bit, ready to swing with his left. I bring my leg up, kicking him in the spleen. He lets out a low *oomph*, curling over for only a moment. I step forward, punching him directly in his corded neck. I watch his bowed head freeze, his eyes blazing up to mine.

He's angry now.

He stands to his full height, towering over my five-two frame. He hits me in the chest, and I swear if I were a normal person, my entire body would've shattered. It'll leave a bruise, but bruises heal. I'm fine with that.

He steps toward me quickly, ready to get me down for the count. I expect it, though, and dodge out of the way, slinking beneath his arm and coming up behind him. His back heaves with frustration, and I hit him in the kidneys and kick him behind the knees, making his legs buckle. He falls to his knees and is ready to get up again instantly, but I jump on his back. My arm cinches around his neck, and I pull tight, cutting off his oxygen.

His arm swings back, hitting me in the side of the head. It only makes me tighten my hold around his neck. This is the hardest part. The line between cutting off their circulation to make them pass out and just outright killing them. I could do either. I could do both.

I choose life for him today.

I close in on the pressure point, and his hits to my head jar me, but become softer as he goes lightheaded. He goes up again to hit me, but his hand pauses midway, falling to his side as he loses his fight. He drops forward, and my hands shoot out in front of me to catch my fall.

TWISTED DARES

The crowd goes insane. I don't give them a glance or an ounce of appreciation as I roll off him, getting on my hands and knees and shaking my head clear. Fucker could've given me a concussion from his beefy fists, but I don't feel any of the signs, at least not yet, so I think I'm good.

I stand up, heading toward the back of the ring as my opponent begins to stir. He knows his fight is over, and I can feel the vibration as his feet walk in the opposite direction.

Corgan is there to meet me with a bottled water. I rip it from his hands, uncapping the top and swallowing down half of it.

"You did fucking great, Raven! Your hits are on point!"

I nod, giving him a small smile, only because he's the one that taught me everything I need to know.

"Thanks, Corgan. I appreciate it."

"I'll see you at the gym?" He waits patiently for my answer, and I give him a quick nod before heading back toward the lockers. Back to the silence and into the darkness.

I've had enough for the day.

Finally, I feel like me. But it's only temporary. The moment I put my clothes back on, slipping back into Raven Abbott in her respectable outfit and attitude, I'll once again feel suffocated and so fucking un-me.

The twenty-minute drive home shouldn't be such a dreadful drive. But it is. Each mile that passes from the city to the woods is excruciating. Every turn I take, I leave a little bit of me behind. I leave the real me in the locker room and smooth my face over, becoming an imposter that I'm coming to hate. The only reason I decide to keep going back to the place that brings me the most displeasure is for my cousin.

Aria.

She's what keeps me going. In the world that has screwed me over at every turn, it's my cousin that keeps a thread of me in the light.

She *is* my light.

She is the only thing that keeps me from losing it completely. She's only a few months younger than me, just about to turn seventeen. She looks up to me while also being my best friend. I tell her I'm the last person she should treat as a role model. I'm everything she should fight against. Look at me and know this is who you shouldn't be. Strive to fight against the grain.

But she doesn't see it. She doesn't see any darkness in the light. She doesn't see the evil in my eyes or the venom in my heart. I love her for it, but I also hate her for it.

I don't want her to be anything like me.

Her parents, on the other hand, I know they'd do everything in their power to keep me locked in the basement. Seclude me from the world and pray for me day and night. They fight against the inevitable. They pretend I am one of them. They place the shutters over their eyes and act like they can save me from what I'm to become.

They don't know it's too late. The day I was born was the day I became cursed. I am what I am.

There's no stopping it, no matter how hard they wish the opposite.

Up until this year, Aria's parents have kept us homeschooled. It wasn't until the pastor at church spoke about this school that Aria's parents began to think social interaction might help *steer us closer to God.*

I've never been to school. Even before *here,* I was secluded at home, left to my own resources and finding my own way. I never had communication with kids my own age. I only spoke with my teachers. So, when I moved in with my aunt and uncle, it wasn't any different for me.

But now, the sudden move to an actual school has my stomach in knots. It's not just any school, either. It's a private school without actually being private. I've looked it up. It's prestigious. Highly recommended. The only reason we're able to go here is because the church my aunt and uncle work at, work directly with the school, and we were to get some scholarship. Fully paid. No tuition. Which, I suppose if there was, we wouldn't be going here. They wouldn't be able to afford it.

I'm... nervous. It's something I should be excited about, but I'm not. Not at all. The seclusion over the years has made me grow antisocial. Too many people and me do not mix. When I'm in the ring, I'm able to block it out. Once I'm out of the ring, I flee.

I don't know how I'll make it in a crowd of kids my age.

Blackridge Preparatory School.

I'm not ready. I'll never be ready. But I have to do it, because I won't leave Aria to go there by herself.

Pulling onto our street, I'm instantly covered in heavy trees as I make my way up our long driveway. We live in an older farmhouse between the forests and the city of Portland. It's filled with beauty and also an eerie vibe that you can't escape. Maybe it's just the house I live in, with the religious items decorating every inch. It feels like I'm watched twenty-four seven. Constantly shamed for who I am. Who I originate from.

I see all the lights on as I pull up to the house, the light blue siding looking gray in the night. My aunt's and uncle's vehicles sit next to the house on the graveled driveway, and Aria's Honda sits behind theirs. I pull in next to Aria's and switch my car off. Opening the center console, I grab the small crucifix chain sitting at the bottom.

I'm two different people.

I'm living a lie.

But it's the rules I have to abide by to not get punishment, and as long as Aria is with me, I won't abandon her.

I hop out and leave my duffel in the backseat. There's a bit of blood on my clothes from my opponent tonight, and I know Aunt Gloria would have a fit if she saw it.

They are extremely religious. A constant day and night of praying, church on Sundays, a house filled with crosses and Sister Marys. It's inescapable.

They homeschooled us because they believe public schools worship the devil.

I'm not allowed to listen to the radio at home because they think all stations worship the devil.

We have no magazines from stores because again, they think *People* and *Lifestyle* worship the devil.

It wasn't until their pastor said this specific school would lead us down a path of righteousness that they decided we could spread our wings.

It's all bullshit.

I zip up my sweatshirt to my neck, adjusting my jeans as I make my way into the house. The cross hanging around my neck is cold from sitting in the car all evening. Mandatory at home, though I slip it off the moment I leave.

How can you praise God when your body is made of sins?

Walking up the creaky wooden steps, I gently push through the door, wishing I could be silent, though I know they have sonic hearing. At least when it comes to me. I shouldn't have to walk on my tiptoes around people who should be considered my family. I shouldn't have to pretend to have a job at the library so I can go fight. They'd never allow it. Allowing me to do what I want is the same as giving me control.

Control is taboo in this home. Control equals me giving myself to the devil. They want to wind up the leash and keep me so tight I have not even an inch of slack. They enjoy my struggle.

The small stack of money I get from the Inferno gets divided. Half goes to my aunt and uncle, because it's not enough that they make my life hell, they have to take my earnings, as well. The other half goes to a secret spot in my room. Once I have enough money, I'll be free of them. I'll take Aria, and we'll finally be free.

Until then, I'll stay locked in my cage.

"You're late," Aunt Gloria says from her rocking chair in the living room. She has on a television show, though I think it's just a rerun of last Sunday's worship service. We don't have cable here. Only reruns and prerecorded approved showings allowed.

"Sorry, I lost track of time." I set my keys on the counter, heading through the kitchen that still smells like fresh buttered rolls from dinner.

"You missed your dinner. And you didn't answer your phone when I called." She shoves off the floor, rocking back and forth a bit. She has a roll of yarn in her hand and two needles, making the thousandth crocheted blanket in this house.

"I'm sorry." I wince, knowing she's more irritated than she's letting on.

She nods toward the stairway. "You should head upstairs and shower, say your prayers and get to bed. It's late."

I nod, glancing behind her at the large picture of Jesus on the cross. Bloody. It's morbid. Too visual and graphic to be on the walls, but they want us to have a reminder of what we have in life and why we live in the first place. It's been shoved in my brain since I stepped foot in here.

They could both be considered crazy. Crazier than I am on some accounts, and that's saying something. They used to force me to read a passage from the Bible to them before bed. Usually, you're read to before bed as a kid, but I had to memorize and quote different passages.

The very worst time was after I read a passage and my uncle told me, "God forgives your sins, but if you do not fully give yourself to God, you will go to Hell and Satan will drop the hottest water on your tongue for eternity."

Do you know what that does to a kid? The fear it instilled in my body? It's not something I'll ever forget. Just the thought makes chills break out along my spine.

"Go to bed, Raven. You already missed one prayer this evening, no use in missing another." She tsks, turning her head back to her worship, rocking as she continues making the most hideous blanket of mustard orange and burnt red.

It's atrocious.

I turn around, my hand gripping the worn wooden banister as I make my way upstairs.

At the landing, I glance to my left, seeing my aunt and uncle's room. Uncle Jerry kneels on his floor with his back to me, the straps from his suspenders stretching with each one of his breaths. His hands are folded on the navy comforter as he mumbles incoherently.

He's praying.

I can't make out his words, but he's deep in thought. I don't even think he realizes my entrance.

I slip past his room, not wanting to interrupt and not in the mood to deal with another person bitching to me about right versus wrong.

I keep walking and make it to Aria's room. A large *A* and a cross hang on her old wooden door. I shake my head.

She's brainwashed, just like the rest of them. I refuse to discuss my real beliefs with her for fear of her hating me. I think she knows how I feel, but her own parents who treat her so much differently than they do me love her wholeheartedly and teach her that God is her savior.

And they teach me that I am dirty and must be cleansed and pray and fucking kneel. They push, they push, *they fucking push* some more. Hammering it into my head time and time again.

I will never bend.

I will only pretend for their benefit. No, not their benefit. I do it for Aria.

I am what I am.

I lift my hand, my knuckles rapping gently on the door. The sound of footsteps quickly pad across the floor before the door swings open, revealing Aria in a nightgown. Her eyes widen when she sees me, her hand snapping out and grabbing onto my wrist, yanking me into her room and shutting the door quietly behind her.

"You are soooo late. I thought my mom was going to call the police or something."

I shake my head. "The fight went longer than I thought it would." Which is true. I can usually drop them in a quick minute. This guy had a good move or two.

"Did you win?" She sits on her bed, folding her legs and pulling her gown over her knees. She's anxious and excited, which makes me smile.

She might be brainwashed by her parents, but she's not totally gone. She loves to hear my sinful stories about fighting and being *naughty*, as she puts it. I'm sure the moment I walk out, she prays for her parents and wishes them good health, but at least she can show some excitement while I'm here.

"He was big and strong, but still no match for me." I smirk, reaching out and grabbing her hand to give it a squeeze. Oh, how I wish I could take her away from the evil of the world. But that also means protecting her from myself.

"I wish I could see you up there, sweaty and in your element. I bet you're fierce. Like a wolf or something. I bet you're frightening and beautiful."

I laugh out a puff of air. "I'm mean and gritty and don't give a shit about anyone around me. You wouldn't want to see me like that."

She leans in, nudging her shoulder against mine. "Doesn't matter to me. You love it, and I want to cheer you on."

I sigh, wishing life was different altogether. But I can't, and that makes me release her hand, glancing around her room. Her small, old-school desk has an opened Bible laying on top.

"My mom really was worried, you know? She cares about you, even if she doesn't act like it."

I stand up, the itchiness in my insides instantly niggling at me. The unease that settles in whenever I'm not at the Inferno. Fighting and causing pain to people is the only thing that keeps this emotion at bay. I can't control it, can't fight against it. I need it, and the moment I leave, the feeling comes back.

Sometimes it can stay tampered for a while.

Other times, it seems to hit me the moment I leave.

More than often lately, it's the latter.

My internal clock is running out of time, and I'm afraid that soon enough, I'll lose myself completely.

I'll snap.

"She might care about me, but she also thinks I'm the spawn of Satan."

She says nothing, and I know she won't. Because it's the truth.

"I'm going to go back tomorrow. After school," I say suddenly, knowing I can't wait until next weekend. Every day that goes by, I'm feeling more claustrophobic in this life. I feel like the walls are closing in, and soon, I won't even have an inch of freedom.

It's like myself as a whole is beginning to cease to exist.

"What? How? My mom will never allow it."

"Yeah, well, I'll sneak out. I don't know. I'll figure out something." I run my fingers through my hair, pulling the ponytail free.

"If she finds out… if they both find out." She shakes her head, her skin paling as she thinks about the consequences. She plays with the hem of her dress, nerves making her nibble on her lip. She's adorable, with her soft brown hair and hazel eyes. She looks like an angel in her white gown.

I sigh. "She'll have to get over it. It's just one extra night."

"I don't want her to make you go to the basement again," she whispers, her eyes averting toward the floor.

Oh, yes. The basement where I sit and pray for hours on end. Where they have a shrine-like display of Jesus Christ with so much fucking holy water, Bibles, crosses, and other sacred things that I feel I may burn alive in their presence.

Uncle Jerry has actually touched the cross to my skin one time to make sure I wasn't possessed. I'm guessing he expected my skin would burn.

I frown. "I'm not going down there again. I'm not thirteen anymore. If they try to force me, I'll just leave."

Aria's eyes instantly fill with tears. "You can't leave me!"

I wince, walking up to her and pressing one hand to the back of her head, the other over her lips, silencing her. She can't be too loud, otherwise her parents will come in and find a reason to pin another sin on me.

"I will never leave you, Aria. But you have to know I can't stay here, right? The moment I am able to, I'm out of here."

Her eyes fill with tears, running over her cheeks and onto my finger. I wipe her face and pull my hands off her. "But what about me? Will you take me with you?" she whimpers.

I cock my head to the side, never feeling like she's wanted to leave before. Her parents would never let her. I'll be lucky if they allow me to talk to her once I'm gone.

"Why would you want to go with me?" I whisper.

Her watery eyes narrow, strands of hair sticking to her damp temples. "You really don't think I'd want to stay here, do you? That I don't see how I'm shoved in a box with no room? I'm suffocating, Raven, just as much as you."

I glance at the Bible, feeling so fucking confused. "You've never seemed unhappy before."

Her hand lifts, and she grips the gold cross around her neck. "I love God, Raven. More than you can ever know. But I can love God and be free, can't I? What is the point of God giving his life for mine if I can't even have one?"

My heart twists, an uncomfortable knot that feels like it'll tear my entire body into two. "I can't just take you with me."

Her hands reach down and grip mine, not giving me an ounce of room. A zing of uncomfortableness hits me from the touch, but I clench my jaw, ignoring the burn. It's Aria. It's only Aria. "Don't leave me, Ravy. That's all I'm asking. You don't have to take me forever. Just don't leave me here where I'll rot away between Bible pages."

I can feel her panic fill the air, and I know she isn't far away from having a breakdown. I squeeze her hands. "I promise I won't abandon you, Aria."

Her eyes widen. "Really? You promise?"

I twist my lips into an awkward smile. "I promise."

She lets out a heavy breath, and I feel myself shredding. The high levels of emotion make me lose my grip. Another fingertip over the ledge. I'm holding on. For Aria, I'm holding on. But the fact that she sees me as her savior worries me.

    I may be able to protect her from those around me, but how will I be able to protect her from myself?

chapter two

RAVEN
Age Eight

The sound of humming and singing perks my ears. I glance up from my drawing, my depiction of a bird sitting in a tree looking more like a circle with a face sitting on a stick. I toss my green crayon onto the ground, sliding off the chair and making my way toward the window.

After dark, I'm to stay inside, says Mommy and Daddy. We have a nice dinner, sometimes with just us three and sometimes Daddy and Mommy invite their friends over. Tonight, they had guests, and it was very weird with everyone touching and giving long glances to each other. I wonder why they do that. Why sometimes Daddy leans over and gives their friend a kiss on the cheek.

I don't ask, because Daddy rarely gets mad, but when he does, his neck gets tight and strained and his face turns red. Then he disappears for a while, and I don't see him until he's happy again.

After dinner, Mommy and Daddy usually tell me to either play in my room or watch TV in the living room. It gets boring sometimes, and I wish their friends would have kids I could play with. We live in California, where there is supposed to be many people, but we live with nothing but sand and dirt around us, so I'm not sure where all these people sleep.

I make my way to the windowsill, my fingers pressing against the wood as I watch the big fire in the yard. Their friends sit around it, and my eyes widen when I see their friends rocking back and forth with their shirts off. Music crackles from the nearby radio. Daddy walks up to one of the women, touching her body like he does to Mommy. It makes an icky feeling swirl in my stomach, and my fingers clutch my peach-colored dress, wishing they wouldn't do these things. It doesn't feel normal. It doesn't feel right.

Daddy walks around her, his hands brushing the hair from her shoulder as he leans down and kisses her neck. The lady closes her eyes as she tilts her head to the side, and I watch as Daddy's hands circle around her chest, squeezing the skin and pulling on the pink part of her breasts.

My eyes go to Mommy, wondering if she's mad that he's touching her like that. It feels like it shouldn't be happening, mostly with Mommy there. But she's standing with the other lady, touching her body in the same way Daddy is.

What is going on?

Daddy steps away from the lady, walking to the bench that's made out of big tree logs. He reaches below it, and my mouth drops open when I see him pick up a knife. It's sharp and reflects off the moon. My teeth sink into my lower lip, wondering if I should look away, but knowing I won't be able to, no matter how hard I try.

Daddy walks up to the woman, who doesn't seem scared at all as she lifts her face and arms to the sky, rocking back and forth as they all sing and hum to music that isn't even there.

I watch as Daddy presses the tip of his knife against the woman's stomach, tracing it along her body. He moves between her breasts, up to her collarbone and down again. He moves behind her, his knife going up to her neck. Then he bends down, and I watch as his lips move as he whispers something in her ear.

Her eyes widen, like she's slightly scared but also understands. I watch as she closes her eyes, her voice going louder as she sings to the music.

TWISTED DARES

Daddy shoves the knife into her neck.

My eyes are locked onto her as a river of dark red runs down his arms and her naked body. She slumps forward, and he grabs onto her, continuing to rock back and forth to the music as she takes her last breath.

A small cry comes from the other woman, and my mom grabs onto her tight, her face turning mean for the first time ever. She pulls the woman's arms behind her back, holding her steady as Daddy drops the dead woman and walks over to her with a bloody blade.

He plunges it into the woman's stomach and pulls up. I can barely hear the sound, but I can feel it, pulling against her skin and muscle as he slices the knife through her skin, up between her breasts.

The woman's cries die down quickly as she slumps forward. My mom drops her, and I watch as my dad's hands go into the air, walking backward until he falls onto the log bench. My mom reaches down, pulling her dress over her head to reveal her naked body. She steps over the woman who is sputtering blood out of her mouth on the ground, my mom's dress dropping on top of her.

My dad unbuttons his jeans, pulling out his wiener that looks bigger than I've ever seen it, then my mom climbs on top of him and starts moving. I turn away, forgetting about my drawing altogether as my dinner twists in my stomach.

I walk to my bedroom in a daze, feeling like I don't know those people outside at all. Mommy and Daddy are the nicest people I've ever known. They don't ever get mad and always do the right thing.

Did they just kill someone?

I don't even change into pajamas as I pull my covers back, slipping between my sheets and rolling onto my tense side.

What did they just do? Why did they do that to those women?

My thoughts plague me all night, leaving me in a dreamless sleep that I can't escape from.

When I wake up the next morning, the bodies are gone and Mommy and

Daddy act like nothing ever happened. It makes me wonder, is this the first time, or has this been going on as long as I've been born?

And more than that, if they are evil people, does that mean I'm evil, too?

RAVEN

"I'm kind of excited, but what if everyone talks about us? Or what if the girls are mean? Oh goodness, my stomach hurts." Aria clutches her stomach, her purple backpack squeezed between her knees.

If anyone is mean to you, I'll kill them.

"I'm sure it'll be fine. People are bound to talk. We'll be the new kids." I ignore my own nerves, though I feel them. The first day of school ever for me and I'm seventeen. I feel almost like it's an out-of-body experience. Like I'm watching myself from above.

Aria sits in the passenger seat in her blue girlfriend jeans and floral t-shirt. She has on a pair of new Adidas that her mom bought her for school. I wasn't given the same benefits. I had to wear what I've already had, which is a pair of worn lace-up boots with black leggings and a cardigan.

Then there's the fact that we're going to some ritzy school in my Honda Civic that I know is going to look like a piece of trash next to these nice cars and SUVs. My aunt and uncle would never give me anything. Not like they even have much to give. While we're able to go to this nice school, they don't have much to their name. Their farmhouse has been in their family for generations and their church jobs don't give them much of a salary.

I am worried about my first day. I can put on my mask and pretend I don't give a shit, but the fact is, my mask is thin and cracked around the edges. My knee-jerk reaction is for my feelings to be so out of control that I snap.

I've never allowed it to get that far.

But it's coming closer. Like I'm walking a tightrope and one wrong move will send me plummeting over the edge.

"First days suck," Aria whines.

I bite my tongue as we turn off the highway. By the way of my GPS, we're only moments from school. Our electronic schedules on our phones show we only have our last period together. I won't be able to watch over her. I won't be able to protect her, and I think that's the worst of all.

"You'll be fine." I glance over at her. "But if someone fucks with you, tell me."

She nods. "If someone messes with me, I'll tell you." She winces. "What will you do?"

I want to laugh at the fact that she has never, in her sixteen years of life, sworn. Not even once.

"I'll make them never mess with you again."

She's about to say something when her eyes widen. Glancing toward her line of sight, I see the massive, two-story monstrosity that is Blackridge Preparatory School. The glass, floor-to-ceiling windows expanding throughout the front. The rest of the building is a creamy brick that looks so clean and sleek, I'm wondering if they have someone cleaning the entire building daily.

"Okay, now I'm seriously freaking out." She starts hyperventilating beside me.

I pull into the lot, my gray Honda Civic sticking out like a sore thumb next to the Mercedes and BMWs and fucking Maseratis. Who the hell lets their dumb-ass kid drive a Maserati?

I clench the steering wheel as I drive through the lot, feeling the eyes of all the students turning their heads, sneering, looking down on me like I'm less than them.

Their lives flash before my eyes. I imagine running them over with my little Honda, watching their red blood splatter against my gray, chipped paint. I imagine them screaming and apologizing and me laughing in their misery.

I'm simply cruel. The mania inside me grows with each day that passes. I wonder how much time I have before the crazy takes over completely.

I find a small spot in the back, pulling in and enjoying the moment, hidden between a massive pickup truck and a Denali. I sink into my seat, forgetting that Aria is sitting beside me, close to passing out, I'm sure.

Sooner than I'd like, I blink my eyes open, reaching behind my seat to grab my ratty, black backpack. "Let's go, Aria. Before people start huddling around my car to check out who the poor kids are."

She exhales a shaky breath, and I wish I could pluck the terror from her body. I want to erase it, snuff it out like burning ash and rub it into the dirt. She is so fragile, a glass doll that could easily break with just a knock off her feet. I want to build her up and watch her conquer the world.

Unfortunately, her parents have raised her to be weak and dependent on everyone around her, and it'll be up to me to teach her to be strong. I'll be her big sister. And until she can stand on her own two feet, I'll be the one to watch her and protect her like only I know how to do.

She apprehensively opens the door, grabbing her backpack and slipping from her seat. I step out, my face blank and my eyes cautious as I watch three girls standing over by a convertible. I don't know that much about cars unless I look at the letters on the back, but the cherry red, glossy paint and black rims make it look more expensive than I'll ever be able to afford.

The pavement is fresh, the white and yellow lines perfect and untarnished. I step my dirty boot over a white line, clenching my jaw as I glare at the girls. They look rich and snotty, as predicted, their designer shoes and purses paired with clothes that cost more than my entire wardrobe. The sun reflects off their flawlessly curled hair that lightly brushes their shoulders.

"Wow, they're pretty," Aria whispers as she comes to stand next to me.

The girls lean into each other. The blonde one in the center, clearly the one in charge of their little group, starts laughing as they stare at Aria. *At me.*

I narrow my eyes, allowing a part of my mania to show through. Their laughter dies down, and they straighten, giving us their backs as they walk away.

"They also don't look nice. Stay away from them," I say, nodding my head as I start walking toward the front of the school. The sky is clear today, the air crisp and not a cloud in the sky. The scent of the ocean and the pine trees mingle together in a combination of absolute serenity.

"What class do you have first again?" she asks as we approach the front steps.

I unlock my phone, going to my electronic schedule. "Calculus. Second floor."

She frowns. "I have choir. First floor."

"Don't worry about it. Our lockers are next to each other. I'll see you after every class."

She doesn't say anything, and I know she's moments from freaking out and calling her mom. I say nothing, walking through the front doors that are propped open. The large office sits to the left, with floor-to-ceiling windows separating us. Groups of people stand at their lockers. The cliques. The different styles of people. The artsy people, the jocks, the nerds, the punks.

I wonder where I fit into it all.

A group of jocks stand in a group, their red and black letterman jackets draped over their shoulders. One in the middle turns his head, his brown hair tossed messily to the side. His eyes catch mine. He looks me up and down, his smirk growing as his gaze travels back to my eyes. He nudges his friends, but before he can swagger up to me like I know he's about to, I avert my eyes from his, heading down the hall.

I can't. I can't deal with it. I have no room for guys or friends or anything in the middle. They'll only be distractions, and my sole focus needs to be Aria, and making it through this shit hell without killing anyone.

TWISTED DARES

Don't get me wrong, that guy was literally drop-dead gorgeous, but he also goes to this school, which means he's most likely an asshole, and not someone I'd be even remotely interested in.

I glance down at my phone, looking for my locker number. My eyes flit to the lockers, and I watch the numbers go up as we walk down the hall. I pause when I see mine, knowing that Aria's will be right next to it because of our last names.

We both do our combos, opening our empty lockers and shoving our backpacks inside.

"I don't know what I'm doing," Aria whispers, putting her books on the top shelf. "Do I bring all my books to one class? How long do I have to get from one class to another? Are there bathroom breaks? Should I go now?" I watch her face pale, and I feel so bad for her. I feel like I'm teetering on crazy myself, but she's barely hanging on, and I wish I could help her.

How can I, though? I can barely help myself.

"Aria, you're going to be fine," I mumble, keeping my face inside my locker. "Grab your book for your first hour. If you have questions, ask a teacher. Ask someone that looks nice. If anyone fucks with you, tell me. Tell me *right away*." I slam my locker closed.

She grabs her book and shuts her locker with a much softer click.

"Okay. Okay, I can do this." She takes a deep breath, and we both turn around.

My eyes fall to a group of guys, and I bite my tongue so my mouth doesn't drop to my chest.

My eyes land on one guy in particular. He has this dark aura surrounding him. I suppose all men seem dangerous, in a sense. But this guy, he's something else. So much *more*. He stands there, looking both angry and uninterested in the world as two guys talk to him. He's tall, well over six feet. Built but trim. A pair of black jeans covers his legs, and a black long-sleeve shirt stretches over his broad chest. Even from here, I can see the muscles that sit beneath the fabric. Rock hard. Solid.

The sleeves are rolled up just below his elbows, showing off black tattoos wrapped around his forearms. Swirls and skulls and what looks like powder and sharp teeth. It's a mash of too many different things that it's so fucking chaotic, but it's also the most beautiful art I've ever seen.

I've seen enough art on people at the Inferno, but I also know you can't get a tattoo unless you're eighteen, so how the hell is this guy covered in tatts?

His skin is both creamy and tanned, like his bloodline isn't from here. I trail my eyes up to his neck and across his sharp jawline. A black hoop loops around his nostril, as my leg starts shaking of its own accord. The muscle below his cheekbone clenches, and I swallow the pool of saliva filling my mouth as they drift up to his chocolate eyes, dark eyebrows, and his hair that looks so fucking thick and untamed as it sits in a wave on top of his head.

This man… who is this man?

He shoves off the locker he's propped against, dropping his eyes to the ground as he walks away. I watch the crowd part for him like the Great Sea. They don't even flinch; they don't look at him like he's evil. They look at him like he's a god, like he's the most important person on this planet.

My eyes stay on him until he turns the corner, and then he's gone, and I'm left feeling empty and confused, and even a little angry.

How is it someone I don't even know is able to leave a footprint on my soul when I've never even spoken a word to him?

"Raven?" Aria presses her fingers against my arm to get my attention, and I blink as I glance over at her, wondering how much time has passed. "I have to go to class."

I look around, seeing everyone quickly filtering into rooms and down the halls. I take a deep breath, giving Aria a nod. "You'll be fine. I'll see you after first class."

She gives me a nod back, though hers is much less certain. She is a scared kitten, but at some point, she has to walk on her own two feet.

"See you," she whispers as she walks off down the hall, and I can only hope she survives.

First class was uneventful. I could feel the stares as everyone observed the new girl, but the calculus work was piled on early, so much so that I was able to dig into my homework and not worry about the whispers around me.

Second hour was literature, which I actually didn't mind. The teachers are nice enough, though by the end of class the whispers have started to grate on me.

New girl. New girl.

What is wrong with her?

Why is she dressed like that?

Do you think she's here on a scholarship?

The questions are endless, and none of them are actually directed at me. It's like I'm invisible and they all want to talk about me behind my back. I don't confront any of them, because if they snap, I'll snap back. I keep to myself and internally prepare for the war I'll eventually start.

Now it's lunchtime, and I've been at my locker for five minutes waiting for Aria, and I haven't seen her yet. Each minute that passes makes me more and more nervous. Where is she? Is she okay?

Did someone hurt her?

I shove off the locker, stomping toward the first set of bathrooms. If someone is fucking hurting her, there will literally be blood spilt and I will paint *all* these walls red. I don't care if it's my first day or my thousandth day.

No one hurts my cousin.

I kick open each stall that is so polished I can see my reflection in the light door. This entire place is made of stone and marble. The type of materials that I've only ever seen in movies or TV shows. When I was informed I was going to school, I imagined the smell of body odor, but this place literally smells like expensive cologne and money.

I let out a small groan under my breath as I head toward her last class. It's upstairs, and I take two steps at a time as I make my way to the second level. The light filters in through the windows to the sitting area, and I walk into the pod where her class is, my legs pumping with adrenaline. I hear a snicker around the corner, and I speed up as I reach the library, seeing the seating area filled with the girls from the parking lot this morning.

And Aria.

"Aria," I bark, and she turns around, beaming when she sees me.

A quick glance at the girls tells me what I thought; they are indeed not being genuine with her. Though they must be acting like it by the look in Aria's eyes. "I was waiting for you downstairs."

"Oh! I'm so sorry." She presses her palms to her cheeks to control her blush. "This is Trina, Delanie, and Lorna. They were in my last class and wanted to hang out before lunch. I totally forgot. I'm sorry."

I rub my tongue along the roof of my mouth. "Uh-huh."

"Yes!" The blonde, the head *bitch*, leans forward, her manicured nails lacing together. "Aria was just telling us about the cute little farmhouse you guys live in. You have been homeschooled all these years? How tragic is that!"

Her two friends snicker quietly, and poor, naïve Aria, smiles.

"It hasn't been that bad. I was able to get most of my school done in only a couple of hours."

The brown-haired one on the end, I think her name is Delilah? Delores? Delanie? Yes, fucking *Delanie*, twirls a red lock around her finger. "Those are the cutest jeans. Where did you get them?"

I step in front of Aria, standing over the bitch, so she has to cock her head back at an uncomfortable angle. "Your bloody lip also looks cute."

Her eyes widen. "What?"

Crack.

My hand flies across her face, and everyone in the room gasps as Delanie brings her hand to her lip, split slightly in the corner.

"What the hell!"

"Oh, my fucking God."

"Raven! What are you doing?" Aria screams.

Strong arms come around me, and I'm pulled back. My entire body freezes as I'm pulled out of the library and down an empty hallway. It's not until we're away from everyone that I'm released, and I turn around, coming face-to-face with letterman jacket guy.

The cute guy who was giving me *a look.*

I sneer. "What the fuck are you doing?"

He chuckles. "Saving you from the bitchiest cunts in the school."

"I didn't ask to be saved." I brush off my arms, feeling his fingerprints lingering across my skin when I didn't ask them to even be there in the first place.

His chuckle dies off, but his smirk stays in place. "I was just trying to help. My name is Chad. You must be the new girl."

He's so fucking cute, but his cocky voice and the way he thinks he's my knight in shining armor makes me want to knock him out. "I'm Raven," I grit out, looking over his shoulder as Aria's head pops around the corner, her arms folded over her chest, her shoulders up to her ears.

She looks scared.

"Look, Charles, I have to go." I brush past him, but he reaches a hand out, cinching it around my wrist tightly. He gives me a little tug, and I punch my feet into the ground, whipping my head over my shoulder to glare at him. "What the *fuck* do you think you're doing?"

He releases me, putting his hands in the air. "My bad. It's just… when the prettiest girl I've ever seen comes walking into my school, I can't help but want to get to know her a little."

His school. "Sorry, Chet. I'm not interested."

His eyebrows furrow, and he looks a little put out. "It's Chad."

I frown. *Shit, I'm such a bitch.*

"I have to go. Thanks, but… I'm fine." I walk off, not giving him another moment to play savior or any other type of fairy tale he wants to enact. I don't need a protector or anything else when I have my own shit to deal with.

First thing in order. Aria.

Her eyes are watery, and I clench my fists all over again as I think about what those catty bitches were doing to her. Playing her.

Fucking preying on her.

"They better be gone," I growl.

She nods, sniffling.

I sigh, pulling her away from Chad or Chet and those bitches, straight into the closest bathroom.

She wipes her nose with her sleeve as she looks at me. "They seemed so nice. I'm sorry I didn't meet up with you. I just… I thought I was making friends with the popular girls."

I shake my head, feeling so damn angry and bad for her. "You can't trust these people, Aria. They aren't all good people. They aren't the people at church, or even close to that."

She looks at me, so sad and defeated. "I want to go home. I want to go back to being homeschooled."

I squeeze my eyes shut briefly, and then open them, reaching out and pulling her toward me. I wrap my arms around her, ignoring the uncomfortable burn on my skin from touching someone. "It'll be fine, Aria. We're here, and it doesn't look like we're going anywhere. Just… stay the fuck away from those girls. And when girls laugh, try to figure out if they're laughing *with you* or if they're laughing *at you*."

She sniffles against my chest. "I don't know what I'd do without you, Raven."

I don't even want to think about that.

"You'll never have to know. I'm here with you now." I release her, the instant coolness hitting my flesh. "Let's go and grab some food before lunch is over. I'm sure we're almost out of time."

She rubs at her stomach. "I don't have much of an appetite anymore."

TWISTED DARES

I walk toward the door, pulling it open and holding it for her. "Doesn't matter, you have to eat something." I find myself having to be a mother to her, in a sense. While we're less than twelve months apart in age, her life has been so sheltered. She has lived in a closed box while I feel like I've already lived a thousand lives.

We walk down the hall, and I'm glad I don't see anyone. It's just us, and for a moment, I can breathe.

"You really hit her hard," Aria says after a moment.

I glance over at her. I've never fought in front of her. She knows I'm a bottle of rage; I'm sure she can sense it on me, but I've never hurt anyone around her. I wonder if I scared her.

"She deserved it."

She takes a deep breath, a long one. "I don't want anyone else to get hurt. Because of me. And if it ends up getting you kicked out… I won't be able to do this without you."

Shit. I didn't think of that. If one of those bitches tattles on me and I'm kicked out of here and she is left here by herself? Well, that shit won't be good at all.

I shake my head. "Not going to happen."

She stops in her step, midway down the stairs. "Still… please don't. I don't want anyone else hurt. Mostly over me."

I will fight anyone for her. I will kill for her. I will literally fucking terrorize anyone that even tries to hurt her. Even a little. But I don't say any of that. I put on my face that I always have on around her. The one that leaves everything away from the surface, so I don't show my true colors.

Because they aren't good. They aren't even remotely sane.

"Okay. I won't."

She stares at me a moment, then continues down the stairs. I follow her, and we head to the cafeteria, which feels more like a restaurant buffet than anything else. We walk around, getting actual plates instead of the trays I assumed we would get. There are literal chefs dishing the food onto our plates. No benches or long tables to fit all the kids filling the room. There isn't any of that. There are a few tables and couches, and it looks like the rest of the people are outside in the lounge area. Only one large pane of glass separating us from the outside. It stretches from the floor to the ceiling, letting in every bit of natural light. The trees and forests and mountains surround us. It's a spectacular sight.

I grab my plate and gnaw on my lip as I wait for Aria to grab hers. I'm not sure where to sit, and a quick glance around the tables shows most of them filled. I feel awkward, and I don't want to be standing in the middle of the room with all eyes on me. With a glance at Aria, I mumble, "Let's go outside."

We head out into the crisp air, finding a small empty bench. There are more snickers and talking, but I grip my plate so tightly as we sit down, ignoring them. I don't have it in me to fight with anyone else. I can't do that to Aria. Not now.

I mean, like, fuck, I understand we're the new kids, but is it really necessary to talk about us this obnoxiously? Like we're a fucking disease or something.

I pour my ranch dressing over my posh salad, the lettuce crispier than I've ever tasted. I chew mindlessly, feeling Aria's tension from here as I glance out at the parking lot. My jaw pops, and I stop midchew as I see the guy from earlier.

No, not Charles.

The other one.

The one who left a footprint on my soul.

He sits in his car. Of course, it's a BMW. Black, shiny coat of paint with black rims. He's leaving. I don't know where he's going, but he's leaving, and I wonder what is so pressing that he has to leave in the middle of the day. Or maybe this is normal for him, and he just does what he wants, whenever he wants.

I wonder what his car smells like. Is it fresh leather? Is it cologne?

TWISTED DARES

He talks to someone, his arm bent out of his car window as one of the guys from earlier speaks to him. They look similar. Their skin color the same tan, a creamy but exotic shade. They don't look like they're having the friendliest conversation, and I watch as they bark at each other.

Are they brothers? Or cousins, like me and Aria?

"What're you looking at?" Aria asks, turning in her seat to look over her shoulder.

I drop my eyes to my salad, barely having eaten a bite.

What is wrong with me?

Am I fucking broken?

I don't care. I don't care about anything, yet this one stranger has a cord attached to something in me that is turning me into a puddle of confusion.

"Nothing. I'm not looking at anyone."

She squints, shielding her eyes with her hand along her brows as she scans the lot. "Are you looking at that guy you were looking at earlier?"

I reach out, grabbing her face and turning it toward her plate. "Stop, Aria. It's nothing, so stop asking questions about it."

She lifts her eyebrows. "Whatever you say."

I stab my fork into my salad, shoving another bite into my mouth. I can't help my eyes as they drift back to the parking lot, just as the guy standing near the car walks off, and the stranger in the BMW drives away, disappearing from sight.

Whoever he is, I hope I don't ever see him again. So I can forget this lost feeling in my chest.

But even as I say that, I'm really hoping I see him again. And again.

And again.

chapter four
RAVEN

"Gather hands," Aunt Gloria says, her wrinkled hand extended toward mine.

Aria and my uncle fold hands over each other's as we sit around the dinner table. Hesitantly, I lay my hand in my aunt's. Her cold fingers fold over mine, squeezing tighter than she should as she closes her eyes.

She tries to hurt me.

She wants to.

Her desire is to push the holy into me like it's a physical thing. Like if she could, she would open my chest, set purity inside, zip me back up, and send me on my way.

"Dear Lord, thank you for this food on our table and the roof over our house. Thank you for our health, dear Lord, and thank you for blessing us with all that is bestowed upon us. May we make you proud with all that we do, and we shall teach *those who are struggling* to find the path of God. Thank you, Lord, for you are our savior. *Amen.*" Her head gives a little nod, and her eyes crack open.

Mine never closed. My gaze never strayed from her face, or her voice as she punched the words on how *I'm struggling*. To what, to find the path of

God? She spits the words and repeats them, day after day.

I hear her. I've always heard her.

But it doesn't stop her from rubbing them into my face every chance she gets.

Finally, her eyes shift to mine, the grip on my hand still as tight as it was to begin with. Everyone else's hands have released, though Aunt Gloria still stares at me with such distaste and hate in her gaze it makes my stomach burn.

I pull my hand from hers, and it takes her a moment, but her cold fingers eventually loosen, making my hand snap back and almost knock my glass of water over.

"That hurt, you know," I mumble, questioning myself on how I haven't shoved my fork in her neck yet. These… visions, or desires, grow with every passing day. I want to keep myself sane. I don't want to lose whatever bits I have left of normalcy.

I also want to protect Aria, and even with her speaking the first bit of truth about how she doesn't want me to leave her, I know she still loves her mom. She'd never forgive me if I took her from her.

I love Aria, and because of that, I will protect her.

"Sometimes you have to endure pain to find righteousness." She looks at me like I should be thanking her for hurting me, though I never will. Never.

I think she speaks such words of holiness because she herself knows how wrong she is. She knows the path she walks down isn't one that brings herself to God. She walks the path of darkness, like me. But maybe she doesn't know that. Maybe because she is so fucking toxic, she doesn't even know what is righteous and what isn't anymore.

I don't reply to her, because her words don't deserve a response. I turn toward my plate; my ham and potatoes having gone cold. I lift my fork, spearing a chunk of ham and cutting a bite-sized piece. I pop it into my mouth, my eyes lifting to Aria's. She's already watching me, chewing a bite of potatoes as she stares at me in contemplation. She wonders what I'm thinking.

She doesn't want to know my thoughts. My thoughts would terrify her. She would no longer love me for me.

"Aria, how was your first day of school?" my uncle asks Aria. Neither of them care about whether my day was wonderful or a pile of shit.

Aria's eyes hook mine, and I know she's debating if she should mention the three bitches or keep them a secret. When her eyes drop from mine, I know she's decided to keep the incident to herself.

"It was a good day. I was nervous, but people are actually nice. I'm glad I have Raven there with me." She smiles as she takes another bite, and I know she believes every word she said.

"I think you'd do just fine either way, Aria. You are such a likeable person. I'm glad you had a good day. Maybe you could find some other friends to hang out with, so you aren't only hanging out with your cousin," Aunt Gloria says with a lift of her brow. Her cream and pink floral dress doesn't belong in this century, yet she wears it like every day is church day. Sunday. She's an imposter.

A monster in sheep's clothing.

I drop my hand to the chair beneath me, squeezing the cushioned fabric as hard as I can. It's that or strangle my aunt. This one seems the safer option.

What a fucking bitch.

Aria doesn't say a word, but I know she's hurt by the words. She looks up to me like I'm an idol or something, and I try to play the part as best as I can for her. I keep my darkness hidden from her. She doesn't need to be tainted.

By me.

She knows my plan for the night. She knows to cover for me. Aunt Gloria is always checking up on me. Making sure I'm not committing sins in her house. What would I do? This house is filled with nothing. I have no vices in here. I keep the monster inside me locked away until I'm far, far away from this house. I know Aunt Gloria and Uncle Jerry can see that part of me, at least a sliver of it.

I think sometimes she is hopeful she will catch me in the act of a sin. It's like if she sees the bad in me, maybe I will burn like a witch. She wants me to melt from the cross or my eyes to turn black like a possessed demon. She doesn't know that what's inside of me is much darker than a witch or a demon.

What's inside of me is *death*.

It's that death inside me that makes leaving tonight so important. To protect Aria, to protect myself. What scares me isn't the darkness inside me.

What scares me is how often the darkness is coming to light.

Maybe I should feel guilty for having Aria cover for me tonight, but I refuse to stick around and see the consequences if I don't fight. She agreed to distract her parents tonight. I haven't even let Reggie know I'm coming back tonight. Corgan, either. No one knows I'm coming, but they won't turn me away. I won't allow it.

I eat little because I can't fight on a full stomach. Instead, I cut everything into pieces, pushing it around my plate and taking a bite every so often. I let everyone else finish their food first, even standing up with them and doing the dishes. There's a fog in my head. A whooshing of water as I wait to get out of here. I patiently allow time to pass until it's an acceptable time for me to leave.

"Raven, you look kind of tired. Are you okay?" Bless Aria's heart, she can see my control slipping.

I smile at her, lowering my lids slightly. "I am pretty sleepy. Must have been the busy first day."

Aunt Gloria and Uncle Jerry give me a once-over. Looking to see if there's anything amiss. I wipe my hand on the dish towel. "I might just head up to bed, if that's all right?"

Aunt Gloria narrows her eyes. "Don't forget to say your prayers," she warns.

Like we didn't just pray less than thirty minutes ago? Okay.

Aria gives me a secretive smile, and I now realize how cooped up she really is. I bet she wants to live vicariously through me, be my sidekick, and watch me do all these sinful things. Although I want so badly to watch her spread her wings and be free, because no bird deserves to be strapped in a cage, she shouldn't have to be tainted by everything that I am.

I'd never allow it.

I slip up the stairs, the smell of ham lingering in the halls all the way to my room. Stepping inside, my eyes pass the cross sitting above my headboard, then drift down to the pink and rosy red floral quilt that covers my bed. Everything that isn't me sits in this room. I want the edge. I want the danger in life, a little bit of darkness and grittiness painted on my walls. The light, floral, holy lifestyle isn't me in the slightest.

The girly shit isn't me, either.

I walk to my bed, getting on my knees and digging my duffle out from underneath. I can usually get away by saying I'm working at the library, but both my aunt and uncle know I only work on the weekends. They don't allow me to take extra shifts. They know my schedule because they make a copy for themselves.

Tonight, a Monday, is not my night to work. I have no reason to leave, which means I'm not allowed to. But I can't stay here. I'm cooped up. My fight last night was not a relief like it usually is, which actually worries me a little bit. I feel like I'm losing time. Like the time in between fights is growing shorter, and soon I'll never be satiated after a fight.

What will I do then?

I unzip the bag, peeking inside and seeing my freshly cleaned black sports bra and shorts. Ones I found in the lost-and-found at the gym. They're brand new, and I know Aunt Gloria would never get them for me. That, and a chunk of my paycheck goes to my aunt and uncle. The only money I get to keep, I set aside. It's my secret stash, the money I'm saving for my grand escape. I have thousands saved up, but it still doesn't feel like enough.

I zip my bag up, grab a hoodie and my boots from my closet. Slipping my boots on my feet, I snatch the rest of the things on my bed and head for the window. Up on the second story, there aren't many easy ways to get down. But luckily, the old farmhouse has the roof sloping in so many different directions that if I shimmy my way, I can easily jump without getting hurt.

As I push my window up, the old wooden frame squeaks against the glass. I wince, glancing over my shoulder and expecting pounding feet to be rushing up the stairs.

No one comes, and I take that as my cue to get the fuck out of here. I toss my bag out, listening to the soft thud of it hitting the grass.

Well, time to go.

I shimmy out and turn around, shutting my window as gently as I can. I leave it opened a crack, just enough for me to wedge my fingers underneath to open it when I return.

With a deep breath, I spin around, crouching down and walking as quietly as I can across the roof. I keep my feet light, knowing that this house is old enough, the roof thin enough, they'll be able to hear my footsteps if my steps are too heavy. Or if my feet touch a particularly soft spot in the roof, I feel like I'd fall through straight into the second level.

I crouch down, beginning to slide my way down. The rough texture of the asphalt shingles against my hands scrapes my skin like sandpaper. My skin turns raw, and I clench my jaw in irritation and discomfort.

I can't have injured hands before a fight. *Fucking hell.*

I leap across from one end of the house to the other, becoming low enough that I can jump to the ground. Thankfully, I'm at the laundry room end of the house, and not the living room, where I'm sure they all are right now.

With a swallow, I jump, bending my knees as I land. My body swings forward, my palms slamming into the grass as I catch myself.

"Shit," I whisper, feeling like I was way too loud during my exit.

They don't rush out and chase me down with a crucifix in their hand, though, so I take that as the okay for me to get the hell out of here. I pull my keys from my pocket, swiping my bag off the ground and racing through the dark and to my car.

This is the worst part.

I might be able to get out of the house without them noticing. But will I be able to turn on my car and drive down our graveled driveway without them hearing me?

Swerving in between our cars, I make my way to the driver's side door and use the key instead of the fob to unlock it. My face scrunches as I open the door, jumping in as quickly as I can and shutting the door. I can't risk the overhead light to alert them of my escape. I press my hand over the light, waiting for it to turn off. The warmth heats my palm, and finally, after a few seconds, the car switches to darkness.

I toss my duffle into the passenger seat, and with shaky fingers, I take the cross necklace from my neck, and dump it in the center console.

I hold my breath as I shove the key into the ignition and *turn*. The car rumbles to life, and I can feel my skin dampen with sweat as I wait for them to come barreling out the front door.

They never do.

I pray that Aria just has them sidetracked enough, and they aren't watching me through the windows.

Without turning my headlights on, I shift into reverse and back out of the long driveway. It takes me too long, so damn long, but eventually, the house is blocked by the trees, and I floor it, reversing the rest of the way out.

The moment I make it onto the main drag, I let out a sigh of relief, switch on my headlights, and rev my engine.

My skin immediately prickles, and the rare smile quirks my lips. My blood starts pumping as I make my way toward the Inferno.

I needed this. So damn bad.

TWISTED DARES

Rolling up to the hole-in-the-wall bar, I park on the side of the street and grab my duffle, glancing around the empty alleyway as I make my way to the front door. This bar is a cover-up to the entrance of the Inferno. St. Mickey's used to be hopping back in the day, but now it's abandoned. The walls are barely standing, rot and neglect making the paint and wallpaper peel away, the beams and wood falling apart before my eyes. I don't care about any of it, nor do I pay attention to the state of decay the bar is in. The only interest I have is the door to the basement that leads me to the Inferno.

I pull the door open, stepping through the dusty storage room and making my way to the basement door. It's pitch black, and I switch on the flashlight on my phone as I head down the narrow stairs.

At the end of the hall, behind the empty shelves, is another door that leads to the sewer and tunnels beneath the city. I make my way there, opening the door and coming face-to-face with Barron.

The keeper of the Inferno. The one who allows you in or denies you access.

His eyes narrow when he sees me, his thick arms the size of my head tensing.

"Raven, you aren't supposed to be here tonight."

I tilt my chin up, refusing to be turned away. "I want to fight tonight."

He shakes his head. "You know Reggie only lets you fight on your scheduled nights. You aren't supposed to fight until next Friday."

Grinding my teeth together, I spit out, "I know that's what Reggie says. But people come and fight last minute all the time." I shift my bag over my shoulder. "I can do the same. Let me come in."

His eyes shift from mine. "I should really run this by Reggie first."

Stepping toward him, the top of my head only goes to his pecs. But I tilt my head back, looking at his meaty head that doesn't in any way look like it should be fucked with. "I'm coming through, Barron. I'll talk to Reggie myself."

I don't fuck around. My opponents know this, Corgan knows this,

Reggie knows this, and fuck, Barron knows this. I think they all know I'm a short fuse, and whatever lies inside me has never really been unleashed.

I don't think any of them really want to see it unleashed.

"If Reggie says you're out, you're leaving, Raven. No putting up a fight about this. It's for your own good." He steps aside, and I rush past him before he changes his mind. I really don't want to knock him on his ass tonight.

I lift my hand in a wave. "Yeah, yeah. It's always up to Reggie." It's really not, but I'll play this game if they want.

I live by my own rules. I get nervous when my aunt and uncle are concerned, but it's only because of Aria. I couldn't give two shits about them, but my cousin... that's where my nerves come from.

Everyone else? Poof, be fucking gone.

I raise my flashlight again, walking down the dark tunnels, the smell of water and mildew heavy in the air. I've seen rats and snakes and so many dead creatures down here in this creepy place, it should be enough to keep me away. But it doesn't. Nothing will ever keep me away from the Inferno.

I keep my eyes straight ahead until the glowing lights make it visible enough that I can turn my flashlight off.

The screaming roar of the crowd resonates in my chest. It makes my blood pump through my veins, and I can barely see straight as the thought of releasing this buildup of rage that seems to only be festering overtakes my senses.

I push through the door, the dim lights shining over my head. The heavy bass over the music shakes the lights above me, the rattling metal causing my teeth to grind against each other.

Cutting to the left, I'm not looking to talk to anyone as I head to the locker room. I'll find Reggie eventually, but I'd rather be ready to fight instead of him just finding me with my shit over my shoulder where he can just spin me the other way and shove me out the door.

I drop my duffle on the bench and yank my sweatshirt over my head. Unclasping my bra, I drop it to the ground, turning around to glance at myself in the mirror. My slim curves feel nonexistent. My small breasts seeming juvenile. Everything that I should love about my body doesn't exist. I don't love my body.

I don't love *me*.

My dark hair should be luscious. It should be shiny and make me feel like I'm sexy. Instead, it looks muddy, dull. I don't see the beauty that Aria says I hold. She tells me to become a model. To hitchhike down to Hollywood and become an actress.

Being famous is the last thing I want. The demons that are hiding should stay hidden, and I want nothing more than to keep them that way.

I turn around, grabbing my sports bra from my back and stretching it over my head. I slip my leggings from my legs, swapping them out for my pair of spandex shorts. They mold to my hips, the small definition of muscle on my legs accentuated as I stretch from left to right.

"You better be fucking decent!" Reggie's voice bellows as he slams open the locker room door.

I sigh as I sit down on the bench, pulling the tape from my bag and wrapping them around my hands. He walks up to me, standing above my head and creating a dark, angry shadow over me.

"What do you want, Reggie?" I mumble.

He scoffs, irritated as all hell. "What do I want? You aren't scheduled tonight, Raven. You aren't fighting."

I glance up at him for the first time, seeing his neck and cheeks fire red. His bald head even glows with his anger. A handsome man, though darkened with age and crime. He's slim and built well, someone who could probably still fight in the ring. But he decides to run it instead, watching blood be spilt on his property night after night. He's almost as dark as I am.

"I am. I need to fight tonight."

The line between his eyes accentuates. "Why? What the fuck happened?" The anger in his tone about my safety has developed slowly over time. He has this protectiveness over me that I never asked for. I don't need it.

I can take care of myself.

I shake my head. "It's nothing. I just need to get in the ring, is all."

He frowns. "Not tonight, Raven."

I chuck my tape to the ground, my half-wrapped wrists not nearly as tight as they should be. "I'm fucking fighting tonight. You let everyone else come and fight when they want. Why can't I?"

His mouth screws up in discomfort. I know exactly why he doesn't want me to fight tonight. Because I'm a fucking girl, and he handpicks every person out for me. The weak ones. The ones he knows I can conquer. I don't want the easy. I'm tired of easy.

Give me something good.

"Don't give me the bullshit. You don't want me fighting because you think I'll get my ass handed to me."

He groans, his hands going to his face. "Raven, some of these guys are killers. Like real killers. They'll see you in the ring and pick you apart by your tiny bones. Some of them are three times your size. I can't rightfully put you in the ring with them."

I grit my teeth, my fists clenching. I want to sock him in the fucking mug so damn bad right now. "How fucking dare you not treat me like everyone else. Because I'm a girl! You put me in the ring, and I lay every grown-ass man on their ass without even a split lip. *Don't fucking go there!*" My finger lifts, pointing directly at his face.

He grabs my finger, lowering my hand. "You aren't fighting tonight. Come back tomorrow and I'll fit you in."

I step back from him, sitting back on the bench and grabbing the tape. I continue my wrapping, ignoring him completely.

"Stop, Raven. Stop!" He goes to grab the tape, and I yank my hands out of his reach.

"I'm fighting," I growl, my rage burning so fiercely I feel feverish.

"The fighter tonight… it's *not fucking happening*!" he roars.

I feel ravenous for blood. I bare my teeth, ripping the tape that's finally tight around my knuckles. "Good. Give me the worst you've got."

He narrows his eyes. "You've got a death wish."

"I know my limits."

"You don't know him," he emphasizes.

I grab my bag, walking around him to shove it in a locker. "I don't want to, you know this. I don't want to know any details, ever. Let me get out there, work this shit out in my head, and I'll be on my way."

"Corgan will kill me if you die."

I smile. "Good thing I'm not dying, then."

He smiles, and I know he wants to slap me on the back or do something else that's really damn weird like he does to the other guys, but he knows I don't like to be touched.

I nod, and he walks out. I follow behind him, heading toward the grand ring in the center of the Inferno.

"Good luck," Reggie shouts to me before he turns left. I turn right, squeezing my hands into fists as the ring comes into view. I can feel everyone's eyes on me. They know I'm not supposed to be on tonight. Corgan says I have a crowd that comes specifically for me. I don't care about it, not really, anyway.

I'm not here for them. I'm here for me.

My hands grip the rough ropes around the ring, and I hop onto the mat. I stare at the bloodstains, some fresh and some old. My feet brush back and forth, my body wired and my mind steady.

I'm ready.

A roar starts in the crowd, enough of a scream to make my skin prickle. Whoever my opponent is seems to be popular. He's been here before, and from the sounds of it, he's good.

Really good.

I can feel the echo of his feet as he gets in the ring. I squeeze my hands, my knuckles cracking. I stretch out my arms, my neck, and wiggle my fingers.

This man in front of me, I can feel his dominance. I can feel his strength and his anger.

I can't deny the inkling of hesitation that burrows in my chest, but also the excitement of finally fighting someone who might actually be fair game.

Lifting my head, my eyes widen when I see the man in front of me.

It's him.

The man from school. The one who disappeared halfway through the day. The one who has been flitting in and out of my mind since this morning. He stares at me. For the first time, our eyes connect.

It feels like I'm on fire. It feels like my skin is singeing. My insides are electrified, and I can't look away.

Up close like this, he's like nothing I've ever seen. Dark hair, slightly wavy on the top. Not muddy like mine, but a shiny, almost inky-looking darkness that you only wish you could have. A dark chocolate filled with an onyx to create the most unique and divine color hair I've ever seen. His eyes are intense and glaring right at me. The brown murkiness in them is an endless pit, and my body feels like it trips as I sink into the darkness of them. His jaw is rigid, tensed, and the line from his cheek down to his chin is illuminated in the overcast light. His chest is bare, his ripped abdomen and pecs filled with an array of tattoos, falling over his shoulder and down his left arm. The peek of them I saw earlier was just a tease for the full piece of art.

His body is a madhouse. So much chaos that I don't know where to land my eyes on first. Black and gray carvings with the smallest details trail from the base of his neck and disappear beneath the waistband of his black shorts.

All I can focus on is the dog with the rabid teeth and black eyes, eating what looks to be the entire world expanding across his chest.

His thighs. Motherfucking hell, his thighs.

Tensed and toned, his shorts cut off just above his knees, showing off his muscles and dark hair trailing along his skin. His skin is tanned, and I once again wonder if he enjoys the sun or if he's from someplace other than gloomy Blackridge in Oregon.

This man takes my breath away, and I'll gladly allow my lungs to suffocate.

With no start time, it feels like it's just us. No bell to snap us into the present. No gunshot to make us step toward each other.

Him and me.

How alone I feel but filled completely by this man as he stares at me. By the look in his eyes, he's never seen me before. He never noticed me earlier, and why would he? I'm no one to him, when he seems like just about everything.

He bares his straight white teeth, disgusted as he looks me up and down. Like I'm the vermin living in the tunnels we walk in. Something that belongs in the trash. I can see his judgment, his disappointment that I'm a girl. He doesn't think I'm worthy enough to fight against him.

He thinks it'll be too easy.

I step toward him, and he lifts an eyebrow. The balls he thinks I have. He doesn't realize, metaphorically, they're probably twice the size of his.

I take another step toward him, to the right this time. His eyes follow my every move, but he doesn't take a step, barely shifts his body as he calculates me. He's talented, I can tell by the way he stands.

He's powerful.

I lift my hands to right below my chin, squeezing my fingers as I shift from foot to foot.

I want to hit him, but I have a feeling he's anticipating it.

I step back, allowing him some room as I redirect my steps.

"Get out of the ring before you hurt yourself." I shiver from his tone. Raspy. Manly. Gritty. Filled with an edge and danger that makes me want to hear it again.

Holy fucking hell, what is wrong with me?

I've never, and I mean *never*, felt like this before. No one has ever affected me as much as this stranger does.

"You look like a rabbit bouncing around the ring. What the fuck are you even doing?" he sneers, a malicious smirk lifting his lips when he sees my face flame red. "You can't even fight, can you? I bet you can't even throw a punch."

My nostrils flare, and my eyes literally burn with rage.

"I dare you to try. *I dare you.*"

I dare you.

"Fuck off," I growl, stepping toward him again.

"I'll break you," he taunts.

"You fucking wish." I take another step toward him, and another. Then I step back, acting like I'm retreating again, but leap forward, sticking my fist into his side. He doesn't budge, barely moves as my fist connects with steel.

A pant starts low in my chest, fear finally starting to stick to me. What is this man, a fucking robot? I know I hit hard. I train to fucking annihilate everyone in my path. Even Corgan flinches from my punches.

What the hell is wrong with this guy?

I move around him, waiting for him to come after me, but he never does. "Hit me."

He stares at me, his eyes dead. Blank. Washed away of all emotion.

"Fucking fight me. Or are you too much of a pussy to fight a girl? This is the Inferno, you fuck. Don't be scared away from someone half your size."

His nostrils flare, his jaw clenching in the dark light. I take a giant leap forward, hitting him again. This time straight into his abs. It's like hitting cement. A brick wall. He doesn't budge, doesn't wince.

A regular fight isn't going to take him down. I have to bring out my crazy.

"You're weak as fuck," I snarl, lowering my hands. I'm not going to fight like I'm trained to. I'm going to fight like I was born to.

A fucking savage.

He steps toward me at my words, momentarily forgetting who he's in the ring with. He stalls in his step, though, remembering.

Pity.

"You're a weak man who hides behind his fists. What… you can't hit a woman? You too worried about your image?" I bark out a laugh. "You're pathetic. Men have hit me a quarter of your size. They're stronger men than you are."

He growls, a ruthless noise ripping from his vocal cords as his entire body coils tight.

I made him snap, and relief finally hits me.

A real fight.

He walks toward me, and I dip to the right, racing under his raised arm and coming up behind him. He's quick, but my little legs are quicker. I jump onto his back, my arms going around his neck and squeezing tight. Like I have become possessed, I lean down, my teeth sinking into the skin between his shoulder and neck. My teeth break his skin, and the metallic taste of blood fills my mouth.

He tastes like bliss.

His hand reaches back, and he grabs my shoulders, his strength overpowering as he pulls me off, flipping me upside down and slamming my back to the ground. The wind gets knocked from my lungs, and I stare up at him in fear, his eyes burning with malice, blood dripping down his pec and torso.

He's a monster.

He bends down, and I know he's about to hit me. I roll over, getting to my knees and running across the ring, gasping for air that refuses to fill my lungs. He's quick, though, and I'm disoriented. He grabs me by my ankle, dragging me across the ground. Flipping me onto my back, he gets on top of me, his thighs pinning me down on each side of my waist.

His body ripples only inches from my eyes. Even in my state of fear, my fingers itch to drift toward his skin. It's damp with sweat, coiled tight in tension, and I wonder if he'd kill me if I ran my fingers down his stomach.

Fuck, I must be disoriented.

Finally, I gasp in a breath, my lungs greedy for every ounce of air I can get. I swallow it down, storing it for later as I stare at him above me. The hate radiates from him, and I can barely think straight as his intoxicating scent overwhelms me.

It's salty from his sweat, the smell of a man, but it's so much more than that. It's sharp, strong, overpowering, and so fucking delicious.

"Are you scared yet?" he mumbles.

I smile at him, betting his blood still coats my teeth. I can feel the wetness on my lips, the trail of blood going from my chin and down my neck. "No."

I look animalistic, and I can see in his eyes that he sees it, too. His eyes flare, but quickly go blank, right back to his unemotional stare.

"You should be." He cocks his hand back, his fist flying forward and landing straight into my nose.

Everything goes black.

I cough, fluid sputtering from between my lips as I roll onto my side. My entire sinuses are filled as blood pours from my nose and my mouth.

Fuck. Ouch.

I don't have to feel my nose to know it's broken. The way my entire face is numb and in excruciating pain at the same time is knowledge enough.

A pool of blood grows below me. It's silent, and glancing up, everyone is staring at me with wide eyes and their jaws unhinged.

I lost.

I lost for my first time ever.

I want to laugh, but pain radiates through my entire body. I feel like one massive bruise. A shadow fills my sight, and I lift my head to the side, seeing the man who caused this.

This monster of a man that still imprints in my soul.

I hate him. But I don't want him to leave.

His knuckles are bloody, and rage paints his face as I watch him.

He watches me for another beat, then turns around, disappearing into the crowd. Like he was never here to begin with.

"Shit, Raven." Reggie's voice sounds garbled and muffled. I roll onto my knees, and an entirely new stream of blood pours from my mouth and onto the mat below me.

Finally. *Finally*, I can contribute to the stains on this thing.

I'm pissed that this man won. I don't know him, but I already hate him. The instant pull was unwanted. Whatever fucked-up aura he had surrounding him seeped into my body like a toxin, and it's only now that he's gone does the cloudiness clear from my mind.

I can think clearly again, and I've never wanted to erase someone from earth more than I do that man. If given the chance, I wonder if I'd actually kill him.

Although I'm livid he won, I also can't deny the fact that the pain in my body is a welcome feeling. Not something I've ever felt before, if I'm honest. I'm rarely sick, I don't get injured. I'm too calculated with everything that I do to wind up with a scratch or bruise. I anticipate my moves before they happen.

This feeling. The feeling of an aching body. The feeling of pain. The burning of an open wound. The pounding of broken bones.

It's an unusual feeling. But I relish in it as my name is called again. I glance up, seeing Reggie standing there with a panicked and furious look on his face.

"I fucking told you, Raven!" He reaches for me, and I flinch. He pulls back, his eyes narrowing. "Now is not the time to get all fucking weird when you look like you just got hit by a truck."

"I've got it," I mumble. It's weird to talk, the pain from my nose radiating to the rest of my face.

"Shit," he whispers, shaking his head. I can feel the eyes of everyone still staring at me. I raise my hand, my middle finger shooting through the air.

I drop my hands to the mat, pushing myself up. My palms slip on the mat, in the pool of my own blood. I slam back down, my face soaking in the blood which is beginning to cool.

"Let me help you, Rave," Reggie urges, leaning against the ropes.

"I've got it," I repeat. I push myself against the mat once again, just barely lifting myself to a stand. I'm wobbly, my head twisted and turned around. I can barely see straight as I hobble off the ring, but I can hear the footsteps of Reggie following behind me.

My teeth start chattering, and I'm starting to feel like shit. The adrenaline high and numbness of pain is abating and all that's left is an excruciating ache and a sickness deep in my gut.

"Let me get you a ride home," he says, coming to a stop behind me as I pull my duffle from the locker.

I shake my head. "No. I'm fine."

"You aren't fine. You might have a concussion. I can't have one of my best fighters getting in a car wreck."

I glance over my shoulder at him. "Only an hour ago you made it seem like I'm a little girl who wasn't old enough to play with the big kids."

He sighs. "It's not that at all. This guy you fought doesn't fight just anyone. He wasn't even scheduled to fight tonight. It's weird, it's like both of you showed up unintended and ended up in the ring together."

I grimace. "Don't be weird." I grab my leggings, shoving them over my shorts since I know Reggie isn't leaving anytime soon. I bend over, the pressure from my nose making me gasp, a trail of blood dripping from my nostrils as I shove my feet into my boots.

"You look like fucking shit," he groans.

I tilt my head toward him, watching as he runs his hands over his bald head over and over again. He's not acting like the Reggie I know. The cool, calculated Reggie, who could fuck anyone up from just a look. This guy looks frazzled.

"What's wrong with you?" I leave my sweatshirt in my bag, knowing I won't be able to put it over my face without blacking out.

His face blanks. Retreating from wherever mental case headspace he was just in. "You're a good fighter, Raven. There's a reason I put you on a strict schedule, and that's because one wrong move and you might be out for good. Don't come again unless you're on the schedule. I fucking mean it. You won't fight if you do." With that, he spins around, leaving without another word.

With a sigh, I walk out, my monsters settled for the moment, my mind finally clear. If only for a short time, I'll be okay with it.

I drive slowly as I pull up my house, the gravel seemingly louder than it usually is. The house feels darker than usual. I should be leery about the off feeling. Maybe a little hesitant, but I'm not.

Everyone is asleep.

Aria must have distracted them well enough that they didn't even check on me before bed. Being well past midnight now, I know for sure they aren't still awake.

I park my car behind Aunt Gloria's, switching it off and making my way back toward the side of the house. Going down was one thing, getting back up is another thing altogether. Not to mention, the pain in my face is nearly debilitating at this point.

I know with complete certainty my nose is broken. Shattered. Even a slight touch of my finger against the bridge, I can feel the cracked bone.

Putting the straps of the duffel around my arms like a backpack, I grab the rough branch of a nearby tree and pull myself up, whimpering as even these basic movements create a thumping across the front of my face. I use the trunk to walk up and swing my leg over the branch, feeling winded the moment my legs straddle it.

I feel weak, and with shaky arms, I leap onto the roof, the pounding of my feet way too loud.

Shit.

That was really fucking loud.

My fingers dig into the rough shingles of the roof, my panic taking hold. I never feel this way. *Why the fuck do I feel like this right now?*

Getting to my knees, I crawl across the roof, sweat dotting along my temples as I nearly reach my window. I don't know if I'm on emotion overload or if I just feel like literal shit because my face is broken, but all I want is to crawl under my covers and pass out.

I reach my windowsill, my fingers digging beneath the crack of the window and pushing it up. It groans loudly, awkwardly, too explosive in the middle of the night. I fly through the opening, crashing to the ground.

"Fuck," I whisper, standing up to shut the window.

Light illuminates me, and my face scrunches up in unease as I turn around. Aunt Gloria and Uncle Jerry stand there, both of them with hidden anger on their faces.

"Raven," Aunt Gloria begins, her voice one that leaves a sinking feeling in my stomach. "What happened to your face?"

"I… fell."

"You want us to believe that you fell, and your face ended up looking like that?" Uncle Jerry's finger points toward my face. "Where have you been, Raven? Out robbing people? Stealing? Hurting people? Which one is it, because no one is out after dark unless they plan to sin."

My lip curls back, even as uncomfortable as it is. "I'm not *sinning*."

"You are sinning, Raven. You go out after dark, even when you know it's against the rules. I don't know where you've been, and to be honest, I don't care to know the transgressions of your evening. The only thing I have to say is I had a feeling there was something amiss earlier, and this proves it. You are nothing but a sinful child, and your lessons over the years haven't been as helpful as I believed they were."

"I'm not fucking doing anything!" I snap.

Uncle Jerry clenches his jaw, his eyes darkening in anger. "You curse in this house again, and I'll rinse your mouth out with soap. Your foul mouth is an abomination."

Their hate for me speaks freely in the night when their daughter isn't there to water down their distaste. They truly despise me, whether it be from where I came from or because they had to take me in, in the first place; their dislike is unwarranted, but so real.

I pull the straps of my bag from my back, and unzip it, walking toward my dresser. "It's clear this isn't working. To be honest, I don't think it's ever worked to begin with. I think it's time I go. I can find my own way."

"You aren't going anywhere, Raven. Put the bag down," Aunt Gloria warns.

I shove my shirts and tank tops in the bag, moving on to the next drawer. "I'm not staying here any longer. I don't agree with what you do. Your beliefs are not my beliefs. I shouldn't be forced to conform a certain way just to appease you. I'm nearly an adult, so just let me go."

My bag is ripped from my fingers, and I'm yanked to the side as the both of them grab at me. "Let me go!" I shout, attempting to pull out of their hold. Usually, it would be no issue. I'm stronger than the both of them, no question. I train to lay beefy-ass dudes on their ass. But in my weakened state, exhausted, broken, depleted, their anger and hate toward me is a strength I have no ability to fight.

"We are in charge of you until you are eighteen. You will not disobey our rules as long as you are living under our roof," Uncle Jerry barks at me.

"Then let me leave this terrible place. You guys are fucking insane," I shout in Aunt Gloria's face.

A pinch to the back of my arm enough to break the skin causes me to arch away from them. Their grip is too strong, and I'm instantly pushed out of my room and into the hall.

"Where are you taking me? You can't do this. This is abuse!"

I hear crying from down the hall and grind my teeth to dust as I realize Aria is crying. What the hell did they do? Did they hurt her? Is she getting punished for lying for me?

"Aria! Aria! What the hell did you do to her?" I roar, my heat and spit flying in their faces.

A palm slaps against my cheek, my already throbbing face screaming in agony. "Don't talk to her. Don't speak to her. Don't even think about her. You have caused my own daughter to sin. You are nothing but poison, a toxic being created by the devil himself. If we can't save you, no one can."

I glare at Aunt Gloria, hating her more than I could possibly hate anyone in my entire life. The rage in my belly starts up, and the sickness in me makes me feel feverish. I am manic. I am wild. The beast inside me that I keep locked deep threatens to escape. It wants to be free. It wants to unleash havoc on the world until it is nothing but rubble and ash.

"I will not succumb to your hellish ways to bend me how you want. I fucking refuse!" I snap, bending my body out of their hold. "I will never be what you want, so just let me leave!" I scream, just as Aunt Gloria reaches out, her hands pounding against my chest. I wobble back, my arms windmilling around my body as I glance over my shoulder.

Stairs.

It's no use. The shove was too much, and I am too weak. My body falls into the air, for only a moment. The second my back slams against the wooden stairs, I let out a cry, my body falling and twisting and turning and tumbling as each piece of my body pounds against the wood.

As I hit the landing, my head snaps back, the back of my skull slamming against the wooden beams of the railing.

And everything goes black.

My eyes crack open as my legs slam against concrete. I shift my head, seeing Uncle Jerry pulling me along the basement floor.

"What… what are you doing?" I groan, the pain in my entire body unbearable.

"Don't answer her, Jer. Not a word." Aunt Gloria's voice is demonic as she lashes out. She isn't the nice woman who puts an extra five into the giving basket at church or shakes everyone's hands at the door. No, this woman has so much hate in her body, she smells of it.

"Bring her over here," she croaks.

My head lolls back as Uncle Jerry keeps a tight grip on my wrists as he pulls me against the cold floor. We turn the corner into the storage room, and I cry out when I see everything surrounding me.

Crosses. So many damn crucifixes it hurts to look at. Big, small, gold, silver, wooden. Just about everything you can think of is secured to this wall until there isn't an inch uncovered. There's a blanket on the ground and a bucket in the corner of the room. Otherwise, the rest of this storage room has been cleared out.

"I knew it would only be a matter of time before we brought you back down here." Aunt Gloria reaches in her pocket, pulling out a key. "You can stay here and think about what you've done and how you've acted. Think of your sins and if this is the right path for you. Let God lead you through the light."

Uncle Jerry steps out of the room and comes back with a black, leather-bound Bible. He lays it at my feet. "Let God show you the way. If you don't find the path of righteousness, well, may God have mercy on your soul."

With that, they step out of the room. The heavy sound of a lock twisting on the other side of the door makes my body turn to ice.

I'm locked in here.

In the darkness. With nothing besides a blanket and a Bible. No one is coming to save me.

People have said my life before was one of walking through Hell. The evil and the tainted. They don't realize that I've stepped away from one hell, and directly into another.

chapter five
CAELIAN

Blood drips from my knuckles, the roar of screams sounding like rushing water in my ears. I can feel the warmth of the blood cooling by the fresh air. The man is front of me is barely conscious, though he stays on his two feet, wobbling from side to side as his vision attempts to focus.

I watch him with empty eyes, not really caring about the angry or worried look reflecting back at me. He could be dead at my feet or fucking someone against the ropes; he's nothing but another body for me to destroy and a swipe of blood on my hands.

He's nothing. Meaningless. Pointless.

His weak arm swings out as he tries to deliver an uppercut to my jaw. I step back slowly, and his body gives out as he throws his body into his punch, hitting air and falling to his knees. His hands press against the mat, a stream of blood flowing from his mouth. Either he bit his tongue at some point or he's internally bleeding. Neither is good by the amount pooling to the ground.

"I'm done," he grunts. The man who people say can demolish everyone with one hit, was nothing more than a measly fly that continuously hits the glass window, hoping he can make his way outside. He's too fucking stupid to realize his fight against me was done before his feet even hit the mat. But with the cocky look on his face, he thought he'd win. He hoped he'd win.

There was never any question. What's done is done.

I nod at him, understanding his words, but not liking the way they shatter between his teeth. Like he still has a sense of strength in his tone. Like he's man enough to know when he needs to be done.

He'll wipe his blood clean and patch himself up and go tell his buddies that he had a bad night, but next time he'll kick my ass for sure.

Because that's what they always say, right?

Exactly.

My hands fist at my sides, the blood squishing between my fingers. With a quick snap of my arm, I swing forward, my knuckles popping him beneath the chin. The instant shatter against my knuckles, the sound of his jaw breaking a melody to my ears.

He flies up before tumbling like a boneless body to the ground, blood pouring so heavily from his mouth that I'm wondering if I killed him.

The gasps and cheers ring so loudly that my eardrums feel like they'll burst. I spin around, running my fingers through my hair, knowing I smeared blood into the strands.

People attempt to flock me, but my brothers are instantly on each side of me. I can feel the unease of everyone as they take in the three of us together. The Morellis are a family no one likes to speak of, let alone be around. Our name is associated with death.

The number of times I've heard, *"That Caelian killed someone for just smiling at him,"* should be annoying by now. People whisper it as if it's a rumor.

Except, it's not a rumor.

It's completely true.

I don't give a fuck about anyone or anything around me besides my brothers. My blood. Together, we're a fortress that absolutely no one will tear down. The law is meaningless to us. The police and local government work for us, not the other way around. Everyone is corrupt, not just in Oregon, but in the entire country. Shit, the world.

So, getting a jurisdiction of law enforcement to bend to the Morellis was as easy as taking out the fucking trash.

I should've left this place after my last fight. After fighting *her*. I never fight more than once. But after knocking out a chick that was the size of a fucking toothpick, the beast in my chest has only just woken up.

Who is she? Where did she come from? How is it that someone like her ends up in a place like this? She didn't belong here, but even as I think those words, just one look in her eyes contradicted that.

She had a darkness so toxic I could taste the crazy in her. Each step, each breath from her, was filled with so much pent-up emotion it was stifling. The moment I could breathe was the moment her eyes closed.

She is so much. Too much. Is it her chaos that stirred something inside me? Or is it something else?

I chose not to think about it. About her or whatever the fuck she woke inside me. But I couldn't stop myself from going to Reggie and telling him I'm fighting the next one, too.

One curious look in my eyes and a nod later, and here I am. Another body down, and I'm finally physically fucking exhausted.

"Caelian, can I have your autograph?" some chick shouts in the crowd. I glance over, seeing her blonde curls bouncing against her cleavage. She holds a permanent marker in her hands, extended toward me over someone's shoulder.

I glance away.

I do not, under any circumstances, sign autographs. I'm almost offended she asked me to in the first place.

I head to the locker room to get dressed and grab my things before the three of us walk through the back, and I see Reggie standing at the exit. "See you next time, Caelian. Good fight tonight." Is he talking about my fight with the girl, or my fight with the dumb fuck I just flattened? Most likely the latter, since I could see the way he rushed to help her.

Who is she to him? Who is she to all these people?

"Thanks, man," my youngest brother, Matteo, says. He's the nicest one out of all the brothers, but also the youngest of the three of us. He has a sliver of humanity in him, which is a lot more than the rest of us.

The three of us were born and raised to be killers. Leaders. Fucking rulers of the Morelli mafia. Our destiny is to take the reins of my father's crime organization someday. Unfortunately, whatever is in his DNA has bred three ruthless men.

And me, the psychopath. Sociopath.

When people get excited over school, sports, females, whatever they decide, I don't. What excites me isn't something I speak about. It's not a hobby that I share with others. It's something my family knows about, but only because they are my family.

I'm excited by death.

Humanity and empathy aren't something that come to me often. I lack the feelings everyone else has, except when it comes to my family. I go from zero to one hundred on the rage scale quickly, though, and that's where the Inferno comes in. It eases the beast in my chest so I don't go full-out mass murder on an entire city. Or state.

My father noticed at a young age I wasn't like other kids. I didn't cry or laugh or do things that were considered to be normal. Something in my brain wasn't quite right, and my father figured that out early enough to help me.

He made me my own law. He integrated my need with the business, and together, I can help him, while also helping myself, while also staying the fuck out of prison.

Probably where I belong.

I kill.

I kill *a lot*.

I find those who are deserving of death, and my father finds plenty of people who need a bullet. It keeps my plate pretty fucking busy.

I don't kill innocent. Those people can go when their clock of fate runs out. But those who fuck up royally will usually see the blade of my knife or bullet between their eyes.

My father has made me into this man. He turned my issues into something that I could live with. I'm fucked up so bad that the only thing I want is blood on my hands, but he fucking helped me. He's not a good man. He's not even a nice man, but he's my father, and if it weren't for him, I don't know how fucked up I'd be.

He has his own problems, his own errors that he's made over the years, but he's also a powerful, overly intelligent man that knows how to run a kingdom, and that's exactly what he's done. He's already told me point-blank that I will never rule. I will never be the boss of the Morelli mafia, at least not his. My inability to care will light that shit up in flames, and I have to say, I don't fucking blame him.

The amount of people that would be dead at my feet would certainly cause a stir with the general public.

"Where we headed now?" my other brother, Gabriel, asks.

"Home."

I shove my black duffel behind the seat of my BMW. Our family lives on just the outskirts of downtown Portland. Nestled between the mountains and the ocean is our mansion in the small town of Blackridge. Our other family are scattered within a few miles of the next family member. We all stick close together, the Morellis and their associates making up much of Portland and the surrounding areas.

It doesn't take long for me to pull up to our gate, punching in our unnecessarily long code before it beeps green, and the gate starts sliding open.

"Two fights in a night, Caelian? What's got you edgy tonight?" Gabriel asks.

I clench my fists as I think about the girl. They weren't there for it, showing up only as my sweaty body left the ring and as I walked in for the second one.

Parking my car, I reach behind my seat to grab my bag. "Nothing. The first one was too easy. I thought that second guy would've been at least slightly challenging," I grunt, pulling the straps and dropping the duffel into my lap. "He wasn't. He was weak as fuck. I should've killed him."

"Not everyone has to die, Cae," Matteo sighs, and I sneer at him, wondering why he has to be the most emotional out of all of us.

Not that he cares that much, because he doesn't. That fucker could've or couldn't have died at my feet and we could all go about our night like it was just another day. But Matteo, he's a bit of a loose cannon. It must be youngest child syndrome. The most emotional, because fucking hell, the little fucker can be annoying sometimes. That, and he's a mouthy fuck.

We each have our own traits about us, but together, we're the strongest bloodline of the Morellis.

I'm the oldest. The most fucked up. Eighteen, the sociopath and the killer.

Then there's Gabriel, seventeen years old. Killer and prince to becoming the next heir of the Morelli mafia. He's the rational one. The mature one.

Then there's the youngest, Matteo. The baby of the family, just turned seventeen. He and Gabriel were born only ten months apart from each other. The one who wants everything in one. He wants the girls, and he wants the blood. He wants peace, and he wants to slice throats. He's a fucking maniac, and he drives me crazy, but he's also my brother.

So, whatever is the synonym to love, I have that. Just in a fucked up, distorted way, I suppose.

The three of us are an impenetrable force that is lethal by even the smallest glance.

My phone rings as we pull to a stop. I take it from my duffel, seeing my dad's associate Tino's face pop up on my phone screen.

"No one is a challenge to you." Gabriel laughs.

"Yeah," I grunt, fisting the straps of the duffel as I open the door.

"Need you on South Tenth. Your guy is on the move," he says the moment I put the phone to my ear.

My chest deflates with relief. I've been on this guy for a long time. Whenever I find someone, it's more of a process than just walking up to them and shoving my knife in their gut. It's a lot of time-consuming research and stalking. And between school, the Inferno, and business shit, sometimes I don't have the time.

Which is when Tino comes into play. He does a lot of PI work for the Morelli family and has helped with my kills on countless occasions.

My skin prickles, growing hot as adrenaline hits me. I open my door again, sliding back into the driver's seat and starting up my BMW.

"Dude, where the fuck you going?" Matteo raises his hands, keys jingling from his fingers.

I shake my head at him as I reverse, pulling out of our driveway. "Tell me," I say to Tino.

"I found him leaving the strip club on Fifth. He's definitely on something right now. I'm going to guess heroin. Last time he was this fucked up, he shot one of our men over by Morelli's, our family restaurant. If he's headed that way now, I might have to deal with him before you get here."

"No. I'm on my way. I'll be there in a few." I hang up, tossing my phone onto the passenger seat as I drive back toward the city.

It won't take me long. I'll get there before Tino can catch up with him, and he'll be mine. I've been watching him for a while. He causes fucking problems with our business. He once worked for us, a bottom feeder who uses more drugs than he sells. When our people found out about it, they cut him loose, and he's just been a loose end that's been needing to be tied up ever since. I claimed him as mine, but I know my family has been getting irritated letting him walk our streets.

I can't help it. This drugged-up fuck is somehow stealthier than I imagined. I can catch everyone, no matter how well they hide. But this guy, he seems to turn invisible when he's sober.

But when he's high, he's a dumb motherfucker.

Speeding through town, I count the streets as they climb until I hit South Tenth. I turn into the closest parking garage I can, heading to the parking spot far in the back. Anyone who scratches my car will surely end up with their head in the Pacific Ocean.

I reach under my seat, unstrapping the Glock and tucking it into the waistband of my jeans. Opening the glove box, I pull my two knives and a pair of gloves. One goes into the pocket of my hoodie, the other clipping to the other side of my pants.

I open my door, sliding out and locking it with my fob as I head down the stairs toward the street.

Pulling my hood over my head, I adjust it right below my eyebrows so my face is obscured from the cameras. My gray sweats mold to my hips. I look like just another guy looking to have some fun in the city at night. Nothing to it.

The smell of beer and piss and seduction linger in the air, and I wrinkle my nose. What is it about the city party scene that turns people into crazy fucks on Molly looking for an orgy?

The whole needy, clingy vibe doesn't sit well with me. It makes my stomach twist, and all I want to do is cut their hearts from their chests so I can stop feeling how intense their emotions are.

It disgusts me.

I step over a pile of trash as Barnett's bar comes into view. I can hear the music thumping through my body, the neon lights reflecting across the bar. The door is propped open, and I slip inside, keeping my hood up as I scope everyone out. There are so many damn people. College kids grind on each other. Too many for my liking. The air becomes stifling, thick and hot with breath and sweat.

I walk through the groups of people, slipping into the dark corner and leaning against the wall. My spine presses against the brick behind me, and my eyes scan the room, diving between each couple and group, every single person that grinds against the next.

My eyes stop on a group of guys. Shady, slimy-looking motherfuckers that I'd knock flat on their ass in the ring. I wouldn't even have to look at them straight on for any of them to shit their pants in fear.

I notice the guy I'm looking for instantly. Champlin in his name. He has a cocky smile on his face, and he's wearing shades in the darkened room. He smiles, his bright white teeth reflecting off the neon lights. His hand is on some girl's ass, and he leans over to whisper in his buddy's ear. I bet he's saying how much he's going to destroy her pussy later.

Unfortunately for him, he's going to be destroying no pussy later.

I get comfortable, which means bored, and watch. Wait.

I can't tell you how long passes. Floods of people come in and out. The group of sleazy dudes with their few trashy chicks head to the bar, back out to the floor, back to bar. I watch them endlessly, not moving from my spot. Not moving at all.

The internal clock inside me *tick, tick, ticks*, as I wait for my moment. It feels like hours pass, yet no time passes at all. My blood pumps, hot as flames through my veins as I think of the girl from earlier.

I feel no remorse for the pain I inflicted. She is in the Inferno for a reason, and she wouldn't be between those ropes if she wasn't looking for trouble. The words she lashed at me from her pouty lips were daring, mostly for her. She was a tiny thing. Small but steady. Delicate and destructive. The hidden thorn on the rose. Someone that would strike you before you even knew she was dangerous. Feeling guilty for hitting a girl is a common denominator of good morals, but I have none, and she wanted to knock me down just as badly as I wanted to her.

She was stunning. She kept her beauty hidden behind a thick layer of pain. I've never seen anyone so exquisite yet infuriate me to the point I debated if I should crush her windpipe between my fingers. She was tiny, a miniature human.

How old was she? She couldn't have been taller than five-two, and that's being generous.

If it weren't for her eyes, I would've guessed she was barely a teenager. But the torture bled so easily from her irises, she looked centuries old. She's trapped in her own hell, in her own body, and I wonder if she goes to the Inferno to spill blood or to bleed herself.

Her long hair looked like silk as it cascaded down her back in a long, dark sheet. Her face was dainty, her cheeks sharp and lethal against her crystal blue eyes. So many things to bring a man to his knees, and all it did was harden my hollow heart.

I don't know where she came from, but my blood burned with a warning of danger.

She is a danger I cannot afford.

"Hey, babe. You look lonely over here all by yourself." I snap out of my thoughts, grinding my teeth together as the scent of floral perfume wafts into my nose. It's too sweet, too tangy. Too fucking fake along with her seductive voice that sounds like a dying seal.

I hate women.

They're vile humans that do nothing besides open their legs. The only woman in my life is my mother, and she's almost as disassociated with emotions as I am. Not a single maternal bone in her body.

I turn my face to hers, and I watch as her eyes latch onto my dark chocolate ones. It makes their panties drop, and I wonder if Champlin would let me wear his shades so this woman could leave me the fuck alone.

"Want some company?"

I shake my head slowly. *Absolutely not.*

"Are you sure? No one comes to Barnett's unless they're looking to meet someone." She bats her eyes at me, her fake lashes looking eerily like spider legs.

I shake my head. *Again.*

Her lower lip, red like a crisp apple, pouts out. It could look delicious, but instead it looks rotten. "You're no fun. I'd let you do what you wanted, you know. You wouldn't have to be gentle."

My mouth cracks open, and I wet my lower lip. I'm parched, I realize. Probably going to guzzle a gallon of water once I get home. "If you came home with me, I can guarantee you wouldn't leave alive. Is that what you want?"

Her eyes flare with fear, and I'm finally entertained for the first time this evening.

"Unless you want me to peel the skin from your bones, I'd maybe suggest walking away. Quickly."

She swallows, and I watch the struggle as her throat strains. She spins on her too-high heels, disappearing into the crowd like she was never here to begin with.

My eyes glance back to the bar, where Champlin last was, only to find him missing. A group of bachelorettes sit in their place.

Well. Mother fuck.

My nostrils flare, and for a moment I contemplate going after the dumb bitch who distracted me. But I can't, because I have to keep my focus and do my job.

My eyes scan the crowd, looking for the losers who have almost burned my eyes with boredom tonight.

Nothing.

They're gone.

I shove off the wall, slicing through the crowd and out the front door.

There.

Slowly, they're departing. A few of the guys hop into an Uber. A couple start walking down the street, hand in hand. Champlin and the ugly female he's with wave and start walking in the opposite direction.

Bingo.

I shove my hands into the pouch pocket of my hoodie, gripping the knife in my grip and snapping the blade open. The blade is sharp against my fingers, and I can already taste the blood in the air as I follow them. They're drunk, stumbling around trees and trash cans and air. It's odd to watch. I don't drink often. It's reasons like this—being so fucked up that you aren't even in control. Smoking weed and drinking take the edge off, but getting fucked up like this is not in the cards. Not for me.

The possibility of a massacre happening is very likely under those circumstances.

When they take a right, I turn into the alleyway before them, speeding up my steps. I'll catch them undetected. They have no idea they're being followed, and I'm not exactly being stealthy about it. I don't care too much tonight. Exhaustion is seeping into my bones, and it's time for me to get home.

I take a left at the end of the alley, hearing their footsteps up ahead. I slip my gloves on and pull my knife from my pocket, walking to the wall and leaning against it as their footsteps grow closer.

She's giggling, and I bet if I were to watch them, he's copping a feel of her ass or something.

Acid burns my tongue and I snarl, stepping out just as they come into view. It takes them a moment, long enough for me to grab her by the hair and slam the side of her head against the brick wall. She drops like a rock, instantly unconscious.

"What the fuck!" Champlin shouts at me, growing angry and worried all at the same time. "What the fuck are you doing?"

I turn to him full-on, shining my brown eyes at him. It doesn't take long for the fear to fill his face, knowledge and understanding overtaking his features.

"Shit," he whispers.

"Shit is right."

"Dude, I swear I didn't mean to shoot him—"

I point my knife at him. "Stop talking."

His hands raise, along with his defenses. "I'll leave. I'll never come back. Please, I won't say a fucking word."

I tip my head to the side. No, he won't. I'll make sure of that.

He hears my unspoken words. "Please," he begs.

I take a step toward him, and he walks back. Until his back hits the brick wall behind him and he has nowhere else to go. He glances left and right, like he wants to flee. But he knows who I am. He knows what I am. He stands no chance.

Fucker tries anyway.

He leaps into a sprint, taking off down the alley. He jumps over an overturned garbage bin, nearly tripping in the process. The bang of his shoe against the tin echoes in the alleyway. But his terror keeps him on his feet, his shoes pounding on the pavement.

The heroin makes him quick.

The liquor makes him slow.

Unfortunately for him, he's no competition for me. It takes me only steps to catch up with him, and I reach forward, my gloved hand gripping his shirt. He stumbles, face planting on the dirty ground. I step over him, my shoe pushing against his shoulder blades to keep him pinned to the ground.

"Help!" he shouts, squirming. Still trying. Fucking idiot.

I lean forward, pressing the tip of my knife against his neck. It barely pierces his skin, but it's enough that he swallows his cries, terror shutting him the hell up.

"You know the rules of being associated with the Morellis. How fucking idiotic do you have to be to fuck around with our drugs? Shoot one of us? Do you not think we had eyes on you the entire time? That we didn't know your every move?" Anger bubbles, and I swallow it down, so I don't explode. It expands my chest, constricting my breaths. My rage is a beast even I don't like to confront. It leads to a messy death.

Tonight, I don't want the mess.

I just want death.

All I feel right now is a relief and adrenaline that I've finally got him. He's been on my radar for too long, and my fingers itch to spill his blood. A tremble starts deep in my bones, and I want nothing more than to watch the black pavement turn a dark crimson.

"I told you I wouldn't say a word," he weeps.

I shake my head. "You've already said that. Don't you have anything different to say?"

"I just want to go home. Please."

I grunt, lifting my shoe from his back. He intakes a large breath, his chest lifting off the pavement as he inhales all the air he can get. I lean forward, my fingers gripping his shirt and flipping him onto his back. Sweat sticks to his shirt, his body so overwhelmed with fear, the bitter smell of body odor sticks to every inch of his skin.

"No," I whisper, plunging the knife into his gut. I dig in until my wrist connects with his shirt, then pull out, the silver blade now covered in blood.

My eyes go dark, my body running hot, and *I lose it*. The mania comes out to play.

I shove it back in, pulling it out, only to stick it back into a different spot. Over and over again, I stab him in quick succession to the point the only sound in the quiet alley is metal slicing through skin.

Champlin starts spitting out blood, his whimpers turning to gurgles as his insides turn to shreds. Blood splatter makes its way to my clothes, and finally—*finally*—the acidic smell of blood fills the air. I can nearly taste it on my tongue.

Once Champlin's head lolls to the side, I know he's gone. A slow river of blood trails from the corner of his mouth, making a small puddle on the pavement. With my gloved hand, I reach forward, prying his mouth open and gripping onto his dark red tongue. I pull it out as far as I can, my knife digging into the tough muscle as I cut it from his mouth.

He will never, ever say a word. I promise that.

Once it slices free, I stand up, slipping his tongue into my pocket. I could do something with his body. Maybe try to make it look like a mugging or something, but it doesn't really matter. If anyone suspects it's us, not a word will be said about it. It'll be covered up in one way or another, so the point of me wasting my time and energy would be completely useless.

I close the knife and stick it into my pocket as I glance over my shoulder, seeing his slut still knocked out clean. I wander up to her, stopping once the toe of my shoe hits her back. I nudge her a little, and she wobbles, still in a dead sleep. Leaning down, my hands go to each side of her head. With a breath, my hands tighten, and I flick my wrists in one quick motion.

Snap.

Her spine disconnects from her skull, and I drop her to the ground in a heap.

I peel the gloves from my wrists, keeping the clean side on the outside as I shove them into my pocket. Reaching back, I pull my hood over my head again, then steer back down the alleyway.

Time to head home

Pulling into my garage, I switch my BMW off, stepping out and taking the knife and gloves from my pocket. I leave them on the table next to the door, knowing I'll have to clean them later. Gabriel is a germaphobe and hates when we bring someone else's blood into the house. Well, mostly me. We all end lives, but I'm the one who typically has someone's blood on my hands on a daily basis.

I step inside, the sound of nails on wood making my eyebrows lift.

My boy.

The one thing in life besides my brothers that keeps me sane. My German Shepherd comes into view, his hair raised and ready to attack, but the moment he sees it's me, his tail shakes in a rapid wag. I bend down, burying my fingers in his hair and scratching behind his ear. His head tilts to the side, tall enough that his back reaches my waist. He's a tall fuck, half mixed with a wolf. An illegal dog, but he's mine.

My guard dog. My companion. The closest thing I'll ever get to love. *He's mine.*

"How are you, Rosko?" I ask, and he butts his nose against my thigh, smelling the blood so easily against my skin.

He's as filled with madness as I am. He enjoys the kill just as much as I do. My perfect companion. I take him with me at times, let him tear the jugular from someone as easily as meat from the bone. He's a carnivore, and blood is what makes him wild.

Blood is what makes me wild, too.

"I'll take you with me next time. Promise. But, hey, I got you a treat."

I reach into my pocket, pulling out the tongue that's been dried from the fabric of my jeans. I present it to him, and it only takes a moment of his nose against my fingers before he snatches it from my palm and walks off, his nails clacking on the wood as he goes wherever the fuck he feels like to enjoy his snack.

If Rosko can't come, I at least try and bring him something he can enjoy.

I toe my shoes off before going any farther into our oversized two-story house, tall and wide, nestled between the woods and sitting close enough to the Pacific Ocean that I can smell the salt in the air. Mixed with the pine, it's an aphrodisiac that could satiate my thirst for blood, even if only for a moment.

I walk down the hall, the dark wooden floors freshly polished. Our open floor plan expands from the living area to the kitchen, the dark gray and black appliances, and cabinets, a stark contract to the eggshell white countertops.

I'm thankful no one is around. I'm not in the mood to answer questions or deal with my brothers or parents. Matteo talks too much, and Gabriel inspects too much. My mother mostly keeps to herself. More than likely, she's upstairs in the bath or drinking wine in her bedroom. My father is usually working and very rarely home. He is fiercely protective of my mother, though both of them are cold, detached.

TWISTED DARES

They're more business partners than they are a married couple.

I turn the corner, heading up the stairs that curl around the side of the house. The stairs are wide and grow wider once they hit the second level. Matteo's door is closed, but a low rumble of music thumps from beneath the door. Gabriel's door is next, and only silence comes from his room. Not a sound.

Walking past, I head toward my room at the end of the hall. My door is opened, and Rosko lays on my bed, his chin resting on his paw as he stares at me. Waiting for me.

I stop in my doorway, staring at him and his perked ears as he waits for me to get into bed. I pull my clothes off, dropping them into the hamper, then go into my en suite bathroom. I step into my shower, turning the water to scalding as I wash away the day. The sweat, the blood, the toxic air that constantly surrounds me. I wash it all down the drain until my skin is red and numb. It's only then that I step out, toweling myself dry and flicking my light off, heading back to my bed.

Rosko hasn't moved an inch. His eyes watching me sideways as I walk to the bed. I slip beneath the sheets naked, the cool silk against my skin refreshing and clean. Rosko finally gets up once I nudge him, moving only enough to give me room and then curling directly against my side.

My hand falls to his neck, digging into his hair and scratching at his skin. He huffs, getting comfortable and falling asleep within moments.

I close my eyes, my mind exhausted and my body wired. It's a complicated mix. Where all I want is sleep, but the adrenaline after a fight mixed with a kill leaves a combination of chaos brewing beneath the surface. It should mean that I step away, let my mind and body relax for a few days.

But I know that's the exact opposite.

It's my night off from fighting tomorrow, but I know I have to go there, and I have to fight again.

A flicker of a brown-haired, blue eyed girl flickers through my vision. *That girl.* She's bloody, but beautiful. She's strong, but weak. She's Heaven, and she's Hell. I don't know why she invades my thoughts, because I don't want them. Yet they fester, and she becomes a disease in my mind.

I don't need her infecting my thoughts. I only want to focus on my priorities.

Fighting. Family. Death. Blood.

Blood brings me chaos, and blood brings me sanity.

Tonight, it brings chaos.

Tomorrow, it'll bring me sanity.

I hope.

The sound of gurgling, coughing, and sputtering fills my ears, and I nearly roll my eyes at the fucker in front of me. An early released prison inmate of someone who has wronged us.

He should've known he wouldn't have escaped without any repercussions. He stares at me with a tear on his cheek directly over a tattooed tear right below his eye. Fucking idiot loser. I mean, honestly.

His hand reaches up, shaky, attempting to reach toward my shirt. I bat his hand away, using my other to twist the knife embedded deep in his belly. Any farther and the handle will sink beneath the skin.

Blood whooshes through my ears, and I lick my lips, so hungry and ravenous for another kill. I shouldn't be this hungry after my kill the other day. My hunger should be satiated, but it's not. It's worse. An insatiable need to just *fucking murder*. I don't care who it is; I don't care what they've done. I want to tear everyone limb from limb for even breathing the same air I am.

I can't stop.

The man coughs below me, blood splatter spraying across my face. I flare my nostrils, my free hand going to his mouth. He garbles and gasps around the blood, but it's filling his body too quickly. Too many liters draining from him that it won't be long until he's gone for good.

My fingers curl around the bottom set of his teeth, and I press down, cranking his mouth open as wide as it will go. His eyes widen when he realizes what I'm doing. He fights against it, his jaw locking up as he refuses to let me crack him in half.

He has no choice.

I use my weight to press into the knife, and it sinks down as far as it can go, plunging into his organs and leaving him with no choice but to die. There is no alternative for him. Not today. Not tomorrow. *Not ever.*

He gasps, his jaw slackening for a second. That's all it takes. With all my force, I yank his jaw down, listening to the satisfying crack as his face breaks in half.

His eyes darken, the fear fading, and his body sinking into the ground beneath him. Rosko pants behind me, pacing back and forth. He's just as hungry for blood as I am.

"Rosko, come," I order.

He listens immediately, his large feet cracking the branches as he walks through the woods. He ends up beside me, his head at eye level as he waits for my next command.

I pull the knife out of his stomach, the blade covered in dark, thick blood. The broken man below me will never fuck with the Morelli family again. And unfortunately for him, he's now dinner for my dog.

"Eat."

He chomps his teeth, his paw stepping on the man's leg as he leans forward. I turn around, glancing at my two brothers as they watch me with bored expressions.

"You could've just dropped us off, you know." Gabriel sighs.

"There was no time. He had to be dealt with."

"Where to now? I need a fucking shot after watching that shitshow." Matteo's lips curl around his teeth, and I know it's because he hates when I draw this shit out. He could bathe in someone's blood, but he fucking hates the sound of snapping bones. I don't know why. My little brother is weird as fuck sometimes.

"I'm heading to the Inferno. I'll drop you off on the way."

"Again?" Gabriel's face scrunches in confusion. "What the fuck would you do that for? You were just fucking there." His face is similar to mine, though he's shorter by a few inches. His brown eyes are milkier than my dark ones, and his nose is a bit wider, getting those features from my dad's side.

Then there's Matteo. He wears his curly hair longer. His nose is like mine, and his jaw is sharp as glass. He's the same height as Gabriel, but he'll be taller than him, maybe as tall as me. We take after my mom. She's a fucking beautiful woman, even if her heart is hardened stone.

I must get my inability to care for anyone or anything from her cold ass.

I can't answer him on why I go back. Because I refuse to answer it myself. I don't like the direction my thoughts are going, so I pretend they don't exist in the first place.

"Just checking out some new fighters." The lie is effortless from my lips, and I stare at him as he stares at me, looking for a white lie.

He'll never find one.

"Are you fighting?" This comes from Matteo.

I shrug. I guess I could, though I haven't fought since the night with her. The spitfire who thought she could fight me and survive it. She tried. She tried so fucking hard. I have the teeth marks on my neck to prove it. "Maybe." I probably should get in the ring. Maybe it would help my tightly coiled body.

I need to release this fucking tension.

"You're acting weird." Matteo shakes his head and turns around as he heads for my BMW.

I glance over my shoulder, not wanting to get into why they think I'm odder than normal. They wouldn't be wrong. I'm not normal, not in the slightest. My brain doesn't work as it should. My internal clock ticks counterclockwise. I'm off.

But since my last fight last week, it seems like I'm hanging upside down. This unease in my gut doesn't feel good, and I'm not sure how to stop it.

"Rosko, come." His face is buried in the man's gut, and when he lifts his head, he has a piece of meat hanging from his mouth. "Come," I order again, and he leaps off the man's body, chewing his last piece of meat as he runs toward me.

"Good boy. Let's go." His face is red, his snout and chin covered in dripping, cold blood.

I put him in the trunk, and he starts lapping up water from his bowl in the corner. Grabbing the jug of water in the trunk, I pop the top off and pour the lukewarm water over my hands, rinsing off the blood.

Once my hands are clean, I close the trunk and hop into the driver's seat. Turning on the car, I watch the man, his stomach cavity wide open to the elements. I don't have to bury him out in the woods. The animals will find him, have their last meal before he rots. If he somehow is found, then they will suspect an animal killed him anyway. No one will suspect foul play.

And on some odd chance that they do, well, it's a good thing I'm a Morelli.

I pull up to my typical spot downtown, the parking garage that is strictly reserved for the Morellis and other high-profile names. Those spots usually belong to actors and actresses from Hollywood who are looking for a night full of illegal activities.

People deny it. The government hides it. The world pretends it isn't real. But the places where you go to watch people bleed, to die, to suffer and writhe in pain, they exist. And only the high rollers can afford it. There are ritzy places and run-down joints. The Inferno runs somewhere in the middle. It's a place to go when you want a taste of the real world.

A place where you go when you're okay with the dirty. Accepting of the possible blood splatter on your cheeks as people kill each other only feet in front of you. There is no glass barrier to keep you safe. You are just as at risk being in the ring as you are being out of it.

I head to the back of the parking garage, opening the back door to let Rosko out before I head down the hidden stairs that lead directly to the Inferno. There is no security or guards this way. If you know this way, it's because you were meant to. Simple as that.

Opening the heavy door, a waft of sweat and the sound of screaming hits my ears. It's packed tonight, even though it's nearly the middle of the week. Not out of the ordinary, but usually there isn't this type of crowd unless it's a Friday or Saturday night. When the nine-to-fivers can turn into the greedy, blood-thirsty animals they really are.

I pull my hood over my head, not in the mood to be ambushed tonight. Girls flock to me like a bitch in heat every time I'm here. Having Rosko with me doesn't help. I'm the only person that has a wolf dog in the city.

Slipping through the crowd with Rosko walking against my side, I make my way to the front as I watch two people I'm unfamiliar with wail on each other.

One tall man and one short man. The tall one has brass knuckles, and the short one has a blade, no handle. Almost like one of those old-fashioned razors that you'd put directly against your skin to shave. The man with the blade has a broken cheekbone, and blood flows from his nose in a steady stream.

The man with the brass knuckles is clutching his side, blood oozing between his fingers as he tries to both cover himself and fight at the same time.

It's peculiar, the feeling inside me. I'm fascinated by the fight in front of me, but that isn't the peculiar part. What confuses me is I'm disappointed the ocean-eyed girl isn't here tonight. At least, not at the moment. I don't know why she would be, considering I've been here every night since and haven't seen her.

TWISTED DARES

Maybe I killed her, after all.

Oh, wouldn't that be a pity.

But it shouldn't be. Not in the slightest. She's as meaningless as these people dying in front of me. She serves no consequence to me. Though, killing people is my greatest hobby, and ending her life doesn't feel the least bit satisfying.

I don't like where my thoughts are heading, so I focus back on the ring just as the man with the brass knuckles falls to his knees, the blood loss too great. He can't stand any longer. You can tell from his face, pasty white and covered in a sheen of sweat. The poor man won't survive unless he gets to the hospital soon.

The man with the blade steps forward, plunging the blade directly against his Adam's apple. He chokes, his hand leaving the wound on his side and going to his neck. Blood sprays out in quick spurts, and I nearly laugh at the people behind me as they gasp, some disgusted by the sight. Others amazed.

This scene in front of me gets a ninety-nine score in my book. Fucking pleasing as hell.

The injured man collapses onto his stomach, and within seconds, a puddle of blood surrounds him, filling up more and more of the white mat.

"Hey," I frown as I glance to the side, expecting to have to fling someone across the room, until I see Reggie, the owner of this place.

He's decent enough. He lets me fight whenever I want and stays out of my way. I know he's got a past of his own, a fucking double homicide is what I found out after doing some digging, but he's turned it around and now owns billions of dollars from watching other people murder each other.

"Let's talk." He nods his head toward the back of the Inferno, and I lift my brows, following him through the crowd with Rosko beside me and into an office that looks like it belongs in an executive suite instead of an underground tunnel. The floor-to-ceiling windows give him the perfect view of the ring.

He can watch death from the comfort of his cushioned chair.

"How can I help you?" I ask, keeping near the doorway. Rosko stays on his feet, his eyes on Reggie. He doesn't know whether or not he can trust him.

I feel the same.

I could take him out easily, no questions asked. I'm not a very trusting person. Not after the lifestyle I've been brought up in. Trust isn't given.

It's earned.

"You fought with one of my best fighters last week. Yet, she hasn't responded to her trainer once, and he's tried multiple times. When my best fighter goes missing, I grow concerned. And then I see you, who isn't scheduled to fight tonight." He scratches at his bearded jaw. "Any idea of where she might be?"

Oh, so this is about the girl.

She's missing?

She's one of his best fighters? I want to laugh at that one.

"Haven't seen her. Don't even know her."

He stares at me a moment, then nods slowly. "She was pretty messed up when she left here, and I'm a little concerned something's wrong."

Why the fuck is he talking to me about this? Like I give a shit in the slightest.

"Go to her house?" I pose my statement as a question, because I'm a little confused, and to be honest, irritated that he'd think I'd have a clue where she is.

Does he think I killed her or something?

He runs his hands over his face. "Forget I said anything, Caelian. She's probably just recovering." His face softens a moment. "I care about her, you know? I act like I don't give a shit about anyone, but she's different. She's not like the usual fucked-up people that walk through my door. She's on a different level. That girl… she's about as fucked up as they come. I think me and the others kind of think of her as a daughter or something."

I blink at him. "Okay."

TWISTED DARES

He clears his throat, standing up abruptly and running his hands down his shirt.

Wow. This guy acts like a fucking hardass, but he's a big-ass softy for some chick that probably gives less than two fucks about him.

"Thanks anyway."

I nod, heading out after possibly the weirdest conversation I've ever had in my entire life.

CAELIAN

Age Ten

The sound of an arm breaking makes a smile pop onto my lips, and I laugh silently as the wailing in front of me intensifies.

"Please stop." The sobbing is labored, choppy, and choked as the little asshole Henry from school decided to fuck around with Matteo. He was sorely mistaken.

The bone at his elbow pushes through the skin, white and tinged in red. Tears flood his face like the Niagara Falls, or at least, what I imagine it would look like. They look like a cartoon as they flood down his face before falling to the dirt beneath him.

Tears. What the fuck are tears? I've never experienced them. Never cried. Not for as long as I can remember, and even before that, my parents told me I never cried. Not even once as a baby.

I'm odd, as my mother puts it.

Unique.

She says it with a forced smile, then turns to my dad with wide eyes, having some secret, silent conversation behind my back.

It doesn't matter, my *lack of emotion*, as they put it, makes my ability to sense emotions that much stronger. That, and I've got good as hell hearing and can tell my mom's bitching to my dad that something's wrong with me.

Then my dad says there's nothing wrong; I'm just a sociopath like she is. Then he calls her a *cold bitch*.

Whatever.

My greatest hobby is causing pain, and when stupid Henry decided to take Matteo's lunch box and hide it in the bushes so he couldn't eat at school today... well, Henry deserved much more than this.

But I'm being lenient for some reason.

"Caelian? Caelian! What are you doing?" I roll my eyes as the voice of my level-headed brother, Gabriel, comes running up behind me. I can hear his shoes crunch on the leaves as he sprints through the woods. His angry steps overpower Henry's cries.

Gabriel steps up behind me, glancing over my shoulder at a nearly delirious Henry.

"He took Matteo's lunch box and threw it in the bushes. Matteo didn't get to eat lunch today," I growl.

Gabriel clenches his jaw. "Where is Matteo now?"

"Home. Because he was fucking hungry." I twist Henry's arm, the bone sliding even farther out of his skin. He screams like a banshee.

Gabriel steps around me, his tennis shoe swinging back and then forward, landing directly into Henry's nose.

The sound of a crunch makes my blood hot, and a flow of blood mixes with his tears, turning the dried leaves on the ground from brown to crimson.

"Come on, we have to go before someone finds us." Gabriel pulls on my arm, but I'm not ready to leave him. Not yet.

I want to kill him.

The need buries in my gut and makes it ache to the point that I wonder if something is wrong with me. Why do I constantly feel the need to hurt everyone around me? Everyone except my own family. Someone can literally walk past me and this need to take their breath from their lungs is debilitating.

"Come on, Caelian!" Gabriel pulls on my sweatshirt, and I glare down at Henry, spitting flames from my eyes.

"You speak a word about this to anyone, and I'll stab you in the stomach next time," I growl, throwing his arm to the ground and making him start a whole new round of screaming from the change in position.

"And don't fuck with my brothers!" I shout, walking away and heading home.

"Caelian, is that blood on your sleeve?" my father asks.

I curl my hand beneath the table, averting my gaze from his as I take another bite of my dinner roll. "It's nothing. Had a bloody nose."

I can hear the sound of metal clanking against metal as my dad sets his fork and knife down on the table. It's a large wooden thing, sitting in the middle of our dining area with patterned wallpaper and a large, brass chandelier over our heads. Our house is extravagant, made with gold and bronze and silver. Everything is shiny and overdone. But that's what happens when your dad is a powerful man. He has more money than he knows what to do with.

Our table is a masterpiece. The carvings around the edges had to have taken days, weeks, months; I have no idea. But they are so intricate and detailed that I imagine it took more time than I would ever bother with. Our chairs match the table, high and wing-backed, with patterned cushions that make you feel like you're sitting on a throne. Each one as large as the next, except for my father's, whose is just that much taller, that much more expensive.

He is, in roman terms, king of the fucking castle.

"Look at me, Caelian."

I do as he requests, bringing my eyes up to his. He glares at me, then looks around the table at my brothers, who have similar, sheepish looks on their faces.

"Someone tell me what happened."

"Henry took my lunch box at school," Matteo mumbles.

My dad whips his gaze toward mine. He knows. There's no need to even ask *if* I did anything. He immediately goes to the *what I actually did* conversation. "What did you do, son?"

"Nothing!" I shout.

"He broke Henry's arm," Gabriel says.

I turn my face toward his. "*Shut. Up.*"

His arms fly into the air. "He's going to find out anyway!"

I growl under my breath. There's a reason I don't tell Gabriel everything. He's an asshole like me, but he also respects my father the most out of all of us. He wants to do what's right, and in his mind, that means being truthful with him, all the fucking time.

"He took Matteo's lunch box!" I shout.

My father leans forward, grabbing onto my wrist and yanking me toward him. My chest brushes my plate, a tip of the fabric dipping into my gravy.

"What did you do?" His command for answers is lethal. He doesn't like to ask twice, and each one of us knows this. My father isn't a patient man. Not in the slightest.

"I broke his arm," I mumble, my eyes so badly wanting to fall, but they don't. At the end of the day, I don't care. I did what I thought was right at that moment, and nothing else matters to me.

The emotions of remorse and sadness that a normal kid would feel are all pretend for me. What I feel is anger. So much anger that everything else is washed away. My eyes see red, and my chest burns with a need to inflict as much pain as possible.

All other emotions are removed for me. Happiness is rarely felt, and sadness is an oddity I don't understand. I feel anger, irritation, and any other emotion I should feel, I just… *don't*.

My father squeezes my arm, and the sound of a throat clearing comes from the other end of the table. From my mother.

"Do you have something to say, Lucia?"

"I do not." She barely spares any of us a glance, looking uncomfortable yet bored as she takes a sip of her wine. I'm most like my mother out of all of us siblings. We are both very, very removed from life.

My dad pulls on my arm, and I turn back to him, his emotions so much different from my mother's. My dad has the temper of a short wick. It's literally only a few heartbeats from when he first gets angry before he explodes.

"Is he alive?"

My eyebrows lift. I've never killed anyone. So why he would ask such a thing is unnecessary.

"Of course. I just broke his arm."

"Broke his arm, agh!" His hand slaps on the table, rattling our plates and glasses. "Don't you think at all, Caelian? What happens if he goes back to his parents, huh? What if he goes to the school, with his shattered arm, and tells them that you snapped it without a care in the world? What then?"

I shrug, because I don't know. Nor do I care. I know my family gets away with a lot of things, and they'll protect me just as easily.

The groan of my father's chair pushing back makes me jump. "Come with me, Caelian."

"Where are we going?"

He nods his head. "Come. Now. I want to take you somewhere."

A sense of unease sits in my gut, like something bad is about to happen. I'm not scared of it, just uncomfortable with the unknown. With what I can't control.

"Gabriel kicked him in the face!" I point at Gabriel, who looks at me like I broke *his* arm. His nostrils flare, and I watch as his fingers whiten around his fork. Maybe he's imagining stabbing me. I don't care; he ratted me out when he was just as guilty. He should get whatever punishment I'm about to get, too.

My dad starts walking out, knowing that I'll be following him. "Gabriel stays here. You, Caelian, come with me." His voice echoes down the hall.

I glance over my shoulder, at everyone behind me. No one can look at me, each of them watching their plates with interest. Like they've never seen food before. Well, this is fucked up.

"You guys suck," I grumble, following my dad to his car.

And to the unknown.

We pull into a parking garage next to our family restaurant.

"What're we doing here?"

"Quit asking questions and follow me, Caelian."

I bite my tongue, following him from the car to the back of the building and into the staff door. The restaurant is closed for the night, lights off and door locked.

He pulls a key out of his pocket and shoves it into the hole, unlocking it before opening the door, waving me to step through. My heart bounces around my rib cage, and I want to grab onto it, hold it in place. The unknown unsettles me, makes me feel erratic. It's not a good feeling.

My father takes me straight to the basement, the place that's off-limits to me and my brothers. My heart pounds in my chest as I watch my surroundings turn from our family restaurant to what looks like it should be an abandoned building, with the barely functioning lights, as my father takes me underground. A door is at the bottom of the stairs, one that I've never been through. He pulls a separate set of keys from his pocket, using a giant one to unlock the door with a noisy grind of metal against metal.

He opens the door, and my eyes widen when I see we're in some underground office or warehouse. I'm not sure exactly how we ended up going from Morelli's to this secret underground lair. My eyes widen when I see some familiar faces of my dad's business workers as we walk down the hall. They give him a quick nod, but otherwise, everyone just goes about their work.

How was this going on underneath my feet and I never knew a thing about it? Do my brothers know about this place? Most of all, what the hell is it that they're doing down here?

My father walks without saying a word to me, his hands folded behind his back, his black suit expertly tailored to his body. Everyone says we look alike. That my brothers and I are replicas of our father.

Our slim builds, our sharp jaws and slim noses. Our dark eyes and dark hair. Our tanned, Italian skin. We all look similar, and I feel like I'm too young to determine whether or not that's a good thing.

We head through the basement that feels more like a tunnel than anything else. There's even a slight rumble above me, and it feels like it's the streets of Portland right above us. Which they very well may be.

It feels like there's not enough circulation down here. Like the air is thick and humid. But it's a cold humid. One that leaves a stickiness on your skin and a chill in the air. Each inhale brings the scent of old water into my nose, and even though the floors are dried in here, the walls have a dampness that give way to the earth surrounding us.

Eventually, the people disappear as we make our way to an even darker part of this strange place. I so badly want to ask my dad where it is we're going, but he hates being questioned in public. That's one of the things I've learned over the years, and I'm very determined to follow his orders.

"This way," he says quietly, walking up to a door and opening it. It's quiet, and the moment I step inside, he turns around, closing and locking it. There's a door behind us, and my dad opens that one, closing it as I'm through once again. His hand goes to the wall, and he turns on the light, his hand slapping the switch.

A humming sound starts before the lights flicker on, casting the room in a low yellow glow.

My eyes widen.

In the middle of the room sits a man in a chair. His ankles are tied to the legs of the chair, and his wrists are tied together behind him. The way his shoulders are bunched together, I'm almost certain they're throbbing with an aching pain. He has a navy blue blindfold over his eyes, and a dark gray piece of duct tape, shredded at the ends, stretched across his lips.

"What?" I ask myself more than anyone else.

"This, son, is where I wanted to take you." He steps farther into the room, walking to the man who seems slightly familiar but not enough that I'd know his name. I don't think I've even spoken to him before, but his face looks like I've seen him at least once.

"Who is that?" I nod toward the man.

He seems to be sleeping, but as my dad walks toward him, his nice Armani shoes tapping on the floor, the man's head swings up, and he looks from side to side.

The man starts panicking behind his tape, mumbling incoherencies that I can't make out.

My dad says nothing to him, continuously walking around the chair while talking to me. "You are different, Caelian. I'm sure you've realized this."

He glances at me, a dark shadow cut across his face, and I nod, unsure where he is going with this.

"For people like you, you need to make sure that you keep whatever is inside you at bay. If you don't, you might be uncontrollable. You might lose yourself if you don't learn how to control it."

My eyebrows furrow. "How am I supposed to do that?"

He smiles, his teeth shining brightly in the dim light. "That is why you're here." His finger points up, and he walks to what looks to be a tool bench. Shelving lines the walls, along with a row of cabinets and drawers. I'm so confused as he walks over to them and opens a drawer, pulling out a small blade. "I've had this man in this room for a few days now, unsure of what

I wanted to do with him. I was debating whether to let one of my men deal with him or just let him starve and die. But it clicked at the dinner table, that you are exactly the answer I've been looking for."

He runs his finger along the blade, testing the sharpness. Once he's satisfied, he turns toward me, walking with the blade extended in my direction. My heart double thumps in my chest, and for a moment, I wonder if he's coming to end me.

His problem child.

That's until the last moment, when he spins the blade around until he's holding the tip, the handle pointed toward me.

"Take it, son."

I do as I'm told, grabbing the knife from him. I test the weight in my palm, wondering what I'm supposed to do with it.

"I want you to take this and go do whatever you want to do."

My eyes widen, and I look up at him. "What?"

He points to the man, who's listening to us intently. I can sense it. His worry. His terror building. "To that man."

I swallow, my hand slightly shaky. "You want me to… kill him?"

My dad laughs. "I don't care what you do, Caelian. I just want you to do whatever you want. Let that monster in your chest free, son. But only for a minute. Control him. Let him loose when you say and reel him in when you say. *Find. Your. Control.*"

I can feel the monster. With his snappy teeth and his sharp claws. He demands so much of me. He claws and claws at me until I can do nothing but what he orders.

Like breaking Henry's arm.

"If you aren't ready, just give me the knife and we can go home." He grabs for the knife, and I pull it toward my body.

He smiles, like he's known all along. "Of course."

I lick at my lips, a tension building in my spine. I want to sprint toward the man and sprint away from him. I've never completely, wholeheartedly, let the monster free. I wonder if I let him out of his cage, if I'll ever be able to get him back in it.

"Go do what you want, Caelian. This moment is yours." He lifts his arm, patting my shoulder before dropping it back at his waist.

He knows I don't like to be touched. By no one. Not even my own mother.

With a deep breath, I step toward the man. Then another step, and another.

His chest starts shaking, and he once again starts mumbling behind the tape on his lips.

I stop for a second, and his head lifts, his eyes covered, but he can sense me. He can feel me.

He's talking to me, but I can't hear a word he says. His words are muffled, but the terror is still there. The pleas for his life are still clear in his tone.

"Caelian, this man is a bad man. Do you know what he did to one of my workers?" my dad asks from behind me.

The man groans deep in his throat.

My father continues, not even waiting for a response. "This man cut off my worker's fingers and toes and mailed them to the restaurant. Your grandmother opened the package. Imagine how she felt."

My nostrils flare, imagining my grandmother, who hasn't been well lately, opening a package of bloody fingers and toes.

My mouth cracks open, and I let loose a shaky breath. The monster in my chest grabs the bars and shakes at the cage, so wishing he could be free.

My free hand goes to my chest, and I rub there, knowing exactly what I want to do. Exactly what I need to do.

"Go ahead, son. You won't get in trouble."

The man's screams grow louder. He's shouting at me, I realize. Begging me to help him. To save him from his fate. He doesn't realize his fate was written the day he decided to wrong my family.

The Morellis do not fuck around.

I don't listen to him, a low hum starting in my ears. Anticipation. Adrenaline. The need that barrels through my chest all day and night is roaring to the surface, so fiercely, the knife shakes in my palm.

The man can sense my nearness, quieting down, the one sound of his shaky breaths rushing through his nose.

I take one more step.

His body tenses and his head tips back, letting out the most bellowing scream he possibly can behind the tape. His nostrils flare as wide as they can, his cheeks somehow paling and turning a bright red.

It does something inside me.

Flips a switch.

It feels like I wet myself, though it's through my entire body. A flush of heat runs from the tips of my ears to my toes.

The sound is wretched. It's terrible.

I step forward, the knife in my grip stronger than ever. The dampness from my palm drying as my hand slams forward. The tip of the knife sinks through his shirt, into his skin, and buries in his gut.

The ringing in my ears turns to a full roar, and my mouth salivates as I pull the blade out, seeing the thick red blood covering the silver.

My hand doesn't shake. It doesn't falter. It's steady as I plunge it back in. In and out. In and out.

In and out.

I stab him so many times. My arm begins to ache to the point I can barely hold it up. But I keep going. I go until he's a lifeless body, and the monster in the cage is satiated. Finally, for the first time in my life.

I'm content.

A hand on my shoulder makes me jump, the knife in my grip pulling back as I spin, the blade nearly plunging into my dad's dark suit. His eyes widen a fraction, settling on my face.

He looks… happy.

Pleased.

"You did well."

I feel nothing as he reaches forward and pulls the knife from my grip. "You are unique, Caelian. Like I've said before, you aren't like other people. But that's okay, because what I have planned for you will be just what you need."

My eyes narrow. "What?"

He steps away from me, heading to the wall with the knife and placing it on a metal tray. It looks like one that would be in a dentist's office. It doesn't even look new, but instead old and dented and scratched a million times.

"You will grow up to be a man that doesn't live like other men. You are not like them, Caelian. You need certain things in life, or you might find yourself one day on the verge of snapping. That's why we're here. I'm here to show you there's a way to live."

"To... *kill people*?"

He smiles, his face darkening a few shades. He looks like the businessman he is. Not someone you want to mess with. "How much do you know about our family business, Caelian?"

A lot and not much. I know we own a restaurant, and my family owns a few other businesses. I know that we're powerful, but I don't know why that is. "I don't know."

"Our family does things that not everyone would find acceptable. But what we do also serves a purpose. We get rid of men like that"—he points over his shoulder—"ridding the world of the toxic scum. We just did the world a favor." He straightens his suit jacket, his face blanking out. "I think you would serve well to help me get these bad men. What do you think?"

To kill people? To do what I've just done, time and time again?

I look down at my hands, covered in blood, as well as my shirt. My forearms are splattered, and licking my lips, I can taste the metallic flavor. I'm covered in it.

And I feel... satisfied.

"Yes. I will." Because what other choice do I have? This feels right. This feels like what I'm supposed to do.

He smiles, a genuine one this time. "I knew you would choose correctly, Caelian. I'm proud of you."

My father is proud of me. I don't think I've ever heard him say the words. The first time he's proud of me is when I've taken the life of another person.

At only the age of ten, my father chooses me to be such a significant part of his business. An important piece. One of the most important, I think.

At the age of ten, my father makes me a murderer.

RAVEN

My eyes crack open, my entire body weepy in agony. It aches like I've been sleeping on rocks, but I suppose sleeping on a cement ground wouldn't be too different.

I sit up, letting out a whimper as my bones and muscles scream in protest. Hobbling on my knees over to the bucket, I pull my leggings down, sitting over the rim and letting out the small trickle of pee that's in my bladder. I don't have much. They don't give me much.

One glass of water.

One slice of bread.

That's my meal per day. Nothing else.

I contemplate eating the pages of the Bible just to spite them, but I think that'll only dry my mouth further.

It's been… I don't know how long. *Too long.*

Days.

I feel like it's been over a week, but I've been sleeping so much that I can't be too sure. The noises above me have been minimal. Aria must be in trouble too, because I hear Aunt Gloria and Uncle Jerry's footsteps the most, and rarely do I hear the light footsteps of my cousin.

Has she been going to school without me? What have they said to the school? Is Aria being attacked by the other students? Have those girls bothered her without me there? Or have my aunt and uncle locked Aria in her room, and she hasn't been to school either?

I hope they haven't hurt her. I worry about my actions—if they've laid a hand on her body. If they've done even a fraction to her of what they've done to me.

It's been brutal. Inhumane. That's the only way to put it.

I stay here in the dark for most hours. Only one hour of the day consists of pain.

The hour of penance where I plead for forgiveness because my body is one huge, disgusting sin.

That hour is filled with such immense pain that I see nothing in the darkness of this basement. My vision fades and my throat constricts. The hate filling my body only intensifies to the point that breathing is an impossibility.

I hate so deeply; I wonder if I'll ever find a way out at the end of this.

I pull my leggings up, falling to my knees and sliding down until my cheek presses against the cool concrete. My backside hurts. My entire body hurts.

Aunt Gloria is angry. She is spiteful and rude with her punishments.

Uncle Jerry isn't as harsh, but with his punishment comes a lingering touch that makes my stomach turn to acid.

I know the reason I'm awake right now. Any moment, I'll hear the footsteps of either my aunt or uncle, followed by the door opening.

And my penance will commence.

Just as expected, my shallow breathing is interrupted by the sound of footsteps upstairs.

Two sets of footsteps.

My body tenses against the ground as I anticipate the pain. My body already twitches, my mind building an invisible wall that I can mentally hide behind. Taking on their punishments, as raw as they are, is traumatizing. I have nothing to protect myself. It's skin on skin, brutality against brutality. I'm nothing but exposed down here.

TWISTED DARES

It's wishful thinking to believe they would let me go free today, but with how slow their steps are, it's almost like a warning, or a threat. What is to come will be so vicious, the aftermath surely causing trauma.

The door opens, the hinges creaking loudly before the sound of footsteps on the wooden stairs grows louder the closer they get.

They are silent. They don't speak any words as they walk toward me. I keep my face planted on the ground, my eyes facing the wall in front of me.

I can feel them standing over me with malice emanating from them and hate seeping from their eyes into my already burning back.

"Undress." The words come from Aunt Gloria, her tone demanding and lashing as she spits them at me.

I push against the cement, feeling weak, completely lacking any fight in my bones as I get onto my knees and pull my shirt over my head. The cool air against my back gives me relief and pain. The wounds have no time to heal before new ones take their place. Cuts over scars. The burning and throbbing mixing together gives me such pain I can barely feel anything at all.

During their punishments, I find myself going to that place. The place that runs deep in the hottest parts of my blood. The bloodline that is filled with madness.

There is so much madness inside me.

It's only during times like these that I give into the mania. I let it overtake me because without it, I wouldn't survive. So, I let it swallow me. I let each bit of hysteria inside me consume me completely.

Until it ends, and then I want to go back to pretending it doesn't exist.

"All of it today," Uncle Jerry growls from under his breath, and my eyes widen.

They want me to be completely nude?

"What? No!" I scream, wanting to keep the last bit of dignity I have in me.

Aunt Gloria takes a step forward, and I shrink back, feeling the venom seep from her. "Do it, you little whore."

I wonder if I would survive if I fought against them. If I weren't in such a weakened state before they brought me down here, I'd have a chance. But between my broken nose, and them throwing me down the stairs, and now their beatings, I'm a fractured glass just waiting to shatter.

I want to choke and gag as I get to my feet, pulling my pants and underwear down my thighs, kicking them to the side. I fold my arms over my chest, keeping my back to them as I bow my head.

I know what they see.

Slim body, pale skin. Large, angry welts covering my back and ass. Some open wounds, some on the edge of splitting. Purple bruises and green ones. My backside must be a painting; it is so filled with pain.

The sound of a belt clanking makes goosebumps pop against my skin, and my breath puffs out in shallow pants.

I close my eyes, letting the darkness consume me. I go to the place inside me where nothing hurts. Where all emotions are blanked out and I care about nothing.

I am nothing.

The first lashing surprises me, but I don't scream. I don't break. I hold my body still as the whipping continues. The heavy slash of the leather belt against my upper shoulders, then the middle of my back. Then around my hips and the top of my ass. My legs twitch as the backs of my upper thighs feel the burn of the whipping.

My teeth sink into my lower lip until the skin breaks, a trickle of blood spilling onto my tongue.

It goes on for so long I lose track of time. I can feel the wetness of blood trickling down my back.

They don't say anything, and I wonder why they aren't requiring me to repent. Why they don't tell me to ask for forgiveness for the sins that they believe plague me so heavily. I don't know if I could speak right now if they asked. I feel like I'm losing myself more by the second. I forget who I am as my body separates from my mind, and I wonder who it is I've become as I watch myself, curled over in defeat, yet also still as a stone as the two monsters behind me tear me apart.

Mentally, physically, emotionally.

The lashing stops. "That's enough, Jer. Do it," she says, her voice forlorn.

My eyes snap open, my bones locking up as her words hit my chest.

Do what?

Are they going to kill me?

My body chills as Uncle Jerry steps closer to me. "Tell me, Raven, are you a virgin?" he asks quietly, shocking me.

My mouth gapes to answer, but all that comes out is a squeak.

"Speak when you're being spoken to!" Aunt Gloria booms, the belt snapping out and curling around my hip. The tip of the lashing hits my belly and pain rips through me.

"Y-yes. Yes, I am." I haven't spoken since I got down here, and my voice sounds funny to my own ears. A dusty cassette in the back of the cabinet. Unused and forgotten.

"Do you know that premarital intercourse is a sin?"

My eyes widen, and I glance over my shoulder. "I haven't… done that."

They look at each other, and I can feel my throat plummet into my stomach. The temperature in the basement drops ten degrees, and I know, without a doubt, that whatever is about to happen is not going to be good.

"I can't trust your sinful mouth. There is only one reason you'd sneak out of this house. If you are out having sex and getting those STDs and serving your vile body to vermin, well, I think I deserve to know about it," Aunt Gloria growls. "You come home injured, like a harlot in a brothel getting into a fight. Who knows what you're doing in the middle of the night."

"Not *that*!" I cry out, the pain breaking from my chest so real. So raw.

Why don't they believe me?

"That'll surely be the last time you have intercourse while living in this house," Uncle Jerry digs into his pocket, pulling out a yellow rubber glove. Bile rises to my throat, and I swallow it down, the dryness making it burn uncomfortably.

"What are you talking about? What are you doing? I haven't done anything wrong!" I screech, my cool body turning hot as nerves hit me.

"We're going to make sure you haven't been a whore to the devil." Aunt Gloria steps forward, and fight or flight takes hold. My feet punch off the ground, but Aunt Gloria is quick as she wraps her arms around my midsection. Her stiff fingers dig into the sore muscles of my stomach. I'm lethargic and malnourished. Any other day, I'd be able to fling Aunt Gloria's puny body off me with no effort, but lack of nutrients makes me slower and weaker than normal.

"Only a liar and a sinner would run away," she whispers into my ear.

She walks me backward until I'm back in my small square with nowhere to go. She pushes me until my breasts and stomach press against the cool wall, and a shiver breaks out along my body. My arms are shoved above my head, my fingers splayed and palm flush against the wall.

Aunt Gloria kicks at my ankles until my feet slide apart and my body is in the shape of a large X. I feel exposed, disgusting and violated. My backside screams in pain, and I can do nothing except pretend this isn't happening.

Though it is, and at the moment, it's hard to block it out. The pain and rage overtake me to the point I feel murderous. The sickening, manic part of me wants to thrash and spit venom toward each of them until they're dead at my feet.

"Hold still and it'll be done quickly," she grunts. "Hurry up, Jer."

The shuffling feet of my uncle come up behind me, and the snap of the latex glove turns my body to stone.

"No. No!" I thrash, and both Aunt Gloria and Uncle Jerry pin me down, keeping me locked against the wall. The feeling of the rubber glove against my ass cheek makes a wail rip from my throat. "Stop! Please, stop!"

Why do they think I'm a whore? Should I tell them the truth? That I go fight in the underground? Would they even believe me?

But no, I can't tell them. I can't say a thing for fear of them dragging me down there. I'd never survive that. I've been given strict instructions to never talk about the Inferno to an outsider. I refuse to break the rules.

That's my only place. My safe place.

"Please," I whisper as Uncle Jerry digs his fingers between my cheeks. He pulls them apart, the disgusting feeling of latex rubbing and lingering on my skin. Aunt Gloria probably doesn't notice the way his fingers caress me. It's fucking awful, and I can't do a thing about it.

When he gets to my folds, his fingers glide back and forth, and my eyes burn with furious tears as he touches where no one has ever touched before. He can't defile me like this. He fucking can't.

But he is. He's already there.

He dips a finger inside, the rubber squeaking against my dryness. It hurts, the uncomfortable sensation of his rubbery finger sliding against my walls does things to me.

It turns my rotted soul hollow.

"She is intact," he says, like he's a bit disappointed by the fact. It's odd, and I'd question it in any other situation. But I don't want to, because I want nothing more than them to both remove their hands from my body so I can wither away in peace.

I let out a silent gasp, my voice stolen from my chest just as they've stolen my sanity and the only broken, cracked pieces I have left of myself. They've stolen them with no remorse and only hate in their heart.

Aunt Gloria sighs, removing her hands from mine. "Get dressed and go upstairs. You've been away from school too long. You'll have a lot to catch up on. And take a shower. Your vile body smells like the devil's den."

The snap of the rubber glove as Uncle Jerry takes it off makes my body melt in both relief and disgust. I become disassociated with my body as I turn around and stare at them walking up the stairs. My naked body feels tainted as my bare skin chills in the basement air.

As they turn the corner, my body folds over, my knees slamming into the cement as a silent sob rips through me. My body aches from my toes to my face. I feel broken, used, my hollow heart shattered inside the empty cage of my chest. I don't even know who I am, or who I should be anymore.

I play the game and pretend to be who everyone wants me to be, but even that comes with overwhelming consequences. No matter who I am, I'll never be enough. And the truth is, the insanity that is dormant deep within me can only stay tamed for so long. I can only *pretend* for so long. My hate and revenge buried deep in the recesses of my soul stays locked in a cage that only I have the key to.

As I swing it around in my metaphorical brain, I know with a certainty that it's only time on the ticking clock until I unlock the rage and let it free.

There will come a day for revenge. There will come a day when I end the lives of my aunt and uncle.

And when that day comes, I may very well lose Aria. But the manic part of me doesn't care about that. All it cares about is causing pain to the people who have caused me misery.

It's that evil part of me that I let take hold. I'm no longer me.

I am what I am, and now... who I am now is not who I was. I was lost but found myself here in the basement.

I am a reproduction of my bloodline. My bloodline is evil.

Therefore, this is my fate. I make a promise to myself in the dark basement that someday, I will take hold of that evil and let it become me as well.

A knock at my door stiffens my body beneath the covers. I don't answer nor respond. I lay there, my head on my pillow for the first time in a week.

I realize I was in there a full seven days. A quick glance at the calendar in my room tells me I've been out of school for an entire week. I knew all along it was a long time. An entire week of water, bread, and pissing in a bucket was enough to change me.

TWISTED DARES

They've done this before, but not to this degree. When I was younger, it would be for an hour or two with the Bible in my hands and instructions to read scripture after scripture.

The longest I've ever been down there is one day. One day and night where I had to think about my actions for talking back. For being a kid. For just being... me. They think of me as one giant marked sin that cannot be wiped clean. Whatever they see on me through their eyes doesn't reflect in the mirror. The invisible tarnish is unfortunate because it's nothing that I can physically change.

But seven days in the basement has changed me. They've shoved me so far into the dark corner of my heart that I barely recognize myself. The perfection they've tried whipping into my bones has left me immensely imperfect. My imperfections are here to stay.

So is the madness that whispers in my ear, all the dark, terrifying thoughts. Things that I expect my father or mother to say. But to hear my own voice whisper the dark thoughts, my own mind and memories conjuring the evil within me leaves me shaken.

Thoughts of hurting them. Thoughts of brutalizing them.

But, why do I feel so guilty for these thoughts after how they've treated me? After how they've humiliated and tortured me?

The madness that I kept locked away slithered from its cage the moment my uncle shoved his dirty, pudgy fingers into my untouched sex. He defiled me, and my aunt let him. What kind of holy, saintly motherfuckers abuse their family in such a way?

Their own blood?

Now that I go to school, keeping me locked away is going to be more difficult for them. How can they explain repeated absences without raised brows? Being gone for this long is not normal under any circumstances. Even I realize that.

"Hello? Raven?" Aria's soft, hesitant voice makes my eyes shutter. I don't want to see her or talk to her, even though the other part of me wants it more than anything else in the world. I want to check her from head to toe and make sure they haven't laid a finger on her. If they did, that would surely break whatever restraint I'm still holding on to.

"Rave, are you okay?" she whispers, stepping into my room. The click of the door shutting deflates my chest. Nowhere feels safe anymore. Even with my door closed.

The edge of my mattress sinks, and I can feel her hand hover over my comforter. "I've been worried about you." Her voice cracks, worry and sadness in her tone.

I roll over, staying beneath the covers. My ugly floral comforter that I never picked out myself stays pulled up to my neck, and I stare at her with blank eyes. Checking on her with a discreet glance to make sure she's made it through this last week without me. Wondering if I can tell just by looking at her whether she has been at school or locked in her room. She looks to be in one piece, and it makes my rapidly beating heart settle, if only slightly.

My gaze reflects back from her watery one.

"Don't cry, Aria," I sigh.

Her chest hiccups, and she's so damn sad. I can tell she's beating herself up. The way she looks at me tells me she feels guilty about me being in the basement. She shouldn't be. It was never her secret to carry.

"Did they hurt you? Send you to school? Tell me everything," I whisper.

She shakes her head. "They didn't hurt me," she squeaks, her chest hiccupping again. The backs of her hands wipe at her cheeks, but the tears keep flowing. "I was grounded to my room, unless I was at school. Other than that, I've just been... *listening*."

Listening to *me*.

The pain in her voice, in her words, speak volumes.

Trauma doesn't always come in the form of physical pain.

The screams and moans during the first few days as the hour of penance was inflicted on me. I couldn't figure out how to turn it off. How to turn it all off.

Until I did.

"It just... stopped. I thought you died or something. But when they kept bringing you more water and bread, I knew you had to be okay. *Are you okay?*" She so badly wants to touch me, to curl into me and cuddle me like a sister should. But she knows I don't touch. She knows I'm unable to give her the love she so desperately craves.

"I'm okay," I lie, knowing if I tell her the truth, it'll set her off into a completely new spiral. I don't want her to freak or be worried. What she's experiencing has to be stressful. Torn between a cousin who she wants to side with and the parents she loves so deeply. It's a finicky situation and not one I'd ever care to be in myself.

I'm stuck between wanting to take her from her parents and never wanting her to go through the orphan loss that I feel on a daily basis.

"Did you go to school?" I ask her softly, my eyes probing as I look for any hurt in her eyes. If anyone has fucked with her at school, I'll rip them from their desks with my bare, sore fingers.

She nods slowly. "Yeah, I did."

My eyebrows lift. "And?"

Her eyes drop to the bed. "It's been fine. No one has bothered me."

I chew on the inside of my cheek, containing the chaos that feels so unstable inside of me. She is hiding something from me, and I have to determine if I'll be bitching someone out or burying a body sometime in the future. "Tell me what happened."

Her eyes lift to mine, glossy with unshed tears. "No one was mean, but it was hard without you. Those girls haven't talked to me, but it's clear they don't like me. I'm being nice to everyone, but they look at me like I'm a poor loser." Her fingers go to a frayed thread on my quilt, wrapping it around her finger again and again.

I bring my hand down on hers, pulling it away from the string. "But those girls have left you alone, right?"

She nods.

"And no one else is being outright mean to you?"

Her head shakes slightly.

I nod, clenching my jaw. She's going to make friends. If I have to play nice to find her some, I will. She doesn't know anyone besides her church group. She's unsocialized, and it's not her fault. Granted, I am, too. But she's too innocent to understand how to fake it until she makes it.

I'm going to make sure my cousin fits in and fucking rocks the hell out of this school. She's going to succeed, and people are going to wish they were her friends.

I'll make sure of it.

"What are you going to do now? I mean… are you going to keep going *there?*" She ends the last few words so low that I can barely make them out.

She's wondering about the Inferno. She wants to know if I'll be sneaking out again or going against her parents' orders.

It's the one place where I can be me, and I refuse to give it up.

"I will," I say, no hesitation.

Her shoulders sink, and a nod slowly creaks out. I watch her chew her lip as she stares at me. As she stares at my scars and wounds. She wants to know exactly what happened, but also the hesitation means she doesn't. She's scared to know how fucked her parents are.

I'll never reveal how deranged they really are. I won't traumatize her like that. She doesn't deserve it. One look at my back and I can guarantee she'd call the police. She might love her parents, but more than anything, she's just a good fucking kid and wants to see the light in the world.

"I think I'm going to take a nap," I tell her. I don't want to hurt her feelings, but the exhaustion lays heavily in my limbs. They are heavy, and weak. I haven't eaten anything since I got out, but I can smell the beginnings of dinner starting downstairs.

I want to recoup my body so I can gain my strength back. Whatever training I've lost in the past seven days has me feeling weaker than I've ever been before. I need my back and ass to heal so I can get back out there and fight again. So I can go to school with Aria and protect her.

I need to become me again.

"Oh. Oh, okay, then." I can tell she's disappointed, but my fatigue makes me unable to comfort her. At some point, she's going to need to grow up on her own.

I've had to.

"We can talk more tonight after dinner. I'm just really tired." My words do the trick, at least slightly. She nods, pressing her hands into the mattress to stand. In a pair of jeans and a sweatshirt that aren't the least bit hip, you would think my baby cousin is unattractive. That's not the case in the slightest.

With her long, chocolatey-brown hair, and hazel eyes, she is literally one of the most gorgeous people I've ever met. She has fairy features, tiny and petite. She's adorable, a knockout, and unfortunately, her parents will never allow her to flourish in her beauty.

She gives me one more lingering glance before slipping from my room. The click of my door sounds, and I roll over, wincing as my entire backside aches and burns from the movement. Shutting my eyes, I let the darkness consume me.

I need to get back to the Inferno. And I need to get there fast. I worry without it, the rage will continue to build to the point where I'll have only one option.

To kill them in cold blood.

chapter eight
RAVEN

The familiar school sits in front of me, just as large and ominous as it looked on my first day. A few kids watch me in my car as I roll through the parking lot, and I narrow my eyes at them, tired of the fucking gawking already.

Two more days at home and I'm as healed as I'm going to get. My nose has turned from bright purple and swollen back to its normal size, though now it's an ugly green and brown. It's slightly cocked to the side, indeed broken as fuck.

Thankfully, the rest of me is hidden by my clothes. I know everyone would gasp in horror at the lashing wounds along my skin. But the pain has settled enough for me to get around, and that was good enough for Aunt Gloria to send me back to school. In a brief conversation, she let me know the school was notified of my car accident and that I'm doing much better.

That's it. No other words were said about it, though I do have to say, for such a fucking terrible car accident, my car seems to have taken zero damage.

Fucking idiot.

The car they didn't even want me to have. They wanted me to get a job so badly but knew they wouldn't spend the time to actually drive me anywhere. Within a few months, I had my license, and the shittiest car on the lot. I'm glad they got me the car, because instead of going to the library and getting a job like I told them I did, I found myself in front of a gym, which led me to meeting Corgan.

Which led me to the Inferno.

I shake my thoughts clear as I pull into a parking spot in the back, my limbs still a little achy and stiff from this last week and a half. It's Friday now, and tonight I'm planning to go to the Inferno. I'm not ready to fight, my body way too sore to take any sort of beating, but I just need to get out, go back to my element.

Feel fucking sane again after being flooded with all this insanity.

"I'm really glad you're back. It felt weird to go to school without you," Aria says as I turn off my car.

I glance out the window, wondering if I'm going to see the man who broke my nose. I wonder what I'll do if I see him. If I'll chicken out or if I'll give him a dose of my crazy. He deserves it. I can barely smell since he shattered the bone in my nose.

"It kind of feels like it's my first day all over again." I sigh, not really sure how I feel about all of it. I wish I could skip, but after just getting healed, staying away from both my aunt and my uncle is my main priority. Unfortunately, that means following the rules. For now, at least.

Aria sits next to me, not saying a thing as my bones throb and my flesh grows hot. I don't want to be here, but I don't have a choice at this point.

For Aria, I'll do it.

I glance over at her. "Let's go."

We both get out of the car, and I lock the door before slamming it shut. I grip the top strap of my backpack in my hand and tuck a stray hair behind my ear, the rest in a messy bun on top of my head. I couldn't be bothered to try to look presentable today. All I could muster with stiff muscles this morning is black leggings and an oversized Nike hoodie.

Aria walks behind me, her backpack strapped to her back, wearing a burgundy cardigan over a white blouse and dark jeans. Her dark hair sits in soft waves as they bounce against her shoulders. She's trying. She's trying really hard to look as good as she can for these rich kids.

Though she'd never completely fit in. She's too pure, too innocent to get along with them. They're all manipulative, pill popping addicts if what I believe is true. One glance at them, and I can tell their designer clothes and perfect hair are just a ruse to how fucked up they really are.

We reach the front doors, the cool morning making no one linger outside. That means the moment we walk through the front door, the hallways are flooded.

I clench my teeth as everyone looks at me. As their eyes trail up and down my body. I watch their eyes linger on my bruised nose, my tired eyes. My ratty clothes that are more for comfort than anything else.

A few girls scrunch their noses, like I walked through trash on my way to school. I don't fucking stink, and I grind my molars together and keep my feet straight.

Not going over there. Not going over there.

I see the jock group, Charles or Chuck or Chet, standing in the middle. His face brightens when he sees me, and I see him step back from his group. My head drops to the ground, not in the mood to talk to him. Not now.

The students do not part like the sea for me. If anything, they crunch closer together, to the point I'm bumping shoulders with every fifth person I walk past. The jostling does nothing to help my aching body, and by the time my locker comes into view, a headache is brewing in the back of my skull.

I sigh, my hand going to the back of my neck as I squeeze the tense muscles. Three guys stand a few lockers down from mine, and I pause in my step, my headache, my pain, everything fading. Falling down my body and onto the ground like rivulets of water.

It's him.

His back is to me, but I saw him shirtless the last time. My body was attached to his. I feel like I know him so much from just two encounters. I feel like *he's mine.*

I've touched him. I've touched his skin. I've felt the heat of his body and experienced the coldness of his eyes lashing into mine.

"What is it?" Aria leans into me, whispering in my ear.

I bite at my lip, anger pulling at my gut. But that's not it, because I'm feeling so much more. Heat floods my belly, emotions I've never felt in my entire life roaring through my body.

What is this… *fire* that takes over every inch of my skin? I feel feverish, ill, as a rush of warmth rolls through me.

It doesn't take away from my anger or hate. It does nothing to quench my need to knock him and break his bones just as he's done to me.

"The tall one. He's the one that broke my nose," I mumble.

Someone shoves into Aria's back, and she trips forward, barely able to keep her footing.

My blood goes from hot to ice cold, and I narrow my eyes as I step back, grabbing onto the douchebag's backpack and pulling him back. He's strong, a big dude, and it takes all my strength to stop him in his tracks.

"Dude, what the fu—" His eyes widen when he sees it's me. *The new girl.* "What the hell are you doing?"

I keep hold of his backpack while I point at Aria. "You fucking ran into her, you dipshit. Apologize to her, *now.*"

His eyes widen before narrowing into slits. The kid is a punk, and you can see he has issues with authority or being told what to do by fucking anyone.

"*Fuck. Off,*" he sneers.

"Raven, stop," Aria whispers, tugging on my backpack.

"Let go of me, you cunt," he spits at me.

My nostrils flare, and I reel my fist back, ready to pop him in the nose for being the biggest cock on the planet. Probably with the smallest cock between his legs.

As my hand goes forward, it slams against an open palm. Large. Rough.

Warm.

Strong.

Large fingers wrap around my fist, each digit curling slowly around my knuckles. Tanned skin against pale skin. The grip is powerful, and slowly, he lowers it to my waist.

Him.

His other hand goes over mine that is secured around Small Cock's backpack. He unwraps my fingers, his own taking my spot as he pulls the guy toward him. "The fuck did you do?"

His voice is raspy, like he just rolled out of bed. A tone that's meant to be bottled up and stored for the worst of days. Or perhaps, just for any day.

The jackass who bumped into Aria was once cocky and rude to me, but now to this man, he's a weak, weak boy. "Nothing. She just grabbed my backpack and started fucking with me. I don't even know who she is!"

His eyes drop to mine. "What did he do?" His voice is gravel. *Gravel.* Raw and hardened and so, so fucking sexual.

My mouth goes dry, and I forget how to use my words. "He, uh. He, uh, ran into my cousin." My voice cracks on my words, and I feel like a fucking idiot.

His eyes drop to Small Cock's. "Apologize."

He looks at my cousin. "I'm sorry." He doesn't sound like he means it, but he also isn't acting like a dick anymore.

Aria looks over at me, her eyes wide. Frightened. Uncomfortable.

The hallway is starting to flood out, and I know we have minutes before we have to be in our seats for first period. If I'm late and recorded as tardy, Aunt Gloria is going to seriously be on my fucking ass.

I nod, my eyes on my cousin. He removes his hand from Small Cock's backpack, and the man is down the hall within seconds.

He releases my fist, and I instantly drop my hand to my leggings, wiping off the dampness from my palm.

Why the hell am I nervous?

"You're at my school," is all he says.

Fuck him. "It's my school."

He lifts a brow, and I glance over my shoulder, watching his two friends watching me with curious looks on their faces.

"Actually, it's my school."

He stares at me a moment until his eyes drop to my nose. "Figured you died."

I squeeze my hands into fists, my nails digging into my palms. Fucking hell, I want to knock this guy in the face. "You're a piece of shit. You're lucky I don't fuck you up in *your school*. But I won't embarrass you in front of your friends."

His chest puffs out a soundless laugh, full of air and not any humor. "*I dare you.*"

The words. His words that make me want to tear him in two. The ones that got me the broken nose in the first place. He's cruel and malicious, and from the look in his eyes, he doesn't really care about anyone but himself.

Prick.

I walk past him, chucking my shoulder against his, though he's so tall it's almost like I'm slamming my shoulder against his pec, which in itself feels like a fucking brick.

This guy *has* to be taking steroids.

I can feel Aria trembling beside me as I open my locker. My fingers shake, and I so badly want to jump on his back like I did at the Inferno, sinking my teeth into his neck.

I hate that he tasted so fucking good. Salty and manly and so damn possessive. I hate that a part of me wants to bite into him again, not to cause him pain, but to have that taste linger on my tongue.

"Fucking prick."

"He broke your nose? That huge guy did? Maybe we should go tell someone."

I close my eyes, rolling them behind my lids before turning to look at

Aria. "He didn't do anything he isn't able to do. It's part of the Inferno, Aria. Don't be dense about it."

She nods, opening her locker and setting her things inside. "You just look really hurt. I can tell something is wrong. You're walking like your entire body is a bruise." Her faces scrunches in discomfort. "Did my parents do that to you?"

I shut my locker, hating how upset she sounds. This isn't the place or time to tell her that her parents literally wounded me from head to toe.

"Don't ask me about it, Aria. Not here. Everything is fine." Her eyes narrow, and I can see the words working their way through her mind. "Stop, Aria. Stop it," I grit between my teeth.

She stares at me another moment, and I know she wants to press, but the one-minute bell rings, saving me from her interrogation.

"I'll see you after first period." I reach out, gripping onto her fingers that are strangling her notebook in her arms. "Chill out a little. Try not to look like you're walking into a pit of fire. Everything will be okay, and if it's not, you know where to find me."

She wiggles her fingers, her face and spine straightening. "Thank you, Raven. I love you."

I work the words inside my mouth. She doesn't say them often, though I know they're true. I can't remember the last time I've heard the words directed at me.

"I love you, too, Aria."

I wonder if there will ever be a day that I'll go to school and won't be whispered about as the new kid, or the poor kid, or the kid who looks fucked up with the bruise on her face. Even the pound of concealer this morning wasn't able to hide the green along the bridge of my nose.

Aria seemed to take my advice this morning, and she isn't bothered by any words that the people are saying. They aren't even being rude, necessarily. They are just curious and gossipy, which aggravates me more than anything.

"Someone said she got jumped after school last week, do you think that really happened?" some guy at the next table whispers, his eyes stuck on mine as he dips his French fry into a pool of ketchup.

He's preppy, with too much gel in his hair, and I know I could lay him flat on his ass with a flick of my wrist. He's all bones and limbs with no muscle or fat on him. He's not a man.

Not at all like *him*.

"Probably. I heard she has a mouth on her," the guy next to him says.

I sigh, shoving my plate away from me. "I'm going to the bathroom. I'll be right back," I tell Aria, who's working on homework, her own lunch pushed aside, plate clean.

That is the only benefit of this place. The food is immaculate. Everything is catered in by high-quality chefs and nothing—*nothing*—is bagged, frozen, or overly processed.

She glances up, her pencil falling to the paper with a light tap. "I can come with you."

I shake my head, grabbing my bag from underneath the table. "No, stay here. I'll be right back." I need a moment. Just a moment to not have to talk or pretend or listen to any voices.

I'm desperate for a moment of complete silence.

Walking through the cafeteria, I ignore the turning heads and the lingering eyes as I head toward the door.

"Hey! Raven! Wait up!" I quickly glance over my shoulder, seeing Charles or Chad sitting on top of the table he's at. His Converse shoes propped on the bench slide off as he shoves to a stand and grabs his backpack, racing toward me.

No. Please, no.

"Hey, Raven." His footsteps quicken until he's at my back, and I can feel the heat of his heavy breaths on the back of my neck.

Too close.

I barely spare him a glance. "Oh, hey. I'll be back. I'm just going to the bathroom."

"Oh, well, I can walk you, then." He steps in front of me, a cheesy smile on his face.

I smile, though I know it falls flat. "I think I can manage."

He laughs a little, grabbing my bag from my hand and hanging it over his shoulder. I narrow my eyes, not sure why he thinks that's necessary or fucking appropriate.

"I know, I know. You don't need anyone's help and you probably don't even like people that much, but people are talking. And when I say talk, I mean *talk*. I'm going to help whether you want it or not. Pretty much every guy wants to come up and do the same thing I'm doing, and the girls fucking hate you because you're prettier than they are."

I gnash my teeth together. *Fuck, I hate this.*

I also want to laugh, because they're wearing Gucci and Guess and Prada, and I'm wearing clothes that are faded and frayed.

"I really don't want the attention." I glance over at him, hating that he's so damn attractive, yet I feel nothing. It feels like I'm broken. "I appreciate you wanting to help and protect me, but I really don't have the time to deal with"—I wave my hand between us—"this."

"You're cute, Raven. We can go as slow as you want. I'll make you want me eventually."

Cocky ass.

I head to my locker, because I'm halfway concerned he's going to follow me into the bathroom stall. He unzips my backpack and holds it open. I narrow my eyes as my hands dig in, grabbing my last period's textbook. I toss them in my locker and swap them out for my next class.

I shove them in my bag, and a slow smile lifts the corner of his lips, like we've already got a couple routine down, or something. My fingers twitch to slap him in the face for being so arrogant, but I know it won't fly with most people.

He zips up my bag as he leans against the locker next to mine, kicking his foot out. "So, where'd you come from, Raven?"

I shut my locker, sighing as I turn toward him. "California."

His eyebrows lift. "California? What made you come up to Blackridge?"

Nothing I'm going to tell you.

I shrug. "I needed change."

He tilts his head back with a chuckle, his eyes glimmering with humor. "Change? That's it? You really know how to avoid the subject, don't you?" He looks back at me, his face dropping to seriousness. "I can't figure you out. Like, I've always been able to read people like a book, but you're different. I could tell the moment you stepped into the school. A closed book and locked tight." He shakes his head, like he's actually baffled. "It only makes me want to dig deeper. Until I figure out everything there is to know about you."

I can feel myself shutting down.

I stay in the background for a reason. I keep myself hidden for a *fucking reason*. I don't want him to know everything there is to know about me. I want him to know *nothing*.

"Nothing to figure out. I'm Raven from California, and I go to Blackridge Prep." I shove off the locker and head toward the bathroom. "Nothing else to me. Sorry to disappoint."

He chuckles, and I don't like how the sound makes the hair raise on my arms. "I don't think that's true at all. And you know what else?" He comes up beside me, my backpack still in his grip.

I reach for it, but he pulls it out of my reach with a playful smile.

"You should come to my game tonight. We're playing Hearthridge High, and those games are intense. Someone always ends up fighting on the field. They are literally the number one enemy. You never know, you might be my good luck charm."

I reach for my backpack again, and he once again pulls it from my reach.

"I can't. I have plans."

He chuckles. "What if I don't take no for an answer? Maybe I won't give you your bag back until you show up at the game."

Irritation rips through me, and I can feel the heat rolling up my skin. I'm trying. I'm trying so fucking hard to keep my cool, and I really don't want to snap on him, but he gives me no choice.

My mouth opens, a threat on the tip of my tongue, when a shadow moves in front of me. He appears out of nowhere, soundless, in all black, looking like the grim reaper in the flesh. His face is severe, with palpable anger lashed across his features. His hand whips out, wrapping around Chad or Charles's neck. He squeezes so hard I see the tips of his fingers turn white as he slams him against a row of lockers.

It's him. *Again.*

"Get the fuck away from her, Anderson," he growls, and the vibration rolls through my body, straight between my legs.

"Fuck off, Morelli," Chad or Charles chokes out, his face red in both pain and irritation.

My grim reaper growls, like an animal in the forest as his lip curls over his upper teeth, his eyes turning from dark chocolate to black pools of rage.

His hand lowers, and he grabs my ratty backpack from his grip, tearing it from his fingers and tossing it in my direction.

My hands automatically open, and I grab it before it can hit the floor.

I watch as his hands clench, his fingers burying into his neck so deep, I wonder if he's going to crush his windpipe. I watch in awe; the pain inflicted on someone else making my mouth water. I get it, I'm fucked up, but it doesn't stop the fact that this man is hurting someone else for…

For, what?

Talking to me? Walking with me?

I swallow down the knot in my throat as Chad or Charles coughs and chokes, his face turning a disgusting shade of purple.

Suddenly, he whips his arm, tossing Chad or Charles clear across the hallway. He slides on the dirty ground, his letterman jacket filling with dust and dirt until his back slams against the lockers behind him.

"Don't fucking talk to her. Don't even look at her. Stay the fuck away from her," he snaps before he grips onto my arm, pulling me away from wide-eyed Chad or Charles and toward the girls' bathroom at the end of the hall.

My arm burns like it's sitting above a flame right where his fingers clutch me. I've touched him before, and I've touched other people before to know that whatever reaction I'm getting from him… I've never experienced it before in my life.

There's something… different about him. About him and me.

I gasp in a breath when he releases me. Standing flush against the wall, he steps toward me, until we're toe-to-toe and only an air of breath stands between us.

The air is filled with an energy, toxic, and yet it fills me with life. Breathes air into my lungs when they feel like they've been suffocating for so, so long.

"What're you doing?" I whisper.

He hums under his breath as his eyes trail across my face. There's a burning heat in its path, and I wonder if he feels the same or if I'm alone in this abyss.

"I'm wondering how I see you in my ring, and then you're showing up around every corner. Are you following me?"

I puff out a laugh. "Don't flatter yourself." Though even as I say that, I can't help the rapid beat of my heart. One glance at my chest would give it away, the flicker and twitch of my sweatshirt against my breasts wild as if the wind is whipping against it.

"Where did you come from?" he asks, his finger lifting, hovering above my nose. Above the wound he has caused.

I glance away from him. "It's none of your business."

"How is that I have to save you from a jock, but you go in the ring to fight killers and felons and rapists?"

My eyes pierce his. Anger burns in my chest at his words. "I didn't need you to save me. I had it covered."

He stares at me a moment before he shoves off the wall, a waft of his scent trailing into my nose. "Stay away from Chad Anderson." With that, he walks away, leaving me alone in the hall, with my thoughts, my overheated body, and wild heart.

The bell rings only seconds later, and Aria appears around the corner, my innocent, pure cousin snapping that man from my thoughts altogether.

I need to stay focused. I can't let my end goal waver because of a man I don't even know. I need to protect Aria, finish school, and get back to the Inferno. Everything else, even a man who disrupts everything in me, doesn't matter.

It can't.

"Hey. *Hey*, girl." A wadded up piece of paper hits me in the back of the head, and I ignore it, keeping my eyes on my textbook cracked open on the desk in front of me.

Nope. Not falling for it. No fighting. No hurting people. Stay fucking focused.

Another paper hits me, this one tangling in my hair. I can feel it pull on the strands, and I let out a sigh as I turn in my chair, reaching back to pull the paper from my hair. "What do you want?" I grit out.

My eyes pop open as I see one of the guys from earlier. Not my guy, no, this one is the playful-looking one. With curly, wild hair, and light brown eyes. His skin also has the tanned shade, like he surfs for a living or something. He looks very similar to my guy. Are they related?

Morelli. I remember Chad saying that. Is that Italian?

They must be. They *have to* be.

"You're the new girl," he says simply.

I narrow my gaze, not confirming or denying.

"You're creating quite a stir around here." He looks me up and down, humor bouncing in his irises. "Though, I guess I can see why."

I bite at my lip, leaning toward him. His eyes widen before lowering. Then he leans into me as well, until we're only inches away from each other. "Say another leery comment and I'll knock you straight on your ass."

He stares at me, silently, and then leans back in his seat, his tanned neck stretching as he barks out a laugh.

His eyes are glistening as he straightens, and I wonder what was so fucking funny when I was deadass serious.

"Now I see why you're causing such a stir. Not only with this school, but with my brother, too."

They *are* brothers.

I sit up, pushing my shoulders back, then send one last glare his way before turning back around in my seat and grabbing my pencil. "Figures. You're both fucking annoying as shit."

He chuckles. "Okay, baby. You're going to be a lot of fun."

I grip my number two pencil, feeling the wood crack under the pressure. Spinning around once again, my hand goes under his desk, the tip of my pencil pressing against his thigh. "I've just about had it with the crude comments today. I'd rather you keep them to yourself. If you feel like saying any more funny jokes, I think you should direct them at your friends after class and leave me the fuck out of it unless you want this pencil embedded in your leg."

He stares at me, his eyes darkening until they match his brother's. His hand slinks beneath the desk until his fingers wrap around mine. I grit my teeth from the uncomfortable sensation of skin against skin.

"Listen to me and listen good." His fingers tighten, nearly to the point of pain. "I don't know who you are or where you came from, but I don't take kindly to threats. None of my family does. So watch your mouth before I shove a pistol in it."

My nostrils flare, and I narrow my eyes, my fingers tensing until he releases me. I lift the pencil from his thigh, sliding out from underneath his desk and turning back around.

A few people stare, but most of them are unusually uninterested in me. I don't know if this class is that captivating, or if this Morelli kid has anything to do with it. If he does, he must be more dangerous than I thought.

That means the other Morelli is just as dangerous. Maybe even more so. I swallow.

All the more reason to stay away from him. He's nothing but a distraction. A dangerous distraction.

One that I can't seem to get my mind off of.

My duffel is gone.

They must have trashed it after they sent me to the basement. Doesn't matter much anyway, since I'm not fighting tonight. But my fighting and exercise clothes are gone with it, and that really fucking sucks because now I don't know what I'll fight in.

Once I get back in the ring.

The rest of the day was quiet. But it didn't do anything to help the edge I've felt I'm teetering on. My anger is slowly clawing closer to the surface... How long until it breaks free?

When Aria and I got home from school, I was grateful to find both Aunt Gloria and Uncle Jerry working late. That means I won't have to deal with their interrogation before I go to work tonight.

Aka, go to the Inferno.

When I spoke with her early this morning, I told her I'd have a long shift on my first night back. She believed me, and I think that's only because I've been playing it safe these past few days.

I haven't had it in me to try to get out sooner. I've been so fucking weak.

TWISTED DARES

My body isn't what it was, and I'm worried I'll never be as good as I was. Not only that, but when I do get back in there, there will be no way to hide what has happened to me. The torture that was inflicted upon me will be on display for everyone to see, illuminated by the lights above me. Welts and cuts lining me from neck to thighs. They may be healing, some maybe even faded, though they'll be there, and they will be impossible not to notice.

I have one goal in mind, and that's just to get back to the Inferno. Not to fight, but to breathe the violent air and watch the fights. I want the rawness. I need to feel something, and even if it isn't me who is fighting, I can at least pretend.

Until my strength is back, that's all I have.

With my hoodie on my shoulders, and a fresh pair of leggings on my legs, I sit on my bed and pull my tennis shoes from underneath. I'm going incognito tonight. I don't want to be noticed by fans or Reggie.

It's been too long. I missed my last weekend's fight, and I know Reggie is going to have a lot to say about it. There're going to be *I told you so*s and *what the fuck were you thinking*s. I don't want to deal with any of it. I just want to see the fights and forget *everything else*.

I don't want the questions and the hassling to become overwhelming to the point I don't want to be there. My mind isn't ready. My body isn't ready. It's why I don't want to be found tonight.

The fans will beg me to and cheer my name in hopeful chants. They'll be sorely disappointed when they realize it's not happening.

Not tonight, at least.

I will get back in the ring, but I'll be there when I'm strong enough to fight as good as I once was or better. I refuse to allow myself to get knocked down like I was before. I will get strong.

I will be what I need to be.

Who I was always meant to be.

And I will destroy anyone that gets in my way.

I make my way through the civilian entrance and start to think this was a bad idea.

The amount of people hyped up to get a sniff of blood or a drop of sweat on their skin makes them vibrate to the point my stomach twists. The floor vibrates from their pounding feet. The air is electrified, sexually charged, full of rage and a need for skin against skin brutality.

I'm still sore, still feeling off in a way that I want to be around people even less than usual. So, bumping shoulder to shoulder with people left and right as we make our way through the abandoned parking garage and through the tunnels into the Inferno, put me on high alert. It's chilly tonight, and the cool air makes its way into the underground. I'm glad for my oversized hoodie that I have wrapped around me. I keep my head down, my hood up, and my face obscured as I shove my way into the main area.

Aunt Gloria and Uncle Jerry walked in just as I was leaving. I was able to tell her I was running late, so I didn't get blocked by her, but it didn't stop her from staring long in my direction. A warning. A threat.

Don't fuck up.

Don't. Fuck. Up.

I hate that her cruelty makes taking her life someday inevitable. Her hate gives me no choice. I will never be free of her. Aria will never be free of her if I allow her to continue her deranged thinking. She will never stop. She and my uncle destroy just as much as my parents did, in a sense. They fight against the darkness, but they're just as bad.

Maybe even worse, because my parents never hurt me. Aunt Gloria and Uncle Jerry, it feels like their goal is to cause me pain and misery. They care about nothing else besides making my life a living hell. I wonder how she'd react if she realized her days are limited, and there will come a time when everything that she is will be nothing but bones and dirt. I'll enjoy every moment of taking the breath from her lungs. I hate that it has to be this way. I despise that she's trying to save me, but she's only making me worse.

She's turning me into her worst nightmare.

My nostrils flare as disgust hits me. *Why am I becoming this... this person?* The blood in my veins runs hot with a sickness that I've fought against my entire life. I've never wanted to be this person.

But I'm learning, I *need* to be this person.

Aria... she'll never forgive me. She'll never want me in her life once she realizes how demented I am. She'll hate me, plain and simple.

She keeps me tethered to the surface of sanity. Without her, I don't want to know who I'd be.

I'd prefer to not think about it.

I shake my thoughts free as the voices grow to a deafening level. The hype is already top-notch by the time I push my way through the strong arms and stand first in line in front of the ring. My fingers poke out from my sweatshirt, and I brush them along the rough rope of the ring. It's been so long. Too long without pressing my feet against the stained mat. Too long since I've sweat and felt the ache in my bones. *The good ache.*

I promise myself, as I rub my raw fingers against the rope, that I'll be back within the week. I'll get back to the gym tomorrow and work my way back to fighting again. I'll get there.

I have to.

The moment the lights dim, my skin pops with goosebumps, and I glance around, excitement and adrenaline running through my veins as if I'm the one in the ring.

I let go of the rope, pulling my hood farther over my forehead and tucking my hair behind my ears. I feel ridiculous standing in the crowd, next to women who are in dresses and skirts, showing off their stomachs in crop tops and wearing high heels, while I stand here in a baggy hoodie, leggings, and a pair of tennis shoes that have seen better days.

I shouldn't care, because I really don't. But the feminine side of me, the girl that lives beneath the mania, hates that she can't feel, can't experience, like all of them can.

I desperately want love, yet I despise that I want it so bad. I don't ever want to be in a vulnerable position like that, but I also want to experience what the world speaks of.

Love.

Though, at the end of the day, I don't think I would ever know how to make my heart beat to begin with. It's an empty, heavy muscle in my chest that died a long, long time ago.

I watch as a man I've seen one other time before steps into the ring, his shorts slung low around his toned waist, his body looking like it's cut from stone. His tanned arms corded with veins. I've never fought him myself, but I've seen him in passing. He spills blood. He doesn't just fight.

He wants to kill.

That's his only goal, and I can tell as he spins his blade in his hand, worn and faded, it seems it'll snap the moment it hits someone's skin. But I know it won't, because he's an intelligent fuck and knows how to end a life.

He's good-looking, with his five o'clock shadow on his face and his closely shaved hair. It makes his face sharp. His eyes dark, brutal. Slightly crazed.

I know the look.

I feel it in my own eyes.

People cheer and clap and go wild as the man stands there and stares off into the back of the room. Where the lockers are. Where he came from.

He seems... off. Edgier. Angrier.

I don't clap or cheer. I stand with my hands at my sides as I inhale the tension in the air. It's thick and heavy. It burns my nose like nutmeg, and I refrain from bringing my fingers up to rub away the itch.

As if the sound in the room drops, I swear I can feel the sensation of footsteps pounding closer. My eyes glance up, and I squeeze the cuffs of my sweatshirt as a man in the shadows stalks down the hall.

I can't see who he is. But I can feel him.

And I know.

It's him.

It's Morelli.

He's tall. Broad. Vicious in the way he walks. Like the ground is laid for him alone. A precision in his steps that makes my mouth water. His arms stay at his sides, tensed.

Then he steps out of the darkness.

My eyes burn, and I can barely blink as he approaches the ring, his eyes staring at everyone and nothing. His jaw ticks. His hair a mess atop his head. He wears a pair of shorts that cut off above the knee. No shirt.

His abs ripple and tense with each step, the dark tattoos on his torso extending up to his neck, curling around his arm and shoulder. The opposite leg continuing on with the artwork that I don't want to look away from, but I must.

Because they can't stray from his eyes for long.

They are death.

He pushes against the rope and slips under with ease, stepping onto the mat and standing on the opposite side as the man with the blade.

Their postures are both rigid, internally raging as they stare at each other. The man with the knife white knuckles the blade, and I really wonder if it will crack in his grip.

The voices quiet down once again as they stand toe-to-toe.

Then… they move. Well, the man with the blade does. Morelli does the same thing as he did with me. He stands there with almost a bored look on his face. Watching as the man with the knife bounces around him, searching for a weakness, an easy access point.

Sorry, buddy, there isn't one.

He still tries, looking left and right as he grows more and more agitated. His hand snaps out, the blade barely grazing Morelli's arm. I watch the skin grow red, a surface scrape barely affecting him.

Morelli's eyebrows lift, and I can sense what he doesn't say.

Pussy.

The man with the knife jabs at Morelli again, this time cutting deep enough to draw blood. I watch the red bloom on top of his skin, a small bead turning into a trickle as it slips down his tanned stomach.

Morelli's eyebrows lower, like he's confused, or maybe a little shocked at Stabby's bold move. Morelli steps forward, his movement so quick I can barely see him before his hand snaps out, hitting the man with the knife in the jaw with a swift uppercut.

I watch the top half of his mouth move in a different direction from his jaw, my face scrunching up in discomfort as I remember how hard a punch Morelli can throw. My eyes follow the blood splatter as it flies through the air, landing on the mat and the rope of the ring.

The man with the blade stumbles to the side, and I can sense his rage as he rights himself, standing straight as his free hand goes to his jaw. He works it back and forth, stretching out the muscles as absolute fury overcomes him.

He's becoming unhinged.

He rushes Morelli, the speed in which he moves quicker than he's been all night, as he leaps forward and shoves the blade directly into Morelli's gut.

A collective gasp sounds throughout the room, my own gasp included. I blink, watching, waiting to see what Morelli does.

His fingers quickly wrap around Stabby's neck, his free hand going to the handle of the blade and pulling it out of his abdomen. It's covered in blood, dripping dark red, nearly black, across the mat.

He was *stabbed*.

I can barely breathe as I watch a darkness, darker than I've ever felt, surround him. He drops the knife on the ground, his bloody hand closing into a fist as he knocks him in the face.

Once. Twice.

Again, and again, and again.

He hits him as he steps forward, his fingers locked tightly around

TWISTED DARES

Stabby's neck. Stabby fights him at first but realizes quickly he's no fight against Morelli.

No one is.

My skin starts to tingle as he steps toward me, walking across the ring as he hits him over and over again. Stabby's a bobblehead by the time they reach the rope, blood pouring down his half naked body. Even Morelli is covered in blood, a thick mixture of his own and his opponent's. It's a bloody mess, bloodier than I've seen in quite a while.

He keeps moving forward until Stabby's back is pressed against the rope, arching over the side as he hits him one more time.

From this close proximity, nearly directly over my head, I can hear the grunts and groans of Stabby.

Morelli moves his hand from Stabby's neck to his jaw, his other hand moving behind his head as he holds tight.

Snap.

My eyes blink wide as I watch Morelli end his life with nothing but a blink. No emotion, not even rage covers his face as he takes someone's last breath.

My God, it's exhilarating to watch.

Stabby's body lays limp over the rope, his head lolling to the side. Blood starts trailing from his mouth, directly onto my forehead.

I glance up, my breath leaving my lungs as my eyes clash with Morelli's.

He stands there, a blank look on his face as warm blood trails down my temple. I don't step away, having my own share of someone else's blood on my skin. Though tonight, I wasn't expecting it.

I wasn't expecting this.

This… emotion billowing in my chest at such an alarming rate I don't have time to process it. Like the world is seconds from ending.

Like all the emotions I've burrowed deep in my chest for the past seventeen years are raging to the surface with no chance of stopping.

Whatever I've felt in my life is nothing compared to what I feel now.

Morelli's eyes stay locked with mine and forbid me from walking away. His dark gaze flaring as he watches the blood cover me. I reach up, wiping it away, smearing it across my forehead and into my hair. I don't know what to do; I don't know how to act.

I feel... a mess.

My tongue darts out, wetting my lips, feeling like I should speak even though my words won't escape. This moment is nothing like our last encounter. Our last one was hateful, enemies.

This one is all the emotions in the world wrapped up into one.

I want this. I want the ability to be disconnected. The look in his eyes... I want it in mine. I want to be able to kill, take a life, steal someone's breath, without having to worry about the consequences. Everything that is inside of Morelli, I want it in me. I want the emotions to be snuffed out with my bare feet and not feel a thing.

I want to be ruthless, just like Morelli is.

I want him to train me, to teach me, to help me become the killer I'm destined to be. I need his knowledge.

I need it.

Suddenly, Morelli tosses Stabby's dead body onto the ground, then whips around and leaves out the opposite end of the ring.

Our connection is broken, and air rushes back into my lungs at lightning speed. People start going wild, screaming and pushing against my back. I fight against them, but it's no use with the amount of people shoving against me.

He needs to train me.

I wiggle out of the wave of people, sliding beneath the rope and onto the ring, desperate to catch him so I can ask him. So I can plead. I don't mind being desperate at this point. I've never in my life felt as if something is as right as having him show me everything I need to know. I've been lost and confused since I moved in with my aunt and uncle, and for the first time since I stepped foot in Oregon, I feel clarity.

TWISTED DARES

This is right.

I sprint across the ring, my foot sloshing in a puddle of blood. I can hear the whispers, the wonders of who it is. They wonder if it's me, but they can't be sure.

I rush off to the other end of the ring, jumping down and heading toward the locker rooms. I keep my hood pulled over my head, my face pointed toward the floor as I race after Morelli. Just as I'm about to cut the corner and make my way into the men's locker room, fingers wrap around the back of my neck. My eyes widen, and I glance over my shoulder to see Corgan, his face pulled tight with tension and aggravation.

"What the fuck, Rave?"

I frown, shrugging out of his hold, sliding my hood off my head. "What?"

His eyes widen. "The fuck is wrong with you? You disappear for over a week and show back up with the civilians? What the hell happened?"

My eyes shift to the locker room, panic hitting me that I'm losing my chance. He'll slip out, he'll find a way, and then I don't know when I'll be able to ask him. It'll never be the right time.

"Family shit," I mumble half-heartedly. The words are a mistake, though, and Corgan catches on immediately. He knows I don't have a family, not really, anyway.

He barks out a laugh. "Family? Now I really know something was up."

My body screams to flee. I don't like confrontation or being grilled. It's not my thing, and Corgan knows this, yet he doesn't seem to give a shit at this point.

I hear footsteps, and moments later Reggie makes an appearance, his face blank as he looks me over. "I was wondering when we'd see you again."

I clench my jaw, hating the feeling of interrogation. They'd never act this way to Morelli, or Stabby, for that matter. But it's because I'm the only girl that fights. It's because they're normal, and they catch feelings like we're family.

I don't catch feelings, though, and I want to shove every emotion back at them. At least for the moment. At least until I can talk to Morelli.

"I've really got to go." I step away from the both of them, feeling like they'll trap me and grill me. Strap me to a chair and demand answers I'm unable to give them. They'll never get the truth from me. My secrets are mine and mine to keep.

"Where the hell you going so fast?" Reggie barks, his suit tailored so perfectly to his form. His eyes flicker to my nose. "Your nose is healing nicely."

Yeah, if bent slightly is nice. I look like shit.

"I need to go talk to someone."

Corgan glances over my shoulder at the closed locker room door behind me. "I would've never let you in that ring if I knew what he would've done to you."

I frown. "I'm not your problem, Corgan, and you make no decisions for me."

"There's few that I don't want you fighting again, and he's one of them. He's fucking dangerous, Rave. A fucking bomb."

The thought runs tingles through my feet, flowing up my legs and throughout my body. Almost like my entire body is asleep. Those words should terrify me, but they don't. Not at all. If anything, they exhilarate me. I want nothing more than to go in there and demand he insert whatever crazy he has in himself into me. I want it. I want to learn each piece of his brain and let it become my own.

"I'll talk to you later," I mumble, turning around. Turning away from the two men who have been a rock to me for over a year. But right now, they can't be my priority. I'll make it up to them later. I have to focus on the now. And right now, I need to catch Morelli before he flees, and I lose my chance and my courage.

"Wait." Corgan grips my wrist as I walk past, halting me in my step. His fingers are hot, burning flames licking against the forearms of my already heated skin. I bare my teeth, snarling at him as I rip my arm from his hold.

His face blanks, but I know he isn't hurt. They know me. Touching me is forbidden, yet they both decided to break that rule within ten minutes.

"What?" I snap.

Corgan steps toward me. "Are you coming back to the gym?" I can tell they think this is it. That this is the end of me.

They are so far from wrong. This isn't the end.

This is the beginning. This is my rebirth.

I drop my defenses, only a touch. "I'll be back in the gym. And I'll be back in the ring next Friday."

Both appeased, they nod, and I spin around, ready to talk to Morelli. *Finally.*

Nerves hit me as my hand grabs the handle, and I pull the door open, my body instantly breaking into a sweat.

I've only gone into the men's room once, with a promise to myself that I'd never do it again. As I step inside now, I wonder if I'm going to regret this moment.

Or if it'll finally be the moment that fixes every broken piece of me.

Stepping inside, I slow down, my eyes widening when I come face-to-face with not at all what I was expecting.

A large dog. A dog? A wolf? Some weird fucking hybrid? Mixes of brown and gray and white mix in his hair as he stares at me. His paws are the size of my hands, and his back taller than my waist.

This beast is massive.

"Um, hi?" I step toward him, my palm extended to pet him like the good pup he hopefully is, but his teeth bare, and a low growl starts shaking deep in his throat.

"Okay, then." I step back, not sure what to do. If this were a human, I'd just fight my way through them. I might be crazy, but I don't fight animals. Animals aren't bad. They're better than humans. "Hello?" Hopefully, Morelli will hear me, and he can come to me, instead of me having to search for him with this dog on my ass.

I hear a grunt, and then footsteps.

There he is.

Sweat dots his face, his skin pale, his hands tensed at his sides, his upper lip curled back. His nose ring glimmering against his damp nose. He looks lethal.

I take a step forward.

"What the fuck are you doing here?" A shiver breaks out along my spine at his voice. So much different from out there, as he's barking disrespectful comments my way. In this quiet room, his voice is deeper. Gritty, like it's been rolled in charcoal and dipped in hate.

I glance down at his abdomen, at the needle poking through the wound. The gash in his side that still has blood trickling from it. It looks painful, and with the needle through his skin, I'm guessing I interrupted him stitching himself back together.

"That looks painful. Do you need help stitching that?" I point at his stomach, and he steps back.

"What are you doing here?" He ignores my question, his eyes darkening to black pits.

I run my tongue along my top teeth, knowing I would've received his harshness, but having it doled out so brutally takes me aback. "I came to ask you a question."

His eyes narrow. "No." Turning around, he walks around the corner, out of sight and into the dark shadows of the locker room. "Rosko, come," he orders to the dog. Rosko takes one more hesitant look at me before he turns, his nails clacking on the floor as he follows his owner.

"Wait." I walk toward him just as another growl erupts from Rosko. Their shadowed figures move in the darkness, and I shiver again, not feeling as safe as I should. "I need your help."

His hair is a mess, the dark waves damp and tousled. The smell that emanates from him is sinful. Not like the men I fight, who smell of sharp onions and dirty socks. No, my mystery man has his own scent. One that doesn't have a definition, besides being completely, solely, man. Something that I want to bottle to savor for my weakest days.

He keeps his back to me, his muscles rippling as he works the thread through his skin. His back is littered with old and fresh wounds, his battle scars clear he's gained over the years.

My mouth waters as I stare at him. This might be the first time I've ever actually noticed the masterpiece that he is. Across his shoulder blades, from spine to shoulder, are large wings. Dark, messy, devastating wings that also look so strong and angry. The black feathers hold so much texture they look real, and I hold my hand against my side so I don't step forward and touch him.

It's real. It's a masterpiece.

Jesus hell, what the fuck is wrong with you, Raven?

"Get the fuck out of here, kid," he growls, sounding more animalistic than I've ever heard coming from a human. He almost sounds part dog himself, and I dig my nails in my palms, refusing to let him intimidate me.

"Please. This is obviously fucking painful for me to be asking after you broke my nose, but I wouldn't come to you if I wasn't serious. Can you just listen for a second?" It is painful. Terribly so. Asking for help from anyone is against my nature. I didn't even ask my aunt and uncle for things since I moved in with them. Not one thing. They gave me the bare minimum and I've never wanted for anything else. I just want to survive on my own and not have to rely on others.

So, asking for anything from this stranger—this *beast* of a man—is out of my element. It feels foreign, like a weird boulder is sitting on my chest. I want to rip it out and throw it aside, but I can't. Because I need his help. After he trains me, I'll cut ties and run. He'll never have to see me again, and we'll never cross paths.

But until then, I need him. I need him bad.

"Just hear me out." I fold my arms across my chest, refusing to leave until he at least hears what I have to say.

Finally, he turns around, his stomach flaming red from his ministrations. He tears at the thread, and it breaks easily, pulling at the edges of his skin. Gripping the needle, he glares at me. "What do you want?"

I bite the inside of my cheek until pain hits, and I run my tongue along the pinch of pain, watching his dark eyes furiously glare at me.

"I want you to train me."

He says nothing.

I take a deep breath. "I need you to teach me everything you know. Clearly, you know what you're doing up there. You kill people without a second thought. Teach me. Teach me everything you know."

He stares at me so blankly, I wonder if I spoke aloud at all, or if it was all an illusion.

"I'll do anything. Whatever you want, it's yours."

His head cocks to the side at the same moment his dog's does. He doesn't say a word, doesn't respond, not even a flicker of interest rolling through his eyes at my words.

"Please, this is fucking painful, dude. Give me something."

He works his jaw, opening his lips just a crack. "No."

I clench my jaw, knowing he would've said no, but a slim part of me was hopeful he wouldn't. I should've known. *I should've fucking known.* "No, please! I'll do everything you fucking say. I'm a fast learner. Teach me and be done with me. I don't fucking care. We don't have to be friends. We don't have to be *anything*. Just show me how to be ruthless. That's all I need."

He stares at me for another beat, and I would swear he wasn't breathing, but his stitches stretch every few seconds, giving away his shallow breaths.

"No. Come on, Rosko," he demands, walking around me without another word.

"No! Wait!" My arm shoots out, my fingers wrapping around his corded forearm. My fingers immediately burn to the touch, the tingling sensation of falling asleep running through my blood. My breath lodges in my throat, and I glance up, wondering if he feels the same thing I'm feeling.

TWISTED DARES

His eyes burn into mine, the dark chocolate turning murky. My breath escapes me, and I want for nothing except to breathe. But it only takes a second of him staring into my soul that I'm at a loss, floundering for something I didn't know I needed. It's like he can take the beats from my heart that I believed was hollow, pulling them from my chest with such stealth and agility that only he can possess. He sparks a fire to my soul yet drowns it until I'm breathless. I've always felt soulless, worthless, until this moment as I stare at him and realize I'm more human than I believed I ever was.

Rosko lets out a bark, his teeth baring as he gets ready to bite my arm for touching his owner.

"Rosko, no." His free arm shoots up, and my arm is ripped from his. "She wouldn't taste that good, anyway." His eyes look at me like I'm a piece of trash on the side of the road, and I can't help the pinch of pain that shoots through me.

I don't fucking care about anyone, but what is it about this guy that keeps hitting a soft spot?

"So, that's a no?" I step back, needing the space, the air to clear my head. Whatever he's doing to me isn't good, and I start second-guessing this decision.

"That's a *fuck no*. Get the fuck out of here, kid. You're not meant for the Inferno." He turns away, grabbing his things from the bench and walking out, his stomach still half stitched, his massive dog right on his heels.

I glare at his retreating form. "Well, fuck you, too."

RAVEN

Age Nine

I watch the party from a distance, my body alight with tension as I watch everyone dance and drink and take drugs Mom and Dad tell me I'm not even allowed to touch.

People flow in and out of the house, and I watch my dad be the star of the party, as he always is. His long, dark hair flows to his shoulders, his shirtless upper half tanned and toned. The women love him, and I don't really understand why Mom allows it. She says it's not something I'll understand until I'm a big girl.

But I do understand. Love is supposed to be between two people, not four, or six, or an entire party. My dad lets women touch him in ways that make me uneasy. I've heard the word *poly* flit around like a pesky gnat that can't be eradicated. I want to understand, because maybe it would make my discomfort lessen, but I know that's not the only reason.

My parents… they… they kill people.

That first night I saw them by the fire wasn't the last. I've spied on them enough times to see lives taken left and right. Those people don't always want to die. Sometimes it seems like they don't mind death, but some people scream and fight, and my dad gets a scary look on his face that has become a recurrence in my nightmares.

It's like they turn into different people. Ones that aren't my parents at all. But I don't question them, because they're my parents and I love them. They've never hurt me or been mean to me. They love me wholeheartedly.

But, I've seen the bloodstains and the piles of dirt. Small mounds in our yard that weren't there the previous day. There are bodies buried beneath the ground that I play on. I don't understand their way of living, and it makes me feel confused all the time. Like something isn't sitting right inside of me. The worst part of all is that I've become accustomed to watching them take lives.

It's no longer a scary, frightening scene that makes me hide under my covers. It's like your stomach rumbles at five o'clock for dinner. Well, the same goes for me at nine o'clock when they have parties. My feet wander to my bedroom window, and I just... watch.

Am I like them? Are we one in the same?

I watch with an empty mind as they bury others, while some just disappear off the face of the earth. I never see them again.

Where they go, I'm not sure. We're not allowed to watch the news in the house. As I've gotten older, I haven't been able to do much of anything, to be honest. I'm homeschooled, and we stay on our land, and I don't often leave. We live in the middle of nowhere, and there's so much dirt and sand around us, half the time I'm filled with dust. My skin chalky and tinged brown from lack of grass.

"Little Raven, isn't it past your bedtime?" A guy that comes over often, Darren, runs his fingers over my dark hair as he sits on the couch beside me. I set down the book in my lap, knowing I wasn't focusing on any of the words. Now, with Darren's marijuana-filled scent surrounding me, it'll be even harder to focus.

There are a few people that seem to come back frequently. They don't disappear like the others. Some women, but most of them men. Darren is one of them, and my father's good friend, Brody. Both of them are around my parents' age, and they treat me really nice.

"It's only ten o'clock." I roll my eyes, hating that sometimes they still act like I'm a baby. He leans over, the gold chain around his neck swinging in the air. He's manipulated it, because I know the first time he came here it was completely different. The cross isn't right side up anymore.

It's upside down.

It always gives me an eerie feeling when I see an upside down cross, and I don't really know why. This hasn't been the first time I've seen it or felt this way. A few people have tattoos on their arms of an upside down cross, with a large *C* scripted around it. I don't know what it means.

Maybe I don't want to know.

Darren puts his arm around the back of the couch, and it somehow feels intimate with just the two of us, even when there're a ton of other people in the room with us.

"How's school been for you, Baby Crow?"

I turn my eyes to his, narrowing them at his words. I'm *not* a baby, so that nickname annoys me. To be honest, Darren is one of the younger ones here, probably somewhere in his late twenties to early thirties. He's a good-looking man. Handsome. Darren, Brody, my dad, and a few of their other close friends are the ones who always have girls hanging off of them.

Girls always surround them at parties, and they all have this smirk that flirts across their faces. When I see Darren and Brody do it, my stomach gets a fluttering feeling like wings are tickling my rib cage.

Usually at these parties, they don't talk to me much. It's when there aren't a ton of people around that they come up and hang out with me. They are totally different people around their friends than they are when only I'm around. When there are a ton of people, I'm just their friend's kid, but when it's just us, I'm something more.

I'm their friend.

"School is fine." I lean away from him, even though a part of me wants to lean in for some odd reason. The comfort makes me feel fuzzy on the inside.

"Want to show me your room? I don't think you've ever shown it to me before." His hand drops to my shoulder, his finger pulling on the strap of my flimsy tank. It makes the white fabric stretch against my chest, my barely developed breasts poking through. My cheeks flame. I'm not to the point that I need bras yet, but that doesn't mean nothing's there.

I suddenly feel naked under his gaze.

I can't tell whether I like it or hate it.

"Um, sure." My room is nothing to brag about, but I don't want to be rude. I shrug out of his hold, glancing at my mom, who's kissing one of her friends. It makes me feel weird, so I glance away, my eyes flitting to my dad. He's sitting around a table full of people, the smoke from his joint making them almost unnoticeable behind the cloud.

Standing up, I walk around the couch, heading down the narrow strip of hallway and into my room. My walls are a cream color with a hint of baby pink. There're a few books on my nightstand, along with a coloring set and drawing paper. Besides that, I have my bed, which is covered with a pale yellow quilt.

"This is it." I turn around, my hands slapping at my thighs as I glance up at him. He's not looking at my room, instead staring me in the face with a weird look in his eyes. He takes a step toward me, then another.

His stare goes on and on, to the point my armpits grow damp with nerves. "Um…"

"Have you ever been kissed, Raven?"

I frown and shake my head. I step back, my spine flush with my wall. My palms press against it, and I let out a silent sigh as the coolness of the wall seeps into my skin.

What an odd question to ask.

"Have you ever wanted to know what it feels like?" He takes another step forward, and I have nowhere to go. I'm trapped against the wall, and Darren leaves barely a breath of space between us.

What's going on?

"I-I don't know. I don't think my dad would like that much," I whisper. And it's true, my dad might live an unusual life, but he's always been very protective of me. All of their friends have, so I wonder why Darren is acting like this.

He shrugs. "I don't think he'd mind. His little daughter is growing up, after all."

I chew on my lip, not quite sure how I feel about it. He's really cute, but I feel like he's closer to my dad's age than he is to mine. Eighteen years older than my nine-year-old self.

Is it wrong? Is it weird?

Sometimes around here, the lines are so blurred I'm not sure what's right or wrong.

"How about we try it, and if it's weird, we can stop." His hand goes up, his rough fingers brushing around the apple of my cheek.

"Okay," I whisper. Darren has been around for so long, I know I can trust him. He's always been a good guy. Nice. I shouldn't be afraid of him. That, and he isn't bad-looking. All the girls seem to think he's one of the best-looking, right after my dad, that is.

He smiles, leaning down and pressing his lips against mine. The bristle of his cheeks scratch against my face. It feels funny, almost like a tickle, but also an itch. I don't move my lips, not sure what I'm even supposed to be doing with them. He doesn't move them much either, just holding his mouth against mine.

After a few moments, he pulls back, a smile on his face and his eyes dark as the night. "What did you think?"

I think about it. It wasn't as scary as I thought it'd be, or hard. It was just kind of... weird. "It was okay."

His eyebrows shoot to his hairline. "*Okay?* I need to step up my game, then." He chuckles, his hands moving to my shoulders. He rubs them back and forth, creating a heat on my skin. It makes my face flush, and when his fingers curl under the straps of my tank top, my eyes shoot to his.

"What're you doing?"

He slips them down my arms, and I cover my chest as my tank loosens.

"It's okay, Raven. It's normal to be embarrassed. But you're getting older. You're turning into a beautiful woman." His fingers go to my arms, and he pulls them to my sides. I drop them, feeling uneasy about it as his eyes warm. He stares at my chest, and I glance down, seeing my nipples harden even as the rest of my chest is only barely developed.

His finger brushes my nipple, and it feels weird. It feels kind of… wrong. I glance away.

His fingers continue their assault against my chest, and I stare at my bedspread, wondering how long he intends to touch me for.

"Rave—*what*? Darren? What the fuck are you doing to my daughter?" My dad's voice edges on the tone I rarely hear from him. My eyes nearly pop out of my head as I scramble to pull my shirt up, glancing at him in fear.

Brody stands next to him, both of them with a beer in their hands. Brody's eyes flit from my chest to my face, then his gaze turns to Darren's, a vicious scowl taking over.

Chills break out along my arms and legs, the tension in the room so thick it takes my breath away.

Darren smiles, not worried in the slightest. Not sensing any of the unease that I'm feeling. "Sorry, man. I meant no harm. Raven is just… she's growing up. She's stunning. We were just having some fun together."

"Darren…" Brody shakes his head, stepping into my room, then he stops in his steps, his hands fisting at his sides.

My dad's face blanks, and a smile lifts at his lips. "*She is*, isn't she?" He walks up to me, making certain the straps of my tank top are firmly against my shoulders. "Raven, I think it's time for bed now. Say goodnight to Darren. You can see him again another time."

I glance at Darren, the feeling of his lips still tingling against mine. "Goodnight, Darren."

"Good girl." My dad pats my shoulder, leaning down to give me a kiss on the side of my head. "I'll see you in the morning."

My dad's hand transfers to Darren's shoulder, and they walk out, chuckling about something I can't hear.

Brody stays where he is, and he looks at me like he doesn't even recognize me. His eyes are hurt, angry, accusatory as they glare down at me. After too many unspoken seconds, he steps forward, his hand going to my shoulder, his fingers trailing along the exact spot Darren's fingers were not too long ago.

"I hope I never have to see another man with his hands on your chest again." He fiddles with the strap, making sure it's secure on my shoulder. "Keep your heart closed, Raven. It's not for other men to touch."

With one last glance, he steps away from me and out of the room, closing the door behind him.

It all feels so weird. Like I'm in a strange dream. I stand there for moments after Brody leaves me. Until my eyes grow heavy, and I realize I'm falling asleep standing up. Spinning around, I pull my quilt back from my bed, slipping between the sheets and resting my head on my pillow.

My fingers lift to my lips, and I rub against them, wondering how long it'll take before the tingling subsides. Closing my eyes, I listen to the party still raging loud in the other room. It's not a distraction, though, it's more like a lullaby. Something I've been listening to my entire life.

Soon enough, sleep takes me, and even then, the tingling burns at my lips.

My eyes pop open, and I'm not sure what it is that woke me up. I sit up, touching my lips that are no longer tingling. It's dark in here, which means the party in the next room is no longer happening.

A quick glance out the window shows it's the middle of the night. I'm not sure what time exactly, but with the moon hanging high in the sky, I'm going to say it's sometime after three in the morning.

A low hum has my ears perking, and my mouth pinches.

What is that?

I pull my covers back, my feet falling to the cool wood floors as I tiptoe to the door. The humming grows louder, and my hand falls to the knob. I'm hesitant as I open the door, wincing as the hinges creak ever so slightly.

The house is dark, and I slip into the shadows, sliding against the wall as I walk down the hallway. Once the living room comes into view, I pause, my eyes widening at the scene in front of me.

The majority of the people from the party are in a circle, sitting with their legs crossed on the floor. My dad stands to the side, a long, black robe on his body. My mom kneels beside him, her hands on his leg as he prays.

Praying to God.

I've never seen them do a ritual like this, though I have listened to their readings and scriptures.

My parents think they do deeds to stay on God's path. The dark God, they call him. They think these sacrifices are the way of God. I wonder if they realize this would never be the path of God.

It feels like they are worshipping the devil.

I choke on air as I glance at the center of the circle, seeing Darren lying there, his eyes opened, his chest barely shaking, but he's alive. I can see it. The tremble in his skin. The tears in his eyes.

Brody stands over him, a large silver knife in his hands, dripping with blood.

The blood seeps into the wooden floor, growing with every second. It surrounds Darren completely, nearly reaching their friends on the edges of the circle. Darren's entire stomach cavity is opened and torn apart. Blood streaks across everyone's faces, but most of all, my dad's. His cheeks and forehead, and even his eyelids are covered in blood.

I watch them. I watch him. I watch Darren as he takes his last breath, his blood staining my wooden floor and his body dying in my living room. I watch my father and mother pray to their dark God that feels so much like the devil.

I watch Brody smile as he watches his best friend die.

I watch these people lean forward and worship a body that is a pile of flesh and blood.

I watch it go on so long that my body turns numb. There is absolutely no feeling left in me as I slink back into the shadows and into my room, closing the door behind me.

I slip into bed, pulling the comforter up to my neck. My eyes can't shut, and I'm almost afraid for them to.

The scene was traumatizing, but that's not what has me petrified in fear. The feelings inside me aren't worry, or disgust, or even hate.

I'm… relieved.

I'm… happy.

I'm… comforted in the death of Darren.

I'm glad he's gone.

Does that make me as sick as them? Does that make me demented?

I suppose I must be. The disturbing blood that runs through my parents flows through me. The sickness in them is a part of me, and I know, without a doubt, I'm just as psychotic.

And if I'm not yet, I surely will be.

Someday.

chapter ten
CAELIAN

The bell rings over the door of Morelli's restaurant, and Rosko butts by me, his nose to the ground as he heads to the back. My aunt Mariana always has something for him to eat back there. I shake my head, walking toward everyone in the back private room.

A last-minute meeting is never good, and I've been tense this last week. Taking into account whatever's going on with the business, shit just doesn't seem right.

The door to the private room is shut, and I press down on the knob, the heavy scent of cigars wafting through the door.

"Caelian, the fuck took you so long?" Matteo sighs from the other end of the table.

I barely spare him a glance, taking a seat next to my father. He's a tall man, just about my height at six-three, yet he isn't as broad as I am. His dark hair is mixed with gray peppered around his ears. Always in a dark suit, straight from Italy. He has a tailor come in from his hometown in Sicily. Black suit after black suit, this man is a force who has raised deadly weapons as children. Next to my father are his three brothers, Uncle Marco, Uncle Stefano, and Uncle Angelo.

Uncle Marco is the oldest and owns the restaurant, along with his wife,

Mariana. Uncle Marco does most of the grunt work of the business. He smokes a lot and is heavyset, his dark button-up shirts typically looking moments from popping open.

Uncle Stefano is a year younger than my father; he's a good-looking man who only moved to the United States this last year. He brought his wife, Rosa, with him, getting into the family business after their son, Francesco, died in a tragic car accident in Italy. He has a heavy accent, and sometimes it's hard to hear a fucking word he's saying.

Last is Uncle Angelo. He's the youngest, a little bit of a loose cannon and only recently married. Sofia has attempted to calm him down, but he's a lot like me and my brothers in that aspect. He likes to kill and kills well. My uncles all have children, my cousins that work in the business but aren't part of the table. Our family gatherings and holidays are fucking ridiculous, filled with enough seasoning and cigar smoke to burn down a house.

Because Marco preferred to own the restaurant, my father is the one who took the organization and became the boss after his pop died. His brothers work alongside him, but at the end of the day, they're all under him.

The Morellis are dangerous on the East Coast, and no one fucks with us. We run the largest laundering business, among other things, but the laundering throughout the United States is filtered through us.

We are the core.

So, when shit is amiss, it doesn't just affect our family, it affects the entire country.

"Tell me what's going on." I've been on edge. The last couple of days have been hell. It's Sunday today, and it feels like I barely even have time to make it to school anymore. From doing work for the family, to training, to fucking keeping my mind clear of that goddamn chick… my mind has been scrambling, and school is the last thing I care about.

And now, *she* seems to be there. Around every corner. Walking every hall. Sitting in every chair. She's there, and it seems like I can't escape her. No matter how hard I try.

TWISTED DARES

I don't know what it is about her, but that desperate look in her eyes hasn't left my memory. I don't want to care about her desperation, or the fact that she pleaded for me to help her when I give zero shits about her.

I just want her pathetic face wiped from my mind.

"Where do you want me to start?" Angelo asks from around his cigar pitched in his mouth. A stream of smoke trails from the tip, and he puffs on it, the tip growing red before he pulls it from his mouth, setting it in the ashtray.

They're all so fucking formal sitting in their suits, and I want to ash his cigarette on his lapel to see how he'd react.

"Why is there more than one issue? What the fuck is going on, and why am I just learning about this?" I snap.

My father, Drogo, slides his hand across the dark wooden table and pats my hand. "I didn't find it necessary to alert anyone until I understood how it was all going to play out and how far it'd go."

I pull my hand from his, hating the touch and the emotion. He knows my emotions aren't normal, aren't like anyone else's, so his need to show me affection is exhausting. "But they got far, and now there are multiple issues to take care of. And we all know it's going to fucking be me taking care of them."

"Not necessarily," my brother, Gabriel, says, from beside Matteo. "Don't be such a fucking douchebag, Cae. They're doing their job."

I lean back in my chair, folding my hands across my abdomen, wincing as it hits my scar, still tender and healing. "Just fucking get on with it."

My father levels me a look. "First deal of order is the business. There has been an issue with the Irish. They're causing chaos over in New York, and it's causing a delay in distribution to Canada."

I stare at him. "Send someone over there to look into it." I don't understand. This is a *possible* issue, one that isn't even fully unwrapped yet. Why are they pissing themselves? We've dealt with border patrol before. Worst case, we'll just pay them the fuck off.

Uncle Marco leans forward, his elbows going to the table. "We've had someone over there for the last month, Caelian. They aren't finding anything out of the ordinary. Our guys with border patrol are fucking idiots. They haven't been a lick of help. The Irish are causing a shitstorm with them and the Canadians." He runs his fingers along the table as he stares at me. "Jack O'Clare refuses to work with us. He's doing it on purpose."

I narrow my eyes. "Why?"

My dad straightens out his suit jacket as he leans back in his chair. "Because, Caelian, we're the number one in the United States, and I can guarantee they're wanting to take over that. Their laundering business has nothing on us, and I think they believe if they disrupt us enough, we'll fold under them."

Gabriel laughs. "Fucking idiot Irish fucks."

I blink, not sure why I'm just hearing about this now. "And what is the plan with it? Have you put out a message to O'Clare?"

"I'm putting out a message after this meeting. See if he wouldn't mind paying us a visit."

"And if he says no?" Matteo leans forward, his eyes burning. He wants the hunt. He's hungry for action. He's too hungry, so much so I worry he'll fuck himself up someday.

"Then we'll have to go pay him a visit." Angelo chuckles.

My dad sighs. "That's not the only issue. With this serial killer in the cities, it's gained a lot of national attention. The FBI and CIA have been showing up. The fucking National Guard. This is the worst time to have some serial killer running the streets of Oregon."

Uncle Marco tosses the newspaper at me. I grab it midair, opening it up, and on the front page is a blown-up image of a forehead. The rest of the face and body are completely blurred, but the picture of an outline of a crow on the forehead.

The wound looks familiar. I've seen it before. A few years ago when there was some serial killer in California. It was fucking insane, but they caught the guy. At least, I thought they did.

I point at the bloody outline. "It can't be him, right? The real guy is in prison?"

Marco nods. "Yeah. It's a copycat."

I glance at the article, pulling bits and pieces from the smudged ink that are of any importance.

"Young female victims, younger than thirty. All dark-haired. All living in and around Seattle. All single, unmarried. All sexually assaulted. No suspects, no leads." I slap the paper onto the table, running my hands through my hair. "Well, what the fuck?"

"There're a lot of similarities, but there are a lot of differences too. This guy is sloppier than the original killer," Uncle Angelo says.

"I want you to find whoever is doing this, Caelian, and I want you to get rid of him," my dad says firmly. "We'll take care of the crisis at the border. You find this copycat Crow Killer and do whatever the fuck you want to him."

I look at my brothers, and the excited look in their eyes is almost laughable. I don't understand the humor in this, but I'll let them have their fun.

Emotions are just something I don't understand.

I hear a scratch at the door, and the knob turns, slowly cracking open as Rosko's nose butts through.

He walks in, glancing at me briefly before making his way to the corner to lay down. I found my partner in a dog. Not someone who wants to be cuddled and pet on the daily. He wants to know I'm okay, and I do the same for him. We keep each other company when our minds are nothing but secluded.

"I'll find him." I push back from the chair, standing up and clenching my jaw as my makeshift stitches stretch from the change in position. It's time to take them out tonight, which is going to be a bitch in and of itself.

I'm satisfied at that fucker's death. He was nothing but a waste and a shitty fighter. Anyone who brings a weapon isn't a fighter at all, but instead someone that needs to hide behind a bullet or metal. Fucking losers.

"I know you will, Caelian. Where are you headed now?"

I glance at Rosko, snapping my fingers. His short nap is quickly interrupted, but he moves to my side instantly, ready for my next command. "I'm taking Rosko to the water."

There is absolutely nothing more that I need at the moment. Silence and the absence of everything else.

I need to rid *her* from my mind.

They all nod, understanding that too much of anything will get me unable to focus. And if I can't focus, I won't be able to do my job.

"I'll see you guys later," I direct to my brothers. They give me a nod, and I walk out, with Rosko straight on my heels.

I pull my car up to the abandoned road, to the secret oasis I found last year. It's a place my brothers know little about, but they've never been here themselves. No one has besides Rosko and me. I found it when I brought a kill here last year.

A twisted game of tag where I let the man run with his arms tied behind his back. He was an idiot, running into tree after tree before I caught him, puncturing both of his lungs with my blade before slicing his throat. He bled out, and he was a sprayer, getting blood all over me and Rosko.

Then I glanced up and saw a waterfall tucked up to the side of a mountain, a pool of water clearer than any glass I've ever seen. It was almost meant to be, and I stripped bare and walked straight into the water that was warmer than I'd expected. Rosko ran in after me, and we ended up in the water for hours, until the sun set, and the water cooled.

We cleansed ourselves that day. Of the blood and all the chaos in our lives.

I didn't think I'd come back, until I did. I came back over and over, and now it's a regular thing. Something we can't stay away from. It's a place where emotions don't need to be dissected and words don't need to be spoken.

I can be here in silence, just me and my dog, and listen to water hit water. That's it. It's all I need.

I open the door, and Rosko sprints out ahead of me, dashing into the woods. All I can see is his brown and gray hair dip between the green trees until he's gone.

He finds solace in this place just as much as I do.

I slip out, locking the car behind me before walking into the woods. It takes a few minutes of darting between heavy trees and stepping over rocks before the sound of water reaches my ears. Once the water comes into view, I glance at Rosko, seeing him in the middle already paddling around. His tail swishes back and forth, the water splashing in every direction. He has a long stick in his mouth, his heavy pants heard all the way to the shore.

I peel my shirt over my head, toeing off my shoes and unbuckling my belt. Once I'm down to my skin, my clothes pushed to the side, I walk in until the water brushes my knees, knowing the drop-off is quick. I curl over, cutting into a dive and slicing the surface as I submerge myself.

The water is cool this evening, and the rushing around my ears a relieving and comforting sensation. Drowning out the noisy, emotional world is exhausting. Listing to nothing besides my heart and the flow of water is a necessity that I never knew I needed.

I swim to Rosko, just as he shakes his head back and forth, flinging water into my eyes. I bury my fingers in his wet hair, giving him a quick splash before turning to the waterfall.

It's falls heavy and strong today, the snow from the winter still melting and making the water cascades quicker than usual.

I swim back and forth for a while, floating on my back. My stitches stretch and pinch my skin with my movements, but I work past it as I attempt to clear my mind.

It's difficult, because the girl from the Inferno seems to be a virus of some sort, infecting each one of my thoughts until I can think of nothing besides her. She has swirled into my memory and found her spot to stay.

Her dark hair that runs down her back, as elegant as the waterfall I swim adjacent to. Her small body, tight and firm but not curvy as a woman's should be. She's young, still growing into her body, but her looks are deceiving because there's an age in her eyes that I don't see often. Someone who has seen more than they should have at her age.

I don't even understand the thought process in her question. She wants me to train her, *for what?* She fights at the Inferno, and if she's still alive, even the fact that she came back after I broke her nose, speaks words. I wasn't easy on her; I didn't lessen my strength as I shoved my knuckles against her bone. But she came back, and more than that, she wants me to train her?

It doesn't make a lick of sense.

I'll do anything.

Her words play on repeat. What would I ever need from her? There's nothing she could provide me that I couldn't find from any other person in or out of the Inferno.

So, what would I ever need from her? What do I want from her?

Absolutely nothing.

But it still doesn't stop her from invading my thoughts like a poison.

I lazily swim to the shore, my tattooed arms corded and tense. It disturbs me how much of an intrusion she is.

I don't intend to fight until I get my stitches out, but maybe a night at the Inferno watching other people fight would be settling.

Since apparently, this place isn't doing it for me.

With that thought in mind, I let out a sharp whistle, making my way to the shore. I can hear Rosko panting behind me, his strong legs kicking rapidly below the water.

"Time to go, Rosko."

ns once and for all. And once I do, I'm never going to allow myself to think of her again.

Fucking never.

chapter eleven
RAVEN

"Yes, Mom, of course," Aria says from my doorway. I watch her with raised eyes, my foot propped on the bed as I lace up my shoes. The only other bag I own is next to me on the bed. I hope whatever Aunt Gloria is saying from the other end of the line is good news. Good news for me, not her.

"I will. Yes, she will, too. Uh-huh, okay. Love you, too. Yes, of course. Okay. Okay, Mom. Goodbye. Yep, goodnight. Love you, bye." She hangs up with a sigh, shoving her phone into her pocket.

"And?" I ask, dropping my foot to the ground and bringing my other one up, tying the laces with eager fingers.

"They're gone for the night. It feels weird, actually. They've never left for one of these before, even though the church has them all the time."

I nod, feeling the same. After the last couple of weeks with being locked in the basement, starting a new school, and them breathing over my shoulder at every second, I'm surprised they've allowed us to stay home alone for the night. But I think they firmly believe they've scared me shitless to the point I won't leave the house.

They don't know me. I don't think they ever have.

I drop my foot to the ground. "Well, Aunt Gloria had that lady calling from church all week. Maybe they were short on support staff or something. I don't know." I shrug, not really caring either way. I'm glad they are both gone at this church retreat for the night. There will be teachings with the adults and parents. I don't really care what it's for, I'm just glad I don't have to deal with them and their fucking holy talk, and everything else that has to do with it.

After these past few days of them hovering and barking at me left and right, I finally—*finally*—have the ability to get away. I wanted to go to the ring last night. I was supposed to fight, but Aunt Gloria was too much of a terrorist for me to even get a breath away from her. I was honestly worried that she would have followed me if I left, so I feigned feeling sick and told them that I called into work.

They have been constantly looking for any misstep. I can feel it in my bones that they want to put me back in that basement. They want to lock me up and throw away the key. Possibly forever. They want nothing to do with me, and I really think an untimely death would be the easiest way out for them.

Unfortunately, their scare tactics aren't working. It's doing the opposite, honestly. I'm growing more and more thin with my emotions, and soon I feel like I'll snap. I worry about Aria, feeling like I need to distance myself from her, so she doesn't get hurt in the crossfire. But she doesn't sense the danger on the horizon.

I should keep her at a distance so she can stay pure and good, not be dipped by my toxicity. She's blinded by her own goodness to see my evil.

Maybe…" She glances around, seeing I'm ready to go somewhere. "Where are you going?"

I stand up, grabbing my hoodie, replacement bag, and phone from the bed. "I'm going to the gym for a while, and then I'm going to fight. I'll be back tonight, but don't wait up for me."

She raises her hands to the doorframe, creating a barrier I can't get through. She grips it, and I can hear the uncomfortable squeak of her fingernails against the wood. "Are you sure that's a good idea? Think of what happened last time."

I give her a look. "They're gone this time, Aria. The only way they would know is if *you told them*." She stares at me, and a pit drops into my stomach. "Would you tell them if I went out tonight?"

Her eyes widen. "Of course not! I'm just... what if they have cameras in here or something?" she whispers, looking around the corners in my room. "What if they know you left, then what would you do?"

I roll my eyes. "There's no fucking cameras in here, Aria. Now, I have to go."

I go to move past her, but she steps in front of me.

"What are you doing?" I frown at her.

"Let me go with you," she says forcefully.

My eyes widen. "What? No." I laugh. "That's fucking ridiculous."

Her arms fold over her chest, and I try to picture her in the gym watching me, in her blue jeans and button-up top. Her cross necklace around her neck and her brownish hair pulled into a loose ponytail.

She would absolutely look out of place. Like a dot of blue in a pool of red. Ridiculous. She would look *ridiculous*.

I shake my head. "Not happening, Aria. It's not a safe place. Can you imagine what would happen if your parents did find out? If somehow, they figured out that not only was I out when I wasn't supposed to be, but I also brought you with me? *They'd kill me*."

Her eyes grow watery, and I feel a wall build up around me. It makes me feel uncomfortable to watch other people break down. Going to church on Sundays and watching people cry for the Lord is so fucking uncomfortable, my stomach hurts.

Watching my little cousin grow emotional because she wants to tag along with me is so far from what I want to be doing right now that I could scream.

"Please, Raven. I know what my parents are. They are... they're monsters. Don't make me be stuck and trapped in this jail. Let me experience the world with you. Let me learn to live."

"Then let's go to the mall sometime, or let's go to a movie. Don't come to the gym and watch me be someone you don't want to see me as."

She steps forward, her arm raising to touch mine, but she stalls at the last moment, stepping back and dropping her hand to her side. "You are my cousin. My sister. I could never look poorly upon you. No matter the type of person you are. Don't you know I already know who you are? You're different, and I love you just the same. You don't think or feel like a normal person. You don't like to be touched; you don't like to see emotion. I don't fault you for any of it, Rave. I envy your ability to be so strong."

I want to crush my teeth to dust at her words. The array of emotions is too much. *It's too damn much.*

"Fine, you can come with," I choke out. "But change your clothes and don't talk to people. They like to prey on the weak."

"Are you calling me weak?" she jokes, only half serious.

I pull my keys from the side pocket of my bag, jingling them a few times. "Yeah, to them, you're weak as hell. So don't talk to anyone."

With that, I slip past her, heading downstairs.

Fuck, what am I getting myself into?

"Block your face. Don't want your nose broken again," Corgan barks at me from the other side of the ring.

I grit my teeth, angry and sweating. Tired as hell. One glance behind me shows Aria sitting in a chair. She still looks out of place, mostly with her eyes as wide as saucers as she sees a hidden part of the real me.

The beast beneath the skin.

I'm full of rage, and only in the ring do I allow myself to reveal a piece of it. Only a slip. To completely give away the anger inside me would be catastrophic. To reveal myself to the world around me...

It would be a tragedy.

That's why I keep it locked away.

"Come on, Rave. I know you've got more in you than that."

I growl, stepping forward and throwing my fist into the glove. I keep my other hand in front of my face, blocking my nose from another broken bone.

"Better. Better. Take the gloves. Block me." He throws them at me, and I slip them on, widening my stance and bending my knees. Corgan comes after me, not telling me his moves. He isn't being his normal self. He knows I need the extra brutality, and I'm grateful he's giving it to me. He hits left and right, knocking me back with his forceful steps.

I grunt with each hit, until my back hits the rope. He keeps going, over and over again until anger bubbles in my chest. I chuck him with my shoulder, catching him off guard until he steps back a few paces.

"Enough. That's enough," I snap. "I have to bring Aria home and then head to the Inferno."

He shakes his head. "Take the night off and go there tomorrow. You know you shouldn't train before a fight. Your muscles are too exhausted."

He's right. I never train before a fight. I always go the day before and then allow my muscles to heal and relax the rest of the day. Maybe it wasn't the smartest, but I've been out of the loop and have felt my body getting out of shape since I've been healing from the basement incident.

And the *him* incident.

He's a constant flicker in the back of my mind. A smudge that refuses to be wiped away. I've tried. I've tried so hard to make him disappear, but he's constantly in the background of my thoughts. It doesn't help that I have school tomorrow, and I'll have to see him.

After he denied me. His mind was a brick wall, and he wouldn't even contemplate the thought of training me. What is so appalling about me? What is it about me that he looks at me with such malice?

What if he's there? What if I see him? Will he cheer me on or be on the sidelines as he hopes for my demise?

But I'm not going to put it off. I've been away for too long already. I'm ready. My body is healed. It's tired, but it's healed.

It's time to fight.

I shake my head. "I'm fighting tonight. It was already discussed with Reggie."

He scowls at me. "Foolish."

I don't care. I really don't.

"Ready, Aria? Time to head home."

She blinks rapidly, like she's snapping out of a daydream. "Oh, um, okay." Standing up, she brushes off my hoodie covering her upper half. She gives a quick glance to Corgan, who stares at her oddly.

They haven't said one word to each other. Corgan barely knows about my family. I don't let anyone know where I originated from. I don't speak about my unconventional life. I just don't.

But I think Corgan knows something is amiss. I can tell in the way he talks to me sometimes. The way he treats me. Like I'm a loose cannon. Like I'm Bambi and will flee at any given moment.

Then the way he looks at Aria, like she's a fucking alien or something.

People are weird.

"Are you going to the Inferno tonight?" I ask as I hop out of the ring, laying his gloves on the mat.

He shakes his head. "Not tonight, Rave. Got a class in an hour. You could come, you know. You could teach it yourself instead of fighting."

I almost laugh. *Almost.* "No." I'd rather do anything else in the world than teach a class. My God.

He chuckles. "Mhmm. Let me know how it goes."

I toss him a wave over my shoulder, grabbing the straps of my bag from the ground and looping it over my shoulder. "Come on," I mumble to Aria.

Her feet scatter behind me, her pants heavy like she was the one training instead of me. "That was… that was incredible, Raven. Where have you learned to fight like that?"

I push the doors to the gym open, the cool air drying my skin quickly. "Corgan taught me everything I know." It's the truth, honestly. I wouldn't be here without him.

"That's crazy. You're like... *really good*." We walk to the car in silence, and I swear I can hear her thoughts running wild even when she doesn't say a word.

I hit the unlock button on my fob, and it beeps, the headlights shining momentarily. We hop in, and I turn on the car, switching on the heat and turning to Aria. "Tell me whatever it is you need to say."

She clips her seat belt. "Do you think you could teach me how to fight like that?"

I somehow expected those words and didn't expect them at the same time.

"No." I shift the car into drive, the smell of my sweat and the leather from the seats mixing in the air around us. "Absolutely not."

"But, don't you think everyone should know how to protect themselves?"

I turn to her. "Everyone should know how to protect themselves, I agree. But you don't need to fight like me. My training is a little bit more... extreme." Corgan has bruised and cut me on many accounts. It's the name of the game if you want to learn how to fight in the Inferno.

"Everyone is so... brutish there. Really attractive, too. Are all the guys that handsome?"

I bark out a laugh, flicking on my blinker as I hop onto the highway. "Handsome? Those guys are anything but handsome. They're fucking brutal and will literally snap your neck without thinking twice. Stay away from them. From *all* of them." I glance at the time, knowing I'm cutting it close from when I'm supposed to be in the ring. "I need to just drop you off and fly or else I won't be back in time. I'll be home right after."

"Just let me go with you!" she begs.

My head whips back and forth before she even finishes her sentence. "No. Fuck that. You're lucky I let you come to the gym. That place is shady, but I don't think they'd even let you into the Inferno. It's too dangerous. *No. Nope.*"

"Let me come," she demands.

I turn and glare at her. "No, Aria. No."

"I'm not a child, you know. I know about life. I'm not a baby. I can take care of myself. And honestly, the fact that you're treating me like one is a little offensive."

Her voice is hurt, and I instantly feel bad. I don't want her to be offended.

"I'm just trying to protect you." I sigh.

"Stop trying to protect me! Let me learn how to be a person all on my own. I don't need you to shield me from all the bad in the world. Let me fall and let me get up. It's the only way I'll learn."

I want to scream.

"Even normal people who haven't been sheltered their entire lives don't know about the Inferno. Can you imagine what it would be like to go in there? No, you don't. It smells like blood. Do you know why? Because people die there. Like all the fucking time. It's not a fighting ring like you were just around. Felons, creeps, fucking insane motherfuckers go there on the daily. It is not a place for you."

"If you don't take me there, I swear to the Lord above that I will find a way to get there on my own, and when I do, I won't tell you about it."

I whip my gaze to hers. "Why are you doing this?"

Her eyes water, and I strangle the steering wheel in my grip. "Because I'm capable of making my own mistakes, and I think I deserve to on my own."

I chew on my lip, because I don't know the right from the wrong answer. It feels so, so wrong to bring her there. But am I wrong to keep her from it? Maybe one night is all she needs to figure out this isn't the life she wants to live in the slightest. But if she goes, and I'm not there, I'd never be able to protect her.

I turn on my blinker, hopping off the highway so I can turn around.

"You'll stay where I can see you all the time. If you get out of my sight, I swear I'll never let you come with me anywhere ever again."

A smile breaks across her face, and I swear I can see her vibrate in her seat. "You're the best!"

Shit better not go south, or I will never make it out alive.

"Okay. Stay close to me, don't say your age, don't say your name, or where you're from, or anything like that," I say sharply, shutting the car door and glancing around the empty street.

She shuts her door, glancing at me from over the hood. "This is really serious stuff, isn't it?" The lick of fear in her tone makes me want to laugh. Now she's freaking out?

"Yeah, Aria. It is actually pretty serious. This is why I didn't want you to come with."

Her face blanks out. "I'll be fine. I'm excited to see you in action."

I grimace, walking across the street and into the abandoned bar. It's dark in here, and I step over a cardboard box as I slip to the back of the room.

Aria shouldn't be excited to see me in action. *I'm* not excited for her to see me in action. I'm concerned she'll see me differently, and not in a good way. Maybe that should make me happy; the potential that she'd no longer look up to me, but it doesn't make me feel good. Not at all.

"What is this place? Why are we here?"

"Just passing through." The sound of a glass beer bottle being kicked and sliding across the floor makes me whip around. Aria's arms are crunched against her chest, her face laden with fear.

"Sorry," she whispers.

"Watch where you're stepping. You don't know what you might step on." It's true. This place closed but everything left in it has stayed. It's clear there have been homeless people and criminals here to rummage through the leftovers, but there's still debris strewn around the floors and the bartop. It's a disaster in here and bringing Aria feels like I'm just asking for trouble.

She catches up to me till she's nearly breathing over my shoulder. "This place is creepy."

I grunt, opening the door to the old storage room that'll take us to the tunnels. I can feel Aria's fear, her desperation to ask questions, but she's thankfully keeping her mouth shut. I don't have anything to tell her at this point.

It's just a way into the Inferno. I don't know the backstory, and honestly don't care. It is what it is.

The hulking figure of Barron stands at the entrance to the tunnel, and his lip quirks quickly before flattening into a straight line.

"It's been a while, Raven." He gives me a nod, and I let out a sigh.

"Too long. Ready to get into the ring."

He glances over my shoulder, a curious look in his eyes. "You've never brought a friend with you before. Who do you have here?"

Aria opens her mouth, and I step in front of her, blocking her from view. "It's just my cousin. She's coming to watch me fight tonight. She'll be sitting in the back. I'd prefer no one talk to her."

His mouth forms a stern line, and with a single nod, he turns to the side, giving us a path to walk into the tunnel. "Understood."

That's what I like about Barron. Little to no words. No explanations needed.

"That man was scary," Aria whispers in my ear, her words barely audible but echoing off the walls as we walk through the splashing water in the tunnel.

I swallow down a groan. She thinks Barron was scary? Besides his size and facial expressions, the guy is akin to a fucking stuffed animal.

The noises grow louder as we get closer, and soon enough, the light filters through the door at the end. I stop, my hand on the handle, and turn to Aria.

"You know what to do?"

I can tell Aria wants to be sassy, but she nods, a thick swallow working its way down her throat.

I open the door, the noise and lights blasting us in the face. I can immediately sense the tension coming from Aria, but it's too late. My face blanks out, and I lower my head, walking straight to the women's locker room.

Aria's heavy breaths put me on edge, but I empty my mind of Aria and everything else. Tonight is the night. It's my first night back in the ring. I feel ready, a little tired, but ready. My body is all sorts of twisted since my last fight. I don't know how the crowd will react to me. Last time, I was completely obliterated from the mystery man. Then I went MIA.

Now, I'm here. Ready to fight again. Abused and emaciated for a week, then I healed and became weaker. This last week, I've punished my body more than my aunt and uncle ever could. I've prepared myself for tonight. I refuse to be beaten down again.

I can't deny that I'm a little nervous about what people will say. Everyone bares their own scars in the ring, but I've been between the ropes enough times that they know my body top to bottom. I'll be stepping in there for the first time with new scars. Scars that they'll realize are from more than just a couple hits. These are lashings, beatings that were doled upon my body as punishments. I'm hesitant to take my shirt off. I didn't take it off with Corgan, didn't even feel like explaining when he gave me an odd look.

But in the ring? I have to take it off in the ring, and I have no idea how people will react.

I drop my bag on the bench, sitting down next to it and removing my shoes and socks. I flex my toes, stretching out my legs and feeling this slight ache from training earlier.

Digging in my bag, I pull out the roll of tape and pull at it, the obnoxious groan as it unravels striking through the room. I keep my head down, raising my eyes as I glance at Aria.

"You look like you're about to pass out," I mumble, pulling the tape tightly around my knuckles.

"It's weird seeing you in this element. You don't look… friendly. Not that you usually look friendly, but—"

"Aria," I snap. Her back straightens, and her fingers flex at her sides. "This is the real me. It's why I didn't want you to come, but now that you're here, let's just not talk about it, okay? Before I fight, I just need… silence."

"Silence. Okay. Silence."

I close my eyes and finish wrapping my hands. Standing up, I peel my sweatpants down my legs and rip my shirt over my head. I'm left barefoot, in my spandex shorts and sports bra. My skin is hot, still overheated from my long workout. But I'm ready.

I'm so ready.

My blood thrums through my veins as I pull the elastic from my hair and retie it into a tight ponytail at the top of my head. Glancing at the time of my phone, I see there are only minutes left before I'm supposed to be out there.

When I hear a gasp escape Aria, I close my eyes, lowering my hands to my sides as I turn around. Her eyes stay on my back, even as I turn around and stare at her. I don't have time to explain my injuries, nor do I want to. But the way her eyes water, her lower chin wobbling as her eyes flit to mine, she's broken. And she knows who inflicted these wounds.

"Aria…"

"They're monsters," she whispers, her voice barely audible. The pain is clear in her voice, it floats toward me and suffocates me. Chokes me. I gasp in a breath as I watch her cripple in pain.

I step toward her, forgetting my aversion to touching as I grab her by the shoulders, pulling her toward me. I get in her face, my eyes inches from hers as I speak calmly, soundly. "Aria, you're here because you want to be free. I am here because I want to be free. We can do that. Everything I do, it's so we can live. Do you understand that?"

"How can I live knowing what they've done to you? My own flesh and blood?"

I shake her. "I am your flesh and blood, and I will do anything to protect you." The voices of the crowd grow louder, and I know I'm out of time. "I have to get out there. I need you to be strong, and trust me when I say I'm going to figure this out. Okay? I'll figure it out for the both of us."

Her nose twitches, the tears in her eyes flowing down her cheeks, but she eventually nods, trusting me.

"Okay," she whispers. She runs her hands down the sides of her sweatshirt, and I turn around, cracking my neck as I walk out of the locker room.

I head to the ring, pausing at the corner. "Stay here. Don't move. Don't talk to anyone."

She gives me a nod, and I step beneath the ropes. The roars start immediately, making my ears pulse and my muscles tense. One quick glance behind me shows Aria in the spot I left her. She looks so out of place. So weird standing in the place I feel the most at home. Instead of our real home, where I feel more out of place than I've ever been in my entire life.

My back heats, and I can feel the eyes glancing at my wounds, inspecting, curious eyes putting together their own story of my private life. I block them out, shaking off the feeling of their gaze as I focus on this moment. This fight. This *need*.

My name is chanted, and I lower my gaze to the ground, to the bloodstains covering the off-white mat. My blood now stains the fabric too, and for a moment I wonder which splatter would match my DNA.

It's silly, honestly, but a part of me feels proud that I've finally been injured here. I almost wondered if I was some sort of robotic, unbeatable psycho. I'm glad I'm human, even though I refuse to fall again.

The lights dim, and I can sense my opponent entering the ring. I barely lift my eyes, watching the hulking shadow bend and stretch through the rope. He stands up, and I have to lift my head to be able to see the top of his head.

He's tall, over six feet, for sure.

I pop a smirk. Reggie is upping his game. I'm glad, happy that he finally realized I don't need to be fighting the weakest of the weak. I can withstand to fight someone double my size. Corgan is a big man, and I've laid him on his ass plenty of times.

As long as this guy doesn't have the power that Morelli does, I feel like I have a good chance of walking away from this in one piece.

I can hear the growl barreling from his chest from across the ring. He has a large scar below his right eye, and a shaved head, the lights from above making it glow a yellowish hue. He's bare-chested, so broad his six-pack is no longer a six-pack. He's just… meat. A lot of fucking meat.

His hands clench to fists at his sides, and I watch the veins pop in his forearms. I stretch my arms out, going into position as I back up a step. He goes into position as well, his body tense.

Too tense.

Is he injured? Does he not want to fight a woman?

The notion that he's stiff seems off. If you aren't relaxed in the ring, you won't win in the ring. It's that easy.

Relax, big boy. Don't make this too easy for me.

I go to his side, fake hitting left, then swinging right. My entire strength goes into my punch as it lands in his side. He winces, his eyes darkening as he realizes the strength in my hit.

I've never seen this man before, and he must not have seen me, either. He doesn't realize I'm not a little girl. I can fight.

I can fight well.

He gets ready to punch, lowering the hand in front of his face just a smidge. It gives me the boost I need, and I swing my right arm, hitting him in the cheekbone.

He stumbles back, his neck and face turning red. His arm swings back, snapping forward and hitting my cheek. I stagger back, my brain rocked as I struggle to catch my footing.

His black shorts tighten across his thighs as he stalks toward me. I dip under his arms, still disoriented as I make my way behind him. His back is broad, with messy tattoos scrawled across his shoulders. I hit him in the kidneys, my already sore knuckles screaming in protest as I throw another blow to his side. Three quick jabs until his body flinches on the third time, and he falls away from me.

He windmills, his arm swinging out as he backhands me across the face. I fall to my butt, the pain ricocheting through my spine as my vision darkens a minute.

No. Not again.

What's happened to me? Have I lost my fight?

The hulk of a man falls on top of me, and I bring my leg up, being petty as I knee him in the balls. He freezes, his face pinching in pain as I scramble out from under him. If he pinned me and started hitting me, I wouldn't be able to get out. I'd lose the battle.

He's stunned for a moment, and I wheeze as I jump onto his back, my arm going around his neck as I squeeze tight. His fingers dig into my arms, and I squeeze tighter through the pain. His nails gouge my skin, and I can feel them scrape past layers of skin, blood beginning to roll down my arms. I keep my grip, my other fist going to the side of his head.

Boom, boom, boom, boom.

I hit him over and over, scrambling his brain until he goes lightheaded, his fingers releasing my arm. I don't stop my hitting until I feel his knees weaken, and he's like a Jenga tower, wobbling back and forth a few moments until he falls forward. I loosen my arms around his neck quickly, putting my hands behind his back as we crash to the ground.

I gasp in my breaths as I glare down at the passed-out man. It only takes seconds for everyone to realize I won, once again, before screams start blaring from every direction. I glance over my shoulder, ready to see Aria's horrified face, when I see an empty spot.

What the fuck?

TWISTED DARES

I leap to my feet, glancing around in a frenzy. No one can sense my panic, but it fills me like a fire, burning me from the inside out.

I see a flash of dark hair, my eyes swinging to the right. She's on the edge of the crowd, with a man talking to her, leering at her, his hands on each side of the ring as he pins her against the ropes.

Rage bubbles quicker than it ever has before, the sirens in my mind going from one to one hundred. My blood going from burning to a scorching lava. I rush to the ropes, my hands wrapping around the top section and swinging underneath them, my foot swinging back and kicking him straight in the head. He flies to the ground, shock and disorientation on his face.

But he's a big guy, and he's strong enough to be in the ring himself. He rights himself quickly, getting up and glaring at me with blood dripping down his nose, painting his lips red.

"You little bitch." He turns to his friends, women and men alike who all look rough as graveled dirt, like they were raised simultaneously on the streets. "Get her. Fuck her up!" he roars, and like the ringleader he is, his friends listen on command, turning toward me with such anger on their faces it puts me on red alert.

Aria screams, terror in her eyes as she scrambles to the side. I shove her out of the way as I realize what a mistake it was for me to ever bring her here in the first place.

What a foolish, idiotic mistake.

People pull at my feet, and I keep my hands wrapped around the rope as I kick my feet in an attempt to get away from them. The crowd goes wild, screaming as a mosh pit forms. I've never seen it get this wild, not once since I started coming here.

But my one move started a riot, and the people are already edgy from the fight. I've only stoked the fire.

Too many people grab at my legs, and the burning from the rope rubs my palms raw. My hands slip from the rope, and I fall to my back, sliding to the ground and off the ring.

They pounce.

They all jump me at once, their bodies piling on mine as they each try to get a hit in. I fight my best fight, listening to Aria scream from the top of her lungs as I'm mauled in every which direction. People fight those who are fighting me, my many fans trying to protect me from these fucking barbarians.

But too many of these people are too fucked to care about anyone, and the only thing they desire is blood. Any chance to spill blood creates a frenzy, and all hope is lost.

The cemented ground scrapes my back as I swing my fist left and right, connecting with jaws and arms and stomachs and every inch of skin I can.

Until I hit air, and bodies are lifted from mine.

I gasp in a full breath as I glance up, the body in front of the light obscuring the face, only the outline of a massive form standing above me. My mouth goes dry as a whiff of menacing male enters my senses, and I know without a doubt who it is.

Morelli.

The energy that comes from him is both burning rage and emotionless. Two edges of the sword and I don't know which one is dominant. He reaches down, not going for my hand but my bicep as he pulls me up like I'm a fucking dirty piece of laundry. His fingers burn my skin and turn me to ice at the same time. I'm so fucking angry at him but so thankful.

I glance to the left, seeing Aria leaning against the ropes, as if she can disappear into thin air. Her cheeks are wet with tears and pure terror pales her face.

"You all right?" I pant.

She nods. "You look so bad. Maybe we need to go to the hospital."

I shake my head, my hand going to my face to wipe away the sweat. Only, when I bring my hand down, it's covered in blood.

Shit, I really did get fucked up.

Morelli shifts in front of me, and I turn my head to his, seeing him clearly for the first time tonight. He looks angry, in a black leather jacket and dark blue jeans. His face is sharp enough to cut glass, and a glance down at his hands shows streaks of blood on his knuckles.

Did he fight… *for me?*

"Be here tomorrow. After school. Four o'clock. Don't fuckin' be late," he says sharply.

I blink at him. *What?*

"For?"

"For your training."

"Seriously?" I'm speechless. *What? What the hell changed his mind?*

"Don't be late." He goes to turn around, but panic makes my throat close, and I can barely swallow.

"Wait!" I choke out.

He turns around, his eyes bored and blank.

"Thank you. For helping me."

His eyes narrow. "You have a lot to learn. What I just saw was absolutely pathetic." He couldn't have been more offensive if he spit at my feet.

He spins around, leaving through the back.

My jaw is fucking unhinged. *The audacity.* I watch him disappear into the crowd that's a lot calmer than it was moments ago. Blood splatters on the floor, and random shoes and shirts are left as people start to make their way out.

"Was that… Was that the guy from school? Who broke your nose?" Aria steps up beside me, her nose plugged from emotion. She wipes it with the back of her sleeve.

I let out a shaky breath. "Yeah. It was."

"What did he want?" She watches the crowd with a look of awe on her face.

I shake my head. "I don't know."

"What was he talking about? You're going to meet him tomorrow?"

I watch where he once was, so confused and sore. I'm entirely out of sorts, but I know one thing.

He's going to help me.

I shrug. "Let's get out of here." The vibe feels off, everyone edgy. I can taste the adrenaline in the air. People are more blood thirsty than usual, and that's never a good thing. On my own, I could handle it, but with a trembling Aria with me, I'm just in a weakened position. Mostly because I'm now beaten and bruised.

I nod my head toward the exit when a tall man steps in front of me.

"Hi, Reggie," I say, cringing. I've been his best fighter for a year, and my last two fights have been anything but favorable.

"You're causing quite a stir, Raven." He glares down at me, clearly not proud of the chaos I started tonight. Reaching into his pocket, he pulls out a small stack of cash. I grab it quickly, folding it and hiding it in my palm.

I glance toward my cousin. "Some guy was leering on my little cousin. You know how I feel about them."

His eyes go from the top of Aria's head, down to her toes, and up again. "Maybe baby cousin needs to stay home where she's safe." He licks his lips. "She looks like she should be at a park, not in the Inferno."

My eyes shutter, and I take a step back. "I'm taking her home, now."

"Don't fuck up again, Raven, or I'm going to have to cut you from the ring."

I glance over my shoulder, glaring at him with every bit of spite in me. I get it, Reggie's just trying to protect his place and have as little liability as possible. You fight people, you kill people, but the moment you have immature kids running through the joint, well, all safety is out the window.

Safer to kill than let loud mouths in.

Aria is Aria, though. She's my blood and would never rat me out. She knows what taking this place away from me would do.

If I don't have an outlet for whatever clutches my soul, I'd be worried for everyone around me.

"Won't happen again, Reggie." I turn around, heading from the main area and back through the tunnels.

He's going to train me. Morelli is really going to train me.

I just hope I don't regret this.

chapter twelve
CAELIAN

I roll through the parking lot at school, barely listening as my brothers argue about the Irish as I slide into a parking spot.

I sigh, tired of the noise, inside and outside of my head. I turn my car off and lean back in my seat. I almost didn't come to school today.

Almost.

Between the shit with the Irish, the copycat Crow Killer, and this chick who has infected my thoughts like a disease, my brain has been jumbled. It's not good for me; it makes me feel on edge and agitated.

I should go back to the Inferno. I should take out my rage and messy thoughts on my enemies.

But *no*, instead, I decide to train some girl who looks like she belongs in junior high.

Why the fuck did I say I'd do this? I should've known better than to help her. I don't even know why I did. I just saw her there, beating the meaty fuck in the ring, and seeing her unconstrained rage as the mousy girl she was with was being leered on by a creep. She has no control. No restraint. She is a loose cannon, and she's honestly lucky she's still alive. Was it her bleeding in front of me as the mass of people pummeled her into the dirty ground? She did nothing but cower and cover her body as the screams ripped from her throat. She isn't weak, so what was it in her brain that caused her to crumble so easily?

The other side of her, the monster inside her tiny body, ripped into a man double her size until he was a broken heap of limbs on the mat of the ring. She fights brutal felons in the ring and makes it out in one, albeit bruised, piece. She shouldn't be walking. She shouldn't be alive.

Watching her fight, truly fight to the best of her ability, was both sexy as fuck and horrifying. She fights dirty, and watching the rage in her crystal blue eyes while exuding the raw power bundled into her small frame was seductive as fuck.

The frenzy in her eyes was so noticeable it's written in blood. There was something in me that cracked, and the words escaped my lips before my brain even registered them. It was just something that I couldn't take back, even when I so badly wanted to.

It's not a mystery why people enjoy watching her fight. She's beautiful, but she tries to hide it by being cold and detached from everything around her.

The only time her eyes flared with any emotion besides hate was when she was looking for the girl she was with. Her eyes were a mixture of softness and terror that made me want to dip a paintbrush into her irises and color the world with her emotions.

I don't know what it is about her, but watching her fall apart and weakness fill her created such a rage inside me, I couldn't stop my words even though I wanted to. I should've walked out without another word, but I didn't. *I couldn't.*

But what's done is done, and now I have another issue to take care of on top of my other hundred fucking issues.

"Dude, that chick is fire." Matteo's finger flies past my face as he points out the window.

I follow his gaze, my eyes landing on the girl that has been the center of my thoughts. Her ugly, gray Honda Civic should have been turned over for scrap metal years ago. But somehow, it's still hanging on. She seems to know this as she steps from her car, her jaw clenched as her eyes loosely scan the parking lot.

This is exactly the reason why she needs to train. She acts like she's big and tough, but she can't even sense when three dudes are watching her from the other end of the parking lot.

Where is she from? She looks like she barely owns a penny to her name in her oversized plaid shirt. It loosely hangs over her shoulders, and her pair of black leggings hide the toned thighs that I've only seen in the ring. She has little curves. She's tiny. Petite. But in that small body is bottled-up rage that I know is brewing to the surface.

Her face is busted, even I can see it from here. But the pound of makeup on her face dulls the bruises and cuts. She wants to hide, but the world doesn't want her to. People see her, they want her. I can tell from school and from the Inferno. She's desired by everyone around her. Even if she doesn't want to be.

I glance over my shoulder with narrowed eyes. "How do you know her?"

He laughs, looking over at Gabriel, who also has a smirk on his face. I tense in my seat, hating that they know something about her that I don't. I don't want them to have anything to do with her.

I want to hide her and keep her for my own selfish needs.

"I was teasing her on Friday, and she came at me with a pencil. Almost stabbed me in the thigh." He laughs through his words, and I grind my teeth together as I stare at him.

His smile drops. "Don't worry, big brother. Her threats faded away once I told her I'd shove my pistol in her mouth." Gabriel chuckles at this, and I whip my gaze toward him.

His eyes widen. "What crawled up your ass?"

I glance back at her, watching her walk up to the girl who she was concerned about at the Inferno. The girl looks nervous as she holds her backpack tightly in her grip, the silver cross necklace she's wearing swinging against her collarbone.

"How are they both like super-hot, but also not at the same time?" Matteo leans forward, his head hanging next to mine.

I growl, my hand going to his face as I push him into the backseat. "Stay away from them." And by them, *I mean her.*

Stay away from her.

Gabriel barks out a laugh. "*What?* What the fuck?"

I unlock the door. I need to get away from them. I'm not talking about it with either of them, because I don't even know how to explain what I'm feeling.

I just feel… discombobulated. A fucking wreck.

Before I can open the door, Gabriel slaps the lock button. I turn to him with a fierce glare, and he levels me with the same look. "You aren't getting away that easy. What the fuck are you talking about, *stay away from them?* Who are they to you?"

"They are no one," I growl.

"So why do you look like you want to rip out our throats for even talking about them? Is it the one in the plaid, or the one in the purple?" He leans against the dashboard as he licks his lips, his eyes flaring like he's thinking of them without clothes on. "I bet it's the one in the plaid. Holding a pencil against Matteo's thigh?" He runs his hand along his jaw, and it feels like my teeth are about to crack from the pressure.

"Definitely her. She's feisty. I bet she's a riot in bed. She probably bites. *Hard.*" Matteo chuckles.

I reach back, grabbing the back of Matteo's shirt and pulling him forward, until half his body is hanging in the front seats.

"*Leave. Her. Alone,*" I grit between my teeth.

Gabriel bites his lip as he stares at me with narrowed eyes. "What the fuck is up with you, Cae?"

I stare at Matteo for a moment, then release him as I slap the unlock button on the car. "Nothing. She's just… stay away from her." I step outside, slamming my door shut harder than necessary. With one quick glance toward her shitty car, I don't see them anymore.

Fuck.

Bring Me the Horizon bleeds through my AirPods as I sit in the library, my Mac in front of me, though I'm not doing even an ounce of the homework I'm supposed to be working on.

I tap my pen on the edge of the desk to the beat of the drums as my thoughts stray, once again, to *her*.

They shouldn't. Yet, no matter how much I want her out of my headspace, she only fills it that much more.

I glance down at my bruised knuckles, slices in the skin where I beat as many bodies as I possibly could last night. For hurting her.

For touching her.

There was this innate response in me to speed toward her once I saw she was in danger. To protect her. I've never felt this way before, so having it for some chick I barely know doesn't sit well inside me.

Watching her in the parking lot, with the bruises on her skin, knowing that each step is causing her pain, doesn't cause me any relief, or joy. It makes me angry, and I want to step back into the Inferno and beat those guys all over again for breathing in her direction.

I sigh, tossing my pencil on my keyboard and pushing my chair back. Free period is filled with nothing but fucking around until the next period. When you go to a school that is literally just a platform, feeding you on a platter to a prestigious college, it leads to a lot of unnecessary extra time. Most of my classes are filled with college curriculum, which doesn't have anything to do with me. College is pointless when my family business can't be taught during a lecture.

My sickness and the way I work doesn't fit into their syllabus. I'm deranged and my family are criminals. The fact that me and my brothers get to walk away with a high school degree from a school such as this is enough to make my parents happy.

They'll provide for us, and our family business will keep us wealthy for the rest of ours and our children's lives.

I shove to a stand, stretching my arms above my head in my study room. It's more like an office, with a desk, a nice chair, and even a small couch against the wall. Glass covers the other three walls, giving me a perfect view of the library. Rows upon rows upon rows of bookshelves that reach the second level, where more aisles and bookshelves sit.

It's a larger library than the public one in Portland. This library has just about everything you'd ever need to learn. The school in itself basically shits money, which I guess I can't complain about because the education is unbeatable.

Opening the door, I wander to the back of the library. It's empty today, and the only sounds are the footsteps of my boots against the carpet. The books are loud, though, each one screaming with a story to be told.

I have no purpose as I walk, just waiting for time to pass so I can go to the Inferno this afternoon. A part of me is dreading it, and another part of me can't wait to see her. To see what she's really made of.

How lethal is she underneath her vicious scowl?

I imagine bruising her, though this time she is begging for it.

Pleading for it.

I shake my head and grit my teeth as I head to the back row of books, my eyes locking on my worst enemy. My greatest desire.

Her.

Did I conjure her up, or has she been here this entire time?

She sits in the back, at the other end of the row. Her head buried in a book. She's so unaware of her surroundings.

What a fool.

A quick glance at the cover of her book tells me that she's reading

Wuthering Heights.

A love story.

She really is a fool.

I take a step toward her, and as if she finally senses me, her head shoots up, her eyes lifting to mine.

Her eyes widen as she slams the book closed and shoves it into her bag. "What're you doing here?" She stands up, and this time I see the slight wince of pain as her body adjusts.

I take another step toward her. "At school? In the library? Or near you?"

Her face scrunches in irritation. "Any of them. All of them."

I shrug. "I could be asking you the same."

She squeezes the top of her backpack. "Pretty sure it was obvious."

I step toward her again, and she steps back this time, her back brushing against the books. She wants to hide, but she'll never be able to hide from me. Not even in all the fictional stories in the world.

My eyes fall over the various bruises on her face, and I wonder how she is still upright.

"The bruises… they don't seem to bother you much."

Her fingers raise to her cheekbone, where a reddish-purple bruise covers her cheekbone. I know for a fact that it hurts, the way it's still shiny and swollen. That bitch is probably throbbing like hell.

"I've survived worse."

The way she says it, the way the lilt in her voice is filled with anguish, makes my stomach clench.

Who has hurt you?

Was some guy beating her? Was she in some shitty relationship? Do her parents hit her? What the fuck is her story?

From the look in her eyes, the pain goes further than just skin-deep. It embeds further than her blood and her bones. It integrates into her soul.

"Who hurt you?" I narrow my eyes, my mind grabbing a pen and paper so I can go find the fuckers and tear them into bite-sized pieces for Rosko.

I can hear her breath catch in her throat, like the anger I directed toward her surprises her. She's shocked by my emotion, but to be honest, so am I.

"Who said anyone hurt me? Maybe I'm just talking about the Inferno."

I run my tongue along my teeth, knowing for a fact that she isn't. But she builds a barrier around her heart and along her eyes, shutting me out before I have a chance to see her lies for what they are.

Fear.

"I could dare you, you know. Dare you to tell me the truth. All your worst, dirty secrets."

She sneers at me, and now I know I've hit a nerve. The sensitive spot is her personal life. She doesn't want to go there. Not in the slightest.

"That's one dare I would fail, Morelli. Because honestly? It's none of your fucking business." She shrugs her shoulder, the plaid shirt falling farther down her arm. It's pale and creamy, with a nasty pink scar along the inside of her bicep. It's fresh, but not yesterday fresh.

Someone really is hurting her.

I narrow my eyes, ready to fucking tear into her, when the sound of heels and giggling have me glancing over my shoulder.

The smell of flowers invades my senses before the three bitches of Blackridge Prep make their appearance.

Trina, Delanie, and Lorna.

They cause so much fucking drama and open their legs for literally everyone. Including my brothers.

They try with me, but I'm incredibly not interested in dipping my cock where my brothers have been. And half of the school.

"Hey! Caelian." Trina's eyes heat with a seduction I want to carve out and stomp on. She spends too much of her daddy's money, and her only goal in life is to get a sugar daddy. She's as useless as the leather bag she totes around every day. "What're you doing here in the library?"

"Can I help you with something?" I ask lazily.

She smiles, and Lorna glances over my shoulder, her eyes locking with the new girl's.

"Is that?" She giggles, her eyes flaring. She looks at Trina, leaning into her. "Look who's hanging out with Caelian."

Trina goes on her tiptoes, looking behind me. "Well... I never would've foreseen this." She smiles, her eyes lifting back to mine. "You might want to be cautious with this one."

They all step forward, and I can sense the unease between the four girls. How do they know each other? Something isn't fucking right, and I'm wondering if I should let them tear each other to shreds and just walk away, or if I'm going to be tearing their nails from each of their hands.

"She's got quite a mouth on her. I'm not sure if she's got all her shots, though. She might be rabid." She looks over my shoulder again, a salacious smile covering her face. "Anything else? Maybe a few STDs hanging onto you, too?"

I can hear the thump of a bag dropping to the ground before a gust of wind picks up behind me. I barely have time to turn around before she's shooting past me, rushing toward Trina.

Trina's eyes widen into saucers, and her friends scatter to the side as the new girl pins her against the bookshelf. Her hand goes to her neck, her nails digging deep into the skin. A growl rips from her, ferocious, sexy, not at all like a beast, but a lioness who's been threatened.

She is wild.

Her friends start screaming, coming up behind her and pulling her away from their friend. She whips her hand back, shoving them away with more force than she should have in her small body.

They let out another scream, and it's when Trina's face starts draining of blood, her eyes fading to a dizziness that shows she is moments from passing out, that I realize the new girl doesn't intend to stop.

Fuck, she is almost as crazy as me.

I step up behind her, lifting her away from Trina. Trina gasps in mouthfuls of air as her hands fly to her neck. She sinks to her knees, tears flooding her eyes, as I'm sure her life flashed in them.

The new girl lets out another growl. My fingers sink into her sides as I pull her down the row and through the library. She feels manic in my arms, and I keep her on the other end of the shelves as the librarian and a few other workers rush toward the screams and cries.

Fuck, I'm going to have to clean up her damn mess.

I hurry into the small room I was in, shutting the door behind me and pinning her against the door.

"You trying to get expelled?" I level her a look.

She narrows her eyes. "Fuck you."

"I dare you."

She shoves against me. "You wish. Those girls deserved it. This isn't the first fucking time they've messed around. Next time, she's not going to walk away in one piece." She's in her own world, already plotting her move against a girl whose father is a congressman. She can't go fucking around with just anyone she pleases.

She's too impulsive. Too risky. She has no sense of fucking control.

I grip her shoulders, pushing her against the door. My fingers burn where they touch her exposed shoulder, my thumb brushing against the raised scar. I can't be sure what it feels like exactly, what kind of wound has been inflicted on her skin. But it feels like burning embers roll between my thumb and her skin, a heat so fierce it scalds my insides.

She needs me to help her. She needs to learn how to control her irrational tendencies, or else she'll end up going crazy with the wrong person and get herself killed.

Is it my problem? No. *Should I really fucking care?* Absolutely not.

Does it stop me from helping her? Nope.

"Don't keep me waiting today. Four o'clock. Don't be late." I reiterate my words from last night before removing my scorching fingers from her arm. She releases a breath, like she was captured in the same heat storm as I was. Her eyes flicker from irritation to excitement, bouncing back and forth wildly, like she can't decide which one to land on.

I reach behind her, opening the door just as the bell rings.

"See you tonight," I mumble, just as she slips through the door.

I watch her walk away. I can tell she wants to glance at me over her shoulder, but she doesn't, keeping her body stiff and cold to the world as she disappears into the sea of people.

Fuck, she's a mess.

And I'm only going to make it worse for her.

She's fucking late.

I twirl my keys around my finger, the empty Inferno such a difference from the night before. It still smells like sweat and hormones in here, but every step leaves an echo bouncing off the walls.

Here I am, twenty minutes past four and she's nowhere to be seen. I should've fucking left two minutes after four, because if you're going to be late even a second, you don't deserve my time. I'd split someone in half for disrespecting me in some way, yet I let a girl who's only sneered and scoffed in my direction stand me up.

I clutch my keys in my grip, the metal digging into my skin as I internally hear the clock tick second after second.

Enough is enough. If I see her again, maybe I'll break her nose a second time.

I start walking to the exit, when the sound of quick, small footsteps pound across the floor. My eyes close, and I let out an impatient breath. *I shouldn't stay, I shouldn't fucking stay.*

I turn around, watching her dark hair tumble down her back, not tied up like it typically is. No, this time it flows around her in messy waves.

Not like a fighter. Like a woman. She wears the same clothes she was wearing earlier, though now the plaid shirt is wrapped around her waist, a tiny black tank top fitting firmly around her form. On her back is a nearly empty backpack. Her face is windblown, her cheeks rosy, and her eyes glossy from the breeze.

"I'm so sorry I'm late. I couldn't…" she pants, bending down and pressing her hands on her knees. "I couldn't get out of the house in time."

"I don't have time to sit around and wait on you to get ready for the day, or whatever the fuck it is you do. You wasted my time. I'm done here."

I go to walk around her, and she leaps into a stand. Her arms go out straight on either side of her, and fear laces her face, her chest still rising and falling rapidly in exertion. "Please! I'm sorry I was late. I really tried to get out in time. I just… I couldn't."

I stare at her. I'm fucking bored with her excuses. Of her non-excuses, that really don't make any sense. But I don't care enough to demand an answer. If she wants to spill a pile of bullshit in front of me, then she might as well step into it because I'm not waiting around for her. Never again.

"I really don't give a shit why you're late. The fact of the matter is, you're late, and you wasted my time. Go home, forget I said anything."

"Please!" Her pleas are so desperate, it tugs at my chest. I glance down, not seeing anything out of the ordinary.

Am I sick?

"I'm sorry, but I really need this! There's… something wrong with me."

I turn toward her. "Sounds like you need a doctor."

Her eyes narrow. "I don't need a doctor. I need to learn how to defend myself. And to…" she mumbles the last of her words, but I can't hear a word.

"You what?" I snap.

She stares at me a moment, her lips working the words before she mutters, "I need to learn how to kill someone."

My eyebrows lift. "Do you now? And who are you after?"

Her eyes narrow. "Everyone."

"Everyone," I mock. "I don't think you understand what you're asking. Fighting in that ring is one thing. Spilling blood and bruising people is a different game than taking a life."

"I know that," she snaps.

It feels like a game. I feel like I'm a teacher showing a third grader tenth-grade math. It doesn't make sense. It doesn't feel right. I don't understand why I made my way here in the first place. But here I am, and it was all a mistake. Talking to this girl in the first place was a complete, and utter, mistake.

"No." I turn around, ready to walk out when she jumps in front of me once again.

"What do you mean, *no?* You told me *yes*. You told me that you'd meet me here today and show me. You can't change your mind at the last minute because you want to. You have to teach me. I feel like… I feel like I'm out of control!"

That is the thing. She *is* out of control. I see her blue eyes flickering in fury. Will she become a killer whether or not I show her the way?

Maybe. Most likely. If the way she attacked Trina today is any indication. But if I don't show her how to control her rage, she'll likely be in prison in the next year for her recklessness. She'll kill everyone in her sight and get locked up for getting caught.

Is she my problem? No. Not at all. Not in the slightest.

"You are," I seethe.

"So, help me," she urges. "I need help. I don't fucking ask anyone for help, but I'm asking you. *Please.*"

I stare at her a moment. She's pathetic, really. But something is off, because as badly as I want to throw her on the ground and tell her to fuck off, my brain doesn't let me. "Come with me."

I turn around, leaving her in the darkness behind me.

It takes a moment, and I know she's stalling because she doesn't know how to respond, but then I hear her little feet pad after me, and my skin heats.

I have a feeling this might be the biggest regret of my life.

TWISTED DARES

"Where are we?"

I glance at her, these being the first words she's spoken since she hopped into my car. She decided to stare out the window, and I could tell she was nervous, but tried hiding it. She didn't want to give away that she's scared of me, but every bit of tension coiled in her body gave away to the fact that she doesn't trust me, doesn't fully want to be here.

But her need overtakes everything else.

Turning into my driveway, I pull around the side of the house, going toward the back where our attached gym sits. It's hidden, much like the rest of the house. Our house is a monstrosity, two levels with sleek, black lines and sharp corners. It's modern and eco-friendly, hidden in the trees and between rocks. No one will notice it as they drive by, they'll only see the massive iron gates with an *M* for Morelli in the center. The long driveway will take you to our house, and around the back is the gym that was built only a few years ago.

Once I got into high school and started going to the Inferno, I realized a gym was a necessity, and going to a club or gym in the cities was not on my fucking list. It was an easy decision, and within a few months, I had a gym that easily replicated the Inferno, but on steroids. This gym is a beast and has everything I'll ever need.

Both me and my brothers use it, but it's also the place where most of my training is. My father had hired a trainer back in the day, multiple, actually. Until I realized I could handle more than every single one of them could.

So that's when I decided I would just train myself. And here the fuck I am.

"Are you going to just sit there and ignore me?" Her voice grows with an edge to it, and I grit my teeth.

Mouthy.

"Watch your tongue."

She rolls her eyes, and her hand goes to the door handle, ready to escape me and my brutish manners. I turn to her, tired of her antics and drama, and we've barely spoken a sentence to each other. "You want me to teach you. What the fuck do you think we're going to do?"

She glances up at my house, which I'm sure looks like a mansion to her. I have no idea what kind of house she lives in. Nothing like this, that's for sure. This house probably doesn't look nearly as inviting to her as it does to me. But the uninviting always looks the most inviting.

"Well, I don't understand why we're at a house. Is this your house? Shouldn't we be going to a gym, or something similar? If we're training in your living room or something, I might as well just have stayed at my house to practice."

I sigh, done with her complaints. Would it be disrespectful of me to tape her mouth shut while I train her? Tell her to not speak at all?

What the fuck am I doing being a teacher? I don't even fucking like people.

"How about you shut the fuck up and stop asking questions," I grunt.

I park, immediately turning off the ignition and stepping out. Slamming the door shut, I walk toward the gym without glancing back to see if she'll follow. I know that she will. There's something about her.

Something that piques my interest, and I know she feels the same. She seems just as disturbed, maybe more than I am.

And that's saying a lot.

Soon enough, I listen as the door shuts and her light feet rush to catch up to me. I step up to the door, punching in the code that is too many numbers for any normal human to remember.

The lock disengages, and I pull the door open, the smell of disinfectant and bleach slapping me in the face. The large, open area is filled with training equipment of every type. Regular exercise machines, weights, and even a training ring similar to the one at the pit.

My eyes shutter as I glance over my shoulder, seeing the girl peek around me with wide, innocent eyes. They are those of a fake innocence, though, because the innocence clashes with a bleak darkness that she hates almost as much as she hates me.

"What is this place?" she gasps.

"Where we'll be training." I step inside, waiting for her to step through the doorway so I can shut and lock the door behind me. Her eyes flare once she hears the lock click, but I walk past her without a care to give her any reassurance.

No, baby girl, it's not even slightly safe to be alone with me.

And if it was pussy I was after, which I'm not, hers wouldn't be it.

"Do you realize I need to know more than just to fight? I want you to teach me to… do things."

I step up to the table next to the ring, grabbing the tape and tossing it to her. I notice she wraps her knuckles; she needs the protection that I don't.

She catches it with ease, but the hesitancy stays in her gaze.

"If you can't even say the word *kill*, then you aren't ready to actually do the fucking deed." I toe my shoes off, lifting each foot to take off my socks. I'm already dressed in a pair of joggers and a white tee. This will do for the day. I would never fight this, but today I feel like I'm teaching elementary basics.

She doesn't say anything, and I glance over at her, watching her wrap her hands with her face scrunched up, so much displeasure and unease pinching her skin. Does she even want to be here? Why is she doing something she doesn't want to do?

"Why the fuck are you here?" I snap.

She stops her wrapping, glancing up at me with conflicted eyes. "How do you know killing is something you're meant to do?"

I squint my eyes curiously, cocking my head to the side. "What's it about me that makes you think I kill people for a living?"

She tears the tape, flexing her hand, then starts on her other one. "Well, for one, you killed someone in the ring without a second thought. Got blood on me, too, you know. You looked almost… pleased. Like you enjoyed every second of it."

"I did," I say, not at all put off by her comment.

She takes a deep breath, her eyes not straying from mine. "Then there's the fact that you have this look in your eyes. Like you've ended lives. Not just one or two, not just in the ring. It's like I can see each breath you've stolen. Each body you've torn apart and buried. The blood you've drained. You don't seem remorseful, either. It's like it gives you life."

I say nothing. I feel nothing. I have no response for her because I don't understand what she wants from me. Reaffirmation that I do these things? Denial? A fight? I don't know what she needs.

"You have this control that I need. I'm desperate for it. I have this… need to take life. I'm so fucking angry all the time, and I just want to take it out on everyone around me. I'm scared that I'll make a mistake I'll never be able to take back. That's why I'm here." She sniffles, her head dropping to the tape as she finishes her second hand. "I just want to learn how to control it and be… like you." Her voice drops off at the end.

I clench my fists. "Get in the ring."

She drops her bag to the ground, her nerves making her arms shake as she unties her shirt from her waist and tears her tank top over her head, leaving her in only her sports bra that clings to her chest. She keeps her leggings on but bends down to shove her shoes off her feet.

Standing up, she stares at me a moment, already in the ring. Waiting for her.

"I'm ready."

chapter thirteen
RAVEN

Walking into the opposite end of the ring, I slip under the ropes, this mat clean and white, unlike the stained one at the Inferno. This one has been bleached enough times that I can still smell the chemicals.

My eyes lift to his, and I stare at him, his lean physique that is also viciously firm. He looks like a weapon, lethal and ready to snap at any moment.

"What is your name?" The mean girls from earlier said it, but their voices were too quick for me to catch on. I realize his last name is Morelli. But that's all I know.

"Caelian." *Sea-lee-un.* "Caelian Morelli."

Caelian Morelli.

I test the words around my mouth. His name is said with certainty and power. He isn't someone to be fucked with. Each letter is filled with brutality. His name is one that only would be given to someone who could rule the world. Someone who could break a spine with only the flick of his wrist.

He's someone I should never, ever, fully let my guard down around.

"Where are you from?" I ask softly. I'm suddenly unsure of my place here. He sounds like royalty. Death wrapped into a body made of muscle and art. His skin is tanned, rippled with tension. I watch the tattoos on his arms dance against the muscle.

"Sicily." He doesn't offer up anything else. Doesn't ask me for any information in return. He doesn't ask me *anything* in return. He just stares at me, like he's been over with this conversation since before it started.

Caelian Morelli from Sicily, Italy.

He opens his mouth to speak, when the back door opens, one that we didn't come through. My eyes widen and my body tenses when two older people walk in, each of them standing with such authority I wonder if I should bow in their presence.

Caelian's body stiffens next to me, and that makes me all the more nervous.

Who are these people?

"Caelian," the man says, his body dressed in an expertly tailored black suit. His back is snapped intensely straight, his hands in his pockets as he watches Caelian.

"Dad. Mother." Caelian nods, and I try my best to not let my jaw drop, as my eyes widen.

His parents?

Somehow, I never would've guessed these were his parents, but I do see the resemblance. His father has his same skin tone, but he has his mother's beautiful hair, and dark brown eyes.

"Who do you have with you, Caelian?" His mother's voice is silky and feminine, yet there's a hardness in her tone. She isn't friendly. She doesn't have the motherly connection like a mother should.

Maybe she would get along with Aunt Gloria.

Maybe this woman can't be trusted.

Caelian steps in front of me, blocking them from my sight.

Or, maybe he's blocking me from their sight.

"She is no one," is all he says.

Heels clack closer and closer until her voice is next to me. "That isn't very nice, Caelian. Introduce us."

I can hear Caelian growl slightly, before his hand reaches behind him and he grabs onto my arm, yanking me out beside him. "These are my parents. And this is a girl from school. I'm teaching her a few things. Now, if you don't mind, I should get back to it."

"Caelian." His father's lips turn down in a severe scowl.

Caelian sighs, and I know his temper is running thin. I glance up at him, seeing his clenched jaw, his corded body.

My eyes flit to his mother, looking at her dark brown hair, the waves tamed and combed to perfection. She has on a creamy blouse, tucked into a pair of dressy pants that look so sleek and shiny, I wonder what the fabric feels like as it brushes against her skin.

I reach my hand out, my fingers wrapping around Caelian's bicep. It's so large, so tense in my grip, my fingers barely make it halfway around his arm. The tips of my fingers burn, and I gasp as I feel the electricity between us. I turn my gaze to his, and see him already watching me, a ruthless look on his face. One that should scare me. It should absolutely frighten me.

But I squeeze his arm again.

"I really do have to go soon. We should get back to work if we're going to finish in time." Where my strength comes, I have no idea, but I'd like to pretend Caelian is giving me even an ounce of courage at this moment.

I'm not afraid of him.

I'm not.

His father clears his throat, and the sound of heels retreating makes me turn my gaze to his parents.

"We have a dinner meeting we must attend. We won't be back until later tonight," his father says.

Caelian tenses once again. "A dinner meeting?"

His father's lips press into a tight line. "Yes, a dinner meeting. We can discuss later. Have a good night, Caelian, and Caelian's *girl from school*," he says, before he and his wife walk out. Caelian's mom glances over her shoulder at the last moment, giving me a curious, slightly cold look before the door shuts, and it's just us.

Us alone, once again.

My fingers tingling alerts me that my hand is still on his arm, and I release him, shaking out my fingers as I bring my gaze to his eyes.

He watches me for a long moment. I see his jaw clench, the twitch in his cheek somehow fucking attractive, and I have no idea how.

"Get into position," he orders, backing up and going to the opposite end of the ring.

His command snaps me into action. My feet jut out, my knees bending as my fists go up to my face. I block my nose, the place he shattered into pieces. My other hand gets ready to hit him, because I have no idea what he has planned.

"Your form is shit," he announces from the other side of the ring. My eyes narrow, and my hands drop to my sides.

"I've laid grown men on their asses with my form like this. I've been trained by one of the best, and he's made my form fucking perfect, thank you very much."

He shakes his head slightly. "Your form is shit," he repeats.

I step toward him, my hands going up again. I swing my hand out, because he pushes every button there is to be pushed inside me. He doesn't only disrespect me, but he also disrespects Corgan?

Fuck him.

His hand snaps out, grabbing onto my wrist, his fingers tight and unforgiving against my skin. His grip is firm, and his other hand swings out. His knuckles hit my jaw, not gently but not forcefully, either. Enough for a lick of pain to hit, but it doesn't knock me on my ass.

"Your. Form. Is. Shit. You think you know what you're doing, but you don't. Corgan and Reggie put you in with amateur fighters that know less than you do. That's why you get them on their asses. What happens when you run into someone like me? What happens when the moment you're ready to kill someone, they are so fucking erratic you can't expect their next move?"

He steps forward in the blink of an eye, his hand going around my throat as he lifts me off the ground. I grapple at his hands, trying to pull his fingers away. I can't even gasp in a small breath of air. He cuts off everything. Completely.

"It takes nothing to sweep you off your feet." He sets me down, and my hands go to my throat. I suck in a lungful of air, lightheaded and so fucking angry at his words.

I know I'm a good fighter. *I know I am.*

He grabs onto my shoulders, turning me around so my back faces him. He pushes me toward the other end of the ring, and I stumble forward, walking away from him. He's quick as he moves behind me, bending down and pulling my feet out from under me. I land on my face, my forehead smacking the mat so hard I see stars.

"You can't even protect yourself from an attacker that is coming up behind you. How would you escape? How could you ever kill someone if you don't know basic fucking instinct?"

I growl into the mat, sweat instantly beading and dripping down my back. It's not from exertion. It's from fucking rage.

I spin around, leaping off the ground and jumping into his arms. My legs wrap around his waist as I claw at his face. He's stunned, but quickly recovers as he fights me off him. I'm not to be deterred, though. I'm so angry that I cling to him like a feral cat as I claw at every inch of skin I can find. My elbows hit the side of his face, and I do any and every move I possibly can. "I hate you so much," I growl.

He drops to the ground, my back slamming against the mat. The wind is nearly knocked from my lungs as I stare up at him, his face dark and obscured in the shadows. But I can see his eyes glaring down at me as he pins me to the mat. Almost every inch of his body presses against every inch of mine. We're tangled and twisted and intertwined so intimately it would feel sexual if there wasn't a raging hate between us.

"Your form is shit, and you fight like a fucking kitten."

I push against him, but it only makes him press against me harder. I can feel his hips, his legs, his fucking cock as he grinds his body down on mine. Not sexually, but possessively. Like he knows who holds the cards. Who is more powerful. It would take nothing to end my life. He is too strong.

"Instead of overpowering me, why don't you fucking teach me?" I pant.

"I am teaching you. Sense people around you. Sense their moves, their strength. I'm coming up behind you and you can't even tell I'm there. Fucking figure it out, or you'll never be able to do what you so badly want to do. *Kill.*"

He lifts off me, walking back to his side of the ring. He bends his neck back and forth, a vicious crack echoing through the room. "You should already be on your feet. The moment you have the ability, you should be in stance, ready in case your attacker is coming after you once again."

I leap to my feet, embarrassed at how weak I feel. I thought I knew what to do. I thought I had everything together, but I've never felt as in pieces as I do right now.

I step back to my side of the ring, keeping my hands at my sides. I don't know how to stand. Apparently, I've always had it wrong. So, what is the right way?

"Don't face me fully. Your body is open for strikes in any location."

I pivot to the left, turning my body so my right shoulder faces him.

"Don't bend your back leg so much. It looks like the wind could knock you down."

I scowl at him, but his face doesn't change.

"Put your hands up," he orders.

I do as he asks.

"Not that high." I lower them. "Not that low." His voice becomes sharp, and I want to snap at him, but am afraid he'd just tell me to get the fuck out.

"For fuck's sake, are you completely useless?" He stomps over to me, his hand grabbing mine in a searing grip. I want to whimper at his burning touch, and I wonder if third-degree burns will be left in its place. My heart jumps all across my chest, bouncing from rib to rib. I clear my throat, glancing through my lashes at him. He doesn't seem to notice my unease, or he's hiding it well. Either way, I feel like a bottle of overwhelming emotions while he just seems so… emotionless.

He shoves my arms all over the place, positioning them exactly how he wants. His body is too close to mine. I can smell the spiciness of his scent, how strong it is. Does he know how he smells? Does he know it's an aphrodisiac? What it does to people who are in his proximity?

I could fall to my knees. I want to, but I lock them in place to stay upright.

His foot lifts, and he kicks behind my knee, putting them into a bending position. "You'll break your fucking legs if you keep them locked."

I'll fall if he doesn't step away from me.

What the hell is happening?

I don't like anyone. I don't want to like anyone.

"Keep your hands like this." He positions them in the same position I had them, but it doesn't matter, because I know he's the type of man that always gets what he wants. He crowds my space, his body molding to mine.

My heart stops jumping against my ribs, and this time it feels like someone released one million butterflies in my chest, their soft wings fluttering against each part of my insides. I swallow down my gasp, and even his breath stops. For only a moment.

Does he feel it, too? Can he possibly be experiencing the same erratic feeling in his chest that I am?

He takes a deep breath and continues. *If only it were that easy.* "When you step toward me, watch me. Sense me. Smell me. Figure out everything about me before you make your move. If you're missing one—*even one thing*—you're fucking dead. You got that?"

"Got it," I choke out.

He steps back to his side, standing with his hands near his waist. "Come get me."

I look at his stance, his feet pointed to my weak side. His hands poised to get me in my stomach. His body taut, tensed and ready.

Where is his weakness?

He tilts his head to the side, exposing his neck ever so slightly. He's helping me, I realize. I step forward, watching his weakness open. I walk toward it, acting like I'm going to the opposite end, but my arm strikes out at the last moment.

He grabs it.

"You're too fucking obvious. I knew you were going to hit my neck before you even thought it yourself."

"You did not!" I shout, my other arm swinging out and cracking him in the cheek. I can feel my knuckles hit bone. And though he doesn't flinch or falter from it, I know it had to have hurt. My rage is burning right now, and I want to tear him to pieces. He's creating emotions I've never felt before, and it's not a welcome feeling.

I feel even more twisted than I've ever felt before.

I surprised him with my hit, and he knows this. His hand goes out, his fingers twisting in my hair as he pulls me to the ground. I fall, my back slamming onto the mat with an *oomph*. I glare up at him, pissed he once again got the upper hand.

"Tell me who you want to kill," he says from above me.

"None of your business," I growl.

His foot goes over my chest, and he pushes down. "You want to be trained, tell me. Do you have a boyfriend from wherever you came from? Your parents piss you off?" His eyes are burning and mocking, and I bring my foot up, kicking him as hard as I can.

"My parents are dead." This isn't the total truth, but it might as well be. "I want to kill everyone. But most of all, I want to kill my aunt and uncle."

His brow lifts, curious and surprised. "What did your poor aunt and uncle do to make it on your hit list?"

TWISTED DARES

I grit my teeth, fury burning in my gut. *So many things*. They have done so many things for me to hate them, but this last week they have fucked me up beyond repair.

But I won't tell him a word about it, because he doesn't deserve the truth of my situation. I don't trust him. I don't trust anyone.

"They did nothing," I say instead.

He glares at me, and I hold firm with my stare. He can take it or leave it. If he doesn't want to train me because I won't give him my honesty, well, then I'll just have to figure something else out.

I really hope that's not the case.

His foot lifts off my chest, and he turns around, giving me his back.

His weakness.

I leap to a stand, jumping on his back and bringing my arm around his neck. I squeeze tight, and he grabs over his head, lifting me and flipping me around. I end on the other side of the rope, and he pins me there, his front to my back. He molds to me, and my body melts against his.

His fingers dig into my skin along my rib cage, and they trail down, little by little, until he's past my sports bra, his fingers pressing against my bared skin. It's seductive, intimate, yet aggressive and dominating.

"Your body is littered with scars," he mumbles, his voice a rasp as he breathes into my hair.

My body tenses, and he digs his fingers in more, until I'm certain his fingertips will leave a mark. I can feel his erection, strong, thick, angry as it presses against my ass.

"My scars are none of your business."

He hums against me, and I can feel it caressing along every inch of my skin. "I think you are becoming my business every moment you stand in my home."

I go to pull away from him, but his fingers stay embedded in me, and I know I have no chance of escape unless he sets me free.

I'd be lying if I said a part of me never wanted to be set free.

Here, in this moment with him, I feel the chaos settle. My mind rests and my body relaxes with Caelian standing next to me. He is here, this monster, this beast of a man who has torn me down physically and mentally, but he's also constructing me into a stronger version of myself.

One who can conquer. One who can survive.

I don't know who Caelian Morelli is, but I'm beginning to realize, he is mine.

His fingers dip lower, spreading across my abdomen, my muscles twitching from nerves. His pointer finger dips into my belly button, pressing, molding, engraving himself into me. Then he dips lower again, his fingers trailing along the waistband of my leggings. They toy with the fabric, slipping beneath my pants an inch, and retreating. He plays this game with me until I'm a trembling mess in his arms, eager and craving his touch.

He says nothing.

His fingers reach beneath my pants again, this time going farther, beneath my panties and touching where no one has ever reached before. They brush against the small bed of curls, and I hold my breath, my eyes squeezing shut as my aunt and uncle's words come back to haunt me.

Whore.

Slut.

Daughter of Satan.

I spin around, chills breaking out along my arms and a hot flash hitting me at once. I look at Caelian with wide eyes, but he's ever the cool and collected one, his eyes shuttering and becoming unemotional once again. He withdraws his hand and steps farther into the ring, leaving me on the outside.

"You are a fast learner. Put your things on. That's enough for the day."

I step off, my feet hitting the floor as I glare at him, unsure of what just happened between us. What would have happened if I didn't turn around, and the fact that I wanted it to. So I focus on the reason why I came here in the first place. "But you barely taught me anything."

His eyebrows lift as he walks off the ring, to the opposite side of me. "I taught you everything. It's up to you whether you took anything from it."

I'm speechless as he puts his socks and shoes back on. I walk to my things, pulling my clothes on with irritated, jerky movements. Then I grab my bag, feeling a little bereft. I feel like this should've been such a longer session. I feel like I should barely be able to walk out of here.

I feel like there should be so much knowledge in my head and so much ache in my bones it would be overwhelming. I wanted him to teach me how to be a killer so I could walk out of here and into my aunt and uncle's house, ready to take their lives just as I feel like they've taken mine.

But I don't feel that way. I don't feel at all ready to kill.

"I thought you were going to teach me how to… you now, *kill* someone?" I say to the ground, listening as his steps come closer to me.

The heat of his body warms my back, and I stand up, my eyes widening once I realize how close he is to me.

"You are the farthest thing from ready to kill someone." I spin around, ready to snap on him when his eyes clash with mine. They pull me in and hold me hostage. He locks me in place and I have no chance of escape. His eyes trail over my face, my slender features and hair that I'm sure is damp and a complete mess. "Tell me your name."

I small smile quirks my lips. That's the most humane question he's ever asked me. I almost wondered if we'd go through this entire training process without him knowing my name.

"My name is Raven."

His eyes flick over my dark hair and pale skin. "The bird."

A sickness trickles through my blood, and I can feel my veins cool to ice. "No. My name is just Raven." I slink away from him, giving him my back as I walk to the door.

I don't want to get into my life, my past, or my family. That's an off-limits topic, and I'm hoping my cold demeanor was enough of an answer for him.

He walks behind me until I reach the door. I step out of the way, and he punches in a code before pushing it open for me to walk through. We're silent as we head to the car, the only sound the smooth beep as he unlocks his black BMW. It's crisp and clean, like it just ran through the car wash. I slide onto the leather seat, anger bubbling in my chest. I wanted so much more than what he gave me, more of everything. And that makes me question if this was really a good idea in the first place.

Pulling my phone from my bag with a sigh, I check the time.

Wow, more time has gone by than I thought.

Telling Aunt Gloria that I had a project to work on with girls at school was easier than I expected it to be. At first, she wanted names, parents' names, and phone numbers. Of course, fucking stupid me spit out the first names that came to mind.

Trina, Lorna, and Delanie. Once I gave her those names, she let me go with the promise I'd be home before dark.

Well, by the time I get home, it'll definitely be dark outside. I swallow down my groan. *Fuck, I better not get in trouble for this.*

I glance at Caelian as he slides into his seat, his face is blank, which is what I'm realizing is the norm for him.

"I can give you this address and you can be here in two days, same time."

Dread seeps in. I can't be here on Wednesday. I never work on Wednesdays. I'm rarely able to go anywhere on the weekdays. The only times I'm allowed out of the house are Fridays, Saturdays, and Sundays for my *job*, which means the Inferno. I was lucky enough to get out of the house this evening, but I don't know how many times I can tell them that I have a school project to work on.

I can only get away with it so many times before it'll start to raise their red flags.

"I-I don't know if I can. I'll have to let you know. I can let you know at school, okay?"

His fingers stay on the ignition, confusion lacing his features. "Why?" He glances up and down my body. "You're in high school and don't know if you can go out after school? What the fuck aren't you telling me?"

My skin pales. I can feel the blood drain from my face, and my skin prickles as it grows cold as ice. I refuse to divulge my secrets. Talking about my aunt and uncle will lead to why I'm there, which will lead to who I am and who I come from.

No.

Absolutely not.

"Nothing," I mumble, my eyes darting to my lap.

"You're fucking lying," he growls, and I can feel it in my rib cage.

Fuck.

I whip my gaze out the window. "I'm not lying about anything. My aunt and uncle are just strict. I can't always get away. I can let you know about Wednesday at school. Sorry, that's the best I can do."

The car rumbles to life beneath me, and his voice is just as smooth as his engine. "Let me know. I'm not going to wait around and shit."

I nod, feeling a relief in my chest that he's not going to keep digging. I glance out the window and bite my lip. The rage inside my blood is tamped down, only slightly. I'm not sure if he's calmed it or if he's the cause of it, but it's something I don't think I'm even ready to inspect.

Caelian drives through the city, weaving with ease and control. It's droolworthy, but I refuse to swoon. I'm sure he has his own bevy of women at his feet. Probably a slew of them, ready to meet with him at the drop of a hat. I bet one phone call from *Caelian Morelli* and he could have anyone in the Portland area at his doorstep within an hour. I wouldn't be surprised if he didn't blow through more than one in a single night.

It feels like only moments later when he pulls up beside my car outside the Inferno. How he knows it's mine, I have no idea. But he's there, stopping and not even shifting into park. His arms flex against the steering wheel. His face doesn't even turn in my direction. "If you're late again, don't bother showing up because I won't let you in."

My nostrils flare, and the calm I felt only moments ago is swept away by his callous words. "I told you it wasn't my fault." Grabbing my bag, I go to open the door when the lock clicks.

I turn to him with wide eyes, and he's staring at me blankly. "I know you're hiding something from me, Raven. I know whatever fucked-up shit you're dealing with at home is your own shit. But don't bring it around me, don't involve me, and don't let your shitstorm touch me. If it does, you'll be the next one beneath my blade."

I swallow air. How the fuck does he know? Are my emotions that transparent? Do I look like a wounded animal, or a beaten child? I try to keep my face strong, my demeanor cold. I wish he wasn't able to read me so easily, because now I feel like I shouldn't come back at all. If my aunt and uncle somehow found out what I'm doing, if word ever got back to them…

Fuck.

"Bye, Caelian," I say hesitantly, not sure what to do. Not sure what to even say.

He unlocks the door, and I slip out, walking around the back of my car until I reach the driver's side. My hand makes it to the handle when something fluttery catches my eye, and I glance over, seeing a piece of paper flapping underneath the windshield wiper.

Someone gave me a ticket? I've never gotten a ticket while parking here.

I reach over and lift my wiper as I pull out the sheet of paper, letting the wiper slap back against the windshield. Unfolding it, my eyes glance at the words, taking in each letter, my veins cooling with each passing second.

Oh, fuck…

My eyes widen, and my entire body trembles, my fingers loosening their grasp. The paper flutters from my fingers, blowing to the ground and becoming a tumble weed as it begins to fly away.

It can't be…

A shoe comes down on the piece of paper as Caelian steps on it. I can barely catch my breath as he bends over, snatching it up between his fingers. Standing, he uncrumples it, staring down at the scratchy writing scrawled across the page.

I'm hot. I'm cold. I'm numb. I'm in excruciating pain. I can barely see straight as he walks up to me, turning the paper around and sticking it directly in my face. I squint, the drawing bringing back so many memories that I feel a panic attack beginning.

How? How is this possible?

"Why the fuck is the copycat Crow Killer sending you shit?" He flaps it in my face, and I backhand it away, stepping back until my spine hits the brick wall of the building. It's only us in this alley, and I can feel the walls shrinking in on me, growing smaller, tunnel vision darkening my sight.

"Get that away from me," I grit between my teeth, my voice shaky and my eyes burning with shocked tears. I feel like everything I've ever tried running away from just unveiled itself.

My past is like, *ha-ha, you thought you saw the last of me? Think again.*

"What the fuck do you know about the copycat Crow Killer?"

I narrow my eyes, swallowing through the nerves. "Copy what? Copycat Crow Killer? What the fuck is that?" My voice sounds like it's not even here. Like I'm watching myself from the outside.

He steps toward me again until his body is nearly flush against mine. "The copycat killer of the Crow Killer. You know who the Crow Killer is, don't you?"

"A little," I grunt.

"Have you heard of the copycat?" he barks, the paper still firm in his grip.

I shake my head.

"Are you sure? Or are you fucking lying to me about something else?" He looks down at the paper again, reading the word over and over again. "Why the fuck did he send this to you?" His voice is steel venom in the empty alley. I glance at the paper, so similar to the drawings of an outline of a crow that I've seen.

I've seen it many times. *So many times.*

My eyes go to the corner. To the childish handwriting of an adult. Messy on purpose. Immature letters written together to make a disease on paper.

Hello.

That's all it says. A simple word with too much meaning on a piece of paper, along with a drawing, a messy outline of a bird that brings back so many memories.

Good ones, bad ones. Traumatic ones.

"I don't know," I whisper, a shiver breaking out along my spine. I feel weak. This isn't me. I'm not weak, and I haven't been for many years. I'm no longer this person, and it makes me furious that one piece of paper can put me back to where I used to be.

A weak, broken child. Frightened and confused.

He stares at me a moment, crumpling up the paper in his hand as he takes a step away from me.

Then he's back in my face. So close his breath brushes against my skin, soft and featherlike. His lips are plump and wet as they brush my ear, his voice rumbling and commanding as he speaks his words. "I'm going to find out what's going on, little bird. A raven in your name and a crow on the paper. Something doesn't add up to me. Your face speaks differently than your words. You're lying to me about something, and I'll figure it out. I'll figure out *every last detail*." Then he's off me, his back stiff as he walks back to his car. With the paper in hand, he slips inside, zipping down the road until he's out of sight.

What the fuck have I gotten myself into?

chapter fourteen
CAELIAN

Dark red mixes with water, turning a pinkish hue as it runs over my fingers and down the drain. I let the water spray beneath my nails, and soon my tan skin returns to its normal shade, my kill for the night washing away like it never happened in the first place. Where his body goes, I don't know. My dad has people to take care of that.

My part of the job is to end the life, not to remove or destroy the evidence.

This… *job*, I guess you could call it, is more than just something I need to do. My dad has used my needs to make it worth his while, too. He assigns me to people he needs taken out, an assassin, of sorts. It's grown over the years, from the occasional person when I was a kid, and now that I'm eighteen, I'm a full-blown killer. My Friday nights aren't filled with movies or dates, they're filled with taking the lives of those around me, whether I found them myself or it's someone my dad found necessary to remove from the world.

It used to be simple; the people who work with my dad would strap the victim into a chair in the basement, going so far as to place the weapon straight into my palm. All I needed to do was put the knife into the chest and my job was done.

Just end their life, my dad would tell me.

After the first time, it only got easier.

Each life I take with my hands is more of a thrill than the last. The moment I moved into high school, it became more than just death. My dad put the hunt in there. It was no longer a body to drain, but a game to play.

These games, they keep me interested. My dad knows it's the games that keep me intact. Without them, my body and mind become a mixed bag of shit that no one wants to find themselves in.

If you end up there, you will not get out.

My mind is death. I am not normal. I've always known this. I don't have the needs and desires of regular people. The emotions I feel are very little, if at all. Anger is the biggest emotion of any of them. Everything else is miniscule in the realm of emotions. Even my brothers, who are my greatest allies in the world, are more on the normal scale than I am.

I get that there's something wrong with me, and I just don't care enough to fight against it.

My family accepts me for me.

Though, would *she?* Would she accept me for my faults, my darkness, the pieces of me that aren't quite whole?

What do I want from her, even? What is it about her that clings to my mind? Holds tight and refuses to let go?

What is it about her?

I've never wanted a girl before, not like this. I've never felt the need barreling against my chest. No girl has ever held my interest. They're all the same in my eyes—boring, bland, needy. All cut from the same cloth.

Until her.

Raven.

Filled with such pain and anger that she tries to suppress and hide from the world. But it's never been clearer. I've never met someone like her. Is it her rage that draws me in? Or maybe it's the fact that she's like me. We're both so fucked up, our evil is what keeps us going.

I don't know what is going on inside me, to be honest. She's flipped some switch in me, and I haven't found out how to turn it off. How to treat her like I do everyone else. A nobody. It's not as simple with her.

She's anything but simple.

I grit my teeth as I wipe my hands and prepare myself to go upstairs to Morelli's restaurant. Today's kill was easy, someone already captured and waiting for me in the basement of the restaurant. But now I'm needed upstairs, where the rest of the family waits for an update on what I've found on the copycat Crow Killer.

Nothing, if I'm being honest. I'm usually fucking knee-deep in facts. Shit, sometimes I've even caught the guy already, walking in there with my hands bloody and his head in my grip.

But I haven't found anything. Not a damn thing. At this point, I'm just as useless as the fucking detectives that roll through the city. I haven't had time to even sit in front of a computer to dig into the fucking case, my mind too distracted on everything that is Raven.

She even *looks* like a Raven, with the secretive way she watches everyone around her. She has a lot of secrets she keeps locked tight. There is so much I don't know about her.

So much I'm bound to learn about her.

Maybe that's what has me nearly obsessive. I want to pick away at her secrets until everything is uncovered. She is a closed book, with a latch securely locked. Nothing will be revealed, not if it's up to her. She doesn't want anyone to know about her past or her life, and I don't usually care. Her life is her life, just as I don't walk around telling people about my own.

Because people wouldn't understand.

Is that why she doesn't tell me? Because she doesn't think I'd understand the fucked-up-ness that is her life?

The thought alone is bothersome. She wants me to train her and teach her the ropes of who I am, yet she doesn't allow a single slip of her own life to escape. I don't work like that. I don't live like that.

For someone to be even slightly integrated into my life means I'm going to know every detail, down to the time they wake up in the morning. The fact that I'm allowing Raven to stroll into my life without even giving an inch is unacceptable.

And now, I'm going to have to take matters into my own hands.

Which fucking means I have double the research to do.

I let out a sharp whistle, and Rosko's nails clack up the stairs as we head up to the restaurant.

I open the door from the back, and Rosko slips in beside me. Aunt Rosa walks around the corner with a bin of dirty dishes clutched to her hip, a towel slung over her shoulder. "Hello, *mio nipote*. They are waiting for you."

I nod, heading to the room and opening the door. My uncles and father are already half a cigar down, my brothers watching me with an impatient look in their eyes.

"I'm late." *Again*, is what should be added, but I'm not going to apologize about it.

"No shit," Matteo growls.

Gabriel is just sitting there, staring at me. I know he wants to get the fuck out of here. Both he and Matteo are going to a party, and I'm just holding them up from getting pussy. They don't even ask if I want to go anymore. They know I'm going to say no. I have no interest in the noise, the chaos, the fucking fumbling idiot teenagers.

No thanks.

I sit down next to my father, lifting the cigar from his ashtray and taking a couple of puffs. I rarely smoke. But every once in a while, it's a good deterrent of tearing whatever room I'm in into pieces.

My little Raven dances in my vision, and I take another puff, the dark hair and sweaty skin as rage burns in her eyes like a fucking drug. Watching her in front of me, seeing her anger and feeling as her burning skin touches mine. It's like she's constantly feverish as she attacks me. She can't reel it in. She's uncontrollable. She isn't weak. I tell her she is, but she has strength in her small bones. It's the fact that she has too much frenzy inside her. Someone like that is bound to shred the world the first moment something around her collapses.

I haven't seen her since I left the alleyway yesterday, her face pale and clammy. I knew something was wrong then, but I haven't had the time to uncover what's really going on. I wasn't able to go to school today, with my father calling this morning and telling me he had some work for me. I knew that meant a kill, and with Raven constantly on my thoughts, I needed it now more than ever.

I wonder if she knew I was gone. Did she look for me? Did she sit in the library, hoping I'd show up again? Or maybe she didn't notice my absence at all, and she hung out with Chad Anderson all afternoon.

I set the cigar down in the ashtray, so I don't crush it to a pile of tobacco.

After this meeting, I'll be digging deep, both into the Crow Killer and Raven. And tomorrow, when I train her again, I'm going to tell her every little detail I discover about her.

"What do you have for me, Caelian? It's been so quiet, I almost wondered if you found the guy, but after all these things still happening on the news, you haven't mentioned anything. Have you found out anything at all, son?" My dad's voice edges on irritation. He hates waiting, and a part of me wants to knock him straight on his ass. He has everyone do the dirty work while he sits and puffs cigars and barks orders.

But then I swallow down my thoughts, because he's had his fair share of dirty running back in the day, and he's helped build this business and expand it into what it is now.

I reach into my pocket, just as the sound of a paw scratching on the door interrupts us. Uncle Marco stands up to open the door for Rosko while I pull out the white scrap of paper I've been staring at for the last day. The dirty scrawl of a crow and the word *Hello* on it.

I toss it on the table.

My father grabs it, flattening it out.

"Where'd you get this?" he asks with caution.

"Found it on a car in the alley near the Inferno." I refuse to speak an ounce of information about Raven. Not until I know about her. Right now, it'll only raise suspicion.

"This isn't typical copycat Crow Killer material. How do we know it's even him?" Uncle Marco asks, inspecting the paper with narrowed eyes.

"It's him." I don't know how I can tell, but I can. The way the strokes of the crow are nearly just as similar as they are when carved into the foreheads. Yes, you can replicate, but not like this. I've looked at the paper until my eyes burned, and I know it's spot on.

"Why would he put this on someone's car? Do you know whose car it went on?" Gabriel asks from the end of the table, barely having glanced at the drawing.

I shake my head. "I'm working on it."

He stares at me a moment, our brother connection too fucking strong for me to lie to him. He knows something is amiss, but he won't bring it up. Not now.

He nods, his eyes flitting away from mine.

"So you find this piece of paper, don't know any kind of fucking detail about this shit, whose car it went on, or why it was delivered? What the hell have you been doing?" my dad barks at me.

Rosko walks up to me, his stiff body standing against mine. He senses the tension in the room. My hand drops to his back, and I give him a comforting pat. He'd never act up to my family; they are his family, too. But at the end of the day, he's mine, and he'll ravage anyone who tries to fuck with me.

"I'm going to go figure it out now. I just gave you an update. That's what you wanted." I reach over the table, grabbing for the crumpled piece of paper and shoving it back into my pocket.

Uncle Angelo lifts his brows. "Come back with a real update tomorrow, Caelian. We need to know what's going on with this guy and get him taken care of. No more slacking."

I grind my teeth, giving him a sharp nod as I scoot the chair back. He does need to be taken care of. They are all right. I should quit fucking around and take care of business. Quit worrying about the sneaky bitch who's invaded my mind since I laid her flat on her ass.

"I'll be back tomorrow." With a whistle, Rosko and I leave the restaurant, then head back to my car and make our way back home.

I've got some digging to do before tomorrow. Not only to update my family, but also when I train Raven. Because when I see her, she's going to tell me.

She's going to tell me everything.

Dark-haired girls.

Small.

Young. Between sixteen and twenty.

No notes left.

All of them have been raped or sexually assaulted in some way.

There's barely any evidence of this guy. Even tapping into the FBI network that we conveniently have access to, there's just nothing out there. This guy is a fucking enigma. He's stealthy and leaves no DNA behind. There's nothing.

Fucking nothing.

It's alarming, honestly. And after frustrating searches that only lead to dead ends, I decide to set that aside and go through my next search.

Raven Abbott.

Yes, I was able to get her last name by her license plate number. Easy enough. Except, putting her name in the database is surprisingly another dead end.

It's *never* a dead end.

Going through page by page, finding out she's been homeschooled since she moved in with her aunt and uncle six years ago. That's an easy enough find. Her cousin, Aria, also lives with her. That must be the mousy girl who was at the Inferno. An idiotic idea to bring her there. I'm sure it's the worst one she's ever had, and I doubt she'd ever be stupid enough to do it again.

Except, it's like before the age of eleven, she never existed. There's no hospital record, no birth certificate, nothing with social security. She showed up at her aunt and uncle's house at eleven and began her life.

Who are you, Raven?

My eyes burn and my fingers ache from clicking through every database we have. There are so many. I could find out anyone and anything in the world that I want to. The fucking elite Hollywood stars that are pedophiles, and the politicians that do shit no one wants to know about.

I have it all at the tip of my fingers.

But *Raven Abbott?* She's a fucking conundrum.

I slam my laptop shut with a groan, knowing any more searches will lead me absolutely nowhere. It'll be up to her to tell me about herself. If I'm to help her or protect her, she'll need to give me everything. No matter how painful it is, I'll pull it out of her.

Bit by bit, until I've unraveled her completely, and every secret is revealed.

I watch her in the distance, though she hasn't noticed me yet. My Reuben sits untouched on my plate, the smell of Matteo's blunt filling my senses from outside the cafeteria. It's a relatively nice day outside, the rain and clouds having departed just in time for the sun to arrive. It feels weird to have the sun on my skin when all I'm used to is rain and clouds.

Gabriel nudges me, the blunt pinched tightly in his fingers. I grab it from him, taking a hit as I watch Raven and her cousin, who I now know from my research is Aria, walking through the cafeteria for a place to sit.

This is the first time I've seen her today, and I have no idea if she'll be coming over later, but I'm counting on it.

TWISTED DARES

They find a table right in the middle, and Raven sits down, acting like she doesn't give a shit about anyone or anything. Her cousin is the opposite, though. She's craving acceptance by everyone, yet doesn't have the self-esteem to even know where to look. She looks lost, like she's missing a piece of herself and doesn't even know how to find it.

I take another hit before passing the blunt to Matteo. One glance at him, though, I realize Raven has caught both of their attention as well.

"What is it about her?" Matteo mumbles around a hit. "She's hiding something."

Gabriel gives me a side-eye. "Cae? You know something we don't?"

I lift my eyebrows. "What would I know?"

"I don't know, but you sure seemed to be fucking defensive about her the other day."

I say nothing, my teeth grinding together.

"Caelian just wants to fuck her. Don't worry, big brother, I think we all do," Matteo chokes out, his lungs full of smoke. "I'm honestly just glad to know your dick works."

I close my eyes on a sigh.

"There's something else, isn't there, Caelian? It's not only the girl that's hiding something," Gabriel says, the warning in his voice making my eyes pop open.

I glare at him, giving him a warning of my own. He doesn't want to go there. Not about her.

I don't keep things from my brothers, so I know Gabriel feels pissed that he's left in the dark, but until I know what the fuck is going on, I can't give him half-truths, not about a girl that's taking this much of my headspace. It doesn't look good.

It's dangerous. *She* could be dangerous.

"Oh, look. She spotted us." Matteo chuckles.

My eyes fly to hers, and she's already standing from her seat, her and Aria's plates abandoned as they walk toward us. I sit up straighter, my back straightening as her eyes lock with mine.

A portal of blue that's a mixture of both light and dark. There's a sharpness to them that dares you to look away. She looks at me like she's ready to rule the world. Like she isn't afraid of what comes next.

She should be. She should be *terrified.*

"Caelian." She says my name with a familiarity that has both my brothers stiffening beside me. I stiffen alongside them, looking at her with a blank face.

Her cousin appears nervous as she glances at all of us. Like we're famous celebrities, or maybe her worst enemies. I can see the tremble in her jaw. She can't look anyone directly in the eye.

I say nothing.

Raven's eyes dance from mine, to Matteo's, to Gabriel's, and back to mine. She's trying to gauge how much she should say in front of them. Her eyes lock back with mine, and I could read every one of her emotions, but I look away from her, not wanting to dissect what she's trying to tell me. Not now.

Later. Definitely later.

"Tonight is a yes." I glance back up at her, and her face is closed off. "Just wanted you to know."

I give her a nod, and she grabs onto her cousin's arm, then they spin around, walking away from me without another word.

My chest deflates with each step she takes away from me. She doesn't turn around to look at me, but I can tell she wants to. She wants to see my face. She wants to ask me questions. There're too many emotions, her mind churning too fast for her to be as simple as she was.

Don't worry, baby. I'll make sure I get every inch of information out of you later.

I watch them head back to their table, and it's almost slow motion as they make their way through the crowds of people.

My eyes dart to the left, and I see Trina sitting at her usual table. Finger marks are bruised on her neck, and I'm not in the least bit shocked. Raven meant to cause her harm, and she was successful with her attempt.

Though now, I can see the revenge in Trina's eyes as she grabs her plate of food, and because she's predictable as fuck, she stands up as Raven pulls her cousin near her table. My body tenses as I stand up, and I move to stop her, but it's too late.

Trina tosses her dish of applesauce onto the ground, and I can't see their eyes, but both of them freeze.

Aria steps directly into the applesauce, and she tries to right herself, but it's too slippery on the tiled floor, and she grabs onto Raven for support, but Raven just becomes a weight.

They both crash to the ground.

Trina slams her plate against Raven's chest. Sauerkraut and Thousand Island dressing flings into the air with a ton of other ingredients that I know can't smell or feel good against your clothes and skin. I can only imagine what is smashed against Raven's chest.

Gasps make the entire room silent, and then laughter fills the void. So much laughter, the brunt of it coming from Trina's bitch table and those surrounding it.

"Fuck," Matteo snaps.

"Holy shit," Gabriel groans.

I step toward them, heat flooding my blood as rage burns through me.

What kind of a bitch move is that? My teeth grind together, livid that Raven has found herself in only another pile of shit that I'm going to have to clean up.

My eyes widen as I watch Raven roll over, her hand reaching for Trina's fork. She fists it in her grip, prongs out. *The perfect weapon.*

Fuck, she's going to stab her.

I speed up, and just as Raven leaps to her feet and takes her first step to charge Trina, I'm there. I wrap my arm around her waist, hauling her back against my chest. My hand goes to her wrist, and I pull it against me, hiding the fork from everyone's view.

One glance at Trina tells me she definitely saw what was about to happen. Once again, her life was hanging in the balance.

"Next time, I won't hold her back," I growl, just as my brothers reach me. I nod toward the cousin, who looks confused on the floor as she glances at me and then Raven.

My brothers help her up, and we leave the cafeteria, into the empty halls and straight into a darkened classroom.

Gabriel shuts the door, and I pull Raven into the corner, my hand still holding her wrist that clutches the fork. I squeeze hard, until her fingers release, and a light clank of metal hitting the tile is the only sound in the room.

"Fucking bitch," she spits, wiping her shirt of the orange dressing. "You should have let me end her miserable life when I had the chance."

I stare at her. "And you would've done it unseen… how?"

She stares at me, like she didn't think about that little bit. Realization shifts in her eyes, and I'm relieved she has at least a little bit of self-control and humanity still inside her.

"Shit. I never thought of that," she breathes.

"Of course, you didn't," I growl. "You're fucking impulsive and think about nothing except in the moment. You would've stabbed her in the cafeteria, and everyone would've seen you. They would have locked you up. Her father would've made you get charged as an adult. Would you like that? Being locked up in prison for the rest of your life? Maybe you'd get away with going to the looney bin, but I can guarantee that wouldn't be any better."

"I get it. I get it!" she groans, stepping out of my space and running her hands through her messy hair. "I wasn't thinking. Obviously, that's why I came to you in the first place."

I glance over my shoulder, seeing Gabriel helping Aria with the mess on her clothes. He has two rolls of toilet paper in his arms, and I know he doesn't know whether to touch her or not. She seems frightened by everyone, but eventually Gabriel doesn't care, stepping forward and wiping a large glob of applesauce from the sleeve of her shirt.

My eyes shift back to Raven's, and she looks a mixture between livid and completely lost. "Yeah, you obviously need it." She scowls at my words, and I drop my tone for a second. "You need something? I can have Matteo go get some clothes from the locker room."

Raven's face scrunches up in disgust. "No, thank you. We're going home. No way am I sitting the rest of the day covered in that bitch's leftovers."

"Raven! My mom won't like that." Aria's eyes widen, and I narrow my eyes at her.

Her mom won't like what?

Raven's jaw tenses, and she shakes her head. "I don't care, Aria. Let's go."

Aria pauses a second, and there's some unspoken communication between the two of them. I understand, I have the same discussions with my brother. Though I wish I knew what they were telling each other.

"Four o'clock, Raven," I order.

She nods, walking away from me and grabbing onto Aria. "Thanks for helping her," she mumbles to Gabriel, before they both slip out of the door, closing it behind them.

"What the fuck was that?" Gabriel barks at me once the door closes behind them.

I give them a look, Matteo finally putting away his phone and giving me a similar look Gabriel is giving me.

It's accusatory.

I narrow my eyes at the both of them. "I'll tell you later." Matteo opens his mouth, but I cut him off with a glare. "Later."

I'll give them something when I have something to give them. Right here, right now, I have nothing.

Nothing besides a jaded girl with a shit ton of baggage and a past so hidden, not even the FBI sources can uncover it.

The alarm above my head sounds, and I glance at the security monitors on the wall of our office, monitors upon monitors hooked to the wall, seeing the ugly, shitty Honda Civic pulling up to the gate.

I wait a moment, then hit Enter and watch as the gate rises above her car.

She's once again late, but not nearly as late as she was two days ago. Only a few minutes today, and that could be for traffic or another number of petty reasons that I keep telling myself. I should just blow her off like I want to.

I know the real reason I'm letting her through the gate, though. It's because I want to get to the bottom of Raven. Today is the day I'm going to find out who she is, and what she's hiding.

With resolve and determination, I get out of the black leather chair and leave the dark room, Rosko hot on my heels as I walk through the house. No one is here this afternoon, and I'm fucking grateful for it. Another run-in with my mother and Raven is not on my list.

I don't need to talk to her to know she isn't fond of Raven. My mother isn't fond of anyone and doesn't think anyone is good enough for us. It's fucking weird, because it's not like she dotes on us constantly or anything, but she sure acts like we're fucking gold. Anyone who comes near us gets my mom's bad side.

It's not a side any of us want to see.

Our two-story house is long and designed with so many curves and secret passages to other ends of the house that it's more of a maze.

I make my way to the gym, stepping around the ring and opening the door. The sun from earlier quickly dissipated to the clouds and a chilly drizzle drips from them. Raven has a scarf wrapped tightly around her neck, bundled around the lower part of her chin.

TWISTED DARES

She glances up at me at the sound of the door opening. Her eyes flicker with uncertainty, and I wonder what emotion it is she just felt running through her veins. Was it hot and electric, or cold and achy?

Why does she look nervous to see me when I only saw her hours ago? What happened between then and now to put the guard up?

"Hi," she says, standing in the breeze.

"Come in." My curiosity and wonder want her to keep coming back, but the other part of me also wants to frighten her so she never shows her face again. I've never had a friend, never had a girl that I liked. I don't know what she is, but my innate reaction is to claim her, and I barely know her. I have too many questions. I need too many answers to let her walk away before our path or story is written.

For now, I'll keep her at arm's length, just as she should be.

She ducks her head as she walks past me, stopping when Rosko steps in front of her. Her eyes widen, and she squats down, letting her backpack slide off her shoulders and settling it to the ground behind her. "You're a really big dog," she says softly.

Her hand goes out, like she wants to pet him, but he takes a step back, settling on his butt as he stares at her.

If only she knew this is much friendlier than Rosko ever is to anyone. He doesn't like people. He's basically me, in dog form. So, the fact that he's even allowing her to talk to him is astounding.

"Can I pet you?" Her hand goes out in front of her again, palm up, as if she's hoping for some type of connection.

Anything.

Rosko gets off his ass, taking a step forward, and shockingly, drops his wet nose in her palm. His tongue slips out, and he licks her skin, before glancing up at me, his face blank, but his eyes are speaking to me in a language only him and I know.

He likes her.

I stare at him until she gets to her feet.

"Sorry, he's just… really big. Is he a German Shepherd? Because he kind of looks like a wolf."

"He is a wolf. And a German Shepherd."

She glances back at Rosko. "Is that legal?"

I shake my head.

She stares at me a moment, like she wants to say more. I can see the words bubbling. But she doesn't, instead toeing her shoes off, and then lifting her feet to peel off her socks. With her bare feet against the vinyl floor, she curls her unpainted toes as she waits for my command.

"I don't have long. My aunt and uncle are sticklers when it comes to me being late."

I lift my brows. Interesting. "Well, take your fucking scarf off, then, and get in the ring."

Her hands go to the light fabric, keeping it secured against her neck. "I'll be fine. I'm kind of cold today."

Lie.

It is cold, but her twitch gives away the fact that she's lying between her teeth. I hate liars.

Walking up to her, she can instantly tell my intent, her hands going to her neck as she steps back from me. "What're you doing?"

I don't listen to the fear in her voice as I walk until I reach her, my hand going to her shoulder as I start pulling the scarf from around her neck. She fights me, but I'm stronger, pinning her hands behind her back as I unveil her neck.

What the fuck?

"What the hell is this?" I look at the burn on her neck. Like she's put her skin to a stove burner.

And it's in the shape of a cross.

"How the fuck did this happen?"

She turns away from me, her hand cupping the fresh wound. I watch her entire body rise and fall, like she's taking in giant breaths. Trying to control her breathing. On the brink of a panic attack.

Suddenly, her body tenses, and she bends down, ready to grab her bag. "I'm sorry, I have to go."

I reach down, grabbing her around the thighs and lifting her in the air. She squeaks, slapping my back as I walk her to the ring. I step inside, dropping her back against the mat. I place my leg on top of her thighs and use my hand to pin her hands above her head. The cross on her neck, right by her collarbone, is burnt and red, like it was done only moments before she arrived.

"Tell me. Now."

I feel like I'm sick, like there's something wrong with me. Almost like I'm having a heart attack or have pneumonia or something. I can't breathe correctly, and something feels different in my chest. Kind of makes me want to vomit.

She stares at me in anger, a shadow over her eyes like she doesn't trust me. I get it; we should never trust anyone in our lives, but I'm not letting her step into my ring and be around me if she doesn't give me every detail about what just happened to her.

And who the fuck she really is.

"It's my aunt and uncle," she whispers as she tells the air. Her eyes refuse to connect with mine. "They aren't good people."

"They did this to you?" My thumb touches the burn, and she winces, hissing through her teeth.

She nods her head.

"Why would they burn you with a cross?" I don't understand who they are or what their motivations are, but if this manic girl who is strong enough to bring down grown men can't stop this, then she is in a worse situation than I thought.

"Because they hate me," she sighs.

I want to shake the shit out of her; this emotionless, quiet kid is so much different from the strong, wily girl who always looks like she wants to rip my throat out.

This girl looks... defeated.

"Why do they hate you?" My body settles into hers a touch, knowing this conversation might be bigger than I thought it'd be.

She says nothing, her jaw clenching and unclenching as she stares at the wall. Whatever she's hiding, it's nothing she's proud of. She hates her secrets, and maybe her secrets hate her as well.

"What is your relation to the copycat Crow Killer?" That's the biggest question. And possibly a question that would get me some information into her past.

Her head shifts, her eyes locking with mine. She no longer fights me, like she knows I'll get my answers no matter what.

"I don't want to tell you," she whispers.

"Little Raven, you don't have a choice in the matter."

The vessels in her eyes pop red before they begin to water. "It's my father."

I narrow my eyes. "What's your father?"

She swallows, and I see the struggle as her neck stretches, like the words are fighting their way from her throat. "Crow Killer."

Fuck. What?

"Your father is the Crow Killer?" I think back, through all my memories to remember what I can about the case. I was a child when he first began killing, and only a young teenager when he was caught. I never dug into it. All I know is that he killed.

He killed a lot.

He killed men, but he mostly killed women. He was a cult leader who ran a fucked-up sex club and fucked everyone. So did his wife.

That might be the most fucked-up part.

He was a married man, and his wife was just as deranged as he was. They both have a hit list that could nearly fill an entire city. The mutilated people. They fucked them, then mutilated and left them for dead.

TWISTED DARES

Until someone tipped off the police, and all it took was putting a few puzzle pieces together to figure out who the serial murderers were. Cash and Nancy Crow were lovers and lived in a small, run-down shack in the middle of the desert of California.

What they found was horrifying to the detectives and law enforcement. I remember seeing the picture in the paper of Cash Crow covered in blood. His hair, his skin, his clothes, all a dark, thick, crimson red. The only other color was the pits of his eyes, which were as dark blue as the deepest depths of the ocean, a nearly black color as they stared through the paper.

Like he was possessed by the devil.

The same crystal blue as Raven's.

He didn't put up a fight, but what was the most horrifying part was the fact that this couple had a daughter, and both the daughter and wife were missing when he was caught. It was a question of whether the Crow Killer snapped and killed them, or if they fled and got away. It was never questioned, and eventually the story became flushed out from all the other news stories in the world.

I look down at her. Raven Crow. She's not Raven Abbott. She never has been. Raven Abbott is fake.

This girl lying in front of me with her dark hair and wild eyes. The young child of the Crow Killer isn't at all what I picture she'd look like. I don't know why, but I didn't picture her to be such an untamable girl. Someone so… beautiful. Raven is gorgeous and unique and absolutely fucking crazy, yet so powerful.

Looking down at her, I see how she could take down the world. She has the ability. It runs in her blood. But she'd be taking down herself with it. She needs to learn how to destroy without destroying herself in the process.

"My parents are the Crow Killers," she says, a furious tear leaking from her eye, running down her temple and into her hair.

"I can smell the murderer in your blood," I murmur.

She looks at me with such pleading and desperation, the feeling of a heart attack in my chest only getting worse at the sight.

"Do you see why I want you to teach me? I feel like I'm becoming unhinged, and I don't know what to do."

I watch her, how she looks like she's nearly in pain from the emotions running through her. It's times like these I'm glad my feelings are broken, because if I could feel, or if my emotions ran as rampant as Raven's did, I imagine I'd be in excruciating pain all the time.

Like her. She looks like she is suffering in an abyss of misery.

I lift off her, stepping to my side of the ring. "Stand up. Scarf off."

She stays lying on the ground for a few moments, confused by my words, then rushes to her feet, heading to the opposite side of the ring.

"Tell me who the copycat Crow Killer is." I stretch my arms out, knowing this training is serious. She needs to know, and I'm not going to fuck around anymore. I'll lay her on her ass until she has bruises time and time again. I'll make her hate me, but as long as she can learn some fucking control, well, then I accomplished something.

"I don't know." She lifts her hands but doesn't step toward me. Her arms look weak; she doesn't look in control, or confident, for that matter.

"Get fucking ready, Raven. You look like a lost fish."

She scowls at me, her face dry but her eyes still red. She's getting angry, and she hates answering questions. But I'm going to get every single one out of her. "Who is the copycat Crow Killer?" I walk up to her, hungry for blood. Ravenous to inflict pain even if she isn't the one I want to delve it upon. I just want someone to pay for her pain. I can't very well go after her father, but someone has to take on her pain, and it makes me desperate to cause a massacre at her feet.

I would slaughter the world if I had to.

"What do you know about the copycat Crow Killer?" I ask this time.

"Nothing!" Her arms swing out at her sides, and I use her weakness as a learning moment. I reach forward, my fist knocking into her side. I hold back, not giving as much strength as I have in me, but enough to where she stumbles back. "Hey! You were asking a question."

"I'm also training you. Figure out how to multitask, Baby Crow, or you'll never get to where you want to be."

Her face pales, her body coiling tight at my words. "Don't call me that."

Mmm, I hit a soft spot.

"I'll call you whatever I like, *Baby Crow*. Learn to pick and choose your battles, and fucking deal with the rest of it."

She swallows a growl, and I watch it work down her throat. It's the moment it hits her stomach that her hands go up, and she gets ready to hit me back. "I know nothing about the copycat killer. That note is the first time I've ever heard of him."

She swings forward, but her eyes gave it away before her arm moved, and my hand reaches out, blocking her hit before she can connect with me. My free hand extends, punching her in the ribs. Pain lances across her face as she hunches forward.

"Stand up. Don't show your pain. You show even an ounce, and you'll keep getting hit in that weak spot. Has your trainer taught you nothing?"

She snaps her spine straight. "Shut up."

I shake my head in disgust. "Quit showing your anger. You're overemotional, and it's just another weakness. Straighten out your face and pay fucking attention to me. You're all over the place."

"Because you're asking me all these fucking questions when I'm trying to pay attention to your moves!"

Fuck. Is she really this hopeless?

I walk back to my side of the ring, nodding my head for her to do the same. Her spine hits the rope gently.

"I get that you were trained, but you were trained wrong. Your trainer taught you how to fight in the ring, but that's as far as it went. It's not his fucking fault, but you have to forget about everything you've ever learned. Start from scratch. If you don't listen now, we'll never get anywhere."

We go into a standoff, each watching the other, our eyes zoned in. Barely breathing. Just staring at each other and waiting for whoever to make the next move.

"Okay," she breathes. "I'll listen,"

"Good. Pay attention to every single detail. Smell me. Hear me. Sense me. My weaknesses, my strengths. Know which moves I'm going to make, not at the direction my body is, but fucking sense my every move. Until you feel like you are not an opponent, but until you feel like you are a part of me."

I move toward her, and I watch her eyes dance over every inch of my body. She's doing what she's told, and the constant tightening in my chest relaxes a little bit.

What the fuck?

"Now, I'm going to speak to you, and you're not going to get distracted by my words." I walk back and forth, and her eyes flit up to mine for a moment before going back to my body. "Tell me, do you know who the copycat Crow Killer could be?"

She shakes her head, keeping her eyes trained on my body.

"Anyone from your past that might be out for revenge?"

Her face shutters. "Everyone is out for revenge."

That, I can agree with. "Anyone who would be out for you in particular?"

She gnaws at her lip, and I can see the hesitation in her gaze, the glazing over of her eyes, and I know she's losing focus.

"Pay attention, Raven. And tell me." I continue stalking around the ring, changing my movements as she stays pinned against the rope.

"A man… he touched me when I was young." Her voice is barely audible. But the words may as well have been screamed at the top of her lungs. I hear them, and they make me feel like a toxic venom is dipped into my stomach.

"A man… touched you, *as a child?*"

She nods, her focus barely hanging on.

"What happened to him?" I keep my voice calm, though I want to demand it, rip it from her throat painfully and go find him myself. I'd rip him into pieces and sew him back together, only to do it a second time.

"He's dead. My father... he—th-they killed him."

So, I agree with the Crow Killer on that.

I make my way to her this time, faking left and swinging right. Her hand snaps out, her palm slapping against my knuckles. I raise my eyebrows in surprise, and her right hand snaps out, punching me directly in my spleen.

"Good girl," I murmur, and watch as her eyes flare at that simple praise. Her body trembles, and I swear I can taste her desire in the air.

"Thank you," she whispers.

I step forward, crowding her against the rope. I should keep going, testing her limits time and time again, but my feet move on their own. My entire body doing whatever it wants. And right now, it wants to push Raven against the ropes, and just... fucking touch her.

Her spine arches back, and her neck cranks up so she can look me in the eyes. They're curious, worried, fucking hopeful, and I want to douse it in a fire and let it burn me alive.

She should never feel any type of hope around me. I will only take and take and never give her an ounce of what she yearns for.

I see her differently now that I know who she really is. Like she is a new person. She's no longer just a girl that wants to get into trouble. She's a natural-born killer who wants to learn how to control her urges.

I can't stop myself from pressing my body against hers. My heat against her heat. I have so many more questions, but most of all, I just want to see if her darkness matches my darkness.

If we're one in the same.

"What are you doing?" she asks, her voice mostly air at this point.

"I don't know." My words are the truth. I don't know why I'm doing this. I've never acted... never pursued anyone besides a kill. Never even wanted to go after a girl.

So, what the fuck am I doing?

Her hand goes up, brushing against my damp white shirt. My muscles flex beneath the fabric, growing taut and corded as I hold myself back. I'm on the verge of losing control, and I don't trust myself. I'd break her bones.

I'd break that fragile little beating muscle inside her chest.

I hate touch, I hate the feeling of skin against skin, yet I can't stop myself from pressing my body against hers. This desire, this craving in my veins has been locked in a cage, and Raven held the key. One moment of our skin touching and she unlocks it all, and my beast is finally set free.

My hand goes up, and I place it on her waist, her skin shuddering against my palm.

"Is this wrong?" she questions, seemingly unsure of even herself.

"I am wrong." Which is the truth. I am so wrong, and I don't know much besides the fact that I'll never, ever be able to provide her with anything more than an emotionless fuck. I should step away. I should step away now and not put her through this shit.

But my body is craving her right now, and it feels so foreign to me.

I don't want to, but I get ready to pull back when her hand goes to my waist, pulling me toward her. Molding my body against hers. Her eyes plead. *For what?* For liberation? For freedom? Salvation?

I don't know. But it's begging for something, and I so badly want to deliver.

Her free hand goes to the back of my head, and she leans up, pressing her lips against mine before I realize what she's doing.

It feels akin to the burn on her neck. I scorching sensation rolling through my lips as we connect. She's cautious, nervous, and uneasy about her movements, and it feels like I'm possessed by a beast, a growl ripping from my throat as I press into her, my cock instantly turning rock solid as I grind against her.

Her hands fall from my head, my dominance overtaking her. She doesn't push me away, but instead curls against me as I ravage her mouth, nipping at her lips like I'm fucking starving.

I've never felt this wild, this out of control when it comes to a woman.

I take every bit of her for myself, leaving nothing of her but a beating heart.

My hands trail up her waist, over her slim form, and end beside her breasts. Her skin burns through her flimsy shirt, and I go to squeeze her breast when she tears away from me.

"I… I… *fuck*." She shakes her head, her thoughts just as jumbled a mess as mine are. I can see the confliction in her mind, her entire mentality scrambled. I feel the same, but I also feel hungry, and I have to hold myself back from pouncing on her again.

"This is too much. I don't think this is such a good idea. Can we… can we just train?" she asks softly, her eyes unable to connect with mine. She slides out from under me, standing up and walking to the opposite end of the ring. I watch her grab the ropes, suffocating them between her fingers.

Her confliction also causes her rage. She feels torn in half by her feelings that aren't as clear as she wishes they were. Her muddled emotions only cause her more confusion.

I understand it, but it doesn't make me feel any less angry.

I want to tear into her for turning away, but I also want to lick her from head to toe and see if her body tastes as sweet and salty as her lips did.

Anger rolls through my body, along with an emotion I've never felt before. It's like my blood is boiling to the point my veins split open. Is she turning me down? Does she not want me? Is it the crazy inside me? Does she want someone normal to ground her? Someone like Chad Anderson?

"We're done here today." I give her my back, trying to rein in whatever is wrong with me, so I don't literally snap her in half. Am I disappointed? What the fuck is wrong with me?

"Caelian…" My name on her lips is a knife to the thread, snapping whatever control I have over myself. I spin around, seeing her stare at me with so much desperation, she bleeds it. Stalking across the mat, I wrap my arms around her again and lift her off her feet. She squeals as worry runs through her eyes. I don't care. *I don't fucking care.*

I whip around, slamming her back against the mat. I fall on top of her, leaving not a sliver of air between us. My head bends, until our lips are barely touching, and I growl into her gasping mouth, "When I say we're done, we are done. Don't test me, don't play with me. You put your lips on mine and then push me away. I don't play games, Baby Crow. Don't do it again or you won't like the consequences."

Her eyes flare, her lower lip butting out to brush against my lips. "I'm sorry, I-I just... I felt like..." There are millions of emotions running through her eyes. I can see them, and bending down, securing my lips with hers, I swear, I can taste them.

Her need. Her desire.

Her regret.

Her indecisions.

Everything in her seeps from her skin, and I can feel it against my fingers as they dig into her sides.

She exhales from her nose, her many emotions mixing together and clashing, breaking into dusted shards around us.

She wants this so bad, yet she also wants nothing to do with it.

My hand goes up, and I thread my fingers through her messy hair, pulling it back as I slip my tongue into her mouth. She whimpers silently, darting her tongue out to brush against mine. My cock starts pounding, and I feel so fucking aroused I wonder if I'll fucking come in my pants.

That is not an option.

It's me this time that rips my mouth from hers. I leap to a stand, and her eyes immediately go to my gray joggers, the obvious bulge pressing against the seam. I reach in the waistband, squeezing my cock right in front of her.

Her cheeks flame an apple red, and she turns her head away from me.

"I think you should go, Raven." I warn. Because if I were to be honest, if she doesn't leave, I don't think I'd be able to hold back the next time.

She nods, getting to her feet in a daze. She stumbles as she makes her way to her shoes and socks, re-wrapping her scarf around her neck.

"Raven."

TWISTED DARES

She glances up at me, her eyes wondrous and cautious.

"Your aunt and uncle, they hurt you a lot?"

She freezes, her entire body locking in place. A small nod breaks free.

That sickly feeling of my blood on fire starts up again. "You want to kill them?"

Another nod.

"I'll teach you how. And if you decide you can't, well, I hope you know that I'm fucking doing it, one way or another."

With that, I let out a sharp whistle, walking out of the gym with Rosko hot on my trail.

RAVEN

Age Nine

There are moments in life that change the trajectory of how everything will play out. Life-altering moments. Moments when you have no idea that what's about to happen is about to carve a path for your future. I always knew my life was different from most. I knew the standards in which I was raised were probably not the safest or the healthiest, but I was alive. My parents were fucked in the head, but they still cared about me. They loved me and wanted what was best for me.

So, I know a few months ago when they killed Darren for touching me, that was their way of showing me they cared. They'd never let some creep put his hands on me. Ever since that moment, things have changed. My parents no longer treat me like a child, but instead have started to treat me like an adult.

They gave me the sex talk, and knowing they are so open with sex with each other and their lovers, they wanted me to know sex is a normal thing, but sex at my age with a grown man isn't. They told me how much they loved each other, but God wanted them to share their love with other people as well, and that when I find someone who loves me enough, they will do anything for me. It might be one person and it might be many people, but it was up to me to choose, and I didn't have to pay attention to what is right and wrong in the world.

They told me that our blood was precious and unique, and we will never live like normal people.

They told me that they made me, and therefore I was just like them, and that was okay.

They informed me that they were aware I knew they took the lives of other people, and they did it because they were told to by God. They told me they take their lives because it is their calling to help heal the world and sacrifice those whose are deserving, and God tells them who those people are.

They taught me so many things, but it wasn't until they had me watch them kill someone, their body only inches away from mine as they took their last breath, that things really changed.

"Raven, would you meet your father and I out in the shed, please?" Mom calls from outside.

I set down my colored pencil and paper, then head out of my room. My parents have me stay in my room now when they have friends over. I'm not sure why they still have people over if they don't trust them around me. Doesn't matter to me anyway, the constant contact high of marijuana and watching people touch each other in front of me is only growing more uncomfortable the older I get.

I head outside, my bare feet barely feeling a thing as I walk across our graveled driveway and to the shed that sits in our yard. It's a bit off from our house, and honestly, the thing has seen better days. Its walls are half caved in, and the roof sinks a bit. The wood is faded and chipped in spots, but my parents don't have a ton of money, so fixing up the little things isn't on the priority list as repairs go.

My dad stands in the doorway, his white t-shirt turned a dirty gray. Like he's been working hard all day, which I know he hasn't. My mother stands beside him, a flowing skirt that brushes the tops of her feet matched with a tan halter top that only covers her breasts. Her flat stomach is tan and toned, her waved hair tumbling in the light breeze over her shoulder.

My parents are so good-looking, so I wonder why they always have us hide out here way in the middle of nowhere.

"We have something to show you, Baby Crow," my father says from the doorway.

I give him a nod, sudden nerves making my tummy jump around. He sounds so serious right now. I have no idea what they could possibly need. Am I in trouble? Have I done something wrong?

I think back to everything that's happened lately, but I can't for the life of me figure out what I did that could make them bring me to the shed.

Unless they want to kill me.

I want to laugh. They would never do that, but even as I think the words, I still have the uncomfortable pit in my stomach.

My mom grabs onto my hand, her warm fingers lacing through mine, and she gives me a gentle squeeze. "Nothing to be afraid of, Rave. Everything will be okay."

They pull me inside the dark shed, and the separation between the weathered boards allows thin streams of sunlight to filter in. There is some sort of bench or table in the center. The room is dry and hot, and I can barely breathe in anything besides rotted wood or stale air.

And a woman, one of my dad's girlfriends, lays naked in the center. Her breasts bounce with her nerves, her mouth taped shut with a thick piece of gray tape. The small amount of makeup she wore runs down her temples. Her skin is red and scratched. It looks like she was in a fight. Her ankles and wrists are secured tightly with a thick, frayed rope, the skin red and raw.

I look up at my parents with wide eyes, wondering why they want me to see the stuff they usually keep from me. Why I have to look at this woman who has a dampness on the inside of her thighs, her naked body wiggling only inches away from me.

My dad lifts his hand, a sharp blade in his grip. He passes it off to me, but I don't take it, my hands firmly cemented to my sides. "What are you doing?"

"Take the knife, Baby Crow."

With a shaky hand, I listen to his command, grabbing the rusty blade and dropping my arm to my waist, once again.

"You understand we don't want to do these things, but we have to, right? You understand that this is our calling in life?"

I nod. I do, but I don't. I don't understand how killing anyone would be right, but my parents say to trust in God—that they are part of God's plan.

"God came to us last night and asked us to make you part of our ritual. We want to create a brand. So the world knows we work with God and are cleaning the earth and ridding the bad."

I feel like crying and running away, but also, I just want to please my parents and do right by God. I want my parents to be proud of me.

"What would you like me to do?" I ask on a whisper, fear and desperation to be accepted and loved by my parents strangling my voice.

"Cut her, Raven. Cut her anywhere you'd like. Give her your mark, so the rest of the world knows their sins will only lead them down the path of death."

I kind of feel sick, but I step forward anyway, knowing my parents wouldn't like if I refused to do it.

"Do something meaningful, Raven. Something that is meaningful to this family," my mom urges, a happiness in her voice. I don't really understand any of this. It feels wrong, but my blood also warms, like an excitement is rolling through me. I don't understand my feelings, so I push them away, focusing on the task at hand.

I think of my colored pencil and paper in my room. What I've been drawing over and over again all these years. Trying to perfect the edges and curves. The outline needs to be precise, or it doesn't look good at all.

I lean over the girl, her tears mixing with her makeup as she looks at me. There's a pleading in her eyes that I refuse to speak back to. If my parents have her on this table, there has to be a reason for it.

They would never hurt an innocent person.

The tip of the blade touches her forehead, and her skin twitches, tensing up. I ignore it. I ignore everything around me and cut into her skin. The first dollop of blood that leaks through the skin is exhilarating. The instant scent of metal in the small shed makes me dizzy.

I carve left and right, a simple but intricate outline. It doesn't take long, though it also feels like it takes hours, and when I'm done, there's blood pouring down her forehead and into her eyes. It's on my fingers, smeared and faded to a dark pink.

A crow.

Our last name. The significance is something that only my family will understand. It is us. It is our family. Our blood.

I hand the blade back to my dad, and he takes it with pride in his eyes. Both he and my mom stare at me, pleased as pie.

"Good work, Baby Crow," my dad says, leaning down to kiss the top of my head. His long hair tickles at my cheek, and I look at the girl, barely conscious from pain. I don't know what they're planning to do with her. I don't want to know, honestly.

"I'm proud of you," my mom says, her mouth beaming from cheek to cheek.

I smile, and they let me go back to my room.

For the first time, in I don't know how long, I feel accepted by my parents. The three of us can finally connect on something, something that is meaningful to them.

They're proud of me.

Pride blooms in my chest and makes my skin tingle. I head back to my room with a smile so bright on my face, my cheeks hurt hours later.

It was that day that felt like the real beginning. It was no longer my parents that were monsters, but I was also a monster. I was a part of their ritual that couldn't be completed without me present. It didn't matter if I was asleep or awake, tired or alert. I can't count the number of bodies I carved the outline of a crow into. There were many deaths before that day, but that day…

That day was the beginning of the Crow Killer, and we were all part of that death.

chapter sixteen
RAVEN

My lips burn and tingle the entire twenty minutes home. I can't count the number of times my fingers drifted to my mouth, and I brushed them across the soft skin of my lips. My entire body burns, feverish from his touch, even after it's gone.

Whatever happened today was a turning point for us. We can never go back to the unknown of each other's touch. I know what he feels like. I know how my body reacts to it.

I know what he tastes like.

Fuck, my very first kiss.

Well, besides my *first* first, which I refuse to even think about.

I wonder what his thoughts are on it. Did he think my lips were too small? Too stiff? Did my breath stink?

I don't know why I care, honestly. I could never be with him. I could never be with a man like him. He reminds me of my past. I can't tell whether that's a good or bad thing, though all I know is that someone like him would absolutely destroy someone like me.

But every time I say those words, I feel them with certainty. Then I end up back in his presence, and it becomes more than that. He clutches me with his gaze, with his strong fingers. I become enraptured by his mocha-colored eyes, and all thoughts of right versus wrong flee my mind.

I shake my chaotic thoughts free as I peel my scarf off, feeling my skin dampen and my mind off-kilter. My hand goes to my neck, and I wince as I brush the crucifix burn. It was a brief encounter, but horrible all the same. My aunt and uncle, they're getting worse. As the days go by, I'm feeling them hovering closer and closer.

A part of me feels like death is the answer to them before my eighteenth birthday. Maybe they never intended for me to leave their house. Maybe they see the murderer in me. I wouldn't be surprised. I can feel it in me too.

But it feels like, with every day that passes, they're one more step from getting what it is they want out of me.

Retribution.

"Where are you going?" Aunt Gloria asks from the bottom of the stairs. I grip the railing, so badly wishing I could've just left without her noticing. That's never the case, though. All she does is wait for my next move.

Checkmate.

"I have a school assignment to finish. I was going to go to the library." I should've known this would be an issue. The moment Aria and I arrived home early, I could see her grow more and more agitated.

Then she started cleaning the already sparkling kitchen, and I knew I was in for a hellish encounter.

"After pulling my daughter out of school in the middle of the day, I'm surprised they haven't expelled your deceitful, selfish soul. If you think you can corrupt my daughter, only for you to go and get good grades, you better think again," she snarks, turning around and making her way into the kitchen. I hold my breath as she grabs a knife, going to her pan of banana bread and cutting herself a slice.

"I can promise you I'm trying to do no such thing. I only knew the rest of the day for either of us would be distracting to ourselves and others with us covered in someone else's lunch. I'm sure the teachers will excuse us and allow us the time to make up for any late work." If only I could cut a cold remark in her direction, but if I do, she'll never let me go.

"I think it might be a good idea if you stay home for the evening. Focus a little more on your time with God. Lord knows you need it," she says around a mouthful of bread.

Dread sinks into my stomach. "Please, I can't."

She dusts her crumbs off her shirt. "And why not?"

I cut my nails into the handrail on the stairs. "I'm enjoying school, and I don't want to fall behind in my classes. Please. I'll spend more time here focusing on God."

She nods. "Yes, you will. If you're living in this house, you will be connected to the Lord, and I get the feeling you're anything but."

I smile at her, not sure what kind of answer she's looking for, but refusing to give her one.

I walk down the remaining stairs and head around the table, on the opposite end of the room than Aunt Gloria is standing. I'm only steps from the door when my name is called again. I stiffen, looking over my shoulder and seeing her standing there, hand raised and pointer finger wagging me over to her.

Shit.

I turn around, walking to her with ice-cold dread washing through my bones. I can guarantee my red blood turns icy blue.

I walk around the corner, where she still stands with the sharp knife on the counter. I swallow down my fear, glancing at the stairwell and wondering if she'd stop if Aria was home. She went out with my uncle, heading to the store to pick up some groceries. I should've left then. I'm rarely home alone with Aunt Gloria, and if I am, it's never felt like this.

Like I'm in danger.

Once I approach her, she reaches around my back and places her hand on my waist. "I feel like there's something you're not telling me. Are you keeping something from me, Raven?"

I whip my head back and forth, worry and terror filling me. Are they tracking me? Does she already know, and she's testing me? I don't know how to answer her question without feeling like I'm answering wrong.

"Would you like to tell me why you're hiding another bruised face? What on earth are you doing to get banged up? Are you getting into fights at school?"

I keep my face neutral as possible as I look at her. "I promise I'm not getting into fights at school."

"Do you realize that God knows every single time you lie? You are committing a sin for every lie you make. So, I'd be very careful with how you answer me, Raven. So, tell me truthfully, are you keeping something from me that I should know about?"

Her grip grows painful, burying so deep into my skin, I feel like her fingers will pop out the other side.

"I'm not keeping anything from you."

Her free hand goes into her pocket, and she lifts it out, dangling my cross on a gold chain in front of me. My eyes widen. I took it off and couldn't find it. I'd looked and looked, but figured it'd turn up sooner or later.

I should've known something more sinister has been going on. They play these games, make me look like the bad guy. I didn't do anything wrong, but here they are, and I feel fucking terrified that I misplaced my necklace.

"If you aren't keeping anything from me, why have I been holding on to your necklace for days? The necklace that shows your devotion to God, and you take it off. The only reason I can conjure up in my mind is that you're committing vile sins out of this house. Now what is it, are you using drugs? Underage drinking? Are you seeing a boy?"

I choke on air, pain spearing my fingers as it feels like her grip is going to break me into pieces. How can a decrepit old lady have this much fucking strength?

She pulls me with her over to the stove, turning the flame on high. I back up, but she pins me to her side, and my fear has me weak.

"Tell me, Raven. Which one is it?"

"None." My voice trembles, and I feel like falling to my knees. I lie but tell the truth. I'm not doing what she accuses me of, but I'm not being honest with my actions. I'm committing sins, I realize this. I'm bad blood, I also realize this. But to her, even me breathing is sinful.

She glares at me, her shaky eyes flitting back and forth to each of mine. With my gold chain in her firm grip, she holds it over the flame, until it glows a fiery orange. "Keep God with you for your sake. If you refuse him, there will be grave consequences. Even me and your uncle won't be able to save you."

With quick motions, she pulls the cross away from the flame, sticking it to the skin of my neck. I let out a wretched howl, and I can almost swear I hear her chuckle in my pain. It's a terrible thing, the pain not focused on my neck, but spreading throughout my entire body. It feels like I'm doused in flames, completely engulfed in fire.

I drop to my knees, pure agony rolling through me. Aunt Gloria moves around me, and I can barely focus on her clasping the slowly cooling necklace around my neck.

"Only God can save you, child. Go do your schoolwork. You better not get any bad grades while living in my home." She moves away from me, and it takes me a few minutes, my face drenched in tears as my pain slowly subsides.

Once the pain is abated enough, I rise to my feet, wiping my face as I rush up to my room, grabbing a scarf and running out of the front door before she can stop me again.

I barely take a breath as I hop into my car, reversing from the lot so quickly dust puffs up in its wake. It's not until I'm down the street from my house, with Aunt Gloria completely out of view, that I pull onto the shoulder of the road. My forehead goes to my steering wheel, sobs breaking from my chest. My hands go to the back of my neck, to the tiny clasp of my necklace. I take it off, chucking it onto the passenger seat.

I try to stay faithful to God. It's not that I hate him, but it feels like he fails me time and time again, when I need him most.

A gut-wrenching scream breaks from my chest, and I lean back, pulling the visor down and looking at the cross-shaped burn on my neck. The sight only makes my heavy sobs start all over again. Grabbing the scarf on the floor beside me, I lift it, wrapping it around my neck securely.

With a deep breath, I swallow the rest of my sobs. I shift into drive and make my way toward the city.

Toward Caelian.

He'll teach me what I need. And then I'll be rid of my aunt and uncle, once and for all.

I snap out of my thoughts as I pull into my driveway. It feels like so long ago, yet it was only hours.

I feel like a different person than who I was. Leaving Caelian just now, he changed me. In just a moment, with his lips against mine, with his large body molded against my small one.

And this was after he knew who I was. This is once he knew I was tainted. An abomination to the world, yet he still came after me like he wanted me.

He. Wanted. Me.

No one has ever wanted me.

No one besides the evil man when I was a child. Besides that, everyone has treated me like I'm a leper. Like I'm someone who should be looked down upon. No one has ever touched me intimately, grabbed me sexually, looked at me sensually. He makes me feel like a woman instead of a monster.

I don't know what tomorrow will bring, or the day after that. But I feel like I'm already addicted. I want more of him.

I want all of him.

Grabbing my necklace on the passenger seat, I clasp it around my neck, and rub at my lips once more because they still feel swollen from earlier.

With a sigh, I step out of my car, walking through the dark and into my house.

I unlock the front door, letting out a sigh of relief when I see the living room empty. Thankfully, my aunt and uncle are in bed for the night. I slip through the dark, making my way upstairs. I dump my bag on my bed and walk to the next room, seeing Aria's door open a sliver.

She knows that Caelian is training me, and I don't know if I should be telling her what happened today, but I feel like I can't *not* tell her. She's my best friend, and to be honest, I have to tell someone.

"Aria?" I whisper.

She glances up from her book, already tucked in bed. Removing her glasses, she sets them and her book on her nightstand, sliding to a seated position as she smiles at me. "Come here. Shut the door." She pats the spot next to her on the bed.

I smile, closing the door quietly and making my way to the empty side of the bed. Pulling the soft pink comforter back, I slip under the sheets with her, a smile instantly making its way to my lips.

"What has you smiling like that?" she whispers, leaning on her side, her cheek resting in her palm.

I glance toward the door quickly before leaning into her. "He kissed me."

Her eyes widen, and she rears back in surprise. "What?!" she whisper-shouts.

I bite my lip as I slap my hand over her mouth. "Well, actually, I kind of kissed him. But then he kissed me."

Her mouth pops into a surprised *O*, and I can't stop the blush from making its way up my cheeks. "I know. I know." I don't know what to say, but I feel like a little girl who had her first date, though it wasn't that at all. I was just meeting a man—*a grown man*—who kills people. Who's teaching me how to kill.

"Do you like him? When are you going back to see him?"

I shake my head, feeling so out of sorts. But I also feel alive. For the first fucking time, it feels like my heart beats in life, not for death. "I'm supposed to see him on Friday, and I'm fighting on Saturday. But I don't know. I don't know if I like him. I just feel… different."

"You look different." She squints her eyes at me, looking me up and down. Her eyes pause on my neck on the way back up, and her eyes widen. "What is…" Her hand reaches out, and she pulls at my scarf before I realize what it is she's doing.

"Aria, no." I shake my head, tearing her hand from the edge of the scarf, but it's too late. She's seen a shred of it, and now she's going to be persistent as hell.

"No, Raven, let me see what's on your neck." She gets to her knees, pulling at the fabric until it's loosened from my neck. She gasps, her eyes going wide as saucers as her hand goes to her jaw-dropped mouth. "What in God's name happened to you?" Her eyes shoot up to mine, and tears spring to her eyes. "Did my mom do this to you?"

I look away from her, sadness and shame hitting me. She loves her parents so fucking much, and I hate to have her see the truth. But at the same time, when will she ever learn the cruelness and true evil of her parents if she never sees it with her own eyes?

"It doesn't matter, Aria. Just leave it alone."

"I'm not leaving it alone! Why do you have a burnt cross on your neck, Raven? This wasn't an accident. Someone did this to you! Was it my parents?"

Tears roll down her cheeks. I want to wipe them away, but I feel frozen in place as she comes to terms with reality.

Her parents are fucking psychos.

"Oh my gosh, they really did, didn't they? They hurt you like that? For what? What did you do wrong?"

I can do nothing but shrug as my poor cousin breaks down in sobs.

Her hands fold in front of her and she looks toward the ceiling, praying for a God who has never done me any favors. "Lord, please—"

The door swings open, and both Aria and I jump about a foot in the air as we look behind us.

Fuck.

Aunt Gloria and Uncle Jerry stand there, each with equally irritated looks on their faces.

"What in the world is going on in here?" Aunt Gloria shouts, her ruthless eyes instantly going to mine.

Aria scrambles off the bed and to her feet. Walking around the foot of the bed, she stands in the middle of the room, her arms flinging at her sides. "Mom, please tell me you didn't do that to Raven!"

Aunt Gloria's eyes narrow, like she wants to decapitate me on the spot.

"What are you talking about, Aria?" Uncle Jerry walks into the room, looking at my neck. His eyes flare in surprise, but a pleased look enters after he realizes what happened. "*Oh.*"

Aria looks rabid as she glances back and forth between her parents. "Why are you hurting her? Why?"

Aunt Gloria steps toward her, her arms extended like she's about to give her a hug. Aria scrambles back, and Aunt Gloria's face turns a fierce red. "Aria, you wouldn't understand. Some people are beyond being saved by God, honey. It's hard to explain."

"She's a bad seed, Aria," Uncle Jerry says, his eyes spitting hate in my direction.

Aria looks at me, her eyes wide in horror. "I'm so sorry, Rave. This is so messed up," she says through a tortured sob.

I shake my head, not wanting to speak or say anything that would get me or her in trouble.

"Don't feel sorry for that devil's spawn, Aria. She's born out of bad blood."

Aria whips her gaze to her mother. "If she's bad blood, then so am I! We're blood-related, don't you realize that? You can't sit here and tell me she's the devil's spawn! What kind of monsters are you guys? Hurting her? I hate you! I hate you both so much!"

Her screams are painful as they rip from her chest, and I can feel the tension rising in the room until it's stifling, and catching a breath feels like sucking in a hot gust of air.

Aunt Gloria and Uncle Jerry look at each other briefly, and my body locks up as Uncle Jerry walks toward Aria. I'm about to sprint into action, knock his ass unconscious, when he pins her against the wall. She thrashes against him, and he holds her there roughly. I scramble off the bed, rage burning in my fingertips, and all I can see is red as I watch her scared, horrified, fucking terrified.

Riiip.

Aunt Gloria tears at my hair, pulling strands out and grabbing for more. She yanks me out of the bedroom, and I let out a scream as she tugs me down the hall. I grab at the doorframe, but she's unnaturally strong right now, and I can do nothing but scream and fight against her.

She walks down the stairs, and my back pounds against each wooden step. I howl, howl like a tortured animal as she takes me down the stairs and through the kitchen. I grab at the kitchen chairs, wincing as they fall on top of me. I pull at the lace cloth on top of an end table, listening as glass shatters across the floor.

The front door creaks, and Aunt Gloria leans down, lifting me and tossing me out the front door. "You can sleep outside tonight, you little witch. You try to convince my daughter I'm the bad guy again, I'll kill you myself." She reaches into her pocket, pulling out my car keys. She slaps them against my face, the edges of the keys digging into my cheek. I whimper as she puts her shoe on my hip, shoving me down the front steps and into the grass. "Or never come back again, for all I care. I almost hope you die out here; it'll save me the hassle of dealing with your spiteful self anymore."

The door slams, and then the familiar sound of the lock latches.

I roll onto my back, the stars in the sky twinkling back at me.

I should leave now. I should leave and never come back here. From her words, I'd be doing us both a favor.

But... *Aria.*

The look on her face as her dad pinned her against a wall makes my breath escape me. A wicked hand sliding into my chest and peeling apart my heart. I can't breathe.

Her eyes.

Her eyes were so fucking tortured.

My neck arches, my head tilted nearly upside down as I let out a tortured scream. I want to go back in there, but my fear is that Uncle Jerry will have a gun. His only gun. Will he use it on me? On Aria?

A shiver runs through me.

I'm not ready. I'm not prepared.

I don't know what to do, but I know I have to get out of here before I do something I'm going to regret.

An image flashes in my mind, and my chest settles. I immediately know where I'm going. It was settled before my brain even knew where to go.

I scramble to my knees, grabbing for my keys laying in the gravel. I get to my feet, wincing as pain hits in just about every ounce of my body.

Limping to my car, my eyes narrow when I see a piece of paper pinned beneath the windshield wipers. I lean against the hood of the car, lifting the wiper and pulling the paper from beneath the rubber.

My heart pounds out of my chest, thumping in my ears as I unfold the paper. A whimper breaks from my throat as I read the writing on the front.

One, two, three,

I see you. Do you see me?

My eyes widen, and I look around our dark yard, expecting to see someone standing around in the darkness. *I can feel it.*

Their eyes.

The heaviness, the malevolence in them as they burn down on me.

A shiver breaks out, and I glance back at the paper, seeing the crow—*my crow*—staring back at me.

I crumple it in my fist, rushing to my car and starting it up, flooring it out of there before whatever hides in the darkness comes to find me.

CAELIAN

I sit in my kitchen, listening as Rosko's teeth grind on a bone in the living room by the fireplace. The sound of wood crackling fills the room and the scent of pine mixes with the joint pinched between my fingers.

I'm alone, and I usually enjoy the silence. I need it when everything else in the world makes so much noise. But right now, in this moment, the silence is louder than the voices.

I can't get her off my mind, no matter how hard I try. What I should do is go have a meaningless night with someone else, like my brothers seem to do on the daily, try to forget about her, if only just for a moment. But it won't help; if anything, it'll just make it worse.

Irritated with the fact that this little kitten has clawed her way into my brain.

It makes no sense.

Not to mention the burn mark on her neck, the cross that should mean so much good, but is burnt and scarred into her skin with so, so much fucking bad. Evil people find solace in things they believe are right, but are actually filled with such toxicity and wrongdoing that there is not an ounce of purity in their soul.

It's just bad people wading through the bad, and good people pretending to be good, when all they are is fucking despicable.

I meant what I said when I promised that if the day comes when she wants to kill her aunt and uncle and she can't, she better believe I'll be one step behind her to behead their asses. Those scum of the earth don't deserve to take another breath, and it'll be my fucking pleasure to let Rosko feast on their flesh and bones.

My tongue runs one last swipe around the paper before I fold it over with my fingers, creating the perfect joint. I stub it between my lips, grabbing my Zippo lighter from my pocket and sparking it up. The instant scent of marijuana fills the room, and I let it roll through me, my muscles and tension fading, if only slightly.

The alarm makes a quick beep, and the front door opens, the sounds of my brothers and parents pounding down the hall, a complete opposite from the complete silence I was just engulfed in.

"Caelian, aren't you fighting tonight?" Gabriel slaps me on the back and swipes the joint from my fingers, bringing it to his lips. I glance at my parents, dressed to the nines, as usual.

"What're you doing home?" I ask my dad, leaning over and setting my elbows on the kitchen island. Our kitchen is one massive chef's kitchen. Which doesn't make much sense, considering my parents rarely cook a meal. If I'm looking to eat something, I'll have to go down to Morelli's.

The chrome and black appliances are just for show. Everything is new and updated, from the smart refrigerator to the soft-close drawers. It's shaped in a large *U*, which overlooks the oversized living room. Every detail is high end, all the way down to our bamboo floors.

"Uncle Angelo is heading out to New York tonight. We dropped him at the airport and were heading back to the restaurant, but apparently the Crow Killer struck again, and they have mandated a curfew in the city. No use in going to a restaurant that is closed."

I stare at him, grinding my teeth together at the thought of another innocent victim. "Fucking hell."

"You look conflicted about something, Caelian. What's got you in your head?" My mother steps up to me, her eyes narrowing as she stares at me.

"Caelian is upset about a girl, I'm betting," Matteo says as he grabs the joint from Gabriel. I grind my teeth as I watch it wither away to a small roach.

There goes my fucking joint.

"Is this that girl you were with in the gym?" she asks, her voice turning frosty.

"You brought her to our house?" Gabriel grits out.

I scowl at him, reaching over to grab my joint from Matteo's fingers. "I'm fucking training her. Would you give me my damn joint?" I take a hit, stubbing it out in the sink after one measly hit. "It's nothing. Don't overthink it."

"I'm hoping you aren't being distracted by some girl when you should be focusing on your work," my father reprimands. Of course, his only focus being the business. Finding the copycat.

I close my eyes on a sigh. Fuck, that one moment of silence I'd take back in a second.

"I'm in the process of getting information. I'll update you as soon as I know more." I lift my eyebrows at my dad before turning to my mom. "Don't worry about Raven."

Finally, I turn to my brothers, who look at me like I shit in their cereal. "Both of you can fuck off and quit assuming shit you have no idea about."

My father sighs, his hand cinching around my mom's wrist. "We'll let you guys be, then. Have a good night." Together, they walk off to their side of the house, where we won't see them for the rest of the evening. The house is split in a way that it's basically two houses combined into one. The only space we share is the kitchen. They have their own living area, entry to the garage, and everything else they could possibly need.

"So, no fight tonight?" Gabriel asks, scratching his stomach while walking to the refrigerator.

I shake my head. "I'll fight tomorrow night." And just like that, Raven infiltrates my thoughts once again.

It's been a few days since I fought, and I'm feeling the effects. To say I'm on edge is an understatement. Whatever is going on with Raven is something I've never experienced before. It's grating on me like a phantom ache I can't escape from.

She actually kissed me. Like I was a normal kid in high school; she lifted herself onto her toes and planted her soft lips on mine. It caused the animal in me to break free. I couldn't be contained, though I tried. She spoke to me and like quicksand, I quickly fell into her trap. One step and I fell, deep. Savagely, brutishly. Unforgiving.

Her blue eyes screamed for mercy, and I could do nothing but deliver. I gave her the only kind of penance I knew how to give, and she wept into my mouth with so much glory it flowed from her fingertips.

"Dude." Matteo chucks my shoulder with his own. "You look sick. You okay?"

I shake my head. "I'm good. Fucking long-ass days."

"What have you been doing? Find anything out about the copycat?"

"Besides hanging out with *Raven*," Gabriel mumbles, his head stuck in the fridge.

I shake my head, not sure how much I should spill. Giving information about the copycat Crow Killer is one thing, but to explain you're training the daughter of the OG is a totally different story, and not one I'm sure I really want to get into right now.

"Not much, honestly. I'm surprised at the lack of details about the case. There are a lot of similarities, but also a few differences. The original had both male and female victims, whereas the copycat targets only females. The copycat also wrote that strange note, which makes no fucking sense to me." I can't explain the connection until I know what I'm working with. Something's not right. There's something going on that I can't put my finger on, and I need to figure it out. Soon.

I have a feeling I don't have much time before something big happens.

"This is fucked up. Something big like this happening in our city. Like, what the fuck is the motive? Where is the pattern? It just doesn't fucking make sense."

It doesn't, but it does. It makes perfect sense.

They are after Raven. I just have to figure out why. And who the fuck it is.

Our alarm dings again, alerting us of someone pulling up to our property. Both of my brothers narrow their eyes in suspicion, reaching behind them to pull out their Glocks. I rarely pull out my strap. I barely ever need it.

If I need to kill someone, I'm fully capable of doing it with my bare hands.

Rosko instantly gets up, his bone forgotten as a growl rips from his throat. The hair on his back stands up aggressively. He knows too. No one comes here at night. No one comes here *at all*.

"Who the fuck is that?" I ask, stepping around the island and going to the living room to turn the security camera on the TV.

"No clue," Matteo says as he heads toward the door. I look over at Gabriel, who shrugs his shoulders. I don't fucking know who it could be, but what I do know is that if it's someone who's even slightly suspicious, he won't be walking off the property.

I turn on the camera, but the gate is empty. No car. Nobody. Nothing.

"Is Caelian here?" The voice ricochets through my body, my eyes widening in surprise.

What the fuck?

I whip around, seeing a terrified Raven standing there, with nothing but her keys and her phone, a piece of paper crunched in her grip.

Rosko goes up to her, his hair settling down as he sniffs at her ankles. He starts panting, like he can tell how stressed she is.

"What're you doing here, Raven?"

Her eyes dance to my brothers, then land back on me. "Can I talk to you?

Alone?"

I blink at her, not sure how to fucking react. Her eyes are so hurt, so tortured. Her spine curves over, like she's been beaten down. So much different from the Raven I usually see.

"Okay, sorry if I'm being a dick, but how the fuck did you get through the gate?" Gabriel steps up beside me, looking between the two of us. "I've been feeling like something is off about you since I first saw you, and now you're showing up at my house at night? Some real fucking explanation would do you some good right now, kid."

She stares at him, and I can see the aggravation building in her. It's funny how we are the same, but so different. Both clearly insane, yet me with broken emotions, and her with too many.

"I parked on the street. Walked up." She says the words so simply, like it's the easiest thing to do. And maybe it is, but people never do it because of who we are.

Raven doesn't seem to have the same fear normal people do. She doesn't seem to fear much at all.

Matteo chuckles, impressed. "The balls on you."

"So, what? Caelian is training you? Training you for what?" Gabriel asks.

I can see the impatience growing on her face. She's here for a reason, yet they have too many questions that need answering before they'll let her go.

"To fight," she states plainly.

Matteo raises his brows. "Fighting, what? Martial arts? Boxing?" *Shut up, Matteo. Shut up.*

Raven whips her gaze toward his, and I kind of want to see her react. See what she does. See if she's learned anything from our training. "The Inferno. In the ring."

"Wait, you fight?" Gabriel guffaws.

Her eyes narrow. "Yes. I fought Caelian."

Matteo lets loose another cackle. "And you're alive? You really went easy on her, Caelian."

"I didn't—"

"He didn't," she interrupts. "He broke my fucking nose."

Gabriel laughs this time, and he rarely laughs. It's cut short quickly, though, and his eyes blank out. "Why are you here, Raven? No offense, but my brother doesn't have friends. So, the fact that you come here at night, looking all kinds of fucked up, has me on edge. What is it you're here for?"

She sneers at him, stepping forward. I know she's about to hit him in the face, but I step into the space between them. I turn toward Raven. "What's going on?"

She lifts her hand, her fist still closed tightly with the piece of paper in it. "Here," she whispers.

I narrow my eyes, my teeth grinding as I lift it from her shaky palm. I think I know what this is, though I'm hoping it's not. Just as the paper touches my fingers, I know.

I know it's another note from the copycat.

I unwrap it, reading the words slowly.

One, two, three,

I see you. Do you see me?

The pathetic scrawl of a crow sits on the paper, and I glance up at her. "Where'd you get this?"

"My house." The words are choked out of her, and I know she's telling the truth, and she's terrified by that fact. Whoever the copycat is, he or she knows where she lives. That makes her entire world unsafe.

This changes the game.

"What the fuck—*what?* You're the one getting messages from the copycat?" Gabriel shouts. "What the fuck is going on, Caelian?"

I shake my head, knowing a can of shit has just been opened with my brothers. They'll never stop until they learn every last detail.

"I'll tell you guys later," I growl, reaching forward and latching my fingers around her wrist. I pull her up the stairs and down the hall, ignoring the complaints from my brothers. I'll never get anything out of her if they're barking fucking questions the entire time. I need to figure out what's going on, and with one look at her, it's more than just this letter.

Once we get to the top, I cut right, and we head down the maze of my house until we reach my closed door. With my hand on the knob, I turn it and walk through, tugging her in behind me. I close the door behind us and slap the light to my bedroom on.

I've never had a girl in here before. Not once. My brothers are rarely even in my room. It's just me. This is my safe place, only for me and Rosko. But right now, for the first time, Raven is in here, and it feels really fucking odd.

My room is filled with nothing but gray walls. My king-sized bed sits in the middle of the room, with a dark gray fur comforter covering the top. My dresser is filled with guns and knives, and the rest is blank.

I have no sentimental things. I've never needed or cared for them. Clutter is meaningless to me. Will she hate the lack of humanity in my room?

Probably.

I spin around, pinning her against the closed door before her eyes can trail around my room.

"What the fuck is going on?" I growl in her ear.

She sniffles. Fucking sniffles. Then her knees give out, and she sinks to the floor beneath me. "I can't do this." She buries her head in her hands, her voice muffled and so fucking distraught.

I don't know how to deal with this, so I step back, running my fingers through my hair as she sobs on my floor. "Tell me what happened."

Her head lifts from her hands, her eyes tear-stained and her cheeks blotchy and red. "My cousin found out about the burn on my neck."

I nod. Okay, so the mousy chick realized that her parents are psychopaths.

"She freaked out, and my aunt and uncle heard and went in her room. They freaked out. My uncle pinned my cousin against the wall while my aunt pulled me down the stairs by my hair."

"She *what?*" I roar.

She nods, another sob choking from her throat. She stands up, wincing on her way. Lifting her shirt slightly, she shows me her hips and back, red and purple from ugly bruises.

My blood goes from boiling to explosive. I've never felt this way before, which seems to be a common theme lately when it comes to Raven. I want to tear my room apart.

I want to fucking *detonate*.

I walk to my dresser, lifting my gun and picking up the silencer sitting next to it. I screw it on, popping the clip out to make sure it's loaded before locking it in. "They're dead," I say, walking back to Raven. I place my hands on her shoulders to push her out of the doorway. She slams her back against the door, her arms outstretched to block my exit.

"No! You can't. Please."

My face scrunches up in confusion. "Why would you protect the motherfuckers that hurt you not once, but twice?"

Her face crumbles, and I instantly know this isn't the first, or second, time this has happened. This has happened many times before.

"Move out of my way, Raven, or I'll move you myself." My rage calms down, and in its place is a dangerous calm. Their death is inevitable. A certainty that I'm more than okay with.

"You can't hurt them. Trust me, I want to more than you realize, but not now. Not yet. My cousin is there."

"They could be hurting her in there."

She shakes her head as her eyes turn watery, though I can see in her eyes even she doesn't totally believe her thoughts. "They wouldn't hurt her. At least not like they hurt me."

"Okay, you don't want me to kill them now. When would be an appropriate time, after breakfast tomorrow?" My snide comments aren't needed, but her reasoning for letting pieces of shit like those two take any more air off this earth is appalling.

"I have to go back. For Aria."

I lean forward, my hand pressing against the door behind her as I get in her face. She thinks she has the ability to do what she pleases and there are no consequences. She has no idea that with each passing second, she's becoming more and more engrained in my thoughts, in my fucking bones. It's an irritating feeling, but she has to realize that it's happening, right? She has to understand that her coming to me wasn't for no reason at all.

She feels the exact same way.

I press my torso against her chest, her breasts heaving against my pecs in an erratic motion. She glances up at me, like she doesn't want what's happening to happen, but her breaths speak otherwise.

She wants so much, but she fights against it.

Why? Am I a monster in her eyes? Does she think I'm only a beast to teach her how to become just as crazy as her blood has painted her to be? Maybe she doesn't crave me, but only craves the feeling of want and need.

Maybe I'm just a body to fill the void.

"If you go back there, what will happen?" I murmur, my lips brushing the softness of her cheek.

She swallows audibly; her hushed whimper like a fucking siren's call in my ears. "I'll do what I have to do to make it out alive. To make sure Aria makes it out of there alive."

I shake my head. "You aren't ready for death. To take a life."

Her body settles against mine. "I know."

"Will they kill you?"

"They want to." Her eyes scorch mine, and my hand can't help itself as it secures around her waist, her tiny frame hot like a burning flame.

"How can you save your cousin if you can't even save yourself?" I tilt my head to the side. Does she not realize she isn't only at risk of her aunt and uncle, but also the monster of the unknown? How can she think she is safe anywhere she goes, except for being with me?

"I will fight to the death for Aria. I will gladly die for her to become safe." Her eyes shutter, a coldness entering them that I've only seen in my own eyes. They don't belong in hers. She may hold a darkness that not many can handle, but the low glow of humanity can't be snuffed out completely, or she'll never get back to the person she was.

The distaste sits bitterly on my tongue of her fighting a battle alone, but she hasn't asked for help, and she's refusing to let me do it on my own. I don't know how to help someone who hasn't asked. I barely understand the concept of anyone asking me for help, ever. Helping her is a foreign concept, yet it also feels like something that is a necessity.

I shouldn't care. Care equals emotion, and I've never fucking had any in my entire life, so why start now?

"Death is inevitable for all of us, but it seems you are walking straight into the fire."

"For her, I will gladly burn." With this, she looks into my eyes. They open, like she wants me to see her struggle. The way in which her eyes are an open book is almost painful to look at. To know her history, her past that is so screwed up that no kid should ever have to go through.

My father taught me how to murder in cold blood. To wipe the earth of the scum. My father showed me how to rid people like her parents.

Raven's parents taught her how to kill everyone and anyone. They fueled the urges in her blood and left her to stumble through it on her own.

If they weren't locked up right now, I'd surely find them and rip them to pieces.

Feed them to Rosko.

"I'm not afraid of death," she adds, her own hand going over my heart. It beats steady, strong against her palm; I can hear its vibrations in the silence around us. Her other hand goes to my chest, her fingers clutching the fabric of my shirt, scrunching it between her fingers. "It doesn't scare me."

I tilt my head back until our eyes are aligned. "Death should frighten you." With that, I dip my head only a hair forward, our lips molding together in a kiss filled with so much tension I feel like it sucks all the air out of the room. She gasps, pulling in air as her lips part.

My fingers dip beneath the fabric of her shirt, digging into the skin of her hip. I squeeze, feeling her body tense against me. Her hand slides up my shirt, across my neck until her fingers grip my jaw, the slight scruff along my jawline scratching at her skin. My other hand burrows into her hair, pulling her head back until I can manipulate her mouth exactly how I want her.

My fingers loosen on her hips, traveling up her slender hips until I meet the fabric of her sports bra. Brushing along the hem, I slip them beneath, her small breast bouncing into my palm. I exhale through my nose, never having felt this aggressive for a woman in my entire life.

She arches her breasts into my palm, and I grab at her nipple, giving it a sharp pinch. She lets out a squeak, and I brush my thumb across her nipple to ease the pain, making a small moan crawl up her throat. I slip my tongue between her parted lips, feeling out her hesitant tongue. She doesn't know what to do, barely sweeping her tongue against mine. She's so inexperienced. Unknowing in anything about a man and a woman. I can tell by the way she looks at me. By the way she touches me.

She hasn't done this before.

She's never had a chance to live a normal life.

Her eyes flare, like she knows what I'm thinking. I run my tongue along my teeth, and that does it for her. Her irises show me every inch of mania in her bones.

It makes me hard.

A crackling, tension-filled moment zings between us, the temperature in the room cranking to an inferno.

I wrap my arms around the backs of her thighs, lifting her in the air as she dips her mouth to kiss me again. She initiates dipping her tongue into my mouth this time. A grunt escapes me, and my teeth sink into her plush lip until the skin breaks, a dollop of blood sliding onto my tongue.

Suddenly, her hands press on my chest, and she releases her lips from mine. "I… I can't…"

My entire body shutters, and I snuff out any and all emotions that even attempted to make an appearance in my mind. I drop her, and she barely lands on her feet.

"I'm not a whore," she whispers to herself.

I whip my gaze to hers. I want to rip her head off her shoulders for saying those words.

What the fuck is she talking about?

My mouth pops open, ready to question the shit out of her, when a beeping alerts. Her eyes go wide. "Shit, I forgot I had my phone."

She reaches into her sweatshirt pocket, pulling out her phone. She unlocks it, and I watch her eyes dip in sadness. "Aria says my aunt and uncle want me to come home now."

"Tell them to fuck off."

She starts typing out a message and shakes her head slightly. "I can't. I have to go home." She looks up at me, fear and worry in her eyes. *"For her."*

I shouldn't fucking care whether the girl in front of me lives or dies, yet I do. For some fucking reason, I do.

I reach around her, my hand going to the knob. "Go ahead, then."

Her eyes glimmer with tears at my cold tone. I refuse, and honestly don't even understand how to care about someone, and whatever weird fucking virus is going on inside me, I can't let it take over. She can go deal with her shit, and we can go back to training and nothing else.

The clicking of Rosko scratching at the door snaps us both out of our trance. I open the door slightly, and he instantly walks up to Raven. She smiles sadly, squatting down to the floor.

And oddly enough, Rosko steps forward and licks her face.

She sniffles, petting him on the head, which he also doesn't fucking allow anyone to do—*ever*. She shoves to a stand and gives me one more glance. "I'm fighting on Friday. Will you be there?"

I grit my teeth. "Maybe."

She drops her eyes to the floor. "Okay. I'll see you later." She goes to walk off, and I snatch her phone from her hands. It's still unlocked, and I go to the keypad, typing in my phone number and dialing myself.

My phone goes off in my pocket, and I hit End, handing her back her phone.

"See you later." It's a fucking promise, and she knows it, her eyes lighting ever so slightly before she bows her head, slipping down the halls and out of sight.

Rosko looks up at me, his dark brown eyes curious. He can sense something's off, and he sniffs the air, as if it'll tell him why the tension is so thick.

"Don't even fucking ask."

He turns his head away from me, walking over to my bed and jumping on top of it.

He'll grow restless soon, just like I'm feeling. It's time for both of us to get a kill, probably why I'm acting so fucking out of character.

chapter eighteen
RAVEN

I pull up at home, nerves hitting my stomach once again. Should I have listened to Caelian? Maybe I should've never went back.

What if it was my aunt or uncle texting me and not Aria? What if they are luring me here to finally kill me?

I feel nauseous as I turn off my car and slip out of the front seat. It's pitch black outside, the only sound the gravel crunching under my feet. I received another text from Aria on my way home asking me where I was. I decided to not even respond. Whether it's really Aria or my aunt or uncle, I couldn't tell them where I was.

The lights turn on in the lower level as I walk up the steps, and before I can grab the knob, the front door opens, Uncle Jerry standing there with a blank look on his face.

"Where were you tonight, Raven?"

I narrow my eyes. "You kicked me out."

"The fact that you had somewhere to go makes me wonder who you have to go see in the middle of the night."

I chew on my lower lip as I slip past him, the house empty and silent downstairs besides my creepy fucking uncle who I hate more and more as the days go on.

"I didn't have anywhere to go. I was just driving around."

He says nothing, and I walk around him, heading toward the stairs. He stops me with a hand on my shoulder, hovering over my back. Too close for comfort. His warm body against mine makes me feel dirty.

"If I find out you're lying to me, it won't just be God who you are asking for forgiveness."

His tight fingers release my shoulder, and I don't respond as I rush up the stairs, not even glancing in Aunt Gloria's room as I head to my own room, closing the door quietly behind me. Even though any encounter with Uncle Jerry is unwanted, it went better than expected.

I see my bag where I left it earlier this evening, and I grab it, shoving it under my bed. Toeing my shoes off, I kick them to the side of my room and slide between the sheets. I pull my phone from my pocket, yanking the comforter over my head as I glance at the new number in my phone.

I have his number.

Why did he get it? Is he going to call me? Am I supposed to use it? A part of me wants to text him. Just to talk to him, not anything else.

What is going on between us?

He doesn't seem like someone that dates, but I suppose neither am I. And what I said in his room is true.

I'm not a whore, and doing what I'm doing is what I was taught against since I moved in with my aunt and uncle. The way he touched me, the way he gripped my skin was so possessive and exhilarating; I only want more, but I know it's frowned upon, and something that's been ingrained in my mind the last few years is hard to just shove under the rug.

I shouldn't let it go further. Us together is a fucking disaster. Most likely, he'd just sleep with me and then never talk to me again. Then not only would I lose my virginity, but I'd also lose the only trainer that I believe can teach me how to survive in this world.

Mostly now with this killer... this... copycat of my parents running around.

Who is it? I have no idea who it could be, and I don't know how to figure it out.

Everything is a fucking mess, and it's turning my brain into a fucking thunderstorm of chaos.

I close my eyes, though his number is already embedded in my brain.

I'll fight tomorrow, and then I'll get back to training. No more fighting. No more sexual tension. I want him to teach me how to take a life, and then, once I've perfected everything he teaches me, we'll be done.

And I'll never have to talk to him again.

"Raven." My name being whispered rouses me from sleep.

I roll over, my eyes popping open to see Aria hovering over my bed.

I glance outside, seeing the night sky still dark behind my curtains.

"Aria? Is everything okay?"

She smiles sadly, sitting on the edge of my bed. "I just wanted to see how you were. I'm sorry that I got you kicked out." Her voice is shaky, nervous, a little worried. She looks like a beaten dog, and it instantly puts me on edge.

I remember her face, how terrified she was as her dad pinned her against the wall. The absolute fear in her eyes.

I slide up until I'm sitting, leaning forward so I can get a good look in her eyes. "What the hell happened? I've never seen your dad be that… aggressive with you."

She glances toward the door. "It was scary," she whispers.

I nod, able to see it in her eyes. "I'm sorry."

Her eyes instantly water, and I grow uncomfortable. I know she can see it. She can sense it. "I'm sorry, it's just. You can't be sorry. It's not right for my parents to treat you like this. They were so willing to take you in after what happened, but why do they treat you like this? I don't understand." Her voice cracks at the end, and I feel so bad for her young, naïve soul.

I shake my head. "It's not something you really have to understand." And it's not really something I can explain. They treat me this way because they hate me. And why do they hate me? That's not something even I comprehend, and I don't know if I want to.

There shouldn't be a reason to hate a child, yet they do, they hate me for it.

"I just… I want it to stop."

"It will. Eventually." I can't tell her what my plans are, and the truth is, there's a large chance she's going to absolutely hate me after it happens. But I can't not do what feels so damn right just for her. I will protect her at all costs, and by protection, that also means I'll take them from her. I'll eliminate them from earth if I have to.

And I will.

She nods, probably thinking I mean when I move out or something simple like that. "Did you go see him?"

I stare at her for a moment, then give her a slow nod. Just a single one.

Her eyes soften. "You like him, don't you?"

I narrow my eyes, not really knowing exactly what it is I feel. But it's different from anything I've ever felt before. I've never felt this connected to anyone. Not even my own parents. This is on a level so deep it frightens me.

I shrug.

She smiles, her fingers brushing over mine slightly. "It's okay. I can see it in your eyes, Raven. You're changing. Maybe he's the one that can get you away from all this stuff."

Maybe. Or maybe he'll just teach me how to eradicate it myself.

Fuck, what is going on at school today?

"Is there some party I wasn't aware of?" I mumble under my breath.

"Yeah," Aria sighs. "It's the pep rally and then homecoming tonight. You didn't know?"

No, I didn't. I haven't been paying attention to school, *at all.*

"I don't know. I must not have heard about it."

Aria laughs, all the problems from the last few days for her having washed away with last night's rain shower. She's totally excited and upbeat, and I swallow down my petty attitude. She deserves the teenage experience, even if I feel like I'll never get the chance.

Blue and white streamers hang outside the building, and people drive into the parking lot with their cars draped in an insane amount of decorations. It's not cheap stuff that's taped to the bumper of their cars. These people spent a lot of time and money getting ready for today.

What is a pep rally? What is homecoming?

I pull into my normal spot in the back and step out of my car, for the first time feeling like hundreds of people aren't watching me. They're focused on their friends today, on whatever's happening that seems like such a big deal.

I've finally faded into the background. Where I want to be.

"Apparently, there's going to be some big thing out on the football field today, and there's going to be a party, and then tonight, there's a dance."

"A dance?" My eyes widen, my chest burning with something akin to jealousy.

Jealousy that maybe *he's* going, and he just didn't tell me about it. Why would he have to? It's not like we're together, but maybe that's why he didn't say with certainty that he'd be at my fight tonight.

Maybe he has other plans. Maybe he's had a girlfriend this entire time, and he didn't tell me.

I feel ridiculous walking into school in a black cardigan and jeans while everyone else rushes in with their crop tops molded to their breasts and leggings or cropped jeans. They all match, and of course me and Aria didn't get the memo.

Why would we? We're on the most popular girl's shit list. No way would we be invited or included in any conversation about having fun.

Fuck that.

When we walk into school, it's only a bigger production than it was outside. The lockers and walls are filled with so much school spirit, the *Blackridge Prep Panthers* making a massive production.

"This is actually pretty cool," Aria says, running her fingers along the streamers hanging from the lockers. "It's like one big celebration. A party, or something."

I smile at her, knowing she wants to fit in and realizing the problem isn't about her or what she thinks or even how she dresses. As long as her parents have control over her, she'll never be free from their grip.

We make it to our lockers, and I swish some of the streamers out of the way as I start twisting the combo on my lock. "I wonder why they even have school on days like today. It's not like anyone is going to be learning anything." I'm on edge, as I always am the day of a fight. My body, my muscles, my tendons, can all sense the upcoming adrenaline. *Am I ready? Have I learned anything from what Caelian taught me?*

Will he be there to watch me? Will he be cheering me on with the rest of the crowd, or will he silently observe and criticize every move I make?

"Hey, Raven!" I grip the door of my locker as my name is called from down the hall. I peek around the door, seeing Chad and his group of buddies all half dressed in their football gear. He looks happy to see me, like Caelian never threw him down the hall only last week.

"Hey." I smile, realizing at the least I could be friendly.

"Where's your school spirit?" He lifts his arms at his sides, getting the attention of everyone else in the hallway. People finally start glancing, and I no longer feel like I'm in the twilight zone, or invisible. I'm once again the new girl.

I pull at my cardigan, feeling like I'm wearing neon colors instead of black. "I guess I didn't get the memo." I shrug.

He laughs, slapping his friend on the shoulder before he walks over to me. His hair swooshes back and forth, and he has streaks of black painted along his cheekbones.

He's such a damn jock. I momentarily wish he was my type, instead of my heart beating like a wild drum the moment Caelian walks into a room.

"I might have some extra stuff in my locker if you want to borrow it," he says once he reaches me. His fingers wrap around my locker door, and he pulls it open, stepping right into my space.

He looks at Aria, a cheeky smile brightening his eyes. "Hey, I'm Chad. I don't think we've met yet."

She looks a bit starstruck as she stares at him. "Aria."

His smile grows wider, like he knows the exact effect he has on women. "Are you guys coming to the pep rally today?"

"Is it required?" His face screws up in confusion, and I internally wince. Okay, this guy takes it seriously. "When is it again?"

"After second period. If you want, I can save you guys a seat so you can sit by me. I figure being the new kid isn't the easiest thing in the world."

"It's not fun at all," Aria whines.

His eyes flicker from Aria's and back to mine. "Great! I'll save you guys a seat. See you in a bit?" His hand lifts, and he goes to brush a stray hair out of my face. I tilt away from his hand, bringing my own up to comb through my hair.

"Thanks. See you then."

He's not deterred by my obvious shut down of his advances. He doesn't seem to care in the slightest. Either he isn't afraid of Caelian and his words, or he's just trying to be the nicest guy on the planet.

Regardless, what he's doing feels risky. And the risky part of me is excited to see how Caelian will react.

My spine snaps straight as a horn blares over the loudspeakers. I look at the ceiling, scowling as some dick bag screams his announcement. "It's time to pep, motherfuckers! Get your sexy asses outside before I drag you out there myself!" I hear a shuffle, and the speaker goes out.

People start laughing and clapping, putting their things back in their bags before flooding out of the classroom. I shake my head as I grab my things, not nearly as excited to go celebrate with a ton of kids who don't necessarily want to even be around me.

I toss my backpack over my shoulder as I stand from behind my desk, making my way to the door.

I see a shadow in my peripheral, my gaze shooting up to see Chad leaning against the doorframe, a smirk on his face.

"Fucking hell, Chad. What're you doing here?" I bark.

He laughs, shoving off the doorframe and reaching out to grab my bag. "I figured you'd find a way to get out of it, so I thought I'd come meet you and bring you down there myself."

I bite my lip. This guy knows a thing or two about me, it seems.

"Okay, now that is something I'd do. Except, Aria is down there, and I'm not going to leave her there by herself."

He spins around, and we start walking to the stairs. "She's... what? You guys are related? Sisters? Cousins?"

I nod. "Cousins."

He bobs his head, taking two steps at a time as we head downstairs. "She seems nice. Though, a little piece of advice?"

No. Not needed. "Sure, okay."

"Let her spread her wings a little bit. You're spending all your time thinking you need to protect her, but you're only putting yourself in a cage and her in an even smaller cage."

I frown as we get to the same level. Am I inhibiting her? Shoving her in a box so she can't breathe or see the light of day?

Am I her parents, but on a different scale?

Chad's hand goes down on my arm, and I flinch, looking over at him with a scowl. "I'm sorry. I didn't mean to make you upset. I can see you care about her."

"I do." I pull my arm out of his grip gently, not liking the warmth he spreads through my skin. "She's my cousin. I'd do anything for her."

He smiles softly. "I can see that. Don't worry. We'll make sure no one messes with her."

I lift my eyebrows. "If that's your job, you've already failed. That bitch, Trina, and her minions have already messed with her on multiple occasions."

He winces. "I heard about the cafeteria incident the other day. Sorry about that. If I would've been there, I would've put a stop to it before Trina could've done anything." He shakes his head, irritation clear on his face. "Trina isn't a good person. She and her friends think they rule the school, but people just don't want to be on her bad side. With her dad being a congressman, she thinks she's tough shit. When in all reality, I don't even think she's all that pretty."

I laugh as we walk to the front door, feeling like, for just a moment, my life is normal. I'm just a normal girl who goes to a normal school and has normal friends.

It's all a sham, though. Me, here, now, I'm living a lie.

My life is much more complicated than this.

It's fun to pretend, though.

It's cloudy outside today, the crisp fall air beginning to turn the colors of the leaves. The air is bitter in the mornings and nights, though it never gets too cold here by the ocean. I wish I would've brought a chunky scarf with me this morning. I would've, if I knew we'd be spending time outside. I didn't think I'd need one, my cardigan oversized enough to hide the wounds from my aunt.

Aria's brown hair catches my attention outside the football field, and her face brightens as she notices me.

"Remember to let her fly," Chad mumbles.

TWISTED DARES

Let her fly.

"Hey! What took you so long?" Aria asks as she steps up to us.

"Sorry, my class was on the opposite end of the school."

Aria smiles, her cheeks blushed a rosy pink from the fall air. "Doesn't this look crazy?" She laughs, her arms waving toward the stands.

Indeed, it does.

It looks akin to the Super Bowl with all the people, their feet pounding on the metal stands. Blue, white, and black pompoms swishing in the air. The football field is set up with a stand in the center, and drinks and party supplies are set up in the field. Along with a few games arranged for people to play in every direction.

Fucking hell, this is wild.

"You haven't seen anything yet. Come on." He nods his head for us to follow him, and we walk through the throngs of people and onto the field. The football players swarm around us, and I feel like we should be sitting in the stands with the rest of the students instead of on the field with the football players. It's unlike anything I've ever seen, and my mind filters it out as the screaming and noise around me fills me completely.

It's a similar feeling to being in the ring. So much excitement that I compartmentalize it from everything else. I drown out the noise and let the chaos consume me.

Aria loves it. She swallows it and chooses not to drown in it. She wants the energy; it builds her up instead of draining her. She thrives.

"Come on, follow me!" Chad shouts over the noise as he walks toward the podium in the center of the field.

I shake my head, my eyes popping wide. "No, that's okay! We'll go sit in the bleachers."

"Nah, I don't think so!" He reaches out, grabbing onto my sleeve, his other hand still securing my backpack in his grip.

Fuck. I need that back.

"Welcome, Blackridge Prep Panthers! To the fifty-seventh annual pep rally!" The coach of the football team stands in a suit as he makes his announcement. Chad stays next to me, crowding my body next to the rest of the football players who stand off to the side.

We're the only ones that aren't actual football players on the field. It's weird, and I feel like I'm drawing attention to myself by standing here.

The coach keeps talking, but Chad leans down toward my ear. "You know, I was wondering. After the game today is the homecoming dance. If you don't have any other plans—" He cuts off his words as his eyes narrow, at the same moment a warm set of fingers curl around the back of my neck, and *squeeze*.

A chill breaks along my spine, and warmth finally hits me in the crisp air.

I know who it is without having to even turn around. I'd wondered where he's been and how long it would take him to find me. I should've known he would've eventually, even though a part of me wondered if he really cared.

I glance over my shoulder, seeing Caelian, barely hanging onto his composure as his fingers dig into the skin of my neck, my dark hair draped over his wrist.

"Caelian," I breathe.

"I didn't think I'd need to explain again who it is you belong to." I don't know if he said those words for his benefit or mine or Chad's, and I'm not even sure if Chad heard the words, but they hit me right in the chest. Straight through my rib cage and into my empty heart.

He might as well have ripped my flesh apart with his bare fingers and let the world feast upon it. That is how he makes me feel; with his possessive touch and his commanding tone, he leaves nothing for me and takes everything for himself.

He consumes *everything*

"I'm not—" I start to complain, to give him an excuse, anything that says why I'm standing on the field next to Chad like we're… a what? A couple? Friends? It definitely doesn't look good.

"Don't speak, Raven. There's nothing good that you can say right now.

Unless he drugged you and dragged you out onto the field himself?"

He twists my neck, until my gaze clashes with his. Black orbs swirling with such menace, I'm surprised he hasn't obliterated everyone on the field.

I'm surprised he hasn't obliterated *me*.

I shake my head.

He narrows his eyes, spitting hate and brutality toward me before turning his gaze to Chad.

"I thought I warned you, Anderson. Stay the fuck away from what's mine."

At this point, he's garnered the attention of the other football players. The coach still speaks, but the players circle around us, with Chad, Caelian, Aria, and me in the center.

"She's not yours, Morelli. She hasn't so much as stated that fact. I think you're being fucking ridiculous, and maybe need to ask her what it is *she* wants." Chad puffs out his chest, like he's the king of the field. King of the school. I don't think he realizes the war he would initiate if he went up against any of the Morellis.

Mostly Caelian, who seems like the most dangerous one of all.

Caelian pulls on my neck again, and my eyes once again clash with his. "Is that true, Raven? You haven't given him the truth?"

My mouth pops open, and I wonder what it is about him that sucks me in. A black hole that I never even want to find my way out of. He's a dangerous man. Potentially destructive. Most definitely sinful. Yet when it's him and me, I see nothing else.

I see no one else.

It's only us against the world.

"Tell him, Raven. Are you going to speak the truth, or continue with your lies?"

It's a painful feat to tear my eyes from his and glance over at Chad. His face is a mixture of wanting to save me and wanting to just destroy Caelian. Back and forth my eyes turn, and for the life of me, I can't figure out where they should land.

They land on Caelian's.

"I'm yours," I whisper, listening as Chad sighs, and Caelian shows his teeth, snapping and vicious, and so incredibly pleased.

"I know," he mumbles, leaning down to kiss me briefly in front of everyone. I gasp into his mouth, shocked and surprised at the public display of affection, but it's over before it starts. He pushes me aside, turning toward Chad with a lethal look on his face.

"You come up on Raven again, and your football arm won't even be a fucking arm." He lets out a sound that sounds like a half growl as he steps up to him until they're nearly nose-to-nose. "Mine. She is *mine*," he snarls. Then he steps back, and I let out a sigh of relief, hopeful it's over, when his fist snaps out so quickly, his knuckles connecting with Chad's nose. I can hear the crunch, can see the blood splatter in the air.

It feels like I'm watching a movie as the entire football team coils tight, like a slingshot pulled back fully, before it snaps forward, and everyone attacks each other. It feels like the Inferno when I was jumped, except this time, it's Caelian against Chad.

It's about me.

They're fighting... *over me.*

I stand speechless as Caelian's brothers appear out of nowhere, and an all-out brawl starts. Kids start running from the bleachers, their shoes pounding against the metal stands echoing in the air.

"Holy shit," I whisper.

"Seriously. And you're *dating* him?" Aria sounds shell-shocked as we watch Caelian tear everyone apart. There is no contest, no question who would win.

His body moves with ease and control as his fists slam against Chad and anyone else his knuckles can connect with. His body bends and folds, his back muscles rippling through his shirt. The smooth features on his face are dangerous, deadly. I know what he speaks without saying the words.

He's claiming me. In front of everyone.

I turn to her, watching her stunned expression as she stares at the fighting crowd. I say nothing as I look back at them, not even sure what answer I could supply to her.

The Morellis are weapons, Caelian the most powerful. Putting them in a battle, there are no hesitations on who would win.

It'll be Caelian. *Every. Single. Time.*

Eventually, the teachers and staff break it up, the coach blowing a horn that startles most of the students. Caelian and his brothers listen to no one as the coach starts barking orders. His eyes instantly capture mine, and he walks toward me, his knuckles dripping blood, his hair a mess, and his eyes like black pools that I dive straight into. My breath gets caught in my chest, and I can do nothing as I wait for him to come to me.

He does, walking straight into my space, his hands wrapping around my waist and pressing my body against his. He lips sink into mine, and he kisses me roughly before pulling away. His thumb goes to my lower lip, and he swipes across the plumpness. "No more games, Raven. You're mine now."

And then he's gone, taking my breath, my mind, and my fucking soul with him.

Aria: Good luck. Please don't stay out too late. My parents seem on edge. It's kind of freaking me out.

I stare at her words, rereading them a few times before I shove my phone into my bag. I refuse to let the words get to me before a fight. I need to focus on my fight, and what Caelian has taught me. I can't let Aria's concern or the behaviors of my aunt and uncle worm their way into my head.

"Rave!" The voice of Corgan both settles and puts me on edge. It's been too long since I've seen him, and I feel bad, but I also can't be too upset over doing what I need to do.

He walks in, handsome and ripped in a pair of jeans and a dark shirt that molds to his form.

"Hi, Corgan." I grab the tape from my bag, sitting down on the bench to begin wrapping my hands.

He sits beside me, leaning forward and placing his elbows on his knees. "Where've you been, Raven? You haven't come to the gym."

I refuse to look at him as I wrap my hands. Is he upset? Relieved? Angry? I don't really want to deal with any of those emotions, I don't know how to.

Do I tell him the truth? Or do I lie to him?

"Don't beat around the bush, Raven. I'm not a fucking girl."

I sigh, tearing the tape with my teeth and flexing my hands to test the tightness. "That guy... Caelian?"

His face blanks out. "Morelli? What about him?"

"He's been training me. But not the shit you've been doing. More... intense. So don't think I'm just looking for someone else. I'm just looking for... something *more*."

He doesn't say anything, and I chew on my lip. "Well, fucking say something."

He blinks. "I was wondering when I wouldn't be enough for you."

I narrow my eyes. "What do you mean?"

His fingers go together, and he cracks his knuckles. "You're a unique kind, Rave. What you need is more than I can provide. You've been walking circles around me for a while now. I've done all I can do. I've known you needed more. I just... I guess I wasn't ready to give you up."

I feel a pull in my chest. *Guilt.* "Give me up?"

He chuckles. "You're a good friend, Raven. And fun to train. There isn't another girl that I've ever seen walk around my gym ready to tear into grown-ass men. But I refuse to turn you into one of them. I hold back, I guess. I see the good in you."

There is no good in me. *I am tainted.*

"I'm sorry, Corgan."

He shakes his head, shoving to his feet. "You don't need to be sorry. Just don't be a fucking stranger, all right? You can come by the gym anytime."

I turn toward him, a part of me not wanting to see him go. "You haven't seen the last of me. I can promise you that."

He lifts a brow. "I'm holding you to it. And if…" He scratches at his head, and I'm almost worried about what he's going to say. "If shit is ever going on at home that you need to get away from, I'm always here for that, too."

I nod my head, knowing he's being so fucking truthful. It hurts. He's a good man.

"Now hurry up and get out there. Show me what you're learning from Morelli."

He slips out, and with a heavy sigh of both relief and guilt, I wrap my second hand, refusing to let emotions get to me. With everything in me, I blank out his words, focusing on my fight.

I hope it's someone good.

I know I've only had a couple of training sessions with Caelian. But during those times, I feel like I've learned so much and completely changed the way I think about fighting.

Caelian doesn't hesitate to hit back. He doesn't worry about it being man versus woman. He is fighting human against human, and that is what I've always strived for.

With one last tear of my teeth, my hands are wrapped, and I stand up, ready to go fight once again.

The cheers are loud, and I wonder if people are expecting me to conquer or fail. I've had my ups and downs lately, but it's time I get back to my old but new self.

With a deep breath, I walk out, the bright lights and the wave of the crowd making the air thick. I ignore it all as I head toward the stained mat, feeling like it's redder at this point than an off-white. I slip underneath the rough, frayed rope, doing a quick glance around the ring to see if Caelian came to see me.

He never said whether he would or wouldn't, but I really hoped he would. I didn't see him the rest of the day, but after the fight, most of the people got back to the pep rally. I was too discombobulated by Caelian. I couldn't focus on anything, so I hid out in the library the rest of the day. My nose in a book. The moment I was able to leave, we did. I haven't seen him since.

I'd hoped he'd be here.

But glancing around, I don't see him anywhere.

The thought leaves a pit in my stomach.

The crowd goes wild as I get to the center of the stage. I don't look around anymore. I don't pay attention to anyone as I stretch out my arms and legs and neck. I want it to be someone strong. Someone indestructible.

I hear another round of cheers, and glancing up, I lift my brows as I see a man step up to the ring who I've never fought before. But I have seen him once or twice, and he's a big man. A strong man who can throw a good punch. A small smirk pops onto my face. Reggie doesn't put me in the ring with men like him, so what changed his mind?

The man growls as he sees who he's fighting. I can sense the disgust rolling off him in waves.

He doesn't want to fight a girl.

A vein bulges in his forehead, thick and purple as it thumps in aggravation. He probably wanted to come in here and beat some poor sack to a pulp. He most likely feels uncomfortable fighting a woman.

I feel sorry for him. He has no idea what he's gotten himself into.

The screams quiet to a stop, and I can hear the anticipated breaths of everyone waiting to see what's going to happen.

With one last glance over my shoulder, I'm disappointed in myself at how upset I am that Caelian isn't here. It's not like he promised me he would be. Something could have easily come up. He could be busy with work.

Or with another girl.

I squeeze my eyes shut as I turn back around and look at the man in front of me.

He's a beefy man, and I watch his shaved head bend as he charges me. His thick arms are taut, his fists clenched so tightly his knuckles turn white.

I dodge out of his way, but he's quick, turning just as I do.

Okay, so he's a fast motherfucker.

I dip under his arm, and his fingers just slightly brush past my side as his arm swings out.

I feel out of sorts, and I barely know how to respond to him or act. It feels like I forgot how to fight as I race around the ring, this big boulder of a dude chasing me.

I run against the rope, a scream lodged in my throat.

What the fuck is happening to me?

I bend over the rope, my heart pounding in my ears.

Time freezes.

Everything just… *vanishes.*

I can barely comprehend the meaning of life as my eyes lock with Caelian's. His face is empty, blank, but his eyes are fierce as he watches me.

Beside him is Rosko. Rosko watches me with the same dark eyes as his owner. Both of them say nothing, but they don't have to.

They are wondering what the fuck I'm doing.

"You're here," I breathe.

His head cocks to the side. "What the fuck are you doing?"

"I don't know," I choke out. Beefy Guy rams into my back, the air in my lungs choking and constricted as the rope digs into my chest.

"Stop thinking. What have I taught you? Pay the fuck attention and quit acting like this is your first time in the Inferno. You're fighting like shit." He licks his lips, his eyes flaming bright as he stares at me. As he stares *into* me. "*I dare you.*"

Beefy Guy sinks his oversized fist into my side, and I grunt out a painful breath. Rosko's hair on his back raises, and his teeth bare, a threatening growl rumbling in his chest.

Another hit to my side.

I dare you.

"Fuck you," I whimper at Caelian. I'm clearly off my game, and he wants to talk shit to me? He wants to dare me and play this game? *Fuck him.*

I lift my leg, kicking my foot out. It connects with the rock-hard muscle of Beefy Guy, but my kick is firm enough to stop him, if only for a second.

"I hate you," I spit, ready to turn around and forget about him.

Firm fingers wrap around my neck, warm and possessive against my skin. My eyes glance toward Caelian, and he has an aggressive look on his face. One that warns me to not speak those words to him ever again.

"Take it back," he growls in my ear.

"Don't be so fucking rude, then."

His fingers tense to the point of pain. "Take them back, Raven. I'm not going to ask you again."

His voice is so serious, a lick of fear enters my blood. I look at Beefy Guy, who's watching me in aggravation. He's going to charge me again. I can see it in his eyes.

By how angry he is, he's going to knock my ass out.

I look back into Caelian's eyes, and I can see how badly he wants me to retract my words. "I take them back. Every one."

His gaze clears, and I swear his lips quirk, just slightly. But then his eyes blank out, as does the rest of his face. "Listen. Watch. Sense. Everything else needs to disappear." He shoves me away from him, and I fly across the ring, my bare stomach scraping against the rope on the other side.

Beefy Guy didn't expect it, his rush still aimed toward the now empty end of the rope. Rosko bares his canines as he almost reaches him, his hair standing on end as he steps forward, a ferocious bark and snap of his teeth echoing over the loud voices.

Caelian stares at him, his fingers wrapped around Rosko's collar as he watches the man with an absolute death stare.

I never, ever want to be on the other end of that look.

Then Beefy Guy lurches back, his feet stumbling as he looks for me, his eyes narrowing once they land on me.

His nostrils flare, and I instantly feel like a different person. Watching, listening, feeling. Every sense in my body is on edge as I watch and wait.

Watch and wait.

He lunges toward me again, and I follow his moves, ducking under his arms. My leg stretches out just as he reaches me, my ankle tripping up both of his feet. He falls to his stomach, landing with an obnoxious shake to the ground.

I jump on his back, my knee plowing into his tailbone. He grunts, and I can feel the pain ricochet through his entire body. I bring my elbows down, grinding them into the meat of his back. He growls loudly, the vibrations louder than the screams as he rolls over, his body slamming against mine and pinning me against the mat.

Shit. Fucking heavy.

I attempt to gasp in air but can't catch onto even an ounce. It's suffocating, and I want to panic.

Don't. Don't panic.

It's Caelian's voice in my ear, even though I know he's on the opposite end of the ring. I don't know when he quit being an enemy and started being on my side, but it happened, and now I want him in my corner. All the time.

Every time.

I bring my mouth forward, my teeth sinking into the skin of his neck. I can feel the skin split, and a rush of warm blood enters my mouth. It's disgusting, foul, tasting tainted against my tongue. I let it drool from my mouth as he lets out a howl, getting off me as quickly as he can. I spit onto the mat, leaping to my feet and stepping toward him, my hand sinking into the back of his head.

Stars. I know he sees them, because my knuckles thump in agony.

He stumbles forward, and I hit him again, and again, until he falls to his knees, his hands going to his head to block my hits.

I grab onto his neck, bringing my knee up and kneeing him repeatedly in the back of his head.

Thump.

His body loosens, and I know he's lost consciousness. He falls to the ground in a mass of muscle, and I fall with him, my muscles giving out as exhaustion hits me.

Shit.

People start screaming so loud the room vibrates, the walls shaking with the force of their excitement.

I gasp in breaths as my heart attempts to slow to a normal rate.

"Raven." His voice calling my name tunnels through the screams in the room. My head turns to the side, sweat dripping down the side of my face as Caelian once again comes into view.

He nods his head toward the locker rooms, turning and walking away with Rosko on his heels.

I get up, stumbling from the ring and ignoring everyone. My hand goes to my forehead, and I wipe away the rolling drops of sweat.

Walking into the locker room, I see Caelian standing there, Rosko at his side. He looks bored as he stands there, watching me. Waiting for me.

"How'd I do?" I ask him, my hands going to my hips.

He lifts a brow. "Do you want me to tell you what you did wrong, or what you did right?"

I shake my head, wondering if what I feel is all in my head. He's a monster, so why I think he's even slightly human when it comes to me is a ridiculous thought. "Never mind."

I bend down, going for my bag, ready to grab my sweatshirt and get out of here. After dealing with my aunt and uncle, dealing with the copycat killer of my parents, and now whatever fucking feelings I have with Caelian? I'm not in the mood for the back and forth, and maybe it's better to just pretend they don't even exist.

His fingers go into my hair, and he clenches his fist, pulling at the root of the strands. He tugs back, my head arching until my eyes clash with his.

"I'm so fucking over th—"

His lips connect with mine, and I gasp out a breath. His other hand goes around my neck, and he squeezes, cutting off my circulation as he flips me around, my back bent over the thin wooden bench. His hand leaves my hair and trails down my body, his arm hooking behind my ass as he lifts me into his arms. He spins us around, my back slamming against the metal lockers. The metallic clank echoes throughout the room.

I grind against him, feeling the tension making this unbearable. I can barely breathe or even think straight with him around me, and it feels like he's two people at this point.

One person wants me.

One person despises me.

Is he just as crazy as I am? Are we both too crazy for each other? Maybe us together will create such a catastrophic event, the world cannot handle it.

"Why are you doing this to me?" I whimper against his lips, feeling the familiar bulge pressing between my thighs. It hits that spot, and my eyes glaze over in lust.

I want him.

I've never wanted anyone, but I want him. So badly.

"I crave nothing, yet you're a fucking addiction that I can't get away from." His scratchy jaw itches against my skin, until his lips brush my jaw, and he opens his mouth, biting down until I know teeth marks will be left in its wake.

I hold on to his shoulders, wanting so badly to find the relief that I've never even searched for, yet every moment with him feels like I'm only moments away from exploding.

His fingers release my neck, trailing down my chest and to the space between my breasts. They dip below my sports bra, along my naked, damp stomach and to the waistband of my shorts. I hold my breath. I know what's happening, or what's going to happen, and my body yearns for it, craves every inch of his touch, yet I don't know if I'm ready for his brutal fingers to go to a place that's never seen pleasure in its life.

The words of my aunt clash in my mind, a war between what I want and what my mind believes is right. My fingers clench on his shoulders, and I know I should push him away. I should walk away from this moment like I promised myself I would. I shouldn't fall down this path with him, but as his hands grip me possessively, full of an aggressive need, I can't find the words to say no.

"The way you fight out there, the way you let go and become so fucking *mad, wild, free,* it's unlike anything I've ever seen before," he rasps against my skin.

I whimper, my eyes burning from the intensity of his words.

"You, Baby Crow, can make grown men fall to their knees. I think you're more dangerous than I ever believed." he mumbles as his fingers tease along my waistband.

Words escape me as heat floods me, and my mouth opens on a gasp as his fingers dip beneath the fabric, teasing the top of my sex.

His fingers spread wide, touching and caressing and teasing every inch of skin they can reach. "Maybe it's time I make you fall to your knees."

"Please," I gasp as his finger slides between my folds, dipping straight into my arousal.

"Tell me what you need," he grumbles, his fingers pressing expertly against my sensitive skin, while I feel so out of my element. I'm high on his touch, on his words, and yet I have no idea what I'm supposed to do.

But I know what I need, and in this moment, it's him.

"I need you to…" I gasp, whimpering when his fingers begin to retreat. "I need you to touch me. To make me feel better."

"How? Tell me what you want me to do." He's teasing, taunting. He knows my inexperience, and he wants me out of my element. Because that's the type of man he is. Powerful. Possessive. Always in charge.

I've never been one to fold. I've never been the type of person to be weak or quiet, unsure of my needs and desires.

I tilt my chin up, staring him in the eyes. "I want you to touch me. Make me come." The words flow from my lips with ease, even with my heart seconds from beating out of my chest. A war rages in me, and I bury it deep, only focusing on what's real. Not my fears or my insecurities, but what my body craves, what my soul beats for so intensely. "I want it to be you that gives me my first orgasm."

He growls, low, deep in his throat. Animalistic and wild. "It would've never been anyone else, Raven. I am the only one that'll ever touch you, ever again. *You are mine.*" His free hand dips, hooking behind my knee and lifting, giving him better access. He uses it to his advantage, his finger sinking inside for the first time. He slides his finger out, spreading my slickness up to my clit. I jolt in his arms, overcome with so many emotions I can barely function. It's too much, my body running on overdrive as he rubs and rubs at the perfect pace and pressure.

Then his finger dips inside again, and the wet sound of my folds around his finger makes my eyes roll in the back of my head. I reach my hands up, grabbing onto his shoulders as I sink my mouth into his.

If I don't, I'm worried I'll start crying out and everyone in the Inferno will hear. My leg holding me up starts shaking as he alternates back and forth from plunging his finger inside me versus rubbing at my swollen bud. Soon enough, a rush of heat starts in my lower belly and spreads like an earthquake over my body. Not an inch of me goes untouched from the sensation as my first ever orgasm roars through me. Caelian bites at my lips, demolishing me completely and swallowing every scream leaving my throat.

"Holy shit," I breathe, the world slowly coming back to me. Caelian sets me down, his mouth finally separating from mine.

He pulls his hand from my pants and lifts it to my mouth. "Open wide." In shock, I do as he asks, and he slips his finger between my lips. "Suck."

I do as he commands, my tongue wrapping around his finger as I taste my own arousal. It's sweet and salty, and it oddly turns me on, knowing that it was Caelian that made me feel this way.

"I knew it," he mumbles, slipping his finger from my mouth.

"You know what?" I ask in a daze.

"That your darkness matched mine. Perfectly."

"Raven!" My name shouted through the locker room disturbs my thoughts, and Caelian adjusts my shorts, but instantly steps closer to me. To protect me.

I run my fingers through my messy ponytail as Reggie walks through, his face filled with annoyance. It instantly puts me on edge.

"Okay, someone's going to tell me what the fuck is going on. My two best fighters are suddenly together all the time. Corgan tells me Morelli is training you? What the fuck, Rave? This isn't like you at all. Are you fucking him?"

Caelian steps forward, his hand going around Reggie's neck as he slams him against the lockers. "Don't ask fucking questions."

"Caelian, stop!" My eyes pop into saucers as I race forward, pulling on his arms to release Reggie. He does as I ask, his fingers releasing, and he steps back, his eyes blanking out as they connect with mine.

"I'll meet you at your car." With that, he snaps his fingers and Rosko walks with him out of the locker room, giving me one last glance before they exit.

Reggie looks perturbed, though not surprised as he rubs at his neck.

"Are you fucking him?" he asks quietly after a moment.

My eyes widen, and I shake my head. "Of course not! What the hell, Reggie!" I walk to my bag, pulling my hoodie out and shoving it over my head. *Does it smell like my arousal in here?* My cheeks flame as the memory of what just happened rushes through me, but I ignore it and give him a look. "I'm asking him to train me. Is it that much of a problem?"

He points at my face. "He trains you while also eating your fucking face?"

I turn around, glancing at the wall with the floor-to-ceiling mirror. My jawline has teeth marks along the edge, each tooth indented neatly into my skin.

I rub at the marks, my cheeks growing warm all over again. "It's complicated."

He laughs, though there's no humor at all. He sounds pissed. Fucking livid, actually. "Let me tell you something, Raven."

I unwrap my hands, flexing them and feeling the ache in each knuckle. I pull out my socks and shoes from my bag and slip them on. "Go ahead, then."

He sighs, crossing his arms over his buttoned-up chest. "You've been coming here for a while now, and I know shit isn't easy for you. Neither Corgan nor I really know what the fuck is going on at home, but we know it isn't good. If you're looking for help, I don't know if Caelian is the way to go with it."

I narrow my eyes. "Why would you say that?"

He stares at me. "Caelian will rip you to shreds and laugh in your face, darling. We don't want you getting hurt."

"Why would I be the victim? Isn't anyone curious if I would hurt him?"

He puffs out a laugh. "You can't hurt what doesn't feel, Raven. That man doesn't have an emotion in his body. If I were you, I'd keep your guard up with that one. What looks good with the eyes might not be as pretty on the inside."

"Good thing I'm not looking for anything. He's just training me, Reggie."

He sighs and gives a small shake of his head. "Whatever you say, Raven."

I zip up my bag, pulling the strap over my shoulder. Heading toward the door, I stop with my hand on the handle, glancing back to look at him. "Though, Reggie. If I were looking for anything, it wouldn't be pretty. My own heart is pretty fucking ugly."

He appears angry at my words, and as I head out of the locker room, his words stop me in my tracks.

"Your heart is the only pure thing in this hellish place. It's beautiful, and if anyone hurts it, I'll kill them." His words warm and cool me to the bone. I wish I could respond, but my bruised heart is lodged in my throat, refusing any words to escape. I bite my lip as I leave the locker room and head down the hall, walking through the tunnels with my mind running a mile a minute.

My mind is a jumbled mess as I walk through the tunnel. I can't decipher what's right versus wrong anymore. Everything feels discombobulated. Part of me feels warm, safe, secure from Reggie's words. Like maybe after all these years, I finally have someone in my corner. That maybe, finally, there's someone who likes me for me.

But what he said about Caelian, about him being wrong for me. I know the words are true, but even as I feel that way, I can't find the strength to walk away. He's a drug and every moment around him is another hit I'm willingly giving myself. Every moment I'm around him, is another glimpse of life that I always believed was so bleak.

Yes, he's wrong for me. Yes, we're toxic, horrible together. How could I even like someone like him? He is a ruthless killer and being with someone who is equally or more fucked up than I am should be illegal.

I shouldn't, but it doesn't stop my heart from filling whenever he's around. Drained without him, filled with him.

Both are wrong. One feels right.

I'm shaken from my thoughts as I hear a grunt near the end of the tunnel. I stop in my tracks. My car is only a few extra minutes away, but I feel on alert as the temperature in the tunnel drops.

I walk to the entrance, hopping around puddles and random objects to not make a sound. I don't want to alert anyone to my presence.

Could it be the copycat? Am I this easy to capture? Will they have a weapon?

My breathing becomes choppy, and I feel so out of sorts as I pause, glancing around the edge and into the parking garage.

Fuck. No way.

TWISTED DARES

Caelian stands there with his foot on top of the head of the beefy fuck I was in the ring with. The most startling thing is Rosko, who lays at the feet of Caelian, with his mouth wide open and wrapped around the neck of Beefy Guy. The one I was in the ring with.

One chomp and his veins will empty into Rosko's mouth.

"Please. I'm sorry," Beefy Guy whispers.

Caelian says nothing as he watches his dog. Rosko does nothing as he sits there like a statue, waiting for whatever command his owner will give.

"I know you're watching me, Raven. You're about the least stealthy person I've ever met."

I step out of the shadows, watching Caelian as he's moments from killing the second person in front of me.

"Release him, Rosko." Caelian lifts his foot from the man's head, and Rosko opens his jaw, his teeth retracting as he gets to his feet. Rosko looks at me, and I wonder if it's relief that I see in his eyes at seeing me. It kind of looks that way.

Like he's starting to like me or something.

The man sputters on the ground, and I walk past him, not sure why Caelian had him in this position in the first place. It feels off; wrong that death was about to be doled out on someone that I don't even know.

Is he a bad guy? I don't know. But who chooses who receives the card of death in this life? I certainly don't know if it's supposed to be Caelian.

What am I talking about? I want him to teach me how to kill people so I can eliminate my own aunt and uncle. My parents decided who received death for dozens of people.

Maybe there is no one person who chooses death, and everyone equally becomes a grim reaper to someone in life. Or maybe to many people.

I hear an *oomph* come from the man before I get out of reach, and soon enough, the nails of Rosko and Caelian's heavy footsteps are following behind me as I walk to my car.

I walk through the broken bar, heading outside and seeing Caelian's car parked right next to my Honda. I hit the unlock button, holding my breath and hoping, praying, that there isn't going to be a note on my windshield wiper from the copycat.

No note.

Opening up the back door, I toss my bag inside and open up the driver's side door.

It slams shut.

I jump, looking over my shoulder at a blank-faced Caelian.

"What're you doing?"

He narrows his eyes. "Why are you acting like that?"

"Like what?" No use in telling him about the twisted puzzle of my feelings. A fucking jigsaw with not one piece put together. That is how I'm feeling.

Manic.

"Like you are upset." He says the words slowly, like he can't even comprehend why I'd be feeling this way.

I sigh. "Why were you pinning him to the ground? Rosko was about to fucking eat him."

He narrows his eyes. "He touched you."

My jaw slackens. "Um, it's called the Inferno? I fight. We touch. Body parts collide." What the fuck is he talking about?

He clenches his jaw, and I can see the ticking of the tension deepening in his muscle. *Is he angry?*

"I don't think you understand. *He. Touched. You.*"

I shake my head, damn flabbergasted at what the hell he means. "No, I don't think *you* understand. You fight in the ring. You aren't going to fight and not touch each other. It's like asking to play basketball without ever touching the ball. It's inevitable."

He steps up to me, and I step back, my body molding flush with my car. "Do you know what's also inevitable? Death. All it would've taken is one small command and Rosko could've torn his throat out."

"Why would you do that?" I shriek.

"*He. Touched. You,*" he growls, repeating himself.

I shove at his chest, but he doesn't budge, only pushing me farther up against my car. "I don't understand why it's such a big deal."

His fingers go to my ponytail, wrapping his hand around my hair a few times, until my head cranks back, and my eyes connect with his. "I don't think you understand. No one lays a fucking finger on you. Not one person. If they do?" His hand goes around my throat, and he squeezes until my air is constricted, and breathing seems impossible. "I'll rip their throat from their neck," he whispers in my ear.

I blink at him, confused. Scared. Slightly thrilled. "Why do you care?"

His hands go to each side of my jaw, and he directs my face only a breath away from his. He crowds me against my car, so I have not even an inch of space to breathe. But he doesn't care, because all I can breathe in is him, and it's enough. It's more than enough.

"Because you're mine. And no one fucking touches what's mine." His words are simple, but so fucking complex. A million reasons come out of his words, and each one is an arrow straight to my chest.

"Training tomorrow. Don't be late." With that, he walks away, opening the door to his car so Rosko can hop in the back.

I open my door again, ready to slip inside when a whimper leaves my lips.

"What?" He's there instantly, at my side as he shoves me out of the way. "You left your fucking car door unlocked?" he growls.

"No. No, I fucking didn't, actually." Panic starts rolling through my veins at what that means. My car was locked and *he* somehow still found a way inside and was able to lock it again.

Chills break down my spine.

A small cardboard box sits in my seat. Black with a red ribbon tied around the top. It looks so delicate, yet I know it's filled with a sinister surprise. I don't need to open the box and look at the contents to know I'm not going to like it.

"Open it," I whisper. There's no way in hell I could. The air is ominous. It feels wrong and eerie as we stand here in the darkened alleyway.

He glances at me briefly before reaching in and lifting the small box out. He pulls on the red ribbon tied around the black cardboard box. It's small, but it feels bad. Evil.

But it also confuses me, because my parents never left any gifts, or evidence, or anything behind. The pattern isn't there. It doesn't make sense. From what Caelian said, there were no other gifts for the other victims.

So why me? Why now?

The red string loosens and falls to the ground. He holds the box tightly, his fingers going to the fold on top. He lifts it, tilting it away from me so he can look inside. I watch his eyes, not able to look inside the dark corners of the box. I don't want to know what it is.

But I know… I know I have to.

"Fuck," he says, and my eyes instantly drop inside, seeing a heart. A real, dead heart, bloody and cold, sitting in the depths of the box. Pinned to the muscle is a small piece of paper, with a drawing.

My crow.

I feel sick, and I glance away from the heart. Whose is it? A victim's? A random stranger's?

"Fuck, this isn't good. Maybe I need to bring this to the police. Tell my aunt and uncle." Nothing feels right. I feel like I need to tell someone, get some protection on me until they can figure out what's really going on.

"No. Absolutely not." He pulls the box out of my reach, picking up the heart with his bare hands and looking beneath it. "Wait."

I squeeze my eyes shut. *There's more?*

"A note," he answers, like I voiced my thoughts out loud.

He hands it to me, and I know he wants me to open it myself. Hesitantly, I lift the tiny, folded paper from his fingers and unwrap it, seeing the familiar chicken scrawl made in a messy black ink.

Four, five, six,

Hear that? Your heart ticks.

Time is running out.

How many more minutes until you are mine?

The paper is ripped from my fingers, and I can feel the air grow hot with tension. He crumples the paper and shoves it in his pocket, setting the heart back in the box and tucking it under his arm.

"Why a heart?" he asks, his voice firm. Like he's pissed at me. Fucking pissed at me for what?

"Tick, tock, like a heart? He's telling me my life is on borrowed time."

"Do you think your dad would know who's doing this?"

I curl in on myself, hating even thinking about him. I haven't seen him, spoken to him, or even tried to think about him in years. I know he's in prison for the rest of his life, but I haven't so much as received a message from him. I tell myself I don't care, though that's just another lie.

"No. He wouldn't." And that's the truth. My dad is a selfish man. He cared about his cult and his murderers and his women. Did he ever even love me? That's something I'll never know.

He probably doesn't even know there's a copycat on the loose. And if he does, I bet he's losing his mind about it. The thought of someone else pretending to be him. It's got to be making him itch.

"I think you need to go talk to him. See who could be doing this."

I whip my head back and forth. Absolutely not. "No. *Fuck no.*" I spin around, sliding into the seat of my car. I'm ready to shut the door when Caelian's hand latches onto it, stopping me from shutting it.

"Caelian, I need to go. My aunt and uncle have been on edge these last few weeks, and I can't be late."

I watch him eye me down. Stare at me and read every little thought in my brain. He looks so uncomfortable, like a knife is embedded in his back.

"Why are you looking like that?"

He glares down at me. "You have a serial killer after you, your psychotic aunt and uncle are abusing you, and you just had some guy jacked on steroids lay his entire body on you and punch you in the kidneys repeatedly," he seethes, and I swear his eyes glow red. "Any other reason you want to add to the list of why I fucking look like this right now?"

He looks so angry. So fucking angry, and I didn't realize he could have emotions like this. He seems so empty and closed off, so for him to look this full of fury, well, I don't know how to react to it.

"Never mind," I mumble.

"I'm following you home. Think about going to see your dad." He sees my face and cuts me off with a snap of his teeth. "This isn't for you, Raven. This is for the other girls out there who will most definitely fucking die if we don't catch whoever is doing this. How many more hearts is this fucker going to deliver to you before you realize you can't just sit around and hope it all goes away?"

I mash my teeth together, the pain shooting up to my ear from the tension. *I can't.*

I can't fucking deal with this right now.

A glance at the clock shows me I should've been home by now. I have to go.

"I have to go, Caelian. I'll see you tomorrow." I pull the door closed, and this time he lets me, walking off like I mean nothing at all.

chapter nineteen
CAELIAN

I don't understand.
I don't understand an ounce of it. Why I'm even driving the twenty minutes to Raven's house is a fucking huge question mark, but just as Rosko's instinct is to attack when he senses danger, my instinct in this situation is to follow her the hell home and make sure the copycat isn't on her property, and that her fucking aunt and uncle don't get handsy with her.

She drives fast, and I can sense her nerves from here. Even Rosko sits in the backseat with his hair raised, knowing that shit is going on that neither of us can't really do anything about.

By the time she pulls off the highway, it's pitch black outside. She drives through the edge of town until the houses spread farther and farther apart. Eventually, it's nothing but trees upon trees. Raven pulls off onto a driveway, rolling down the gravel road and up to an old two-story farmhouse home situated gently between trees and sprawling green grass. I stay a distance away, flicking off my headlights as I watch her pull behind three other vehicles and switch off her car.

The downstairs lights are on, and the front door opens, two shadows lighting up the doorway.

It must be the aunt and uncle.

Her aunt is thin and a few inches taller than Raven. Her hair is curled into tight spirals, and she wears a button-up blouse and jeans. The uncle has a receding headline, and I can see his suspenders attaching his pants around his shoulders. I can't see their faces, nor their expressions, but I can sense the both of them.

They hate her. Despise her with everything in their blood. I watch Raven and how her entire body freezes, tension tight through each of her limbs as she walks up to them. She hates them just as much, and I can feel the hysteria from across the lawn, through the dark trees. She doesn't try to hide her fury, or her distaste for them. She wants them to know.

Her mania is showing.

Her aunt and uncle separate, and Raven turns to the side so she can't touch either of them as she slips into the house. The door shuts, and the lower-level lights turn off.

None turn on upstairs.

I wait for a long time. Too long, if I'm being honest. I hope for the copycat to come. I hope to hear noises coming from inside the house that I shouldn't hear.

But nothing does.

I realize I can't wait any longer; I have to get home. There's so much shit to do, but I'm spending my entire night on the side of the road, watching, waiting, hoping for something to happen so I can fill this need in my chest that's been simmering for weeks.

I need a kill. More than that, I know Raven needs one, too.

I pull up at home, Rosko standing at my shoulders and eager to get out. I open his door, and he leaps onto the ground, heading toward the front door. I follow him inside, shoving the boxed heart under my arm as I walk in and see both of my brothers standing there with curious as fuck looks on their faces.

"Why do you both look like you're about to interrogate the fuck out of me?" I growl, knocking against Gabriel's shoulder as I head to the kitchen.

"I'm wondering why you're spending all your free time with some random chick who's connected with the copycat Crow Killer. Is this some new way you're trying to get information?" Gabriel asks, right on my heels.

I open the dark cabinet and grab a low glass from the bottom shelf. Then I take the bottle of scotch already on the counter and pour myself half a glass. "Why are you so fucking curious?"

He looks at me like I'm stupid. "You don't like people, Cae. You don't talk to them; you don't even look at them. So why are you so wrapped up in this one?"

Why? That's the biggest question of the day. Why is she wrapped in my thoughts as tightly woven as she is? Why do I even care enough to bring her to my house? To train her? To make sure she's okay at home?

I down my drink, instantly filling up a second glass. This one is filled to the brim. I down that one, too.

"Shit, Gabe. He's real fucked up." Matteo laughs.

I scowl at him, not in the mood for either of their shit. "Don't fucking pay attention to me. I'm handling shit."

Gabriel's face blanks out, his eyes becoming inquisitive. "Tell me how she's connected to the copycat."

I look at my empty glass, debating if I want to refill it a third time.

I slide it away from me, knowing they won't stop until I give them at least a little.

"Her father is the real Crow. Cash Crow."

Matteo's eyes grow wide. Gabriel just looks pissed.

"The fuck? She tell you that?" Gabriel asks.

I nod.

"How do you know she's not lying? You don't fuck around with a lot of females, Caelian. They lie all the fucking time."

I narrow my eyes, gnashing my teeth together as I stare at him. Does he think I'm fucking inept? Asking me whether or not someone is lying? I fucking deal with this shit for a living.

"Don't fucking offend me again, or I'll knock you on your ass."

He stares at me, not backing down even an ounce.

Matteo steps between us, his fingers tapping each of our chests. "Okay, so the bitch is the daughter of Cash Crow. What is she doing here? Why is she coming here upset last night, like you can help her? There's more to this than just figuring out who the copycat is."

I run my tongue along my teeth. "I'm training her."

Matteo's eyes go wide. "Training her? To fight?"

"To kill," I snap.

Gabriel backs away, a laugh-scoff mix bursting from him. "What do you get out of this? Training the daughter of a killer how to kill."

"I get nothing." I say the words and hate them as they come out, because they're partially false. It feels like I get so much more than nothing, but I don't know how to articulate the words. Even if I could, I'd never speak them to my brothers.

"It's just weird," Matteo starts, dropping his arms to his sides. "You aren't even this interested in pussy, yet this little Crow walks around and suddenly you can't keep away from her? Fucking odd."

I shake my head. "I don't really give a shit what it is you think about what I'm doing in my spare time." I pull my glass forward, deciding to go back for that third glass, after all. "I do need your help with something."

They stare at me, waiting.

"She needs eyes on her all the time." I grab the box from the counter and slide it across the island toward them. "The copycat left this for Raven tonight."

They both stare at the box with empty eyes before Gabriel reaches over, grabbing the box and sliding it toward himself. "What is it?" he asks.

I nod to the box. "Open it."

He does, folding open the top. They both lean over the counter, peeking inside. Gabriel's eyes narrow as his eyes fall on the heart.

The dead, bloody heart.

"Holy fucking hell," Matteo grunts.

"Where the hell did you get this?" Gabriel snaps, shoving the box away from him.

"It was in Raven's car after her fight tonight," I sigh, not feeling any closer to figuring out who this motherfucker is than I was when I first learned about him.

"And she got the note?" Matteo asks.

I give him a curt nod.

"Sounds personal," Gabriel grunts.

I bare my teeth. "You think?"

He rolls his eyes. "So, what now?"

"The copycat left her a heart tonight, but what's next? A brain? A full body? I'm thinking it's only a matter of time before he reacts and goes after her. I need an eye on her twenty-four seven."

Gabriel starts chuckling, and Matteo slaps him in the chest, but he has a smirk on his face, too.

"What is so fucking funny?" I growl.

"You like this chick." Gabriel's voice cracks over his laugh, and I can't help myself as I step forward, grabbing him by his shirt and pulling him toward me.

"You're a fucking menace," I spit.

His mouth pops open and another laugh comes out. Matteo laughs from behind him, trying to pull him away. "Stop, Caelian."

"I need someone to watch her tomorrow. I'll be busy, otherwise I would. She's meeting me in the afternoon here for training, but I need an eye on her now and in the morning."

Gabriel mashes his lips together, but his eyes are full of humor.

I can't fucking help it.

My fist snaps forward, and I deck him in the nose. I hear the crack and instant gush of blood that leaks over my fingers. "Clean that shit up before it gets in the cracks on the floor," I grunt, walking away from him.

"You fucking bastard," he garbles around the blood. I hear the sink turn on and know he's doing as I ask.

"Text me her address, Cae! I'll head over there now," Matteo shouts from down the hall. I give him a small nod before I turn the corner, heading into my room and slamming the door shut behind me.

My brothers are my brothers, and I'd fucking kill every motherfucker on this earth to keep them safe. But fucking hell, are they annoying as shit.

But if it means she'll be safe, I'll deal with their bitching. Because I have a feeling in my gut. A twisted feeling that the heart in the box was only just the beginning.

Caelian: Bring an extra set of clothes today.

Raven: Caelian…?

Caelian: Yes.

Raven: That's an interesting way to greet someone. Why do I need an extra pair of clothes?

Caelian: Training.

I pocket my phone with a sigh, ignoring the next vibration that alerts me to an incoming text. She'll bring an extra pair of clothes regardless of if I answer her question. She's eager, and I can't help the sigh of relief I had earlier when Matteo told me there was no screaming and no random visitors in the middle of the night.

Though, if the copycat is as intelligent as I think he is, he knows we're on to him, and he's going to be stealthier than he's ever been. Being able to carve out a heart and keep it intact, no nicks or injuries in the delicate muscle, is a job that an amateur can't fulfill. This guy knows what he's doing, and he's going to plan his next attack with great care.

It's unfortunate I'll be one step ahead of him.

Grabbing my keys and my leather jacket, I give Rosko a nod as I head out. He hates being left behind, and I know he's growing edgy for an attack, just as I am. He doesn't need to be upset, though, because he'll have his fun later today.

Hopping in my car, I check the address on my phone and punch it into my GPS. It brings me to the dirty end of downtown Portland. To the disgusting apartments that are ridden with cockroaches and prostitutes. It shouldn't surprise me that my next toy will be here. Those who dabble in the dirty are usually more mixed in with the bad than I initially anticipate.

A simple drug runner likes to catch prostitutes on his spare weekends. It doesn't matter if he's married and has kids, weak knees and big tits always lead to a busted nut.

But this guy, Gregory Champlain. He's known to spend his weekends driving the corners, waiting for his next fill—male or female, doesn't matter too much to him. He brings them back to his secondary apartment that no one knows about except him.

And now me.

Learning about this guy's patterns has been nothing short of interesting. Watching as he brings his victims back to his apartment and put a pill in their drinks. Then he has sex with them as brutally as he wants before hauling them down to the infirmary, which is conveniently located a block from his house, and tossing them in there to burn to a fiery ash.

I've been watching him for a while. The occasional hit has increased with such frequency that I know I can't hold off any longer. It started out with me watching him because he was buying drugs from one of our shady dealers, and I ended up with such a better surprise.

I head into the city, cutting and swerving through the high-end areas until I hit the depilated neighborhoods that are hidden from the normal civilian. They're between the dead ends and the dumpster bins, but the barely standing apartments are near the low-income areas. The smell is atrocious, even with my windows rolled all the way up. It's New York times a thousand. The amount of trash built up and pollution of the city all circulating in this small pocket is like sticking your head into a fat man's sock.

I park on the outskirts, knowing if I passed over the threshold of the dump, I'll stick out like a sore thumb. Locking my car, I slip my keys in my pocket and head down the side of the alley. The shouts from inside the apartment are obnoxious, the paper-thin walls not anywhere near thick enough to hide the domestics going on.

The front door of the apartment building where Gregory lives is propped open with an empty beer case. I pull my hood over my head, tilting my face toward the floor as I walk in. The strong scent of piss invades my nose, and I take shallow breaths as I head up the trash-ridden steps and up to the second floor.

I look for room two-nineteen, the mix of too many smells and my shallow breaths making me lightheaded. I don't know how people can fucking live this way. How people in the city haven't burned this place to the ground. It's a fucking monstrosity and tainted sore for the rest of America.

Ah, two-nineteen.

I press my pointer finger over the peephole and lean my head forward. The fucker better be home. My brief digging showed he doesn't usually leave his house until after dinner time.

Fucking creep.

When no sounds are heard, I press my hand on the knob and turn, wanting to laugh at the easy release of the knob.

He doesn't even lock his door.

My face twists in disgust as the smell of body odor mixed with marijuana and beer smashes me in the face. Better get this over with, and *quick*.

I walk quietly through the apartment, which feels about the size of a shoebox. Through the cube-sized kitchen that is littered with empty beer bottles, and the living room that only hosts a recliner chair and box TV that sits on the ground. Heading to the back room, the door is closed, but I don't wait to listen, wanting to get this over with. I throw open the door, letting the knob crash against the wall.

I sneer, seeing Gregory Champlain with his chubby dick in his hands as he whacks it to something on his laptop on his bed.

His eyes go wide at my entrance, and he slams the computer shut.

Whatever is on his computer is *not good*.

"Who are you?" he shouts.

I step toward him, cocking my hand backward and swinging forward, clocking him in the side of the head. He's out like a light.

Reaching into my pocket, I pull the rope and roll of tape out. I dig in one more time, pulling the syringe of etorphine and jab it into his neck. That'll keep him out for a bit.

I get to work, tying his hands behind his back and slapping a strip of tape over his mouth. I leave his feet untied; I can get those wrapped in the car. Then I glance around his apartment, knowing I can come back to inspect this shithole later. Reaching over, I grab his laptop and shove it under my arm.

Moving the items back into my pocket, I lean down, taking the rope between his hands and pulling him across his apartment. He's a heavy fuck, slightly overweight, and absolutely none of it is muscle. The guy sits in his apartment all day, probably jacking off to pictures of shit he shouldn't have access to.

I open the door to his apartment, pulling him into the hall and kicking the door shut behind me. Then I walk down the hall and down the stairs, his body thumping heavily with each bump. I hear footsteps, and the apartment closest to the stairs opens, a hooker that's had too many bumps of coke stepping outside in only a bra and a red leather skirt.

"What the—*Gregory?* Hey! What're you doing?" she shrieks.

I ignore her, pulling him down another stair when she takes a step toward me.

"I'm calling the police!"

I reach behind me, pulling out my Glock from the back of my jeans and pointing it at her, lazily, nonchalantly. "Call the police. I'll be sure to walk them into your apartment and they can haul you away for all the cocaine you have sitting in there." I'm not a fucking idiot. I know every person that lives in Portland and what their extracurricular activities are.

I know this dumb whore in front of me sleeps with half of the married men in Portland. I know she'll do just about anything for a dime of coke. She's a wasteland, and probably ridden with STDs.

"You son of a bitch," she sneers at me.

I keep my gun pointed at her and continue walking down the steps. "Call them if you'd like. Or walk back into your apartment, take a bump, and act like I never walked these halls."

She says nothing as she stares at me, detecting the power I have over her. She walks backward into her apartment, giving me a scathing look before she slams her door shut. I sigh, shoving my gun back into my jeans and finishing my walk down the stairs.

I head outside, dragging him across the dirty Portland street, and walking behind the dumpster. I leave him there, shoved in the corner, damp from the streets filled with gravel and piss.

I head to my car, jumping in and pulling around the corner and parking behind the dumpster. I pop open my trunk, hopping out and grabbing Gregory, toss him inside, then pull the rope from my pocket and cinch it around his ankles.

Slamming my trunk closed, I hop back into my car, driving out of the dump and back home. With a glance at the clock, I know it's only a matter of time before Raven shows up, ready to start her training for the day.

This next test will be the ultimate test. If she can make it through this day, she'll be able to make it through all the days.

I try to tell myself that she's bad for me. That I can't be with anyone. I'm not the right type of human. My DNA isn't made for a companion. I'm meant to be alone, and I've come to terms with that fact. It's never bothered me before, so it shouldn't bother me now.

But as the days go on, and as I spend more and more time with Raven, I have to repeatedly tell myself she isn't mine. She is *not* mine.

Then I see her, my skin touches hers, I look into her eyes, and the words slip my lips, unabashed, and so fucking true. *She's mine.*

I swallow down my groan at my confused thoughts as I get off the highway and turn onto the long driveway leading toward home, with a body in the back of my car, my chest speaks otherwise. I feel like the alpha of the pack, bringing home dinner for his mate. I bring her the kill.

I provide her the gifts.

I may not be meant to be with anyone, but that doesn't take away from the fact that I know what Raven I have might be toxic. It might be a lethal combination. Two maniacs together doesn't lead to peace and harmony, it'll lead to a futile combination. But it doesn't matter to me. None of it matters. I know what she is.

She *is* mine.

Raven: I'm here.

I pocket my phone, glancing at Gabriel who sits at the kitchen table with Gregory's laptop.

"Raven is here. I'll be unavailable for the next few hours." In other words, stay the fuck out of my space.

Gabriel's eyes shift to mine, like he knows exactly what I mean. "If you fuck her or kill her, you're going to have a shitstorm that you aren't going to want to clean up."

I let out a whistle, and the clicking of Rosko's nails running across the house saves me from having to respond.

Rosko runs up to me, his ears perked and his tongue hanging from his mouth. He's anxious, and more than that, he's hungry.

I walk through the house with Rosko beside me as my blood begins to warm. It seems to whenever she's around, and I haven't determined whether I like it.

I head into the gym, across the empty room and to the back door. Rosko stops near the ring, and I glance at him as I open the door for her. Raven stands there, in a hoodie and dark jeans, her backpack strapped to her back.

"Hi," she says softly.

I open the door wider, stepping aside to let her in.

She walks through, her lips lifting into a smile when she sees Rosko. She pulls the backpack from her shoulders, dropping to a knee and unzipping her bag. She pulls out a ball of tinfoil, unraveling it and holding out a piece of meat. She extends her hand, the meat in her palm.

Rosko's nose twitches as the scent reaches him, and he lunges forward, inhaling the food off her hand in one quick motion.

I look at her curiously, and a little put off. *Why the fuck is she feeding my dog?*

She looks over at me and sees my face. "Why?" is all I ask.

She frowns. "I couldn't go get a real dog treat." She shrugs. "I don't know, I just wanted to give him something. He's been a good boy. He hasn't eaten me yet."

I run my tongue along my teeth. It feels like I'm taking too big of a bite, like I can't quite swallow right. "Don't feed my dog," I grumble, turning away from her and heading into the ring.

"Your owner is crazy." I hear the whisper behind me, and I squeeze my eyes shut on a sigh. I want to throw her on the ground and show her she has no fucking say in anything around her. She lives life too willingly, like everything is just… fine. It's not fine, and she's too much of a wild card to live so freely.

She puts me on edge, more than the copycat and Gregory and Trina all put together. She makes me feel more out of sorts than I've ever felt in my entire life.

She also makes my cock harder than it's ever been. Who the fuck has that say? I've fucked models and fucking TV stars and women who are only dressed in diamonds and crystals. They barely make my dick stir.

Raven? She makes it a fucking stone.

"Caelian?" Her voice disrupts my thoughts, and I turn around, seeing her pull her sweatshirt over her head, only a black sports bra remaining. She has a pair of sweats on her lower half, slim yet comfortable. Her hair isn't in a ponytail yet, a mess of locks tumbling over her shoulders. "Is everything all right?" she asks gently.

I blink at her, hating the soft lilt in her voice. I hate how on the outside she looks so beautiful and soft. Even her skin is soft, clear, so creamy I want to dig my fingers in and bruise every inch. Then on the inside, she's filled with such chaos and darkness. She's so much like me, yet so different.

She is the missing puzzle piece. She is the anchor that I didn't realize was missing. She'll keep me tethered to the earth when the rest of me wants to get lost in the insanity.

"Get in the ring, Raven." I turn around, ripping my shirt over my head as I go to my side of the ring. We're going from start to finish today. The attack, the kill, the cleanup, every single part. If at any time she shows a weakness, she's not ready.

She does as she's told, stepping in with ease and walking to her end of the ring. "I'm not going easy on you today, Raven. Remember what I taught you."

She watches me, keeping her hands down but ready. I stand there, watching her, waiting for a slip, a show of weakness, a blip in her exterior.

I step left, then whip right, my arm snaking out and wrapping around her waist.

First fail.

I lift her in my arm, diving down and slamming her back against the mat.

Crack.

She socks me in the eye, then hits me in the other one, stunting me for only a second. I press into her, a genuine need to cause her pain coming to the forefront. My fingers dig into her hair, and I pull her head back, listening as the threads pop free from her scalp.

She screams, her fingers clawing at my skin as she tries to escape me.

"Look at what you're doing, Raven. Fucking fight me." I loosen my body on top of her, flipping her over so her face mashes into the mat. I press into her again, the hardness in my pants shoving straight between her legs. She moans out a painful, pleased groan as she shoves her ass into my erection. I grab her head and tilt it to the side, exposing her slender, tensed neck. "You aren't doing a very good job," I rasp, bending down and biting her neck. I'm not gentle and can instantly feel the skin break under my teeth.

She shrieks and attempts to get out from under me. I pin her harder, and she brings her hand back, her nails scoring the back of my neck. I grunt as a bite of pain rolls through me. Rolling my hand forward, I bring it down to the side of her breast, feeling the soft skin against my palm. I drag my fingers down over her soft curves until my fingers reach the waistband of her sweatpants.

I yank them down in one quick go, exposing her bare ass.

Fucking hell, is it delectable.

I grab it and squeeze, and that's what snaps her thread of sanity.

With strength that I didn't know she had, she rolls underneath me and brings her knee up, ready to kick me in the balls. I'm fast, though, my hand going to her kneecap and spreading her legs wide, her pants still suctioned around her thighs. Her hand goes up, and she punches me, her fists filled with so much fury it surprises me. She gains the upper hand, hitting me over and over in as many places her fist can connect. She flips me over until she's straddling me. She continues to pummel me, my nose, my eyes, and my cheeks taking the brunt of her force.

She is a force.

My arms snap forward, and I grab her hands, pulling them down at her sides. I'm hard. Harder than I've ever been as I shift my hips forward, grinding into her.

Her eyes glaze over.

"Good job." My face throbs, and she might even have given me a black eye, but it was worth it.

To know she can successfully take someone down that can cause her harm, it's totally worth it.

"Now to the next step," I hedge.

Her eyes go wide. "What?"

I get up, lifting her in the air with me. My hands go to her bare ass, and I give it a tight squeeze before pulling her pants back up to her waist. She tenses in my arms, her hands instinctively going around my neck. Her finger brushes the back of my hair, and she looks down at me, her ankles cinched tightly around my waist. "What are we doing?"

What are we doing?

That is the big question, and one I don't have an answer to. Not an honest one, anyway.

She bends down, her lips settling against mine. She starts soft, but quickly turns aggressive as her tongue plunges between my lips. She isn't usually this dominant, and I can tell by the way she moves that she's still a bit hesitant because of her lack of experience, but she's needy, greedy as she latches her body against mine and takes what she wants. What she is so fucking desperate for.

I bring my hand up to the back of her neck, squeezing and manipulating her exactly how I want her. Pliant. At my mercy. She crumbles in my hand, her dominance weakening until she's a submissive body.

I demolish her.

I bite at her lips and battle with her tongue until she allows me to show her how I want her. Her lips grow swollen between mine.

She starts grinding needlessly against me, and my hands grow tense; I know it's Raven that feeds my hunger.

I need death. I need blood. *I need Raven.*

I rip my mouth from hers, peeling her body from mine and setting her on the ground. She looks up at me like she's angry with me, and I understand her pent-up tension. I feel the same. But I'm never one to take my tension out on sex. That's not the way I'm wired. I take it out with murder and blood.

"Next step," is all I say.

"What's the next step?" she breathes, her voice still winded from her need to get off.

"Rosko," I order, stepping off the mat. He gets up from where he's been laying, and I begin to walk toward the other back door. The door that leads to the basement.

My sanctuary.

"Where are we going?" she asks, her bare feet slapping against the floor as she races after me.

I glance at her over my shoulder. "You ask a lot of questions."

She sighs audibly. "This is part of my training?"

I nod at her as I open the door, the darkened stairwell leading to the place I can be who I really am. And now this is the place I will make Raven who she needs to be.

"Caelian, this is kind of scary." She stalls at the top of the stairs, even with Rosko walking down them and turning the corner without any direction. His tail even wags. He knows what's coming.

"To become what you want to be, you must show me that you can handle it. Can you handle it, Raven?"

She licks her lips, worry and hesitation shining in her eyes. With a slight nod, her hand grabs the railing, and she takes a step down. Then another. Until she reaches me, her eyes wanting so much reassurance that I don't know how to give.

I give her a nod, walking down the rest of the stairway and taking a left. Raven stays close behind me as I head down the dark hallway. I turn one last corner, the basement just a maze of tunnels much like the Inferno. This place is high quality, bulletproof, soundproof steel, and if you're locked in, you will never, ever get out. Rosko sits in front of the door, and I run my hand over his head as I pull the key from my pocket.

"What's in there?" she whispers.

I ignore her as I shove my key in the lock and turn, the click of the lock disengaging sounding loud over Raven's panicked breaths.

I shove the key back in my pocket as I open the door. Raven's shocked gasp sounds behind me as Rosko trots inside, walking up to the wall across from Gregory and sitting down.

I made this scene much like my vision of my first kill. Any and all types of weapons for her to choose from. The only other thing in the room is Gregory, strapped and taped to the chair. His eyes are wide as he watches us, bare, naked with his pale, hairy skin a stark contrast beside the dark room.

Raven steps inside, and I close the door, giving her a moment to take it all in.

"Next step?" she confirms.

I nod. "If you really want to become the person you are meant to become, you have to show me that you're capable. If you can't, you aren't ready."

"And, what, am I just supposed to kill this random man?"

I step forward. "This isn't some random man. He's a murderer, Raven. He's killed a lot of people."

Her brows lift. "Like you?"

I gnash my teeth together. "No. Not at all like me. This man rapes and murders people and lets their bodies burn in the ghetto where they'll never be found. Not only that, but my brother has his laptop and found a lot of child pornography on his hard drive. Go back to that time when you were a child and some man touched you. How does it make you feel, knowing some predator was after you? Think about the scared children, Raven. How does this make you *feel?*"

"Angry." Her voice wobbles. She doesn't have the conviction yet. She's not strong enough to take a life. But she will be. I can see it in her eyes.

"Not angry enough." I step around her, watching her breasts heave against her black sports bra. Her stomach is toned, twitching and damp from our fight only a short while ago. She glares at me. She's angry by my words, but she needs to concentrate on that anger if she wants to take the next step.

"What if this was your aunt and uncle. What if I had them sitting right here in front of you, taped and tied to a chair. How would you react? Would you still be hesitant?"

Her mouth drops open, like she doesn't know how to react. She wants to be angry. *She is angry*. But she isn't angry enough.

"Tell me how you feel, Raven." I step in front of her, blocking her view of Gregory, who is still barely conscious. Only in the beginning stages of alertness, he hasn't even found his voice or figured out where he is.

She looks up at me, her eyes so open and revealing. She wants me to know her emotions, and they're painful to see. To see someone who has the same desires as I do but to actually feel with them.

To want to kill and feel remorseful about it.

I bet it feels terrible.

"Scared. Excited. Like I should feel bad about wanting to kill this man who gets turned on by little kids and who is obviously your enemy. I don't want to kill people who haven't wronged me, but I also don't want to see him leave this room alive."

"So, tell me what you want to do about it." She has to be the decision maker. I won't force her hand. If she wants to take this step, she has to do it on her own. The same decision I was given. If she's not ready, well, then she's not fucking ready.

She turns around, facing the wall of weapons. I watch her gaze go to the knives, her eyes flaring just a touch. She reaches forward, her fingers gliding over each one. The short ones, the tall ones. The ones with long, thin blades, and the ones with short, wider blades. Her fingers pause on an older one. One of my favorites. It's matte black around the handle, worn and slender, with a shiny silver blade. It's feminine.

She lifts it, her pointer finger going to the tip. She pushes down until a dollop of blood falls down the blade. "I've been keeping something from you, Caelian." Her eyes go to mine, and she's so nervous and on edge it raises my guard. I feel like she's about to say something that's going to make me have to kill her.

And I hate the fact that I would really fucking hate to do that.

"This won't be the first time I draw blood."

My eyebrow lifts. "You've killed before?"

She shakes her head, her ponytail loosening from the action. "I've never killed. But I've caused pain. I've drawn blood." She walks toward the man, her steps slow but sure. She's forcing herself to be strong, but I can smell the fear coming off her. "I always liked to draw when I was younger. There wasn't much to do in the middle of the desert, being homeschooled and having no friends. I didn't have anything to do in my spare time. My mom bought me this big drawing pad and some really nice colored pencils, and I'd always draw. Mostly when they had their parties, I'd go in my room and draw to drown out everything going on around me."

Her eyes glaze over, and I know she's in the past. Whatever memory holds her, it's keeping her locked away until she spills whatever secret she's been holding. Whatever it is, it weighs heavily on her. It's a burden on her shoulders.

I keep quiet, not wanting to interrupt or keep her from telling me the truth of her past.

"My favorite part was shading. Holding the colored pencil to the side and shading dark to light. I shaded almost everything that I drew, and I ended up getting really good at it." She clears her throat, and I clench my hands into fists to stop from going toward her. Comforting her. "My favorite drawing was a crow. I thought it was symbolic for our last name. The black eyes and feathers turned out so good. I drew it all the time, to the point where almost my entire notepad was filled with birds. Until one night, my dad and mom called me outside after one of their parties. I knew something wasn't right when they asked me to go to the shed. It was so, so fucked up. My dad handed me a blade that looked just like this one." She holds it up, the blade shining in the dark light, her blood dried on the cool metal. "And asked me, his artist daughter, to draw something symbolic on one of their victims. I wanted to impress him. To impress the both of them. I wanted them to love me so much that I took the knife without thinking twice about it and carved the only thing I perfected. A crow."

She looks up at me, her eyes watery, her knuckles white as she grips the handle of the knife. "I never drew again on my notepad. It gathered dust in my room, but I can't tell you how many times I had to draw the outline of a crow on one of their victim's foreheads."

"Fucking hell," I say after a few minutes. That's fucked up. Like, I know I started killing at a young age. But it was in my blood. From what Raven tells me, she was never meant to kill, but her parents trained her, molded her to become a killer.

She's been fighting it for years, and now here she is, ready to take a life, and she holds the knife that mostly represents her parents.

How fucking symbolic.

"I've never taken a life, but I've drawn blood. A lot of it. I just don't know how to murder someone." She takes a deep breath, her confidence wavering more and more by the second. Her eyes clash with mine, no longer watery, but so, so desperate. "Will you help me, Caelian?"

Without even realizing it, my feet make their way over to her. Gregory is starting to stir, his eyes growing more alert. He watches Raven, his gaze falling to her hand with the knife, his lids disappearing behind his saucer-sized eyes. He mumbles behind the tape, and Raven doesn't flinch, doesn't look fazed in the slightest. Her eyes stay locked on mine, awaiting a response.

I stalk toward her, my bare feet on the floor silent as I step up to her. Her eyes flare, her nose twitching like she can smell me. Smell my power, my dominance, my ability to rip life from this earth like it never existed in the first place. She doesn't realize the monster that lurks beneath my skin is much more dangerous than she could ever imagine.

TWISTED DARES

She wants the danger, but she never asked for the beast hiding in the dark.

I grab onto her wrist, the one holding the blade, and yank it toward my chest. The blade touches my naked skin, right between my pecs. Her hand tenses, and I know she wants to hold back.

"Don't be afraid. I'm not." Her fingers shake as I say the words, but I grip her tightly, and ever so slightly, they settle.

"You can cut to bleed, and you can cut to kill." My fingers slide up her hand until they wrap directly over hers. I press the tip of the blade into my skin, watching it turn pale white from the pressure.

She gasps.

The blade pierces the skin, and a dollop of blood rolls down my stomach. "Only a real monster can do both. Which one are you?"

She flexes her fingers, pulling the blade down until it cuts a line, only on the surface, down my skin. "The blood that pumps through my veins was made by monsters. I may have only touched the surface, but I can guarantee what lies beneath is much darker."

I nod my head toward a moaning Gregory. "So, show me."

"Help me. Please." Her voice is airy, light but full of the heaviest of words. She doesn't have faith she can do it on her own, or at least she pretends. Maybe deep down she understands the depth of what burdens her, but she needs a nudge to break it free.

I place my hand on her waist, spinning her around so her back hits my front. She faces Gregory, listens to his muffled pleas for the first time. I feel her body ripple with tension, a wave that's full of such force it could knock any man down.

Gregory sits naked before us, his face soggy with tears and his eyes rimmed in a dark red. He continues to plead behind his tape, but I don't pay attention to his words. I only focus on Raven's body.

"This man is your canvas. What you wish to do is your choice. Your options are endless."

She steps forward, out of my hold. I think she's about to let go of me when her fingers swing back, wrapping around my pointer finger. She pulls me forward, until I'm once again wrapped around her. She guides my hands around hers, and she's steady now. In control of every ounce of her body.

She squeezes my hand around hers, like she's trying to work the strength from me into her.

I dip my head, my lips going to the sensitive skin right below her ear. "*I dare you*," I whisper quietly in her ear before pressing my lips to her neck. Goosebumps prickle along her skin, and a shiver breaks out. I give her all my strength, all my power and confidence, and press it into her, wanting her to have every inch, every breath. Everything.

"This is for the children." Her voice is raspy as I pull away from her, filled with sexual need that makes my body coil tight.

Her body is rigid, her eyes filled with a rage as she looks upon Gregory. She knows what she means, and she means what she says. Every word that leaves her lips is full of retribution, and they bleed with pain for every child in the world that has been a victim.

Her hand shoots forward, my fingers still locked around hers as we plunge the knife into his chest. She uses all her strength, and only my guidance as it sinks into his skin. She gasps as the blade fills with red, dripping down his chest and into his naked lap.

Gregory gasps through his moans, the blood loss quickly making his eyes unfocused. I can see when he's gone. That moment where his life leaves, but your heart still beats. His eyes glaze over, and the tension in his body goes slack moments before his head lolls to the side, and his lights go out.

It takes her a moment, but she comes back to herself, pulling the blade from his chest. A splatter of blood flings in the air and hits her arm. I watch it paint her skin, my eyes flicking to hers to see how she will react.

Her eyes blink and slowly lift to mine. They flare with need.

Need.

And I know, without a doubt, this Baby Crow is *mine*.

With a glance over my shoulder, I see Rosko sitting in the corner, his eyes on a dead Gregory. He sits so patiently, though the drool hanging from his mouth tells me exactly what he wants.

His meal.

"Rosko, eat," I order, and he gets up, a growl coming from his lips as he leaps forward, a ravenous snarl breaking free as he sinks his teeth into Gregory's skin.

Raven gasps again, and I turn back to her, watching her wide eyes stare at Rosko as he feasts on his food.

"I was planning to show you the cleanup, but I'll save that for another time." I bend down, my hands going under her thighs and lifting her in the air.

"Where are you taking me?" she asks softly, surprised.

"To show you my monsters," is all I say, sweeping her from the dungeon and back to the gym, ready to claim her once and for all.

It was foolish to pretend she doesn't belong beside me. I should've known it all along. The moment I found someone with as much darkness as I had, I couldn't let her walk away.

Not now. *Not ever.*

chapter twenty
RAVEN

The sound of Rosko growling, splitting skin, breaking bones, and blood dripping to the floor makes me lightheaded. But I don't have to worry about my knees because Caelian holds me tightly in his arms as he walks out of the room, through the dark tunnel and back to the training room.

I can barely see where we're going as his legs walk so quickly, with such purpose, through the room until he steps up, then my back hits the mat of the ring. A combination of soft and hard, but the rough surface scratches against my back.

He brings his hand to my hair, tugging on my ponytail until my hair splays around my head. His fingers comb through my hair, a curiosity in his gaze as they slide through my dark locks. He presses his body against mine, and I can feel the hardness. The hardness of his body and the stiffness of his erection pressing into me, and my eyes go wide.

Does death turn him on? Is it me, or is it the scent of metallic blood that clings to our skin?

Maybe it's the fear which cloaked the man's voice and his muffled pleading to be set free. Even with the tape on his mouth, I could hear the words. My parents never used tape, so I heard each word so clearly as they ripped through their victims.

This man couldn't speak, but I've never heard a cry so loud. I could almost hear him clearer, like the fear spoke through his eyes and not his lips.

My first death.

Should I feel remorseful, or relieved? I don't know what I feel exactly, and my thoughts become jumbled as the scent of Caelian takes over everything in my mind and body, and I can do nothing but look into his dark eyes as he watches me, touches me, feels me, and takes my very essence as his own.

"I don't feel things, Raven," he mumbles, seeming to be lost in his thoughts.

I say nothing, knowing this moment of raw honesty is a rarity from him.

"But when I'm around you, something happens inside me. I wonder if this is what emotion feels like. If there's been something broken inside of me and whatever it is about you just… fixed it. Or maybe it's not an emotion but a *fucking certainty* of fate, and my darkness feeds from yours. I'm always hungry for more, yet I'm satiated when it comes to you. Do you feed my darkness, or am I only momentarily blinded by you?"

His fingers trace the skin of my face. Every groove and dip, sharp corners and soft lips. He moves across every inch, until his hands go below my jaw, his fingers wrapping around my slender neck.

"I don't know what's in your head. Is there any light? Or is there only darkness?" I whisper.

"Pitch black," he says, his fingers tensing slightly.

I want him, but a small part of it feels wrong. The words my aunt and uncle have hammered in my head over the years about being a slut. Being a whore. Being a child of the devil. All these words from the Bible and prayers my aunt and uncle have cast upon me made me feel like a permanently tainted girl.

Like I'd never be clean, no matter how hard I scrubbed.

But the needy part of me wants him. Wants his strength and possessiveness.

The way he looks at me like he's listening. The way he touches me like I've always been his. I'm a person to him, not just a sin.

The way his fingers dig into my hips and thighs, each tip gripped with such purpose that it's addictive.

Caelian is an addiction, and every breath is an overdose.

"I shouldn't. We… shouldn't," I whisper.

His free hand runs down the side of my body, my skin twitching from his light touch. "You have no choice."

My eyes widen slightly. "What? Why wouldn't I have a choice?"

"You became mine the moment you spilt blood. Before that, to be honest. Maybe the first moment I saw you. But you have no choice now, Raven."

His words are so certain, so sure of himself. They're intoxicating. Every breath I inhale, his words, his power, fills my chest. I feel like he's inside me, with only his words.

"My aunt and uncle—"

His hand squeezes my neck, cutting off my words. "Your aunt and uncle will die at your feet. And if not yours, they will die at mine."

My eyes narrow, and I work my throat once he loosens his fingers. "They are not yours to kill."

"Everyone is mine to kill," he snarls, leaning in closely, until his lips brush my jaw. "I play by no rules."

I open my mouth, but I don't know what to say. From the look in his eyes, no one could control him. Even if they tried, they'd never have a chance. He is a dangerous man, one that could break even the strongest souls. He can conquer all.

He sees the words in my eyes. Maybe he can taste them on his lips. He looks angry as he stares at me. Ferocious in the way he breathes down on me. But I watch the control shred to a thin thread. Something that nothing can stop.

It's inevitable.

He leans closer, his mouth coming down onto my parted lips. I breathe him in, and he dips his tongue in my mouth, the scratchiness of his jaw rough and aggressive. His fingers go to my sports bra. To my naked sides. He grips and squeezes, looking for anything and everything. He wants, and he fights against it.

My hands lift of their own will, going to his shoulders as I kiss him back. He growls, evil and pleased, as he pushes me into the mat. I squeeze at his muscles, gripping and feeling them flex against my palms.

His hands become hungry as they attack me, tearing at my clothes like a wild animal. He pulls at the waistband of my leggings, dragging them down in one quick go. My underwear goes with them, and the drunkenness of his power clouds my mind, but the air against my naked sex wakes me quickly.

"Wait." I try to sit up, but he keeps me pinned against the ground. "I can't do this," I say as I tear my lips from his.

He scowls at me. Keeping his hands on me as he drags his fingers to my sex.

I keep my knees pinched together. "I'm a... I've never..." I swallow, seeing the confusion on his face. "I'm a damn virgin."

For the first time since I've met him, a smile breaks free on his lips. It looks maybe a little uncomfortable on his lips, but it's also the sexiest thing I've ever seen. One dimple pops in his cheek, to the left of his lips. The small black hoop in his nose is so hot paired with that smile, and I start to feel a dampness between my legs.

"Why are you smiling like that?" I breathe out, feeling winded and turned on and maybe a little disoriented.

"Because knowing I won't only be the first person, but also the last, makes my blood light on fire." His fingers press between my legs, and my body stiffens, breaking in half between what I want so badly and what I feel I shouldn't have. I don't want to be the person my aunt and uncle say I am, but I also know their lifestyle isn't fucking sane. "There is no greater knowledge than knowing that even your *blood* will belong to me."

I gasp in a breath, or maybe I exhale. I can't be sure with his words, and the dark look in his eyes that intoxicates me and makes my veins electrified.

He nudges my legs open, and I finally take a deep breath, letting my body relax as his hot hand covers my sex. I feel embarrassed, wrong, right, everything in between as his fingers touch the tamed curls between my legs.

It's sinful to groom myself, as my aunt would say, because God made me how I am. And only a harlot would shave themselves naked for the world to see. So, I keep the hair between my legs, but now I'm shy, unsure whether he likes it.

The way his fingers bury into the curls, tugging on the small hairs, makes my cheeks flame. I close my eyes, not sure how to feel about being touched by a man who doesn't even seem to like me but claims me all the same.

"This feels so wrong," I mumble, keeping my lids shuttered over my eyes.

"Everything that is right always feels wrong. You have to get used to the pit in your stomach, because after the twist of regret, you'll feel the most euphoric pleasure." He says the words like he understands emotion, like he knows what it feels like to be in pain from the unknown.

My eyes slip open. "Do you know what it feels like? To want something you shouldn't? To want someone you know isn't good for you?" I tell him how I feel without spelling it out. I want him, because pretending I don't would be foolish. But it feels so wrong, like every breath I take around him is tainted in sin.

His fingers slip between my folds, and I gasp out a breath.

"I feel nothing. Even as a kid, emotion was an abyss I've never traveled. Feeling was as foreign as Latin on my tongue. I've never understood it, and I've never cared to." His finger dips inside my sex, and my face screws up in both pain and pleasure. I've become accustomed to his touch, yet this time still feels like the first. My sex is still too pure, too tight for his strong fingers. There's a pinch of pain with each thrust that gives way to a lick of pleasure.

"Then I meet you, and the thought of any emotion goes from a nuisance to a curiosity. I still don't understand," he rasps, his finger dragging out, and dipping back in. His voice is dripping with lust, so wet and raspy it makes my legs squeeze together around his wrist. "Now I wonder what it would be like, to feel. To exist. To inhale emotions. To exhale life."

My eyes flutter closed as he hits that spot. That barrier inside me that's never been crossed. He feels it, too, by the way his eyes darken to an inky black. "I will relish in the screams as I break you into pieces. Only to put you back together again."

His hand on my neck releases, and he drags it down my body, his fingers turning my flesh to a molten lava. Sweat dampens along my temples, the baby hairs sticking to my forehead.

He scoots down, letting my legs fall over the edge of the ring. He lifts my legs, until they're dangling over his shoulders. My eyes pop open, widening as I lean up on my elbows, attempting to pull my legs off him. "What are you doing? Stop it," I urge, though his dark eyes cause me to pause.

He doesn't say anything, just stares at me, but his hands clamp down, not allowing me to move even an inch. "What are you doing?" I ask again.

"Eating. I want to know what a virgin tastes like. I want to know what *mine* tastes like."

Mine. Mine. Mine.

How can I be his when I don't even know who I am?

He yanks me forward until I fall onto my back. Suddenly, his hot breath is between my legs, his long tongue flattening against my folds. He licks and hits a spot that makes my body jackknife off the mat.

His hand goes forward, pressing on my abdomen, pinning me in place. He licks me again, and *again*, ravaging me until my head is whipping back and forth and I'm screaming for mercy. He keeps hitting this sensitive spot that makes stars appear behind my lids.

"Say please, and I'll let you come," he murmurs against my folds, his voice vibrating through my entire body. It ricochets through my legs and chest and I'm weak to everything except his commands.

"Please. Please let me come," I beg.

His finger curls inside me, and he sucks my clit into his mouth, fast, hard, so aggressively that a new sweat breaks out along my temples, and I *break*.

The familiar sensation of my skin starts to heat, and a tingling rolls through me. Pins and needles, like my foot is asleep, only it runs through my entire body. I can't explain it, but it starts slow, then rushes, like a tidal wave of sensations that takes my breath away.

My limbs lock up, and I let out a scream as Caelian pushes two fingers inside me. A whimper of pain escapes at the stretching sensation. It hurts, and my walls clench around his fingers as the flutters subside.

My heart pounds a thousand beats a minute. My eyes crack open, and I look at the tall ceiling above me. Air inflates my lungs as I take a breath, what feels like my first breath in hours, and then he's there.

Hovering over me. His dark hair curling around his face. Long as it rolls over his head, shaved on the sides. He's an enigma as he looks down at me. Untouchable. Hungry. A beast.

His lips are damp, and bending down, I can smell myself on him. It's tastes sweet and arousing as his lips press against mine. It's exhilarating either way, knowing that he likes what I am, what I taste like, what I'm made of.

"It will hurt. Every part of you will ache," he says, his voice sounding like it's rolling over gravel.

I swallow. "Okay."

He shifts around, and I do nothing but stare into his eyes. The sound of a wrapper tearing doesn't even unlatch my eyes from his. He watches me back, our eyes colliding and locking tight. I tell him about my fears without words, give him every worry and hope. I want to be saved, but don't know how. I only hope that at the end of the day, I won't regret this.

He's helped me spill blood, and now he will spill my blood.

After a moment, he's back, his body molding against mine. I feel a nudge of skin between my thighs, and he wraps his fingers under my knees, pulling them apart and wrapping them around his waist. His hips thrust forward, and an instant burning and pinching begins as his erection prods at my folds. It feels like I'm on fire, like he's lit a match between my legs and is watching it burn. I shove my legs together, but they're blocked by his body molded between mine.

"Stop! It hurts," I cry out, my voice echoing in the large room.

"Breathe through the pain. Embrace it. *Relish it*," he grunts, holding still.

I breathe through my nose, the burning not abating as I wish it would. I want so badly to work through it, but I don't know if I can.

"It hurts," I whimper.

His fingers dance along my jaw, and he grips my chin, pulling my eyes to his. "It will hurt. The pain will be brutal. But at least you feel the pain. Live with it. Fucking enjoy it. You're a monster, Raven. Fucking inhale that pain."

He shoves forward, breaking past the barrier. I let out a howl, excruciating agony ripping through me.

"Tear me to shreds, Raven. Give me your pain." He stills once he's all the way in, not moving, barely breathing, just his massive, thick cock stretching my walls more than they've ever been before. I can feel the nerve endings going haywire, every part of me falling off the precipice.

Soon enough, the pain abates and it's like we become in sync. He exhales as I inhale, and I exhale as he inhales. In and out we go, and my breathing slows.

In. Out. In. Out.

We are one, and what I feel is no longer wrong, but it is all right. Every single thing about this.

Is right.

"Move," I breathe.

He does. He thrusts back and forth, to a point where the pain numbs and all I can feel is what he wants me to feel, and that is… *euphoria*.

"Pain is the only thing that gets me off. Pleasure for you, is pain for me, and vice versa. I want to see the fear in your eyes and the pain from your lips for me to enjoy it." His hand goes up again, and his fingers wrap around my neck. "Do I frighten you?"

I swallow, my neck tensing in his hand. "Sometimes."

His jaw clamps together, a click of teeth sounding out. "There should always be a breath of fear on your lips when it comes to me." His hand clamps down, and my breathing cuts off.

My eyes widen, and I gasp in a breath, but I can't. I can't get in an ounce of air as his thrusts speed up.

"You can't breathe, but you can feel. Something I'm incapable of doing. So, feel every inch of me as your life hangs on by a thread."

He speeds up, fucking me just right. Until I'm lightheaded and dizzy, and the edges of my eyesight begin to fade to black. Everything fades.

Life fades.

And Caelian... he focuses. Everything about him comes to the forefront, and he's everything.

Everything.

My body flushes again, though this time, it's different. It's riveting, and blissful, and my soul breaks from my chest as life fades, and everything goes black.

My eyes pop open, and I gasp in a breath. Caelian stands in front of me, his shirt off as he wipes his neck off with it. I sit up, my hands going to my throat, feeling the sore muscle of my neck. "What did you do to me?"

"You passed out."

"You... choked me!" I screech, horrified. But also scared because... *I enjoyed it.*

"Your life was safe, Raven. Chill the fuck out."

Too many emotions to even grasp onto tear through me, and I scramble up, my hands going between my legs to cover myself as I reach for my pants. "I need to go."

It feels so damp, and one glance down shows my inner thighs covered in smears of blood. I wipe it with my hands, but all it does is spread it more. I'm embarrassed, but one glance up at Caelian, his eyes on the darkness of my insides, and he loves it. His dark eyes, the way his tongue darts out to roll across his lower lip, it tells me everything.

"You shouldn't be embarrassed. You should show it off to the world. Maybe it would save me from having to kill everyone who thinks they can get with you," he mumbles.

My cheeks flame, and I pull my clothes on as I stand up. I'm embarrassed, I'm... turned on. *Still.* It doesn't make sense. I feel like I've lost my mind.

I slip my pants up and pull my phone from my pocket. The screen lights up with a missed call.

Unknown.

They left a voicemail, and my aunt and uncle are more and more making me feel concerned. Aria is worrying me, too. What if this is her, and she ran somewhere? What if she needs help?

I unlock my phone, hitting the voicemail button and pressing Play.

Nothing.

Nothing but breathing. Heavy breathing, but from the pants, it's not a girl.

It's a man.

It sounds edgy, excited. Someone that is planning something. Something evil.

Someone like me. Like Caelian.

My phone is ripped from my hands, and I look over at Caelian as he restarts the voicemail and listens to it from start to finish.

His eyes darken with each second that passes. By the end, his jaw is stone as he grits his teeth. He looks through my phone, and I stare at him, watching him flip through it like he's handled it a thousand times before.

Everything hits me at once. The murder. The sex. My aunt and uncle. Aria. The copycat. Caelian. It's like a tidal wave hits my chest, and I know, without a doubt, what I need to do.

"I think I need to talk to my father."

He cocks his head to the side. "And what made you change your mind?"

I nod at my phone, reaching forward and pulling it from his fingers. "The fact that I'm clearly the next victim. Maybe there's something he knows that I don't. Maybe he can… help."

He looks both pleased and irritated. He knows it's something we have to do, but there's something else that's bothering him.

"Why do you look like that?" I ask.

His teeth bare, and he grits out, "Your parents are the type of people I cut into pieces, and I'm sending you to your dad on a silver platter."

I grimace, hating the fact that my heart jumps. I still care for my parents, even though I shouldn't feel a smidgen of emotion for them.

My phone buzzes, and nerves hit me as I glance down at the screen, blowing out a relieved breath as Aria's name pops up. I unlock my phone and open her text.

Aria: My parents are getting suspicious. Come home.

"Shit. I have to go." I search for my bag, rushing around the ring to grab my belongings.

"Why? What the fuck is going on now?" he snaps.

"My aunt and uncle…" I don't stare at him as I pull my hoodie over my head and slide my backpack over my shoulders. "They don't know where I go. They think I'm doing school stuff at the library in Portland."

"What will happen if they find out you're here?"

My face blanks out, and the rarity of emotion I see in his starts to leak through.

"What the fuck will happen, Raven?" he grits between his teeth.

My fingers raise to the faded burn on my neck. It'll scar, but at least it's not as ugly as it was in the beginning. "I'm punished."

He says nothing, but I swear I can hear his teeth crack.

Glancing at him, fear sinks into my gut, and I'm worried he'll take this into his own hands, sooner or later. "Please don't do anything," I plead.

"When will enough be enough for you, Raven? Why do you let them treat you like that? From what you showed me earlier, killing them won't be a problem for you."

I think of Aria, standing over her parents' bodies with a horrified look on her face. Tortured, pained, scared, and alone. She won't be alone, she'll have me. But I know more than anyone, the loss of your parents will always make you feel alone, whether they are monsters or not.

"Aria. When the time is right, it'll be done. But until then… just let me handle it."

He walks around the ring with purpose, with heavy steps, knowing exactly what kind of person he is as he makes his way toward me. "The next time they hurt you, Raven, I will take them down. With or without your consent. Whether or not you're ready, whether Aria is ready, they are fucking dead."

I nod, knowing he's more serious than he's ever been.

"I have to go," I murmur, hypnotized by his possessive nature. The power in his voice, like it's filled with gravel. He hypnotizes me all the time. Every moment, I'm just… enthralled.

"Meet me down the road from your house tomorrow morning at that little broken-down church. We'll go see your dad. Don't fucking be late. If you're late, I'll go see your aunt and uncle."

I nod again, starting to feel like a bobblehead as I watch him. Do I walk away? Do I give him a hug, a kiss? What am I supposed to do with some man who just taught me how to kill and then fucked me into two spiraling orgasms?

"Go home, Raven, before I bend you over the ring and fuck you all over again." He lifts a brow, and I spin around, already feeling sore between my legs. I flee, heading out to my car, and I wonder if it's the wind, or if maybe

I just heard him laugh slightly for the first time since I've met him.

I pull up at home, seeing all the lights on, and I'm beginning to wonder whether it's a good or bad sign.

I turn the car off, the overhead light coming on and illuminating me in a low yellow glow. I look at my hands, seeing my bruised knuckles from Caelian's solid muscles, the hint of blood under my nails.

The evidence.

I flip my hands over, seeing a faint shade of red on my palms as well. It feels odd, like an out-of-body experience as I see another person's blood on my hands. Their heart is no longer beating, and it's all because of me. I haven't even had a moment to reflect on what happened, but now that I sit here in the dark, it feels like it's hitting me all at once.

Relief, excitement, sadness, anger. I feel reborn, but I don't know if I love this life yet or not. *Do I want to take a life from someone? Is this who I'm meant to be?*

All I do know is, hiding who I am for the last few years has been painful. As each day goes on, the need to cut into skin grows more and more desperate. So much so that I've been feeling unlike myself for the past few weeks.

Until today.

Did my parents make me addicted to blood, or was I born to love it?

I've never been so unlike myself, yet I've never felt more like me.

I am what I am.

And I am me.

Maybe I need to put who I was behind me, and fully embrace who I'm meant to be.

Grabbing my bag, I slip from the car, my heart beating hard in my chest as I walk up the steps. It feels like I'm walking in slow motion; every step I take, I feel the crater in my chest shaking more and more erratically. Until my heart beats out of control, and I feel like I can't breathe.

My aunt and uncle are becoming so unpredictable, and I hate the unknown.

I walk inside, wishing I could head right back out when I see my aunt and uncle. They are praying, my aunt holding a Bible in her hands as she holds her other hand over her head. They stand in the living room, their holy shrine lit, with candles surrounding them. Crosses and Jesus figurines fill the nearby tables. It's weird to watch, sense, breathe this air that makes me feel so uneasy.

Believing in something is normal. Obsession and rituals are not.

My aunt keeps praying, and my uncle falls to the ground at her feet, his back laying flush with the floor as he looks up at the sky, like he sees the holy God above him. He starts speaking in tongue, in a language that is unlike anything I've heard before.

It's not a language. It's a cross between humming and words jumbled together.

I've seen them act this way on only a few occasions. Only a few times in my life have they turned inhumane as they speak languages I don't understand and bend their bodies toward a god I don't know if I should believe in.

The door clicks shut behind me, and my uncle keeps bending his body toward the heavens while my aunt whips her gaze toward mine, the blood red, leather-bound Bible in her hands slapping to her side.

"You…" Her eyes narrow. She slams the Bible shut, walking toward me with a purpose in her steps. "You are late."

I glance over at the stove, checking the time and seeing I'm only three minutes late. "Traffic was slow. Construction." It's a lie, but she certainly wouldn't check to see if there was any construction, right?

Fuck, she probably would.

She steps close to me, until I can smell her negative energy radiating from her. I wonder what it is she smells on me. *Blood? Sweat? Sex? Sin? Death?*

"I tried calling down to the library today and the lady I spoke to said she didn't see a girl with your description. It makes me wonder, are you even there at all?" She leans in, her eyes swirling with icy hate. "I can smell the lies coming off of you."

"I'm not lying." The words choke out of me, though I have no choice but to use them. The alternate is telling the truth, and that would lead to punishments. Punishments that I'm not prepared for.

"Next time you go there, maybe I'll stop by. Check in and see how things are going."

"No!" I shout, and her eyes flare with realization. She knows I'm fucking lying. She knows I don't go there. "I mean, do you know how embarrassing that would be? No one's parents check in on them at the library. It's the weekend, and it's going to be really busy. You stopping by would only make things really embarrassing for me."

She smiles coldly at me, and I take a step back, only for her to reach forward, her free hand grabbing my wrist, while her other hand with the Bible slams against my chest, the thick binding of pages knocking the breath from my lungs. "Go by your uncle, and read Revelation until your tongue feels like it will fall from your mouth."

On shaky legs, I walk to my uncle, whose whites of his eyes are prominent as he prays to the Lord. He is no longer on his back, but on his knees in a prayer stance, his neck bent uncomfortably as his head tilts to the sky.

"Do not let me tell you again!" Aunt Gloria screams at me, and I flip the Bible open, going to the last story, Revelation.

The page falls upon Revelation 21:8, and I recite the words. I can feel Aunt Gloria hovering over me, hating me, wanting my pain, relishing in my discomfort.

"But as for the cowardly, the faithless, the detestable, as for murderers, the sexually immoral, sorcerers, idolaters, and all liars, their portion will be in the lake that burns with fire and sulfur, which is the second death."

I can hear Aunt Gloria rustling behind me as I speak the words, and then water is flung at me, burning, hot, fiery drops of water slapping against my skin. I shriek as I turn around, seeing her hold her vial of holy water above the flame of a candle. "Keep reading, Raven! Read the words of the Lord while you feel what hell will feel like if you continue down this path."

She flings another handful of drops my way, and I wince. I swear I can feel the sizzle against my skin.

"*READ!*" she roars.

I go back to the pages, jumping to Revelation 20:10. "And the devil who has deceived them was thrown into the lake of fire and sulfur where the beast and the false prophet were, and they will be tormented day and night forever and ever."

Every few words, there is another waterfall of drops flinging against my skin until it turns numb, and my entire body trembles.

"Mom? Dad? What are you doing?!" Aria screams, and I turn toward the stairs with a horrified look on my face, seeing hers echo the exact same expression.

The silent gasp falls from my lips as she steps off the bottom step, her shaky knees taking her across the floor. "Raven, are you all right? Your skin is blotchy."

Yes, because your shithole parents are tormenting me every single time I see them.

"Aria, get upstairs. This is nothing for you to see," Uncle Jerry says, finally getting off his knees and coming to a stand. He gives me a scathing look, like he hates me more than he can put into words. I'm the bane of their existence, and I know they wish I never came here.

They think I've corrupted their daughter. They think I'm soiling their home.

"No! I can't keep sitting upstairs day in and day out, listening to my cousin scream while you guys hurt her!" A sob breaks from her chest, and I know she wants to come to me.

But she's scared.

I give her a look. *Don't come over. Stop crying.*

It's only going to get worse if we don't stop this. *Now.*

Her father steps toward her, his steps aggressive enough to raise the hair on my arms.

"Stop it." I step forward, getting between Uncle Jerry and Aria. "I'm sorry. I'll do whatever you want, just leave Aria alone."

Aunt Gloria grabs onto the hood of my sweatshirt and yanks me back. My butt slams into the ground, and I hear Aria gasp as she comes to me.

"Aria, stop!" I scream from the ground. I watch Uncle Jerry block her path, his hand raising, and he backhands her with such force that she flies across the room, her back crashing into the chairs at the dining room table.

Rage burns through me, so hot I feel as if I've just stepped into flames. I move to get up, when the large shadow of Aunt Gloria hovers above me.

"You've done it, now." She pulls a heavy steel cross from behind her back. She raises it above me, like she's about to shove it into my chest. I wince, covering my face as it swings down, knocking me straight on the head.

And everything goes black.

I gasp in a breath, my back arching as I come to. Glancing around, I see my room surrounding me.

I'm in my bed.

But how did I get here?

My floral quilt covers my body, heavy and thick and restricting. I whip it off as a shadow catches my eye.

"Aria?" I whisper, surprised to see her on the floor. Sitting up, I clutch the side of my head, feeling a massive knot growing beneath my hair. It's tender to the touch, and thumps in my ear, creating a splitting headache down the side of my head.

She rolls over, and tears spring to my eyes at her face. Black and blue discoloration extends from her jaw up to the apple of her cheek. Even her right eye is a little swollen, like her body couldn't help but react to the pain. She winces as she pushes herself up, tears instantly flowing down her cheeks. "I'm so sorry, Rave."

I slide from my bed, getting on the ground next to her. I don't want to touch her. Touch is foreign, it's uncomfortable, it's unnatural. She knows this, but she doesn't care as she leans forward and buries her head in my shoulder. "Why are my parents like this, Raven? Why are they so messed up?"

I run my fingers through her damp hair, ignoring the ache of discomfort in my chest. I want to flee and hide in my bed, and I also want to run downstairs and tear her parents in half for hurting her.

"I don't know, Aria."

She leans back, looking at me through watery eyes. "I don't know who they are anymore. It's like they're... *getting worse*. Why would they ever hurt you? Hurt *me*? Why would they hurt *their own child*?"

My hands go to the carpet, and I squeeze the fibers in a tight grip, hating how horribly this is affecting her. She's traumatized. "Sometimes there are just some things in this world that we don't understand." Like why I am the way I am, or why my parents are the way they are.

Or why my aunt and uncle are the way they are.

She shakes her head, the tears falling from the edge of her lashes and tumbling down her cheeks. "I don't like who they have become. God wouldn't like who they have become."

I glance away from her, knowing her faith is strong, even when mine is nonexistent.

"I can see it in your eyes. You aren't going to be here much longer. Will you take me with you?" she asks in a whisper.

I look at her, knowing that whatever happens, I can't leave her behind. Not now. "Of course, I will, Aria."

Color blooms in her face as relief hits her. "Oh, my goodness, thank you so much." She bends down, grabbing onto my hand and burying her face against it. "Thank you."

I glance out the window, seeing the sun only beginning to rise. I must have slept throughout the entire night. Today is the day.

The big day.

I see my father for the first time in six years.

I can't tell Aria about it, though. If worse comes to worst, I don't want her to be liable for anything I tell her. Until everything is settled, I need to keep things to myself. Keep her in the dark until we're both safe. It'll be better that way.

For the both of us.

"I'm meeting with Caelian today."

Her face pales. "We're both on lockdown, Raven. Neither of us is allowed to leave the house."

I clench my teeth together. That just won't work for me, because I have things to do. On top of my aunt and uncle, I'm in the middle of dealing with a serial killer who literally is out to attack me.

"I have to get out of here," is all I can say. Claustrophobia hits me, and the walls begin closing in, the mania weighing my chest down like oversized anchors.

"Please don't go. You'll get in so much trouble."

I lean forward, my palms going to each side of her face. My skin tingles, but I ignore it as I look into her worried eyes. "You don't have to be scared for much longer, Aria. I'm going to take care of it. I'll take care of all of it and then we'll be safe. But you just have to hold on a little bit longer, okay? Only a little bit longer."

"What are you going to do?" she whispers.

I shake my head. "It's nothing you have to worry about. Just stay out of their way and stay safe. I'll take care of the rest."

I go to my dresser, grabbing my things that I'll need. It's a few hours' drive down to the prison my father is held at.

Pelican Bay State Penitentiary in northern California. For the worst of the worst. The place where evil goes to die. A place I've never been and never intended to go, but here I am, packing a bag to go see him.

I never thought I'd see the day.

"But... how are you going to get out of here? You can't just say you're going to the library. She won't let you, not now. How do you plan to get out of here?"

I glance at the window.

"No! Don't you remember what happened the last time you snuck out of your window at night? You were locked in the basement for a week!"

"I have no other choice," I grit out.

"So, what are you guys going to do? Is it worth the punishment that will happen after? Because you know if you leave here, there will be consequences." Her voice breaks at the end, a sob working its way to the surface. "And I don't know how much more pain I can honestly take, for you and for me."

I narrow my eyes, glaring at her. "I will never, ever let them touch you again. You hear me? If they so much as land a hand on you, I will make them regret it."

She swallows down her cry at the tone in my voice, taking a deep breath and giving a slow nod.

I zip up my bag after I grab a few things and kick it under my bed. I don't have to leave yet, but when I do, I want to be ready. Because I know, without a doubt...

Everything will change after today.

CAELIAN

I glance at Raven out of the corner of my eye, seeing her stare at the passing landscape. She hasn't said much since we hopped into my car hours ago. It doesn't bother me since I don't understand the purpose of small talk. Though today, she's seemed a little distant.

Not the usual overemotional Raven she usually is.

This one matches my personality. Unemotional, detached, removed from the situation. Is she preparing herself to see her father? Is she regretting yesterday? Did the copycat give her another warning she hasn't told me about?

I've been enjoying the silence, watching blips of the ocean pass by as we head down the coast, but since we've crossed into California, I realize she isn't at all prepared for what she's about to do.

Pelican Bay isn't a prison you just walk into. It's not fucking detention at school. It's literally max security with some bad motherfuckers walking through those halls.

"Raven." My voice snaps her from her daydream, and she blinks, looking over at me in surprise. Though she doesn't see me, not really. It's like she's looking through me.

chest. Like something isn't right, and I don't know how to fix it. Usually, I don't fucking care. But whatever I'm feeling… maybe I do care.

About her.

More than I want to.

"I don't know if I can even understand them enough to articulate them."

"Well, start at the fucking beginning, then. I don't think you've said a damn thing since we got in the car, and usually I want to cut my ears off from your many questions." Not a crack, not even a slight smirk. Yeah, something's really fucking wrong.

"What happened last night? When you went home?" I figure I might as well start with when she left me, because she definitely wasn't this fucking weird when she left last night.

She glances away from me, and I immediately know. *Bingo*.

Her aunt and uncle.

My hand goes to the side of her head to turn her gaze back toward me, and she hisses, shrinking into the door and away from me.

My eyes widen, and I cut off the road without a glance, slamming onto the brakes. Her hand slaps to the dashboard from the impact, her eyes unfocused as she looks at me. "What the fuck are you doing?"

I unclip my belt, leaning over and threading my fingers through her hair, my nostrils flaring as I feel what I thought I'd feel.

A massive—*massive*—fucking lump.

"*What the fuck*, Raven? What the hell happened?"

She whimpers, pulling away from me. "Please, don't."

"What the fuck happened to you, Raven?" I demand fucking answers, because without them, I might massacre everyone in sight.

She stares at me, gnawing at her bottom lip for a moment before it pops free. "My aunt and uncle… they know I'm lying."

I say nothing, wanting her to tell me herself. She doesn't need me to prompt her. She better fucking not need me to prompt her.

"They made me pray. Recite verses from the Bible. A-and Aria came. It started a fight, and her dad hit her. I freaked out, and my aunt hit me." Her hand hovers over her head but doesn't touch it. "I don't remember anything else. I woke up in my bed."

I turn on my blinker. "Well, fuck seeing your dad. I'm going to go take care of your fucking aunt and uncle." I start to turn the steering wheel, and she reaches over, grabbing onto it to stop me.

"No!" she grunts. "Ouch. Fucking hell, my head hurts."

I grab her chin, turning her head toward me as I lean in and look at her eyes. "You have a fucking concussion, Raven. How hard did they hit you?" Her pupils are fucked, but not overly so. I've seen worse and even had worse, but still. I bet she's in fucking pain.

"Not that hard." She winces. "But, pretty hard."

Only a breath away from her, I watch her capture her lower lip between her teeth and I so badly wanting to ravish her. Just as I've wanted to every second since I pulled out of her last night. But I know she's fucked up right now, both body and mind.

"Give me one reason why I shouldn't turn around right now and go rip them limb from limb," I mumble, just ever so slightly brushing my lips against hers.

She breathes out a shaky breath, her eyes dashing back and forth between mine. "Because I will take care of them. I will. But today, right now, I really need to go see who else is trying to kill me. The copycat needs to take priority."

I release her chin, knowing and hating that she's right. I need to focus and take care of the worst. At this moment, I want to say it's her aunt and uncle, though I know if the copycat Crow were to be here, he would most definitely be the worst.

I think of the girls he's killed. Skinned. Cut. Raped. Abused. I think of that happening to Raven, and that's enough for me to turn off my blinker and head back on the road, toward the prison.

"The moment we take care of this fucker copycat, your aunt and uncle are done for," I snap, fucking serious as all hell.

"Trust me, I know it," she whispers, glancing back out the window.

It doesn't take much longer until we're pulling into the lot of the prison, the tall gates, towers, and fences expanding around the entire perimeter. This place is a hell of its own making, a perfect place for her father.

Actually, I take that back. A perfect place for him would be under my blade. It's only then that justice is really served.

"I don't even know what I'm supposed to say." She's nervous now, wringing her hands together in anxious motions.

"Skip all the heartfelt shit. He'll probably spit a ton of stuff and try to catch up with you, but you can't get into it. Let's get in and get out."

She looks over at me, fear and hope in her eyes. "Will you be with me the whole time?"

I run my tongue along my teeth. "No way in hell I'm letting you go in there alone."

She exhales, her entire body melting into the seat. "Okay, good."

I pull into an empty spot and turn the car off. "You ready?"

Her fingers grip her thighs. "No. Not really."

I lean forward, grabbing at the back of her neck, more gently than I'd usually be because of her concussion. I pull her head toward me, smashing my lips against hers. I kiss her deeply, partly wanting to claim her before she walks in there to a ton of dirty-ass men, and half wanting to swallow her nerves for her.

She melts into me, her hands going forward as she grabs onto my scratchy face. She holds onto me like I'm her anchor, like she doesn't want me to let her go, let her drop into the unknown.

"I won't let you drown," I mumble against her lips.

She holds me tighter, like I'm breathing life into her. Like I'm giving her the air to keep going. I'll breathe every ounce of air into her lungs if it means she'll keep breathing for only a moment longer.

Every second that goes by, she burrows further into the part of my chest that's laid dormant my entire life. The part of me that I always thought was broken, but it never was. Not really, anyway.

It was just missing Raven.

She releases my lips, leaning back and dropping her hand. Reaching out, she grabs onto me, lacing her fingers through mine. "Don't let me go."

"I wouldn't even if you asked me to."

With one more deep breath, we get out of the car, unlacing our fingers only to lace them again once we get to the front of the car. She grips my fingers hard, cutting off the circulation as we walk up to the door.

I checked the visiting hours before we came and was glad we were in luck and that visiting hours were today. With a quick call to one of dad's people, he was able to pull a few strings and get Raven on the visitor list.

It feels weird as I walk up to the door with a girl on my arm. I've never had one before. Never held a girl's hand, even. It feels foreign, but it also feels right. Like Raven was always meant to be next to me. A fucking lioness next to the lion. She's ferocious, if not a little wild.

But I tame the mania in her brain as much as she turns on the emotion in mine.

The door buzzes before we reach it, and grabbing the handle, I pull it open, letting Raven walk through ahead of me.

She walks up to the desk, and I hover behind her, watching everyone around me. I don't trust a soul, not one. I don't want even one person to fucking look at her wrong. If they do, I promise I'll be back for them.

Fucking guaranteed.

"I'm here to visit with a prisoner," Raven says, her voice as unsure as her body language.

The woman in the security suit, hair slicked back with a shiny badge, looks at her, turning on her speaker. It crackles a moment before her too loud voice sounds through. "And who are you here to see?"

Raven glances over her shoulder at me a moment before looking back at the woman through the cloudy glass in front of her. "Cash Crow."

There's silence from the other end. Even the crackling turns off as the woman stares at us for a moment.

"Are you on the visitor list?" she asks after a moment. Crackle, then silence.

Raven turns around and stares at me, like she totally forgot. "Oh, shit…"

I lean over her shoulder, speaking into the speaker. "Yes, she is. Raven Abbott."

The woman stares at me a moment before she types on her computer, and I know Raven's name is going to pop up, as well as mine. I have no connection with Cash Crow, but there's no way in fucking hell Raven is going to go speak to that fucker by herself.

She clicks and clacks on her keyboard for what seems like forever, before pulling a piece of paper from a folder and shoving it under the glass wall. "I'm going to need you both to sign on the bottom of the page here." I glance at it, seeing the rules and regulations of visiting hours with a maximum-security prisoner. I sign it without reading between the lines, knowing it's a bunch of bullshit that we don't have to worry about. We're going to make this an in-and-out visit without much else.

Raven spends her time reading it over, her face paling with each line. I want to choke her for bringing her emotions into it. This is the worst time for her feelings to come into play. She should only focus on the task at hand, and nothing else.

But I'm finding that's impossible when it comes to Raven.

The woman behind the glass picks up the phone. "Inmate one-six-seven-six-zero-six. Please bring him to visitor room seven." She taps her pen against the table. "My thoughts exactly. Thanks."

She hangs up and looks over at us. "Please take a seat and you'll be called back shortly."

We walk to the plastic seats that have too many fingerprints and not any amount of comfort in them. Raven sits down in it, though, not even trying to hide her nerves at this point.

"You need to calm down. Stay focused." I nudge her knee with my own, and she looks over at me, her eyes wide with fear.

"I'm about to see my father. I never thought I'd see him again."

There's a battle in her voice of excitement and disappointment. She wants to see him but doesn't. What an interesting war of emotions.

"Do you miss him?"

Her gaze fades off, going into a memory I can't see. "He loved me. He loved me so much, Caelian. He would've burned down the world to protect me. And now that I harbor the same darkness inside me, I understand the rage. The craving. The only difference is, he attacked the innocent, and I only want to rid the world of evil. The people like him."

How difficult it must be to love someone you hate. To hate someone you love.

"Cash Crow?" The monotone voice comes over the speaker, followed by the buzzing of a gate, and the solid steel door opens. A male guard stands there, his gut large and hanging over his belt. How he has the capacity to reach his baton, Taser, or anything else around his belt is a mystery. The man surely isn't fast enough, because he sure isn't fit enough.

Raven stands, and I'm right behind her, giving my warmth to her through her back. We walk to the guard, and I can hear Raven's heartbeat like an erratic drum in the silent air. We go through door by door, pausing every time one opens so we can wait for the next one to close. It's long and unproductive. This isn't the first time I've visited a prison, or Pelican Bay, for that matter. But it feels different this time.

Because I have someone to protect.

I grab the back of her neck, squeezing her tense muscles briefly. She lowers her shoulders, but they aren't anywhere near relaxed.

She's a fucking wreck.

We take a left through the next doors, making our way to the visitor section. We stop at the number seven, and inside is a small table, three chairs, and nothing else. There's a mirror on the wall that I know is double-sided, and the camera in the corner of the ceiling will be watching every movement we make and listening to every word we say.

"Wait here. Inmate will be here in a moment." He turns around to walk out, but pauses at the last moment, looking over his shoulder. "This is the first visitor he's had, you know." His eyes look at Raven, and I want to gouge them out with my fingers. "I'm guessing you're his daughter?"

Raven freezes, then gives out a single nod.

"He talks a lot about you. He'll be excited to see you." With that, he turns around and walks out, the door buzzing and closing behind him.

Raven falls to her chair so roughly, the feet groan against the cement floor. I sit down beside her, already ready to get the hell out of here.

We sit in silence only moments before the door buzzes again, and the sound of chains hitting chains hits my ears.

Raven turns to stone beside me.

The door slowly opens, and the chains, followed by a flood of orange, walks through the door.

I stare at the man who I've only seen on the TV. So much different and so much the same. His beard is longer, as is his hair. Dark hair, just like Raven's. Dark and thick and shiny, even though he spends his days and nights in a maximum-security prison cell.

The guard looks stone-faced as he walks in and makes sure Cash sits in his chair. He locks the chains around his ankles to a cement loop in the ground. He pulls on it, making sure it's secure before standing up, giving Cash a look, and walking out without a word, the door closing behind him.

It's silent for a moment before the chain jingles and Cash raises his hand toward Raven.

I swipe my hand up, cinching my fingers around his chains and pulling his hands back toward the table.

His hands clank to the surface. The air instantly changes in the room, and I know, without a doubt, that if we weren't in these walls, Cash Crow would try to kill me.

    Fuck him.

chapter twenty-two
RAVEN

D*addy.*
He looks the same but so much different. Older. Maybe a little tired. Not as relaxed as he used to be. He has more wrinkles around his lips and eyes, but his bright blue eyes are the same. The same shade as mine. His dark hair, also the same shade as mine.

Though, the rest of me, a replica of my mother.

Mom.

My chest aches as my dad watches me, Caelian on edge as he pins my dad's hands against the table.

"*Don't touch her*," he growls, his voice more ferocious than I've ever heard it.

My dad pays him no attention, his eyes probing mine. "My Baby Crow."

A groan works its way up my throat, but I swallow it down before anyone can hear it.

Caelian's voice echoes in my ear. "Stay focused."

Stay focused.

I clear my throat. "I have a couple of questions."

He stares at me, his face not at all registering my question. "How have you been, Raven? You have grown so much." His eyes glisten, and I feel sick. I've never seen him emotional before. "You look just like Momma."

My eyes drop to the table, and I watch his fingers out of the corner of my eye twitch to touch me. I don't want to look like my mom. I don't want to look like any of them. But he's right. I'm my mom's twin, and my dad's twin, and I really don't want to be associated with either of them.

Though my heart... my heart says otherwise.

The emotional, disturbed child who was trained to draw art into her parents' victims only wants their love and acceptance.

"There's someone out there... in Oregon. He's copying you."

"He's copying *us*, Baby Crow."

My nose burns with emotion, and I slap my hands on the table. "I am not *you*."

He leans forward until I smell the familiar scent of my father. Even years in a prison couldn't take away the scent I can only attribute to him. He smells like... home. "You have Crow blood in you. Your eyes are my eyes. I know a murderer when I see one." He leans back in his chair but is restricted from doing so as Caelian keeps hold of his chains. "Do you feel like life is spinning out of control? Is there someone who enrages you to the point of wanting to set them on fire? Do you feel a little lost, a little confused? Do you feel like you are two different people? What the world wants you to be, and what you really are?"

He watches me, his calculating eyes observing every emotion as they flit through mine.

"You are my daughter. You are a Crow. And you are part of what we were."

Caelian yanks on the chain, leaning forward as he snaps. "Raven is many things, but she will never be a part of what *you* sick fucks were. You are the type of person whose throat I'd rip out with my bare hands and feed to my dog. Now shut the fuck up and answer her questions."

My dad looks at him, maybe for the first time since he's stepped into the room.

"Who is this man, Baby Crow? Is this your boyfriend?" His voice is slightly humorous, like he finds the entire thing funny.

My cheeks grow red as I shake my head. "He's just... we're friends—"

"She's mine, and she's lucky I let her walk through these doors to see you. Now answer her fucking questions."

My dad stares at him for a few beats, then turns his bright eyes to mine. "I've heard of this copycat. A little pathetic, honestly."

"He's after me. Whoever it is. Is there anyone who you know that would do this? Anyone who would be after you? Anyone who would want to hurt me?"

For the first time, I see emotion in his eyes, and it's the same emotion I saw the night Darren was touching me.

Anger. Rage. Protectiveness... over me.

"Everyone is after me," is all he says.

"But is there someone in particular who you think might want to go after me?"

He licks his lips. "Anyone who ever wanted you is dead, Baby Crow."

"Well, clearly, you fucking missed someone," Caelian snaps.

My dad looks over at him. "You have taken lives."

Caelian narrows his eyes. "Many. But I take lives for a very different reason than you do."

My dad looks down at his fingernails, darkened around the edges. Filled with grime and dirt and whatever else he may get into around here. "A life is a life, son. Whether you take it for good or bad, murder is what makes you, *you*."

I know Caelian is holding back from tearing into him. From the way the tension in the room is thick, icy cold, filled with an edgy silence.

"It's time to go," Caelian says suddenly.

"Do you regret it at all? What you did? What you made me do?" I whisper, tears flooding my eyes.

His eyes turn black, and I wonder when I get lost to the darkness if mine will do the same. If what I once was will be completely lost. "The only thing I regret is not killing more than I did."

I bite the inside of my cheek, hating the monster he is, but knowing that he's right. We're one in the same.

"You don't regret that you've lost the only two people who were on your side? You must not regret where your daughter lives, with an abusive aunt and uncle who hurt her at every turn?"

I swing my head to Caelian's, my eyes wide in shock. Fuck, he isn't supposed to bring them up.

The temperature drops in the room. It feels like I've submerged into the deepest depths of the ocean. Complete ice surrounds me.

"Is that so?" My dad turns his eyes to me, death written in them. "Your aunt and uncle hurt you? How so?"

I shake my head. "It's nothing."

"You tell me the truth right now, Raven." His voice is the same as it was when I was a child, when I'd get in trouble for tracking mud through the house or breaking a dish in the kitchen. "They hurt you?"

I squeeze my eyes shut, bowing my head and giving a little nod.

My dad's hand flings forward, and this time Caelian doesn't stop him. My dad grabs onto my fingers, squeezing them tightly, but with the absence of pain. "End them, Raven. Do what I taught you. You know what to do."

I do. I've seen death more times than I can count. It was only yesterday when I took the first soul for myself.

"They will die, but I hope you blame your own fucked-up self for being the reason she's in this situation in the first place," Caelian growls between clenched teeth.

My fingers are released, and he sits back in his chair, his hands going to his lap. "The devil in me is the same devil in you," he mumbles under his breath.

"Let's go, Raven. He isn't going to be any help." Caelian stands from his chair and walks to the door, banging on it. "This was a waste of our time."

The door opens, and I sit there for a moment, watching as my dad stares at me, his mouth mumbling things I can't even hear.

I stand, wanting to say bye, but don't think my throat will even be able to work the words out. This will be the first and final time I'll see my father in here, and I know this with certainty.

As I walk past him, his reaches out to grab me. I stop in my tracks, allowing him to pull me down so he can whisper in my ear. "Into the darkness you go, Baby Crow. Be sure to let the devil catch your fall." He kisses the side of my face, and I can hear the scuffle of guards as they come toward us. "I love you, Raven. Always remember that," he whispers the words as I'm pulled away from him.

I watch as they grab at my dad aggressively, tears filling my eyes as he takes it without complaint. He's so pliant, not fighting at all. This is nothing like my dad. He would have ripped people apart back in the day with only his hands. Now he just sits there, the ugly orange suit covering his body as the chains weigh him down.

I don't realize I'm falling until arms come around me as Caelian catches me. He holds me tightly as he ushers me out, a guard instantly at our side as they help us leave.

I glance over my shoulder as the door shuts behind me, seeing two guards taking my dad down the opposite hall. His dark hair is stringy and long now, a complete mess. He glances over his shoulder at me, as if he could sense my stare. His eyes are as dark as the night, and he smiles, but it looks so sinister and dark that chills break out along my spine.

The doors close.

And so does my heart.

"Raven," Caelian says a few hours later. My name being a constant echo on our way back home.

I've been somewhere. I'm not sure where. My body sits in his nice BMW, but my mind is elsewhere. Stuck in memories, I suppose. Thinking of what used to be. I see things so much differently than I used to.

I realize that my parents and my aunt and uncle have more in common than they believe. My aunt and uncle would hate to hear the words, but it's true.

My parents worship the devil. They worship the darkness.

My aunt and uncle worship God. They worship the light.

But their obsession makes them both filled with a madness that drives them to the brink of insanity.

They are consumed by their faith. Each of them called upon by their own God.

And I feel somewhere in between. Knowing nothing but obsession and evil. Where do I go from here? What is right and what is wrong? I feel like the meaning of life is something unattainable at this point. I feel like I'm just floating somewhere in the middle of everything.

I haven't said even a word to Caelian the entire drive. Lost in my own thoughts. But I can tell he's growing on edge with each mile that passes.

"Want to go to the Inferno with me? I'm fighting tonight. Take your mind off shit."

I glance over at him, and his face is blank and unemotional, not giving a thing away, though I know he feels more than he's letting on. The anger in his tone as he confronted my dad doesn't come from someone who is emotionless.

The way he held on to me as he walked us out of the prison would never come from someone who doesn't care.

The way he's gripped the steering wheel as we've made our way through California and into Oregon wouldn't show in someone who feels nothing. He isn't a sheet of blank paper, no emotion, no anything. He's a black box, padlocked and hidden. There's so much inside, but he doesn't want to show it. Perhaps with other people, he is sociopathic. Maybe he has lived his entire life without an ounce of feeling in his blood. Though, with me, it's the opposite.

He is filled with so much possessiveness in his eyes and hate in his fists. Maybe I waken his dark soul, but he's also woken mine.

Do I go with him to the Inferno, though? After the day I've had? I'm on lockdown, and I snuck out of my window. My phone is on silent, and I refuse to look at it. Aria stayed in my room after I left, but they have to know I'm gone at this point. Right?

So, why haven't they called? Why has no one reached out to me?

I know what I'll walk into is hell. The question is, do I go home now and deal with the consequences, or do I enjoy one more night of freedom before I face my fate? Because I know, without a doubt, what I walk into tonight will be life-changing.

I might never see the light of day again, or they won't.

It'll be one of us, and I'm not ready to gamble on that yet.

"Yeah, I'll go with you."

Walking into the Inferno is like going home. The energy, the madness, it calms me. I can understand that it isn't just my mind that is filled with chaos. The world around me is chaotic, and it makes me not feel so alone.

Caelian left me a while ago, heading to the locker room to get ready. I decided to stand by the ring tonight, watching, feeling like a bystander as I take in the crazy around me. The screams are loud, the vibrations and stomping of feet even louder.

Every once in a while, an elbow slams into my back, shoving me against the rough edge of the ring. I've been incognito tonight where people haven't recognized me, and I'm grateful for it. I still feel in a fog. My head still aches, and my heart continues to weep. It's empty, but so full. Full of pain and regret and so much grief at what I've lost through the years.

I've missed out on so much. My life isn't at all what one should be for a child. I've lived and lost and been through a thousand lives. One thousand lives that should never have been mine to live.

The lights darken and snap me out of my dark thoughts. My eyes shoot to the back of the room, where a body lurks in the shadows.

Caelian.

I could recognize his body anywhere. So powerful and commanding. He will destroy anyone who stands in his way.

The dark locks of his hair fall onto his forehead, messy with a slight wave. His entire jawline is sharp enough to cut glass, tense and tight. His eyes are downcast, but I know they're burning orbs that'll light me on fire.

He is so intense. Like no one I've ever met before. He can send me to my knees and I'm not one to bend. He doesn't treat me like a girl, and he doesn't treat me like a freak.

He treats me like an equal.

His equal.

In only a pair of shorts that sit about mid-thigh, I watch his muscles clench as he walks toward the ring. The hair on his legs is dark and so fucking manly. His fists are clenched and bare, not one to cover himself with tape to protect himself. I think he'd rather feel every inch of pain than use a shield. I hope one day he can teach me to be the same. The ability to fight without fear, without protection, without an ounce of hesitation.

He walks into the ring, not fazed by the hyena screams from the women who want to sleep with him. Or the booming voices of the men as they wish to be him. He's in his own world, his own vortex of power surrounding him.

A pair of panties flings through the air, and an animalistic growl builds in my chest as I watch them land on the mat of the ring. I can nearly feel my teeth crack as I clench my jaw in anger.

The crowd's screams build once again as another figure walks into the room. I haven't seen him before, but he looks deadly. Strong and large, as tall as Caelian and nearly just as built. The look in his eyes screams murder, and my body tenses in discomfort.

I know Caelian is built like a murder weapon, but I don't like seeing him get hurt. I...

I've grown to care about him.

It makes an odd sensation grip my chest. I've never felt anything for any guy before. I've never wanted to protect someone other than Aria. Yet this man makes me want to stand before him and take any wound that is thrashed his way.

The man slips under the rope of the ring and comes to stand before Caelian with not an ounce of fear on his face.

They stand off, each of their eyes alit with the call of death as they watch one another. There is a thick heat between them, like their hate burns as hot as embers.

Do they know one another? Do they actually hate each other? What is it that brews between them?

Caelian's body is relaxed, his face looking nearly bored, yet his eyes are tense. Full of wrath.

The man steps forward, his body moving into the light and showing off thousands of tiny scars. Almost like they are fingernail indentations.

Another step forward, and his fist swings out. Caelian's body folds, dipping down and out of target from the hit. His other fist swings out, this one hitting Caelian right in the jaw.

Caelian's head swings to the side, and he snaps straight, his fist swinging the same moment his foot kicks out. The man's top half jerks back, while his bottom half falls out beneath him, and he slams onto his back so hard the ground shakes. He's quick, though, getting up and rushing Caelian.

Caelian is shoved back to the rope, the skin on his back digging into the rough fibers. I watch his back above me, scraping back and forth, growing raw with each swipe of his skin.

His hands reach out, grabbing at each side of the man's head. He holds it steady as he leans forward, plowing his head against the man's. I can hear skull hit skull, and it makes my skin twitch.

The man leans back, his eyes cloudy and my head aches. *I know that feeling*. The feeling of pain and fogginess and disorientation. The man's head lolls to the side, and I can feel the power of Caelian emanating off him. He uses it, each inch of power rolling through his veins.

I can feel the change in the air, and it's like he charges up, his fist going back and hitting the man in the head so hard I hear the crack of bones. His foot goes up, and he slams it into his knee. Again and again until his knee crunches to mush and he has nothing left but shards of bone. The way his leg bends in the opposite direction causes a collective gasp from the crowd.

I watch in awe and Caelian becomes a monster in front of me, taking everything that he is and exuding it in front of him. He demolishes the man, and though I've seen it before, this time feels different. It feels like he's fighting… for me.

I can see the glow of my phone going off in my pocket, and I want to ignore it, but it doesn't stop, and the alarm inside me goes off. My eyes blink away from Caelian, my hand going into my pocket and lifting my phone out. I see Aria's name on the screen for a moment before it goes black, only for it to light up again.

The alarm goes to a full, blaring horn, and I hear whooshing in my ears as I swipe to accept.

"Hello?" I shout over the excited screams. Blood flies in the air, and it's like it's full of a toxin that turns people into savages.

These people love pain.

"Raven," Aria whispers through the other end.

She sniffles, and I instantly grow on edge. *Something is wrong.*

"What's going on?"

"Where are y-you?" she cries.

"I'm… I'm out. What's wrong? Did they hurt you?"

"My mom knows you're gone. She's been eerily calm. But I'm scared, Raven. Something isn't right. I was downstairs cleaning up when the news came on. You went to see *your dad*?" Her voice is laced with disbelief.

I blink into the phone. *Wait, what?* "How would you know that?"

"Raven…"

My blood runs cold, the hair on my arms standing on end. "Tell me, Aria. How the hell would the news know I went to see him?"

She says nothing, a small hiccup sounding through the phone.

"Tell me!" I shout.

"The news said something like 'the daughter of Cash Crow visits with him just hours before he's killed in a prison brawl.' He died, Raven. Your dad is dead."

The clarity in the room fades to nothing. I see nothing except for cloudy shadows running through my vision, and then my dad is there, clear as day, glancing at me over his shoulder.

"My mom shoved me in my room and barricaded me in. I don't know what they're doing, but they were so quiet when they heard that. I'm scared, Raven! I don't know what they're doing!"

My dad, buying me my first set of colored pencils and a notepad.

My dad, playing with me outside in our yard.

My dad, singing at the top of his lungs to Johnny Cash.

My dad, murdering his first victim by the fire.

My dad, teaching me how to carve whatever I wanted into someone's skin.

My dad, caught by the feds.

My dad, in orange, watching me from across the table with an emptiness and acceptance in his voice. Like it was all over.

He knew.

He fucking knew he was going to die. Did he commit suicide? Did he start a fight? One million and one questions run through my mind, and I can't do anything besides let them overtake me completely.

"I'm coming home," I mumble into the phone, cutting off her rambling by a click of the End button. I shove my phone in my pocket, feeling like

I was injected with all the drugs in the world. The entire universe tilts on its axis. I press my hand against the rope, the vibration of the ring running through my arms and up my body. I stumble forward, nothing clear and everything hazy, as I push through the throng of people. I head to the back, not caring about anyone or anything as my life whooshes in my ears.

He's dead. My father is dead.

A strangled gasp wheezes from my lungs, my eyes burning hot and growing blurry as I escape the stuffy air of the crowd and break through the edge, instantly breathing in the dank, cool air of the Inferno.

Tears fall down my face in heavy drops as I head to the bathroom. Both palms slam on the dented, chipped metal door. It flings open, banging against the wall behind me with a crack.

I rush to the first stall, my mind spinning to the point where nothing looks real. I'm in a dream, a fog, a different universe entirely as my world comes crashing down around me. I press my hand on the brick wall behind the stall, staring at the yellow ring in the toilet bowl.

Disgusting.

The door to the bathroom slams open, and the sound of heels clacking feel like knives against my spine.

Bitches.

I take in a deep breath of the urine and perfume-filled air as their hyena-like voices reach my ears.

"Oh my God, he is so damn sexy, isn't he?" bitch number one says. No, wait… that's *Trina*. I grind my teeth together, my fingers gripping the tin box around the toilet paper roll as I hold myself back.

Don't do it. *Don't do it.*

"I would literally lick the sweat from his abs," bitch number two whines. Lorna. Fucking Lorna.

"Do you think he'd come home with me if I asked?" Trina asks.

"Girl, he's dangerous. You'd be alone with him?" bitch number three gasps. That's the brunette's voice. What was her name? Oh yes, *Delanie.*

"I'd let him break my fucking bones," Trina moans, and the tin starts bending under my fingers.

They giggle. Their sexual tones make me fucking nauseous.

"I wonder how big his dick is," Delanie rasps.

"I saw him get a semi once when he was fighting. Like he was getting turned on by the pain. His shorts got a little tight, and *my God* was it sexy. What I would do to that man." Trina giggles.

"Think he'd let us all have a turn?" bitch number two is so dead serious, and I can feel—*literally feel*—my brain go haywire.

My entire skin tingles, my skin growing hot and cold and everything in between. I feel flush like I have a fever, yet at the same time the skin raises on my arms with chills. I become disassociated from my body, and I'm transported to hours ago, when I was sitting by my father.

We are one in the same.

Into the darkness you go, Baby Crow. Be sure to let the devil catch your fall.

"I don't want to share. I want him all to myself. You know what? I think I'm going to do it. I think I'm going to corner him and see if he wants to fuck. I don't even care where at this point. *That man is mine.* And that bitch at school? Raven? I'm going to rub it in her snarky little bitch face that I fucked the only man that would ever be interested in her prude ass." Trina. Of course, this comes from Trina.

I turn around, my hands clenching into fists as I open the stall door. The three girls by the sinks look coked out as they spin around, eyes wide and skin reddening in embarrassment.

My eyes fall onto Trina, with her fake blonde hair and the jeans that have too many rips. Designer. Too expensive for the Inferno. How the fuck do these girls even know about this place?

I walk up to her, my steps focused and sure. My hand reaches out, tangling in her hair, as I pull her toward me. She screams, and her hands go to her hair as I shove her head forward, directly into the flimsy mirror.

It breaks into shards, falling to the ground and into the dirty sink. Her two friends scream; fear making them scatter away from me.

But Trina, she spits hateful words at me that only spur me on more.

"You fucking psychopath! Stop it! You ugly, dumb bitch!" Her nails scrape my hands and wrists. I can feel my skin shred, blood dripping down my arms and into her milky white hair.

Stupid cunt.

The shards of glass reflect in my eyes, and she looks at me, blood dripping down her forehead and covering her teeth. She smiles at me, conniving and bitchy. "You're jealous, aren't you? He doesn't want you, I bet. Can't stand your freaky ass."

My hand drops to the sink, still damp and sudsy from the last hand wash. I grab a slippery shard of glass, clutching it in my grip. Lorna and Delanie scream again, running from the room as fast as they can.

As soon as Trina realizes what I'm doing, she screams, guttural and horrified. Her screaming turns from hateful to remorseful as she pleads for her life.

"He is mine. *Caelian. Is. Mine,*" I snarl.

I don't give in, my rage and hate and emotions overtaking everything else. Gripping the shard so hard it cuts into my fingers, I shove it down, straight into her neck. She chokes and gurgles, her eyes opening wide and bright, full of pain and fear as blood flows around the shard and down her neck.

I pull the blade out, shoving it back into her neck.

In, out.

In, out.

Quick motions, so fast the blade whistles in the wind, each plunge creating a slurp of blood around the glass.

I keep going until she's limp, blood covering my hands and arms, splatters across my face, my clothes having turned a dark, deep red. A pool fills on the pale tile floor, and my eyes widen as clarity hits.

"Oh, shit," I whisper, dropping her to the ground. The back of her head slams against the sink, the bang echoing in the bathroom before she hits the ground.

She's dead.

She's so fucking dead.

"Holy fuck." I get to my knees, flipping her onto her back. Her eyes and mouth are still open, but only death reflects in her gaze. My hands fall to the blood, and I want to wipe it away, my hands entering the warm substance as I try to clean it. All it does is spread it around as I use her body as a mop. It does absolutely nothing to absorb the red mess.

"Oh fuck, I'm fucked," I whine, rushing to the stall and grabbing the toilet paper. I run back to the body, the trail of toilet paper still attached to the roll. I press the thin squares into the blood, and they immediately turn red, disintegrating from the thick liquid.

"Fuckkkkkk," I groan, pulling more and more toilet paper until it breaks off the roll. A pile of toilet paper floods around me, and my eyes fill with tears.

Holy shit. I just killed someone. Willingly. Easily. With absolutely no hesitation.

I stand up, my body dripping with blood as I bend down to grab her ankles, I start pulling her across the bathroom and toward the stall, having absolutely no clue what I'm doing.

What am I supposed to do with a dead body?

A trail of blood follows behind her, and just as I'm about to pull her into the stall, the bathroom door opens, and there he stands.

Caelian.

He looks full of rage and not at all shocked as he stares at me.

"What the fuck happened?" he roars. He shuts the door quickly, flipping the lock that I had no clue was there.

"I-I don't know," I whisper, feeling numb.

He points at the body. "You don't know why the fuck you're dragging a body across the floor?" He looks at me, his eyes accusing. "You're covered in fucking blood. What did you do?"

My jaw drops open, but I have nothing to say. I think I'm just as in shock as the dead body is. I glance down, seeing my entire body covered. I look like Carrie after she got doused in a bucket of blood. Not an inch of me is untouched.

"Do you have no fucking control? Killing someone with hundreds of fucking people around?" he shouts at me.

I drop her legs, my hands going to the sides of my face as a splitting headache hits. "I'm sorry! She was… she was fucking talking and just wouldn't stop!" I grab at my hair and pull, feeling like I'm losing my mind.

He steps forward, grabbing my hands and pulling them to my waist. "Get ahold of yourself, Raven!" He grips my chin, pinching until pain zings through me. He lifts, and my eyes clash with his. They're comforting and cold, unemotional and detached.

Yet, he's here. He's with *me.*

He protects me.

He wants to save me from myself.

"Are you with me?" he grits through his teeth.

I nod, though his fingers holding my chin make it barely noticeable.

He notices, though.

He notices everything.

"I'm here," I whisper.

He nods, letting go of me.

When pounding on the door starts, my heart flashes a mile a minute. I'm so going to get caught. I'm going to get caught, and I'm going to jail. I'll never see Aria again, and I'll never be able to protect her from her monstrous parents.

"Oh my God," I whisper, tears flowing down my face.

He points his finger at me, "Shut up." Walking up to the door, he slaps it. "Go the fuck away."

"Fuck you!" the female voice shouts from the other side.

He turns around, staring at me with an exasperated look on his face. Then he glances around, spotting a vent near the ceiling. "There.'"

My eyes grow wide. "There, what? You want me to wiggle my way through a vent the size of a shoe?"

He narrows his eyes. "You fucked up, Raven. Deal with the consequences." He shakes his head as he licks his lips. "Do you have any idea who she is?"

I shake my head.

"Trina might be a bitch, but her dad is a wealthy congressman and isn't going to sit back when his daughter never comes home again. This… this is a fucking mess."

Fuck. Oh, fuck. I forgot about that.

"So, I'm going to jail." My hands slap at my sides, and I feel like I'm doomed. My life is completely over.

He sighs. "You have no choice but to fucking deal with it, Raven. I'll shove her through the vent. You'll have to drag her down until you reach the end. It should end by my car. We'll take the body to the woods."

I frown and he scowls at me, his finger coming up and pointing in my face. "You'll fit in there, and you'll deal with the fucking repercussions of your fuck-up."

I swallow down the lump in my throat as I look at the blood. All the blood. Her body has to be nearly empty at this point. "But what about the mess?"

"There's always blood at the inferno. It's you in the bathroom with a dumb bitch that gets harder to explain. If someone went to the cops." He shakes his head. "Reggie would never let them, but I'm not taking the risk."

He walks over to the vent, popping the lid off with no hesitation. Walking back to the body, he lifts her over his shoulder, her form completely limp and dripping red. "Fucking hell, I should knock you to your ass for this," he grunts, shifting her on his shoulders and pushing the top half of her body inside the vent. He grabs her hips and ass, shoving her lower half in.

A hiss breaks from my lips as I watch his hands on her skin, and he pushes her the rest of the way in before turning around and glaring at me with lowered eyes. "You're jealous."

I narrow my eyes at him. "No, I'm not fucking jealous of a dead body."

"You're fucking *jealous*."

My chest burns with anger, and I step forward, seething through my teeth. "Shut the fuck up, Caelian. I'm not jealous of anyone," I snap.

He takes a step toward me, his eyes black as night. He lifts me off my feet, and I kick at his body. "Put me down!"

He shoves me into the vent, directly on top of the bitch's body. "I'll deal with you later. Take her as far as you can go. I'll meet you on the other side."

I attempt to get up, but my spine hits the tin vent on every side. "What the—how the hell am I supposed to drag a body down when I can barely move?"

He sighs like I'm an inconvenience, and I suppose I am. I've caused this mess, and he's the one left to clean it up.

Grabbing the front of the vent, he gives me one last look before placing it over the front. "Go, Raven. Go right now."

I sit there a moment, and he slams his hand against the front of the vent. "I said go!"

I get moving, sliding past the body and lowering onto my stomach. It's uncomfortable, and I have to move like a worm, but I'm able to pull her, bit by bit. Every part of my body causes an echoing bang on the silver cage I'm trapped in.

I'm winded by the time I reach the other end, the smell of metallic blood and overwhelming slutty perfume turning my stomach. I hear an echo behind me, and my heart pounds in my chest a million miles a minute as I prepare for the worst, police, my aunt and uncle, anyone to fucking catch me dragging a dead body through a tiny cube.

Plastic on metal grinds and light filters in as the top pops open behind me. I glance over my shoulder, my head hitting the top in an agonizing slam.

TWISTED DARES

Caelian glares down at me, blood smeared across him in messy splotches.

"How did you get out of there? Did anyone ask questions?" I pant, winded from my efforts.

He ignores me, grabbing onto my ankle and pulling me out. His hands grip me, squeezing all the spots that make my entire body turn to Jell-O. He drops me, though, without so much as a passing glance. I watch him, and his eyes pass over me briefly before he reaches for the body.

He holds her like she's nothing. Nothing but an empty bag he needs to toss into the recycling bin. He lifts her without strain, walking to his car with the trunk wide open.

As he tosses her in, I notice a tarp is already placed around his perfectly protected trunk interior. He folds the tarp over her before pressing the button, and the door lowers, shutting with a quiet hum and click.

His dark eyes turn to me. "Get in."

I clench my jaw, narrowing my eyes as I walk around the side of the car. He's being an asshole to me for no reason. He doesn't understand. Hearing about my dad from Aria, and then this woman, it just… I snapped.

But he doesn't fucking care about the how or why; he can barely even spare me a glance.

My face hurts from clenching my jaw so hard, my eyes watering as I slip into the car. I keep my gaze out the window as he whips out of the parking garage and onto the Portland streets.

My dad… he's gone forever. How could he leave me with so many loose ends? How could he die when there's someone after me? How could he leave me without telling me that it'd be the last time? *The very last time.*

He knew, and he couldn't even tell me.

I sniffle, wiping away a tear before it can tumble down my cheek.

The car cuts quickly to the left, and my eyes focus on the forest around us. How much time has passed that we drove through Portland and are already in the woods on the outskirts of the city?

His hand covers the back of my head, and he pulls me toward him, until his eyes clash with mine. "Why are you crying?"

My mouth opens, but nothing comes out except for a silent gasp.

His eyes narrow into slits. "What the fuck happened?"

My tears fall this time, and I go to wipe them away, when he bats at my hands. "Stop. Your emotions are a part of you. Only hide them when you need to. Right now, you need to tell me what the fuck happened."

"My dad is dead." I whisper the words, each letter and vowel and consonant an agonizing pain against my tongue. The words feel ripped out of me, and now there's a gaping wound in my chest, one I can't cover with a simple Band-Aid.

"My dad is dead!" I scream, bending down until my head hits his chest. The pain rips through my soul, and I feel more agony than I've ever felt before.

I feel... I feel left alone.

I'm so, so alone.

His hand grips the back of my head, and he smashes my head into his chest, his heart is slow, steady, comforting, strong.

He's everything.

I'm nothing.

My guttural screams echo through the car in painful wails. Caelian says nothing, and I don't know if he'd say anything even if he had something to say.

It's hard to do anything when you feel like you've lost everything.

It's hard to exist.

It's hard to breathe.

My face becomes numb from the pain in my heart, and I feel like my soul leaves my body, and I'm nothing but an empty shell left to crack and shatter to a weightless dust.

I have no idea how much time passes. It may be seconds, or minutes, or hours, for all I know. Though, eventually, Caelian pulls my head back, his eyes a mixture that will drown me if I stare for too many moments.

His thumbs go below my eyes, and he wipes away my damp cheeks and tears. "It's time to take care of the body." He releases me, getting out of the car and leaving his door open. He's giving me an option. I can participate, or he will take care of it for me.

It's odd, the feeling in my chest; somewhere between nothing at all and everything at once. Numbness and pain clash together in the most wicked storm that makes me think I could levitate if given the chance.

I slip out of the car, watching as he lifts her dead body out of the already opened trunk. Her body looks soggy, the blood seeped fully into her clothes. He lifts her with ease, though, and I hate watching her in his arms. I hate that she spoke of him, and the way she'll be laid to rest is by him putting her there.

I hate that the last touch while her skin is exposed to the air is from his hands. I hate that she can feel his heart and the heat of his skin. I hate it all.

I hate her.

I hate... *everything*.

I rush forward, my fingers cinching around the fabric of her shirt and pulling until she rolls from his hold, her body falling to the hard ground.

"What the fuck?"

My foot goes forward, and I kick her in the face. I hear the bone crack, and I'm assuming the spine of her neck snapped from the force of my kick.

"Raven! What the fuck are you doing?" He steps toward me, pushing me out of the way.

I dig my nails into her arms. "Don't touch her," I growl.

He blinks at me. "It's a dead body." He steps toward her again, but I snap my fist out, punching him in the shoulder.

"Stay the fuck away from her!" I feel like I'm grasping at straws to stay sane. It's like I'm losing the last bit of humanity that I had left.

Whatever was left of me no longer is.

It is time. What I was supposed to be, I am.

I am now. Me.

I've lost it completely.

I'm a murderer. I feel like an absolute maniac.

"I'm trying to take care of *your* fucking mess, Raven. What the fuck are you doing? You want me to leave? I'll let you dig a hole and dispose of the body yourself. You want to get caught? Leave her ass here. At this point, you could've left her in the bathroom at the Inferno and you would've had a better chance at getting away with it. You wanna do this shit yourself? *Fine.*" He wipes his hands on his dirty pants, ready to walk away.

Ready to leave me.

To leave me more... *alone.*

"No! Stop!" I scream, my voice echoing in the woods.

He stops, his body tense as he stares at me. "What the fuck do you want from me, Raven? *What do you want?* I don't understand your emotions. They're fucking foreign to me, so don't ask me to solve your puzzle."

My heart nearly pounds out of my chest. My eyes flit between Trina's and Caelian's, then stay on his. "She was talking about you in the bathroom. She wanted to touch you and kiss you and... *fuck.* I snapped. I fucking snapped, okay? And I don't want you to be the last fucking thing that touches her slutty ass!"

He stares at me a moment, then gives me his back as he turns around and walks to his open car.

"Where are you going?" I wail.

He digs inside, pulling out a shovel hidden behind the tarp. He walks to a tree and starts digging, while not saying even a word to me. I watch him, working the twigs and pine needles. He moves for a while, digging a hole both wide and deep.

He's dug holes for bodies before. He's buried the dead before.

The sun eventually sets, and the only light is from the moon lingering above us in the clear sky. I've been gone way longer than I ever should've been. Aria is probably missing me, wondering where I am and if I'm okay. I have no idea what my aunt and uncle are doing, but glancing down at my bloody clothes, when I walk inside my home, I know I'll be going head-to-head with the devil.

Caelian leaps out of the hole and looks down at me. "Put her in there."

He won't touch her.

He respects my wishes.

I leap to a stand, grabbing her by the hands and dragging her into the hole.

Thump.

She falls to the depths with an awkward puff of dirt.

Caelian immediately gets to work, shoveling the dirt and plopping it on top of her without a second thought. He's so removed, so detached to her and the entire situation. He isn't fazed by death. He lives for it.

By the time that the hole is filled, and he's covered it to make it look natural, there's a chill in the air, and I know I have no more time left to spare. I need to get home.

He throws his shovel down, straight into the dirt, and gives me a look. A look that says I won't survive. Whatever it is he wants from me, will shatter my already fragile soul. Sweat drips down his temple, the hair around his ears damp while I shiver from the cold.

He stalks toward me.

"Stop," I demand, putting my hand up.

He doesn't listen.

He continues walking toward me, and just as he's about to reach me, I dash. I run as quickly as I can to the car, but Caelian is faster, and in only a few steps, he reaches me, his arm going around my waist as he pins me against his car.

"Please, I can't. I have to go home," I whimper.

He breathes in my ear, and it's a ferocious growl that vibrates through my entire chest. "You should've thought about that before your jealousy got the best of you." He reaches forward, plucking a lock of hair loose from my ponytail and curling it around his finger. "It's a good thing jealousy suits you. You look damn sexy with the fire and rage in your eyes."

I glare up at him. "I'm not jealous."

His finger pulls, my hair locked around it as his hand goes to my neck. He squeezes, pinning me flush against the car. "Jealousy suits you. Lying doesn't, and I can smell every lie. Every single time. Don't do it again or there will be consequences."

I swallow, breathing heavily through my nose as I give him a small nod.

"While death doesn't bother me, you wildin' out, killing any person in your fucking path, does." His fingers go to the waistband of my leggings, and he yanks them down over my ass, until they're stretched around my thighs. "You're a kitten. A wild, young, crazy as fuck animal who knows no boundaries. Who doesn't understand the rules."

His fingers burrow into me, and the pinch of pain only lasts a moment, until he presses into my folds, his middle finger sinking directly into me. "Rule number one, don't ever expose yourself. Nod if you understand me."

I nod, his fingers slowly sinking and pulling out of me. Over and over again until my knees are weak and there's not an ounce of strength left in me.

"You broke rule one tonight. You exposed yourself to nearly hundreds of people by making the foolish mistake of killing in public. That's the most idiotic, reckless fucking idea you've ever had."

His finger pulls out of me, and I want to gasp in pain at the loss. But only a moment later, I can feel the warmth of his hard cock brushing my backside.

I feel needy and wanton as I push back into him, desperate for any affection. I want it so badly. I need it. *I need him.*

While the rest of me feels lost and alone, Caelian seems to be the only one that gives me what I need in the moment.

He fills my void.

His free hand goes to my hip, and he holds me steady as he pushes into me. The burn is there, so much that my eyes water and between my legs is a pinching fire. His head bends, and he sinks his teeth between my neck and my shoulder, focusing the pain on my neck instead of where his cock tears me in two.

"You're not going to take another life until I've taught you how to do it correctly, right?" He plunges to the hilt, until there's nothing separating us. It's his hips to my backside, and his warm against my cold.

I say nothing, gasping out a breath as he pulls out and sinks back in.

"*Right?*" he grits between his teeth.

"Right," I moan, my head tilting forward as I settle my forehead against the cool side of his car. His fingers around my neck tighten as he pulls me back upright.

He tilts my neck to the side, until my lips brush against his. "I'll save you from everyone, but I can't save you against yourself."

I feel so lost, and so found.

"I'm crazy," I whisper against his lips.

"We're all a little wild sometimes."

I look into his eyes, wanting him to fix everything that's wrong about me. Make me normal so I don't feel broken on the inside.

"I feel like I'm not worthy of anyone. Not of you. Not of my cousin. Not of myself. Not even my dad would stick around for me."

He pulls out and shoves back in so hard my hips slam against the car. He growls, leaning forward and nipping at my lips. Pain mixes with pleasure, and I kiss him back, gasping in a breath as I nip at his lips until our separate breaths are one.

"Only you can wade through the chaos. I don't understand your emotions, but I'll grip you tightly as you tread those waters. I'll pull you to the surface when you're drowning in the madness. I'll breathe the air into your lungs as you choke on the overwhelming death. You are a killer. I am a killer. We fight death. We create death. We are the same. I am not going anywhere." He breathes the words against my lips, and I finally feel a calmness in me. My chest settles, and I kiss him fully this time, deeply and desperately as he speeds up.

He fucks me.

In the night, in the silence of the woods, with the moon hanging over us. Nothing can stop us. We're wild and untamed, and we're one in the same.

We both thrive on death. Taking a life settles our souls.

If soulmates are real, I think I might have found mine.

His fingers grip my neck, and the pleasure of his cock inside me is no longer filled with pain, but immense amounts of pleasure. It shoots down my legs and makes my knees weak. My chilled body turns warm from his, and soon we're sweaty as we grip each other in the night.

He speeds up, and we rock against his car until the tingling starts between my legs and his pants turn ragged. His hand grips my hip, the pads of his fingers digging into my side. The pain is welcomed, though, and I revel in it, wanting more of it, greedy for it.

"*I dare you* to come in the night, Baby Crow. With anyone watching, where anyone could see us. Let my name rip from your throat like I am the only thing that gives you life," he growls in my ear.

He is.

I bite my lip as a cry escapes. I can feel his cock twitching inside me, until my walls clamp onto him and he reaches the farthest depths of me. I can feel him in my throat, and his thrusts turn wild. Unhinged.

"Come. Now," he demands, and I let go, my legs giving out. He holds me upright, fucking my limbless body. He comes too, and I can feel the jerking of his cock as he empties himself deep inside of me.

"*Caelian!*" I cry, my voice echoing off the trees.

He holds himself against me until the sweat on his body cools, and then he pulls himself out gently. He yanks my pants back up around my waist, and rights himself before stepping away from me.

The instant emptiness overcomes me. Then I realize what time it is, and my blood chills in my veins.

It's time to go home.

chapter twenty-three

CAELIAN

Age Sixteen

"Cae," Gabriel says from my doorway.

I glance up from my homework to see my smirking brother. His eyes are glowing with an excitement I don't rarely see from him. At least when it comes to me. Me and my brothers are close as fuck, but we don't mess around with shit. I guess they do, but when it comes to me, shit is more serious. So why he has a look like there's an inside joke going on, it just confuses the fuck out of me.

"What's going on?"

He chews on his lip, debating whether he wants to give me the lowdown, but he's already standing here, so I doubt he really has a choice.

"I've got something I want to show you," he says.

"Maybe you should tell me before you show me." I glance back down at my textbook, writing another calculus equation that takes no effort at all to solve.

The footsteps of my brother entering my room make me lift my eyes to him again. I don't know what his plan or idea is, but it's unusual he's walked into my room. No one ever comes into my room.

I set my pencil onto my paper and shut my textbook. "Tell me, Gabe.

Not in the mood for games."

He smirks again. "You'll like it. I promise. But you have to trust me."

Matteo uses this moment to waltz up to my door. "You get him to say yes?"

I narrow my eyes as I glance between the two of them. "I'm not in the mood for pussy. I don't care if it's prime or whatever the fuck you guys think it is. No fucking thanks tonight."

"No, dude. Better," Matteo says, barely able to keep in his excitement. As the baby of the family, he's always bouncing off the walls for some reason.

I lift a brow. "You got me a kill?"

Gabriel shakes his head. "Nope."

Consider my interest piqued. If they think I'll like it more than a kill, well, it might as well be a fucking sea of guns and money.

I stand up, grabbing my hoodie over the back of my chair. "If I'm not into it, I'm bailing."

My brothers beam at me, and I swallow down my irritation and put a semi-interested look on my face.

For my brothers, I'll do anything. Even if it means ruining my night.

"Where are we?" I ask as we pull up into a parking garage in the heart of the city. It's a nicer area, though secluded, with no other cars on this level of the parking garage.

My brother just got his license and my parents rewarded him with a Cadillac. So, of course, he would want to drive his new Caddy instead of rolling around in my BMW.

Matteo is younger than both of us. He'll probably steal a fucking car before he has the chance for one to end up at our house.

"The Inferno," Matteo says from the backseat.

My face scrunches up, and I try to remember if I've ever heard the name before. I haven't. I've never heard of the Inferno or anything that has to do with it. I spend a lot of my time down at Morelli's Restaurant, and my aunts and uncles show me about the laundering business.

The Inferno, however my brothers found out about it, I have no idea.

"Where'd you find this place?" I ask as we hop out of the car. The expensive *beep, beep* of the lock engaging, and the lights flickering are the only sound and light in the darkness of the night. We walk to a door at the end of the garage and Gabriel pulls it open, revealing a stairway heading down.

Down, down, down.

"Someone at Morelli's was talking about it. It took basically no time to learn about this place and figure out what it's about." Gabriel shrugs.

"So, what's it about? What are we doing here?" I ask. The temperature grows cooler the lower we get, and as we hit the bottom of the stairwell, a cement tunnel appears that seems to extend forever.

"It's a place I think you'll enjoy," Gabriel says as we walk down the tunnel.

I glance at them, but their emotions are under lock and key. They give nothing away, and instinct tells me to grow suspicious, even though I never need to be when it comes to my brothers. But when you're wandering the underground city of Portland to an undisclosed location, it starts to look sus.

The echo of our shoes dissipates as the distant sound of screams and cheers and shouts seep through the steel door that grows closer with each step.

"You guys." I narrow my eyes at them. I fucking hate crowds. Like *detest* them. The amount of people that surround you and breathe on you and bump into you. Fucking hell, it's too much.

I stop in my step. "I'm not going to some massive fucking party or something."

Gabriel steps up to me, a blank look on his face. "It's not a party. Trust me, Cae. You'll fucking like it."

I take a deep breath, knowing that I can trust him. He's my brother. They are *both* my brothers.

I give them a nod.

Gabriel grabs onto the handle and pulls, opening to lights and screams and so much fucking shit going on. I squint as I try to make sense of it all.

"Welcome to the Inferno." Gabriel raises his hand and shows me the massive fighting ring. Two men are in the middle, bloody, bruised, and swollen. They fight each other so brutally that my mouth waters.

"What is this place?" I ask.

"This is the perfect place for you, brother. You can spend your entire life burying bodies. But we all see how pent-up you get in the meantime. Why not fucking fight people?" Matteo says from beside me.

"This isn't just any kind of fighting ring. It's more than just MMA or boxing or shit like that. This is like some brutal-ass shit. People can die here. People kill here. This is where secrets stay buried and death goes to die," Gabriel says, his eyes holding an excitement of their own.

I watch the men in the ring, one clearly stronger than the other. One of them falls to the ground, and the other one gets on top of him, beating him senseless and blood flying through the air. Blood splatters across the creamy white mat of the ring, and I can feel my body heat as one man goes unconscious, and the man on top stands, his body covered in sweat and blood as he pridefully takes the win.

It looks glorious.

"I think I might try it out." Matteo seems just as enthralled as I am.

"No," I snap, glaring over at him.

Matteo sneers at me. "Oh, come the fuck on. I can take a handful of these motherfuckers by myself. One at a time? That's nothing."

"Matteo…" Gabriel starts.

I whip my head back and forth. "You aren't fighting, Matteo. Not here."

"Fuck off, the both of you." He folds his arms over his chest, and I glance away, not wanting to get into it here. He'll try to get his way for a long time, but he won't win. My little brother isn't getting in the ring. He's too wild and off the wall. He'll get himself killed because he can't control himself.

"Want to fight? I spoke to the owner, and he said you could get in if you wanted," Gabriel says as he leans into me.

I watch the winner leave the ring, and the unconscious fuck is carried out by two oversized men.

"Does Dad know about this place?" I ask him.

Gabriel smirks, two dimples popping in his cheeks. "Yeah, he knows the owner."

"Who is the owner?"

"I am." The voice comes from behind me. I spin around, body tense as I come face-to-face with someone the same age of my father. He looks just as sharp in a dark gray suit. His bald head shiny, with an array of tattoos swirling around his skull that hook around the back of his ears. He looks menacing, and he smiles at me, his crisp white teeth shining in the dimly lit room.

This entire place has an edge to it. It's dark and damp and a little dirty. It's not swanky or ritzy or anything like that. But it's not run-down and dilapidated, either. It's just… fucking raw as hell.

I'm intrigued by this place, and the man that stands in front of me.

"Reggie Gates. Nice to finally meet the eldest son of Drogo Morelli." He reaches a hand out, and I pause a second before grabbing hold of it and gripping it tightly.

"Caelian."

"I'd love for you to be a part of the ring. The Inferno is open seven days a week. You are welcome here anytime. Drogo has given me some insight about his children, though he says that you, Caelian, can tear someone apart without even taking a breath."

"You should try it, brother. I think it'd be fun," Gabriel says beside me.

I glance away from Reggie, my eyes falling to my brothers. Matteo is still pouting that I won't let him fight, and Gabriel has an excitement in his eyes. He wants me to fight.

"Yeah, I'll try it out."

"Excellent. I'll see you on the other side." Reggie slaps my back, and I grind my teeth together, so I don't rip his head from his shoulders. As soon as he walks away, Gabriel and Matteo are at my side, and we head up to the ring.

"Do you need anything? I can probably get you like a pair of shorts or something to wear."

I glance down at my hoodie, joggers, and Nikes. Not my usual attire I fight or kill in, but it's better than jeans or a suit.

I shake my head. "I'm good." I pull my sweatshirt and t-shirt off my back, and bend down to take my shoes and socks off. All I'm left with is my bare back and black joggers.

I look up at the ring. It's large, bigger than the one I have at my home gym. The ropes are more frayed, the mat bloodier. I'm usually fighting with my brothers or training by myself. I had a trainer the other year, but he became useless when I was constantly able to lay him flat on his ass.

I haven't fought anyone for fun. Pain always leads to death. Pain has never been a game.

Can I fight any of these people without killing them?

I glance at Gabriel. "What happens if someone dies?"

Gabriel's lips quirk at the corners, and I realize he's at ease for me. He knows this is a place I can be myself, which isn't many places, and isn't often. I find myself having to hide my true self from the world, so I don't end up in prison or dead.

"People die all the time in the ring. It's just another casualty here at the Inferno. The bodies here are disposed of discreetly. This is why coming here is almost like a secret fucking society or something. You aren't allowed to discuss this place to anyone unknown. Any tracing back here will fuck everything up. This place doesn't exist in the real world and that's how they want it to stay. Everything is just that… secret."

TWISTED DARES

It's like the place is made for monsters like me.

I grab onto the rope and slip into the ring. Hundreds of people surround me. They're adults, which makes me think that I'm probably the only sixteen-year-old in this place, besides my brothers, that is.

This isn't a place for children.

I can sense the curiosity at who I am. Why I'm standing in the ring when they've never seen me before. I can see them sizing me up. The buff yet trim guy with dark hair and even darker eyes. I wonder if they can sense the death that cloaks my skin, or if they think I'm some foolish kid that's about to bleed out in front of them.

The crowd starts shouting, screaming from their lungs as a form appears in the shadows.

He starts walking toward me, and I squeeze my fists, listening as each of my knuckles crack and pop.

I'm ready. I've been ready for a long time. Between school and the family business, I don't have much time to let out the stress and pent-up tension I feel on the daily. Killing people is a rarity that I can't help, can't execute as much as I know I need to. But as I get older, I'm becoming stealthier, figuring out how I can be discreet in my work. But now I have this place.

The Inferno.

The man falls into the light, and I can see his face, the scruff along his jaw, his ripped muscles so tensed the veins ripple along his arms.

He steps into the ring, and I wonder if we'll hear a ring or a horn or anything that'll signal the start of our fight.

Nothing happens, though. This man stares at me, and before I know it, he's coming up on me, his steps fast and heavy. The ground thumps beneath me, and I duck as his fist comes out. I slide underneath it, my heart pounding in my ears as he steps up to me again, and this time, he does make contact as his fist slams into my back.

I step forward, my stumble awkward and sloppy as I attempt to gain my footing.

My nostrils flare as he hits me again, and it's like a bucket of water falls over me. I'm wiped clean of everything, my mind, my soul, everything.

Empty. Dark.

I focus, darting across the ring so he doesn't hit me again as I turn around and come face-to-face with him.

He smirks at me, like he already knows he has a one up on me. He's a fucking joke is what he is, his fists strong but careless as his knuckles connect with my skin.

I stand up straight, my eyes focusing on his, and his smirk drops, just a tad.

He runs up on me, and my fist slinks out, slamming him in the jaw. He stumbles back, his hand going to his face as he realizes what happened.

His entire demeanor turns red.

He rushes me, his entire body bent forward. He wants to use all his weight on it when he shouldn't. Now his lower half is off-balance.

I swing my foot out, knocking him in the air as he does a belly flop to the ground.

The ground vibrates with his anger.

He rolls onto his back, his leg swinging up quickly and kicking me in the side. I fall on top of him, bending my knees out extra so they dig into his abdomen.

He lets out a loud *oomph*, and I bend over him, socking him in the nose.

Crack.

I bring my fist back, watching as his nose bends off to the side. Blood pours from his nostrils, and he coughs, a spray of blood coming up and splattering across my face.

Sick.

I bring my fist forward, clocking him straight under the chin on a strong uppercut. His entire body shifts upward from the force.

His eyes close, and I know.

He's out.

TWISTED DARES

I breathe over him, his entire body bloody and bruised and broken as he lays unconscious below me.

The room grows silent, then suddenly breaks out in a roar of screams and shouts. The girls scream at the top of their lungs and the ropes shake as they try to get an inch closer to me.

Fucking hell. Too many people.

I stand up, not spending another moment with this fucker as I slip off the ring next to my brothers.

"Holy shit, Cae! That was insane!" Matteo screams in my ear.

Gabriel's hands go to my shoulders, and he jumps up. "You are a fucking beast, brother. A fucking beast!"

I grab for my clothes, slipping them on my body as quickly as possible. The crowds don't die down; if anything, they grow louder. I can see the crowd closing in on us, and I stand up, glancing at my brothers. "Let's get out of here."

With one glance at the crowd, they realize what I'm feeling and give me a nod. We rush out of there, with my brothers shouting in my ear the entire way.

They're excited for me, but I can barely understand a word they're saying. It's all a whooshing combination of voices and words. My blood runs hot, and my skin vibrates with excitement.

That place is made for me. Made for people like me.

I thought I was alone in this, but I'm not.

I found a place where I can go and be me. A monster. A psychopath. Someone who can tear everyone and everything apart in my path.

It's where I can be who I've always been.

Death.

RAVEN
Age Eleven

The sun sets, the sky turning a hazy orange. My eyes grow heavy, but I'm not ready for sleep yet.

That, and my eyes focus on my parents, out in the field. Between the rolling hills and our backyard shed stand my parents with a black tarp in their hands.

Their latest victim lays on top of the fabric, naked and beaten. I know my father had sex with her recently from the white juices between her legs.

Another one of their parties that ends in death. It seems that every party they have ends with another hole dug in my backyard.

I've watched them dig, trading the only shovel we have on and off. The other one stands there and watches, or smokes a cigarette, their fingers stained red and the rest of their clothes brown with grime and dirt. The sun is the only thing illuminating them at this point. If they don't finish soon and get her buried, they'll have to wait for morning, and that's never a good thing.

It's bad to bury in the night, too many wild animals in the northern parts of California. Snakes, wild cats, everything and anything could be lurking in the distance. That, and the stench the next day is atrocious. They've only left the body until morning once, and I know they'll never do it again.

The body the next morning was torn to shreds and stunk up our entire yard. The dry hot air of the desert is not a good place for a dead body to rot.

They work and work, and I watch them until my elbow is sore against the windowsill in my bedroom. My fingers have a lingering red beneath my fingernails. It was only hours ago that I was standing over her crying body as I carved my signature crow into her forehead. The pleading in her eyes was painful to watch, but I've done it enough to become numb to the screams and the tortured cries.

I'm in a daze as I watch them finish their hole. My dad jumps out, throwing the shovel onto the ground and bending down to grab her arms. My mom bends, lifting her legs, and they swing her back and forth like a jump rope before their fingers release, and she falls into the hole.

I swear I can hear her dead body hit the dirt from all the way across the field.

My dad grabs my mom, and he kisses her deeply. My mom grips his shoulders, and it becomes so intimate I feel uncomfortable, and my eyes drop. I don't like watching them when they get like that.

The sound of crackling gravel has my eyes lifting, and I see multiple glows of headlights coming toward the house.

Who could that be? No one ever comes here. Not unless we're having a party.

I watch as my dad and mom release, and I can sense their panic from here. They start sprinting toward the house, their bodies quick in the night as they slink in the shadows. I'm off my bed and into the hallway when my parents burst through the back door.

"Raven! Raven, where are you?" my mom's panicked voice barrels through the house.

"I'm right here!" Cries instantly bubble in my chest as my mom rushes to me. Her arms are shaky as they wrap around her body, and my dad is right behind her, his eyes wild and his skin damp with sweat.

"Both of you, go out the back door. I'm right behind you." His orders are commanding and hold no room for arguments. I glance around my room, wondering what I should take or when we will be coming back.

"There's no time, Raven. Go with your mother. Right now." My father pushes us, literally pushes us down the hall and out the front door. My mom goes to open the door, and just as we're slipping into the night, my father stops us. "Wait." He bends down, giving both me and my mother a kiss. "I love you. Both of you."

"Cash, no." My mother's voice is a warning. *What does she know that I don't?*

She starts pulling me back inside, but he pushes her forward. "I love you. Go!" He gives us one last shove, then slams the door in our faces, locking it behind us.

My mom cries quietly as she pulls me into the yard, behind the tall brush and grass. It only takes another moment before I hear a boom, and the sound of, "Police!" echoes in the night. My mom pushes me behind an oversized bush. The grass is more weeds and is sharp against my bare feet and legs. The air is dry but also cool, and I wish I had on something more than a pair of shorts and a t-shirt.

I squat down, and my mother hugs me from behind as we watch our house in the distance. It's lit bright, as men in heavy uniforms and helmets walk throughout the house and yard. They have big dogs jump out of their cars, and pull the officers to the shed, then all around our yard.

To all the gravesites.

I don't totally know what's happening, but I realize this is bad. This is everything my parents never wanted to happen, and it's happening right now.

My mom lets out a silent cry as they pull my dad from the house. They shove him on his knees with his hands cuffed behind his back. His head is bent to the dirt beneath him, and tears run down my cheeks.

He looks so defeated.

One of them walks up to my dad, a big, black baton in his hand. He swings back, and then forward, the pole whipping across my dad's cheek so hard he flies across the yard and onto the ground in a heap.

Me and my mom gasp, cry, weep as he lays knocked out in our yard for a long time. As they pull the girl out of the gravesite, as they take things from our house, as the yellow tape gets put up around our entire house.

They eventually lift him to his feet, shaking him awake. They have a discussion, and I can't hear a word my father says, though it feels like they talk forever and ever. Bodies slowly start being pulled from the earth, and I can see my dad's realization that he's caught. He's in big trouble.

Once they shove him in the back of a police car, it starts driving away, but everyone else stays. I wonder if they are waiting for us to come back.

"Come on, Raven. We have to go. They'll be searching miles around our house when the sun comes up. We have to be long gone."

With tired legs and a frightened mind, I let my mom pull me to my feet, and we're off. Off into the distance of the night. That was the last time I ever saw my house, the last time my feet ever walked our land.

The last time we were ever a family.

It's been long. A long time.

Almost a full year of articles and news stories about my father and our horrible house. My dad was dubbed the "Crow Killer." A horrifying name and label placed on our house and our family. The manhunt was on for my mother and me, but we were able to stay away. Stay secret. My mom chopped my hair short like a boy and dyed it red. She then dyed her hair, too, and cut it, though hers isn't as short.

We skipped town, and from California we made our way to Nevada, and we've been staying outside Las Vegas in a small apartment. It doesn't even have any bedrooms, but it's all my mom is able to afford from her working at the nearby gas station.

She's… different. She's not as happy or as friendly as she used to be. She's distant from me except when she's crying and wants to hold me and not let go. She spends all her free time watching the news about my father. About a month ago, the trial started, and she hasn't been able to tear her eyes from the screen. She cries every time the camera points at my dad, a big, weepy, soggy woman with a clutter of tissues surrounding her.

I know she's anxious to see what's going to happen.

Thirty-four dead bodies found on our property. From what I know, it's not going to be a good outcome. What they don't know is that there are many more bodies than that, bodies that weren't buried on our property.

But she still looks for any and all pieces she can. My father has already gone through two different public defenders. No one wants to work with a serial killer who admits to the murders. Who explains the sadistic things they have done over the years.

That's the big word. Sadistic.

My father is a sadist.

I had to sneak on my mom's phone when she was sleeping to look up the word, but when I found it, I felt sick for an entire day. I don't like how dark and evil it paints my father to be. I don't know him as the sadistic man. I know him as the guy who would tuck me in at night and play with me in the morning.

I'm definitely a daddy's girl. I was always closer to my father than I was my mother. She loves me unconditionally, but my dad has always loved me more than he loves air. Our love was special, and I've known it for as long as I can remember.

I miss him.

I miss him so much. I wish we could go back. I would do anything to go back to our small home.

But now, now I'm stuck in this place with my mother who doesn't even seem like she's existing half the time anymore.

I roll out of bed, stretching my arms over my chest as I get off the couch.

TWISTED DARES

My mom is supposed to be working this morning, which means I have until this afternoon before I can do anything. I'm told to stay inside. I don't go to school. I don't go outside and play with the neighbors.

I stay in here and talk to no one except for my mom.

I walk up to the TV and turn it on, the voices of the news instantly blaring through our small apartment. I'm about to walk to the kitchen to grab some Rice Krispies to eat for breakfast, when the red breaking news alert stops me in my tracks.

Verdict reached for the trial of Cash Crow, the "Crow Killer."

I barely blink, barely take a breath as I wait for the words. I want to scream and go search for my mom. I don't want to find out what's happening to my daddy without my mom with me. If she hears about this at work, I'm worried she's going to have a mental breakdown. Then people might find out about us.

I really don't want to go on the run again.

A woman comes on the screen, with a dark pink coat on and a white and pink scarf wrapped around her neck. Not a hair is out of place as the oversized microphone sits in front of her face.

"The jury has reached a verdict in the case of The State of California versus Cash Crow, aka the "Crow Killer." The defendant has been charged on thirty-four counts of first degree, intentional homicide. Twenty counts of sexual assault. Thirty-four felony counts of torture. Thirty-four counts of…"

The voice goes on and on, but I can't focus on anything as the carpet meets my knees and I fall to the ground. A sob rips from someone's chest, and I look around, only realizing once I'm alone that it's coming from me.

I want my mom.

I want my dad.

I crawl to the couch, using it as a leverage to pull myself up. I'm never going to see my dad again. I've had only brief talks with my mom about what these different charges mean, but I do know that only one charge of first-degree murder will give you a full life sentence.

He's going to be locked up forever. He's going to die in there.

I sob as I stand up and stumble across the apartment, heading for the bathroom. Wiping my face, I push the door open and turn on the light, my cries getting caught in my throat at the sight in front of me.

My mother, staring at me. Her eyes vacant and cold, her body naked and pruned.

The water in the bathtub a dark, dark red.

Her arm hangs over the tub, with thick, long cuts going from her wrist to her elbow. A sharp knife lays on the ground, covered in red. Covered in her blood.

My sobs dry up, and a numbness fills me.

I fall to the ground, the water and her blood mixing on the white tiles. My hands fill with blood instantly as I crawl across the bathroom floor. To the piece of paper on the closed toilet lid. Written in her handwriting, though it's messy, jagged. Like she wrote in a hurry or was really upset when she wrote it. My fingers touch the damp edges, and I run my finger across her letters, wanting a piece of her to come alive, to breathe from the pages.

I drop the paper to the ground and scramble to my mom, pressing my fingers against her neck and hoping, pleading, that she's still alive. But she's not, and I shouldn't have held out hope that she was.

She's gone.

I glance back at the paper, focusing on the words.

My name is Nancy Crow.

I am married to Cash Crow.

My daughter's name is Raven Crow.

She is innocent.

Please save her.

Nancy.

I grab the paper, holding her handwriting against my chest as a fresh sob rips through my chest. I slide down, the wet floor instantly seeping into my pajama pants as I lay my head against the floor. In the fetal position, I let my mom's words sink into my chest as I spend my last minutes, hours, days, however long I have with her, I just want to have it to myself.

It takes two days. Two days and her work called the police, and they came to do a wellness check. When there was no answer, the apartment manager let the police in, and the smell was an instant giveaway.

Something bad had happened.

The police found me on the floor of the bathroom, covered in blood, dehydrated, cold, hungry, and I wet myself. I spent my days at the hospital and child protective services while the case fully closed. I had no one left. My father was locked away, and my mother couldn't bear to live a life without my father.

It took some digging, but they found my mother's sister and her husband in a small town in Oregon. After a week, I was picked up by Aunt Gloria and Uncle Jerry with the promise that they would take good care of me.

I wish I would have known as I got in their car that I was stepping away from one hell, and into another one.

Only this one would be much, much worse.

chapter twenty-five
RAVEN

"Are you sure you'll be all right?" Caelian asks from the driver's seat. I glance over at him, my house right down the road. I parked in the woods, out of sight from my house and anyone else. Caelian picked me up here earlier before we drove down to California. Now that I'm back, and within breathing distance of my house, it feels heavy and thick with an evil I don't know if I'm ready to deal with.

But the time is now, and it's been too long since I've been away. I was essentially told earlier that I couldn't leave the house, yet I went against their orders and did what I wanted. I wasn't gone for just a fake day at the library, or only a few hours. I left for the entire day, and then some.

I'll be walking back in covered in blood, with death on my hands, and smelling of sex. If I weren't in for hell before, I'm bound to be now.

I nod. No matter what happens, I'll be out of there tomorrow for my fight. I refuse to let them lock me in their metaphorical cell anymore. If that means bringing Aria with me and us never returning, that's what it will be. But I'm done with them. If today has taught me anything, it's that I'm done listening to everyone. I'm done being controlled by evil.

I'm making my own path.

Fuck my father's evil past. Fuck my aunt and uncle. Fuck the copycat.

Fuck all of them.

Caelian has taught me so much in our time together. Most of all, that I can embrace the mania inside me, and I don't have to be my own worst enemy.

I can be me, crazy and all. And I can love every fucking second of it.

I lean over and give him a quick kiss. "I'll be fine. I'll see you at the Inferno tomorrow." I reach for the door handle, but Caelian grabs me at the last minute, his fingers securing around my arm as he pulls me back to him.

"That's a lousy fucking kiss, Raven," he says just moments before his mouth smashes onto mine, a mix of plump lips and sharp teeth clashing together in a battle of unease. I can feel it in him. He doesn't know what's going to happen, and it doesn't sit well with him. He wants to protect me and do everything he can to stop what is bound to happen, but he can't control fate.

And I think that is his worst battle of all.

I lean back, breathless and lightheaded from his possessive mouth. I give him a little smile, slipping from his BMW and into my own car. I turn it on, and he waits for me to leave the woods before he pulls out and makes his way home.

Time to face the music of fate.

I turn onto the main road and quickly pull onto our long driveway. The lights are off, and it should give me relief with the possibility they went to sleep, completely forgetting about me and my faults, but I know they haven't.

It's like the house sits and waits for hell to break loose. I pull up behind Aunt Gloria's car, switching off my headlights and turning off the car. I sit for a moment, listening to the outside crickets and watching the nighttime fireflies circling the air.

With a deep breath, I pocket my phone and head outside. The gravel rolls beneath my shoes and I head up the front steps, taking a deep breath before I shove my key in the lock. It feels more ominous as the loud click sounds from the door unlocking.

I push the door open slowly, barely able to see anything as the night filters in through the windows. It's pitch black, not one light on inside the house. But it doesn't feel empty.

It feels oddly… full.

I slip my shoes off, hanging my key on the hook on the wall as I step inside. My heart pounds in my chest and I exhale a shaky breath. I glance around, feeling the uneasy sensation of being watched, but I don't see anyone. Not anyone.

"Hello?" I whisper, hoping on the off chance that it's Aria, and she's come to warn me of the type of mood my aunt and uncle are in.

But no one answers me.

My skin prickles with goosebumps, and I rush toward the stairs, when a shadow comes out of the darkness.

Fuck.

"You little tramp," Aunt Gloria snaps with a heavy pan in her hand. My eyes widen as her arm reaches up, ready to smack me in the head. I make a dash, when arms come around me, and I look up to see Uncle Jerry holding me in place.

"Time to repent, Raven," he says, pushing me toward Aunt Gloria just as her arm swings down, and the bottom of the pan connects with my forehead.

Everything goes black.

My eyes crack open, and my forehead *thump, thumps*. I open my eyes to the florescent light above me as my hand reaches my forehead. I feel the uncomfortable, painful knot between my eyes.

Where Aunt Gloria smacked me.

I hiss through my teeth. "Fucking hell."

Sitting up, my eyes widen when I see I'm back in the basement. Naked.

Not a stitch of clothing on me or in the cell with me.

Bile fills my mouth at the thought of my aunt and uncle undressing me, looking at my naked body. My uncle's probing eyes and inspecting fingers.

I clear my throat, my stomach turning in disgust.

I pull my hands toward my body and realize both my wrists and ankles are shackled. Also, this isn't where I'm usually shackled. The long, heavy chain extends out of my makeshift cell, secured to the cement ground of the basement floor.

It's like they've moved things around and created a jail cell of sorts in the corner of the basement. Bars surround me on two sides with the brick walls surrounding me on the other two.

Nothing else is in here. No one here to save me. Nothing but a light more fluorescent than one in a doctor's office sits above me, making it impossible to have any comfort down here. I step forward, pushing on the bars that extend from the ceiling to the ground. No budging. They're secured tight.

I pull on the chains, and they clank against the metal bars of the cell, but otherwise no movement from them. It's like they've been... planning this. Like they always knew I'd be trapped down here, naked and alone.

I sit down against the wall, my knees going to my chest and my arms going around my knees. I wonder how long they'll keep me down here this time. Will Caelian wonder where I am? Will they look for me?

Will my aunt and uncle kill me this time? Is this where it ends?

I would have fought them to the death. I would have battled them until I was a bloody body on the ground. I hate that they gained the upper hand, coming after me in the dark, while I was weak.

Caelian would be disgusted.

He's taught me so much, yet when it came time to use my senses and detect when something is wrong, I faltered. I fell flat, even though I knew something was wrong. I knew I was walking into the lion's den, and I wouldn't make it out alive unless I fought tooth and nail.

Yet here I sit, naked and afraid, at their will to do whatever they please.

They could kill or torture or let me sit here and rot until I'm bones and an empty heart.

I sit in the corner, my bare skin cold against the damp cement floor. No blanket, no bucket to use the bathroom. Nothing that would make them even slightly humane.

It's worse than a prison cell.

It's just me, and four walls.

I doze on and off, the shuttered windows making it impossible to decipher whether it's night or day. I feel lost, and alone. I haven't heard a peep of Aria's voice. I miss her.

I miss Caelian.

My heart squeezes in my chest, and my eyes water as I shove my head between my legs. So lost. So cold.

So *alone*.

Footsteps rouse me from a daze a while later. I'm not sure if I slept or if my mind went numb, but my neck is stiff from the awkward position, and my limbs are stiff from being tense due to the cold air of the basement.

The door opens on the other side of the basement. Through the boxes and laundry area and the empty spaces in the rickety old wooden stairs, light filters in from the second level. I'm not sure if that means it's daytime or if they only flicked the light on.

The difference in light causes me to raise my hands to my face to shield my eyes. It hurts, and I know that means it's been a while since I've been down here.

A set of footsteps start heading down the stairs, each step creaking from rot and age. When a second set of footsteps come down, I fold into myself. Both of them.

Both of them is never good.

I say nothing and neither do they as they head toward me. Aunt Gloria is first, with Uncle Jerry right behind her. The looks on their faces could break bones.

TWISTED DARES

They are utterly vicious with the cruelty and hate in their gazes.

"Raven," my aunt says as she reaches the gate. She lifts the wooden cane in her hands, banging it against the bars. "You little tramp." She bangs it again.

I flinch, lowering my shoulders like a beaten dog. I feel so strong when I'm not around them, but falter to the scared, weak little child they want me to be the moment they're near.

My uncle stands behind her, his face a mixture of rage and excitement. This guy is sick. A real disturbed fuck if he gets off on the pain and fear of children.

Says the girl who just stabbed a girl repeatedly with glass from a bathroom mirror and then had sex with the dead girl's blood still on her hands.

My uncle reaches into his back pocket, pulling out a familiar pair of latex gloves.

My eyes widen, my entire body stiffening in fear. "No, please. No." I stand up, my spine flush with the brick behind me. I want to sink into it. Disappear into nothing. I don't want them to touch me. Pain, I can handle. I will live through pain. When he touches me, I feel dirty. Used. His touch lingers, and I know it's his own disturbing secret.

He likes the touch.

My aunt grabs a set of keys from her pocket, dangling them in front of me before she grabs one. "You disobey our rules, you sneak out doing God knows what. You come back covered in blood." She turns the key, looking me in the eye. "You are the spawn of the devil. A demon, just like your father. You go and see him because you have evil blood, just like he does!" she screams, her cane swinging out and whacking my arm.

I whimper, swallowing down my cry.

"Tell me, Raven. Have you given yourself to a man? Are you committing the vile sin of premarital sex?"

I shake my head. The lie might cost me, but I can't say yes. Maybe they won't be able to tell? I don't know, but I fear the consequences for admitting I've had sex.

My uncle steps into the cage, and I shuffle away from him and his gloved hands. Aunt Gloria grabs the base of the chains and begins pulling them, the slack growing taut with each second that passes. Soon enough, I realize the chain to my arms runs upward, and my arms pull at my sides like I have wings. She loops one of the links, around the base, locking my arms in place.

She begins to pull my feet, and my uncle's smirk grows into a smile as my legs start separating.

"No. No!" I shake my head, attempting to get away, when it's no use. My body forms an *X*, and I let out a scream at the exposed position.

It's so uncomfortable, and it's exactly what they want. They love that I'm in a position that is so vulnerable to them. They feed on my fear and pain.

"I'll ask you one more time, Raven. Have you engaged in premarital sex?" Aunt Gloria asks, her hand gripping the cane tightly.

I shake my head, swallowing down my cries. I don't want them to know the extent of my fear.

"Go ahead, Jer. Check." Aunt Gloria nods, and Uncle Jerry stalks toward me. I whip my head back and forth, but it gets me nowhere. I thrash, try to kick, attempt to headbutt him. Anything and everything that I can do, I try. But he's on me in a second, his body flush against mine and his gloved hand on my behind.

"I'm going to go ahead and guess that you've been a naughty, sinful girl, Raven. I can smell the sins on you. I can see them in your eyes. Do you think we want you to be like this? We are trying to help you, but you seem to not want our help."

His hand slides down my butt cheek, using his fingers to probe them apart. I clench them shut, using every bit of muscle I have to protect myself, but it's no use against his alarmingly strong fingers. He slides them between my legs and dips a finger inside. One long finger sinks into the depth of my private area that no one is supposed to touch without my consent. Only a place that Caelian has been, and he is the only one I want there.

But my uncle goes there forcefully, his finger probing in and out a few times before withdrawing.

I gasp, tears flowing down my face in disgust and horror.

He pulls his hand back and looks at me with hate before turning his gaze to his wife. "She is ruined, Gloria. She has given herself to the devil."

Aunt Gloria doesn't say any words, nor does she look at me in the eyes. She brings her cane back and whips it forward, lashing the wood across my breasts and ribs. Pulling the cane back, she whips me again.

"Ahh!" I cry out. It feels like flames hit my skin in a lashing heat. Again and again she hits until stars flicker before my eyes.

My uncle backs away until he's out of the cage. I can hear him take his gloves off, the snapping of rubber making me nauseous. Then he's back, next to Aunt Gloria with a Bible in his hands. He bends to his knees, the Bible in his left hand with his right hand extended toward the sky. He closes his eyes as he starts spouting words. A mixture of English and something I don't understand.

My aunt steps toward me, the tip of the cane pushing into my skin until I can feel a bruise forming from the pressure. "You stupid whore!" she screams in my face. She bangs the cane against my shoulders, my neck, my head, over and over again.

"Please, stop!" I scream.

"I should have never let you come live with me! It was a mistake from day one! Your whore mother didn't want you, no other family wanted you, and we sure didn't want you! But we had to take you, and I wish we never did! You're a whore! You're a sin! You are the devil's child!" she screams at the top of her lungs.

"I'm sorry! I'm sorry!" I wail, my body wet with sweat and tears. I feel wrong, I feel tainted. I feel like the meaning of life is worthless at this point.

Why am I even here?

"Just kill me!" I scream. "If you hate me so much, just get it over with already!" I sob, the lashes continuing on my back and front, my legs, my ass. My neck is hit so hard it feels like my voice is destroyed. My sex is hit so hard it feels like a pool of blood floods my insides.

"Stop! Stop!" Aria's voice filters through my screams, her bellows so gut-wrenching I can feel it in my soul. Aunt Gloria stops her lashings, and Uncle Jerry stops his prayers. Through squinted eyes, I see the trembling body of Aria at the top of the stairs.

"Stop! You guys are monsters! Stop hurting her! She hasn't done anything wrong!" she sobs, her voice echoing down the stairs.

"Go to your room, Aria!" Aunt Gloria shouts.

A growl rips from Aria, so much anger in her voice, and I feel it directly in my chest. "I hate you! I hate the both of you! I'm... I'm calling the police!" She slams the door shut, her feet running across the floor above me.

"Get her, Jerry. Go get her right now!" Aunt Gloria shouts.

Uncle Jerry slams his Bible shut, getting to his feet and barely giving me a passing glance as he rushes up the stairs.

Aunt Gloria steps up to me, until I can smell the hairspray on her hair and the soap on her skin. "You will die down here. You will not eat. You will not drink. You will never lay down again. I will let you die and rot with nothing but these chains attached to your body." She steps back, a low growl emanating from her chest. "I hate you, Raven. I hate everything about you." She swings her cane back, then forward, giving me one last whack to the side of the head.

It hurts. It hurts so bad.

My head lolls to the side, in a daze, as she walks away from me, securing the cage before making her way upstairs.

I grunt, my entire body screaming in pain, the thump in my temple making my body twitch with each beat.

I can feel my nose start to drip and glance down with hazy eyes, watching the blood drip from my nose and onto the cement below me.

I'm almost knocked into a painful sleep when Aria's screams reach my ears. They are painful.

Scared.

Horrified.

So much pain.

My eyes spring open, and I pull against my chains until the skin on my fingers shreds.

"Aria!" I scream. "Don't hurt her! Don't you hurt her!" My vocal cords tear apart with how loud my voice is.

I pull and fight against the chains until every bit of energy is drained from my body.

There's nothing left of me.

The last thing I hear before the pain takes me under is the sound of Aria screaming my name.

chapter twenty-six
CAELIAN

I watch another two men beat each other senseless in the ring. The crowd is busy tonight, as it always seems to be when Raven is around. They like to see her fight. They like her strength, her sexiness. They like how she isn't outright about it and acts like a fucking savage.

There is no one like Raven, and that's what draws me to her.

Except, she's not here.

Raven should've been here an hour ago, fighting in the ring. Overpowering a man double her size. She should walk out bloody, and then I'd take her in the locker room because there's something fucking feral about her when she's covered in blood.

But she's missing, and something is wrong. I can feel it in my gut just as Rosko can. I can oddly tell he wanted to see her, and she has a thing about him. A softness crosses her features. But now Rosko sits next to me, with the same *what the fuck* expression that I have.

Did she ditch me?

Did she get into an accident?

I know none of those are true. I'm holding myself back from losing my sanity because I can feel something is wrong.

I could sense it when I dropped her at her car last night. Something is incredibly off. The sense of dread. The sense of something not sitting right in your chest. I could feel it as she tried pulling away from me last night, which is why I pulled her back for a deeper kiss. I wanted to give her the strength she needed to conquer whatever battle she had against her aunt and uncle.

She's strong enough to beat those old fucks into the dirt, yet with her not here, I know that isn't the case. She didn't beat them.

They've got her.

Rosko looks up at me, like he knows we're about to go do some shit that is going to give him a full belly.

I reach out, my fingers going behind his ear. He tilts his head into my hand, and I scratch the itch for him.

"We have to go find her, Ros," I mumble, my voice barely audible above the pounding of flesh above me. But he hears me, because he can always hear me.

Rosko growls, and I know he's telling me we need to go.

"Let's go."

Thirty minutes later, I'm pulling down her road so fast the dirt kicks up in a cloudy plume behind me. Rosko sits beside me, his body tensed, and his hair raised on his back. The trees grow dense as I drive out of the city and into the wilderness. Her aunt and uncle live on a small patch of land that's secluded from everything else besides a creepy-looking church about a mile away.

Is it a coincidence they live away from everyone? Maybe, but I think it's a good fucking opportunity to torture Rave.

I growl, sounding just as ferocious as Rosko as I cut left and pull into their driveway. The lights are off outside, leaving the driveway and yard in pitch-black darkness.

I park behind her car and take out my phone, sending her another text that goes unanswered.

Me: Where the fuck are you?

I sit and watch the house, tapping my phone on my knee as I wait for a response.

I get none.

Barging in there could be a colossal mistake. I could end up fucking up whatever progress she could be trying to make with her aunt and uncle. Maybe things are good, and she's using the day to smooth things over, and I might just literally tear everything to shreds.

Or... or she could be dead on the floor, staining their carpet red.

"Fucking hell." I rip my door open, and Rosko is right on my heels. I shut my door quietly, and we make our way up the stairs to the front door. I twist the knob, only to find it locked.

I growl, and my fist goes to the small glass pane, shattering it to bits. My hand maneuvers through the opening, and I unlock the door from the inside.

The moment the door opens, the screams hit my ears.

Rosko lets out a low growl.

My skin turns hot as I step on the glass and make my way inside. I'm about to run upstairs when I realize, those aren't Raven's screams. No, those must be Aria's.

I walk through the living room and kitchen, opening the door to the lower-level bathroom.

"Where the fuck is she?" I growl.

Rosko scratches on a closed door, and I open it, seeing the stairs leading to the basement.

The basement.

Rosko instantly races down the stairs, and my defenses go up.

"Rosko, stop." I hop down two steps at a time, flicking on the light as I make my way to the basement.

"*Holy. Shit.*" I blink at Rosko who is scratching at the poles of a cage. A cage where Raven stays trapped.

Naked. Beaten. Bloody. Bruised. Shackled.

Dead? Alive?

"Raven!" I shout. She rouses, her head lifting slightly to look at me through drunken eyes.

Is she drugged? What the fuck is wrong with her?

"Raven!" I yell again. Her eyes focus as she looks at me, disoriented as she tries to figure out what's going on.

When she sees me, her eyes blink a few times before tears flood them. "Caelian, what are you doing here?"

Rosko whimpers and keeps scraping at the cage she's trapped in. I look up and down, seeing it cemented on the bottom and bolted to the wooden beams on top.

I growl, my hand going to the wood and my other one gripping the cage door. I pull with all my strength, and the wood splinters as I toss the metal bars to the ground. I rush to her, not sure where to put my hands.

Rosko starts licking at her legs and side, whimpering as he looks for his own way to rescue her.

I follow the path of the chains, up to the ceiling and to the ground, where a massive metal loop is cemented to the ground, the chains bolted.

"Fucking hell, I'm going to tear these motherfuckers apart."

"Help. Help. Please…" Raven pants as she looks at me, her eyes still crazed, not fully here. She doesn't know what to do, but from her pale face and arms, the lack of blood flow to the top of her body is fucking with her.

I walk to the bolted loop and pull, the chains busting in half. They loosen quickly, and she drops to the ground in a heavy clank of metal. I rush to her, pulling her upright as I look her over. She'll still be shackled to the cuffs, but I can figure that shit out. At least her arms are released now.

"Where are they?" I grit through my teeth.

Raven lifts a weak arm and points up. "Aria. Aria needs help."

I listen, the screams having quieted, but that must be who I heard earlier. The cousin.

The parents are hurting their own child?

My entire body flushes hot and the only fucking thing on my mind is murder.

"I'm going to fucking kill them." I get to my feet, ready to tear up the stairs and chew them into pieces just like Rosko would.

But Raven grabs onto my ankle, weak and in so much fucking pain.

"No. No. They're mine," she moans.

I lean down, releasing her fingers from my ankle. "You can't, Raven. You're too weak right now. Their fucking time is up."

She shakes her head, using my pants as a support to pull herself to her feet. "No," she spits. "I can fucking do it."

I run my tongue along my upper teeth. I'm a greedy asshole and want them for myself, but I'll allow her these kills for everything they've done to her.

"If they do anything—*fucking anything*—to you, or if you falter, you're stepping aside, and I'm taking them out."

She looks pissed, but after a second, she nods.

Rosko sits patiently next to her, protecting her. She leans down, brushing her face against his fur.

It's... weird. To see someone affectionate with my dog. And to see my dog enjoying it. Not tearing their skin off their face.

Another scream tears through the house, and Raven's face grows red as she starts walking up the stairs. The chains clank and drag up behind her. She walks with purpose, though it's slow and wobbled. I place my arm around her naked waist, looking at the welts and bruises all across her skin. Thick and long, like she was hit with a fucking pipe or something.

I can hear my teeth crack from the force of my clenching.

We make our way through the main level, and up the stairs of the second floor. The screams and cries are clearer now, the raw pain and fear coming through Raven's cousin make my stomach jump. This is the one person Raven feels connected to in life.

I can't imagine how she feels. If it was one of my brothers—one of my *family*—making this sound, the people causing them pain would've already been buried.

"Stop it, Aria! Calm down, and it'll all be over soon!" comes a woman's voice that makes my teeth curl over my upper lip.

The aunt.

Raven speeds up, her steps steadier as we get to the second level. She bursts into the room, Rosko right behind her. When I see what's happening, my eyes only fucking see red.

Rosko growls, racing forward and sinking his teeth into the bitch's ankle. I watch as blood squirts onto his teeth, dripping to the beige carpet.

"Ahh!" the aunt screams, releasing her daughter as she turns around. She looks shocked to see us behind her, but immediately goes to the source of her pain.

The cane in her hand—which is what I'm assuming she used on Raven—comes down and whacks Rosko on the head.

Only, Rosko is like me. A normal dog would yelp and cry, but Rosko only bares his teeth, becoming even more pissed.

Raven steps forward, using the chain hanging from her arms to wrap around her aunt's neck, pulling her off the bed and away from Rosko.

"You dumb cunt. I fucking hate you," she spits as she pulls her aunt across the floor. Raven gets her on her stomach, her foot going to the back of her neck as she tugs.

The chain pulls tight, her aunt's back bowing as her head is yanked back, an instant gurgling and choking noise coming from her.

"What—oh my goodness! Gloria!" The uncle shoves off his own daughter—*sick fuck*—and rushes toward her. I bring my hand up, slamming it against his chest. He looks in my eyes, seeing the darkness, the evil, and stops. His eyes going wide as realization hits.

He's fucked.

He tries to leave, but I force him to stay put as my fierce girl kills his fucking wife.

"No! Raven, no!" her cousin yells from the bed, her lower half completely exposed. I grind my teeth and hold myself back from killing this motherfucker in my grip for touching his daughter like that.

Raven is too far gone, though. I don't have to see her eyes to know they're black as night. She's nothing but a dark soul at the moment as she takes the life of her aunt. It makes my blood warm, my bones hum in excitement as I watch the bitch before me take her last breaths.

She chokes, every breath strangled and constricted, her fingers grappling for the chains she used to lock her own niece in the basement. Raven, a fucking force, stands above her, naked, beaten, bruised, her fingers turning white as she pulls, pulls, *pulls* on those chains until her aunt goes limp.

Dead. Gone.

"No!" her cousin cries from the bed, horrible wails ripping from her throat.

Her uncle drops to the ground, my fingers stretching his shirt as he falls below me.

Raven releases her aunt, and her body hits the ground with a heavy thump. Loosening the chains around her aunt's neck, she stands up, her eyes going straight to her uncle.

"You motherfucker," she growls, her voice unlike her own. She sounds possessed, and she is. With rage. With hate.

With revenge.

I let go of the uncle, stepping back but still blocking his exit. He has nowhere to go. He has nothing to do.

"Raven, no! Stop!" Aria screams, sitting up and preparing to lunge at Raven. I step toward the bed, holding her down. Raven is too far gone to even acknowledge her cousin. She grabs the end of the chains, swinging them around before whipping them at her uncle.

They clunk against the side of his head, and he knocks to the floor, his hands going to his skull in agony.

TWISTED DARES

Raven hits him again. And again.

And again.

She bludgeons her own uncle in front of her cousin, not caring an ounce for anything, or anyone. Blood flings through the air and across her naked body.

I should be disturbed by the fact that I grow aroused by the blood coloring her creamy skin. By the fact that she's committing murder and tearing apart the only family members she has.

She is crazed. Manic. Completely turned upside down.

And she has never been more beautiful.

The cousin screams bloody murder in my arms, and I have never heard anyone scream for a sick fuck's life as much as this girl is. Her screams are so desperate, her voice cracks, growing raspy like she's been smoking for fifty years.

I glance down at the uncle. His face is a pile of mush. There is no way to make out his facial features or even his skin at this point. His insides are his outsides.

I lean forward, a hand going out and gripping Raven's shoulder.

Her eyes are unfocused, her face dripping blood, her hair sticking to her skin. She's a mess. Fucking flawless.

"He's dead, Raven."

She glances down, her fingers releasing the chains as she steps back.

"No! Why! Why!" her cousin screams, her body shaking in my grip.

Raven blinks, like she's noticing her cousin here for the very first time. "Oh, shit," she whispers, stepping forward.

Her cousin scrambles backward until her back hits the wall behind her. "Leave me alone! Leave me alone, Raven!"

Raven's face pales and grows red at the same time. "He was touching you, Aria!"

As if just noticing she's naked from the waist down, she pulls her sheets over her legs. "He wanted to make sure I wasn't sinning!" Tears flow down her face and snot runs down her nose. She wipes it away with the back of her hand. "They might not be right… but they were my parents, Raven! And you killed them!"

Raven glances away from her cousin, her eyes connecting with mine, and my chest deflates by the look in her eyes.

Emptiness.

Just pure emptiness.

chapter twenty-seven
RAVEN

Aria hates me.

She honestly, truly hates me.

I can see from the look in her eyes that she'll never forgive me. I glance at the ground, seeing her dead parents lying on the floor. Blood soaks into the carpet, my feet making a disgusting squish every time I curl my toes.

"I, uh…" I swallow, not really knowing what to say. I feel fucked. I feel like this was the true awakening for me. I've not only killed one person, now I've killed four.

I am no longer innocent. I can no longer be saved.

What I've always meant to be is here. I am now me. What I was is no longer. The flesh and blood and bones of my being is cruel. I am a monster, what my father has raised me to be.

I am a murderer.

"I have to go," I mumble, heading out of the room.

Caelian latches onto my wrist, his fingers strong and possessive. "Where the fuck are you going?"

I can barely focus as his eyes probe mine. They are calming and reassuring. He knows what I'm going through. He knows the madness I'm feeling. He can help me. He can walk me through it.

But my eyes flit to Aria's, and I only see hate. She despises me, who I am, what I've done, what I stand for.

I pull my wrist out of his grip. Bending down, I dig into Aunt Gloria's pants and pull out the small set of keys. I unlock the shackles weighing down my wrists and ankles, bloody and filled with the matter of my uncle. Everything is blurry. Everything is wrong.

"I'm a monster," I mumble, feeling like the words are dripped in my aunt's and uncle's blood. They're layered in the pain I've felt my entire life. Everything I've gone through. The emotions that I've been burying, holding in, and building over the years, making me a ticking time bomb…

Have exploded.

"I'm a monster," I repeat. My body grows cold. Empty. Completely void of… everything.

I walk out of the room, ignoring the hate spewing from Aria and the unusual feeling coming from Caelian that's so unlike him.

I can't deal with them when I don't even know who I am right now.

I rush into my room, grabbing the first shirt I can find and tossing it over my body. It drapes to my upper thighs. I can hear Caelian struggling against Aria, but I ignore them as I race down the stairs. I don't know where I'm going. I have no idea what I'm doing.

I just need to… get away.

Once I hit the bottom step, I race through the kitchen. The sound of a boot on the linoleum perks my ears, and I spin around.

My eyes go wide when I see a masked man. Tall, broad, covered in black from head to toe. The mask covers his face, plastic and shiny. The eyes are cut out, and they look black behind the mask.

Black and evil.

I draw in a shaky breath, *petrified*.

Is this the copycat?

I glance toward the stairs, knowing if I made my way upstairs that Caelian would protect me. But the masked man notices, and he steps to the left, blocking my path.

I race to the right, to the front door. But the man behind me is quick, and I feel a pinch in my neck, and a rush of cool flows through my veins.

Fuck. Drugs.

I reach a hand out as my legs turn to sand, my fingers gripping the knife block on the counter. If I could only protect myself, I'd maybe have a chance.

But I don't, because my entire body falls away into nothing. Then my mind.

Then my soul.

I'm left with no bones. Only ash on the ground.

And everything goes dark.

chapter twenty-eight

CAELIAN

I hear a crash, followed by the front door closing.

My eyes narrow, and I glance out of Aria's window, but the roof blocks my sight to the front of the house. I point at Aria. "Fucking stay right here."

I fly down the steps, my eyes flitting around the room. I slap the light on, the room turning a yellow hue as my eyes fall to the kitchen floor. Next to the sink is a block of knives, each one strewn across the floor in a messy heap.

A fucking struggle.

Oh, fuck.

I race to the front door, opening it so fast the glass rattles against the pane. I see Raven's car still parked in her original spot, but glancing at the end of the driveway, I see taillights in the distance before it turns, heading right on the road.

Fuck, fuck, fuck.

I hear the patter of footsteps upstairs and clench my teeth, not in the mood to deal with a bratty kid when in my blood, I can literally feel something is wrong with my girl.

I run back up the stairs two at a time, seeing Aria in Raven's room, pushing her window open and her leg swinging over the side.

"Fuck, no," I grit, stalking into the room. My hands grip her waist, and she lets out a horrified cry. I toss her onto the bed, glaring at her. "Your cousin was just taken."

Her eyes widen for a split second, watery and terrified. "Wh-what?"

I growl, feeling pulled in a million different directions. I want to race after Raven, but I know once I do, Aria will be out of here. Probably to the police, and then I'll have that mess to clean up.

Fuck. Fuck, fuck, fuck.

I pull my phone out of my pocket, dialing Gabriel.

"Yo." His lazy voice, followed by a cough in the background, makes my jaw clench. If he's fucking high as a kite, he might be useless as fuck to me.

"I need you and Matteo here. Right now."

"Where you at?" Matteo shouts in the background.

I glance at Aria. She's squirming, like she's ready to bolt again. I press my hand on her shoulder, keeping her in place. "I'm at Raven's. Get here, like right fucking now." I hang up, pocketing my phone.

Glancing at Aria, I sigh. "Now, what to do with you?"

"Caelian!" My name booms through Raven's small house.

With a quick glance at Aria, I head downstairs, watching as my two brothers step inside. They look around, both of their faces painted in disgust as they look at the nauseating number of holy items placed around the home. The walls, the counters, the tables, everything and everywhere you look is filled with something religious. It's… too fucking much.

"Dude, this is gross." Matteo's face is screwed up in horror.

"What the hell is wrong with these people?" comes from Gabriel.

I shake my head. Now is not the time.

"Follow me." I head through the kitchen, and they both stop as they look at the knives.

Gabriel's eyes widen, and he gives me a pointed look.

I shake my head, walking up the stairs and into Aria's room. The aunt and uncle are where Raven left them, bloody as fuck as everything they once were seeps into Aria's carpet.

"What the—" Gabriel begins.

"You didn't—" Matteo starts.

I shake my head. "Raven killed them." I bend down, picking up the chains. "Those fuckers had her trapped in the basement. Beaten. Naked. I think this motherfucker even touched her." I kick her uncle in the head, blood and bits of brain matter sticking to my shoe.

I wipe it on the carpet.

"Holy shit," Gabriel whispers.

I drop the chains. "That's not my biggest problem." I glance up at them. "Raven fucking ran, and when I heard shit, I went downstairs. The knives were on the ground and some headlights were pulling out of her driveway." I exhale every single ounce of air in my chest. "I think the copycat got her."

"And you didn't go after her?" Matteo shouts at me.

I shake my head, walking out of Aria's room and into Raven's. In the corner of the room is Aria, bound, gagged, tied to the foot of Raven's headboard, circled into a ball on the floor.

Matteo chuckles. "This isn't funny at all, but it sort of is." He runs his hands down his face.

"What the fuck is going on?" Gabriel barks.

"This is Aria." I squat down, pulling the torn sheet from her mouth. "She's pretty fucked up, but I can't let her go. She'll probably run to the police."

"I won't! I won't! I promise, I won't," she sobs, her cries soggy and clogged with tears.

I glance over at Gabriel, and he nods. "She definitely will."

"I need you to take her home while I find Raven," I say.

Matteo's face scrunches. "What about the bodies? You want our help?"

I shake my head. "I'm good. I have an idea. And then I need to go find my girl." It feels weird saying it to my brothers, but they know. And honestly, there's no reason to not make it clear anymore. "Just get her home. But I need to go."

Aria cries, but me and my brothers watch each other. My rocks. My blood. The only people in the world I can rely on.

Gabriel grabs Aria like she's a ragdoll, tossing her over his shoulder before we head down the stairs. I stop once I reach the kitchen, and Matteo looks over his shoulder at me.

"What're you doing?" he questions.

I turn on the gas stove burners, then turn on the oven, leaving the door open. Within moments, the scent of gas starts to fill the house.

Gabriel's eyes widen. "I'm going to get her in the car."

I nod as I head outside, going into their detached garage. My eyes instantly land on the red jug in the corner of the room. I pick it up, walking back out and seeing Matteo and Gabriel watching from outside his car.

I walk back inside, pouring gasoline, from the stove, around the kitchen, and to the front door.

"Here," Matteo mumbles, handing me his lighter.

I open the top and flick it, watching the yellow flame spark.

Tossing it into the doorway, I watch the flame grow, moving from the doorway and into the house.

I move quickly.

I rush to my car, turning it on and reversing out of the driveway. Gabriel is right behind me, and we go to the edge of their property, watching as the flames continue to grow.

Boom.

The gas stove explodes, the entire house glowing yellow before settling in a massive, burning flame.

I glance over, looking into Gabriel's car and seeing both him and Matteo smiling.

They're happy to be rid of weird-ass fucks like that, too.

One glance at the back of the car shows a sobbing Aria, watching her house like she will miss that life. Like she'll miss those people.

Oh, kid, you were living a lie.

I give Gabriel and Matteo a nod before I shift into drive and pull away from this house for the last time. I have no more time to waste.

It's time to go find my girl.

chapter twenty-nine

RAVEN

My neck screams in pain as my eyes crack open. My hands reach up, but they are constrained, blocking me from much movement. I blink as I look down, seeing only the threadbare shirt I have on my back brushing my upper thighs.

I glance around, seeing a room I'm unfamiliar with. It's dark, basement-like. Similar to the basement I just escaped from, but it's not the same. It's different.

This looks like it's inside a dilapidated house, with black streaks and water marks running up the brick walls. Massive cobwebs and dust bunnies clog the corners. This place looks abandoned, and if I'm correct, it really is.

I glance behind me, my hands tied to the back of the chair, my ankles tied to the legs, and from looking at it, the chair itself is bolted to the floor.

What happened?

I think back, and all I see is red.

Me, choking Aunt Gloria to death.

Me, beating Uncle Jerry to a bloody pulp.

Aria, looking at me like she couldn't bear the thought of being around me for another second.

Me, running away. Doing what I do best.

I remember being downstairs and seeing a black figure in the shadows. Chasing me. Stalking me.

Injecting me with something.

And then there was darkness.

My breathing begins coming out in panicked chokes. I wonder if this is the end for me. I wonder if this is my fate, and I was only meant to be evil for a moment. Maybe the world couldn't handle how bad I'd become, and it wanted to be rid of me while it had the chance.

Maybe the copycat is a vigilante and knew I'd only soil the world with evil.

Maybe I was meant to be nothing at all.

A blip in the universe. Something forgettable.

An unmentionable moment in time.

I hear footsteps upstairs, like someone just entered the building, or house, or wherever I am.

A lock sounds, and the door creaks open, a sliver of light filtering in down the stairs.

Footsteps sound coming down the stairs. Heavy. Slow. A man's footsteps. That's the only possibility.

The black figure, the same one that was in my kitchen, comes to stand before me. The black mask that's seen in a horror movie. It covers the entire face, terrifying, almost mocking as it watches me.

Is this the copycat?

"Who are you?" I whisper.

He tilts his head to the side, like my question was complex. It wasn't; it was simple, and the fact that I'm in this position gives me a combination of defeat and rage.

"Tell me who you are!" I shout.

Nothing. No noise, no sound, no words. Not even a breath. Just a mask that looks so devious I wonder what kind of monster lies behind it.

"Let me get out of here! I swear, I won't say a word! Please!" I scream.

Not a peep.

Rage versus defeat. Defeat versus rage. Do I allow the mystery man to break me down, or do I fight him with everything in me? I should let go now, while I've ruined the very relationship with the only person who means anything to me, yet the fight in my blood refuses for me to break into dust.

"If you don't fucking let me go, I swear I'll tear you apart with my fucking teeth!" I snarl.

The mysterious man takes a step toward me, his hand covered in a black leather glove as it lifts, and my eyes can barely blink as it reaches the mask. The fingers wrap around the front, and as if in slow motion, the disguise peels from the face, revealing the person behind the mask.

My mouth drops open, and a shocked gasp breaks free.

What the fuck?

To be continued...

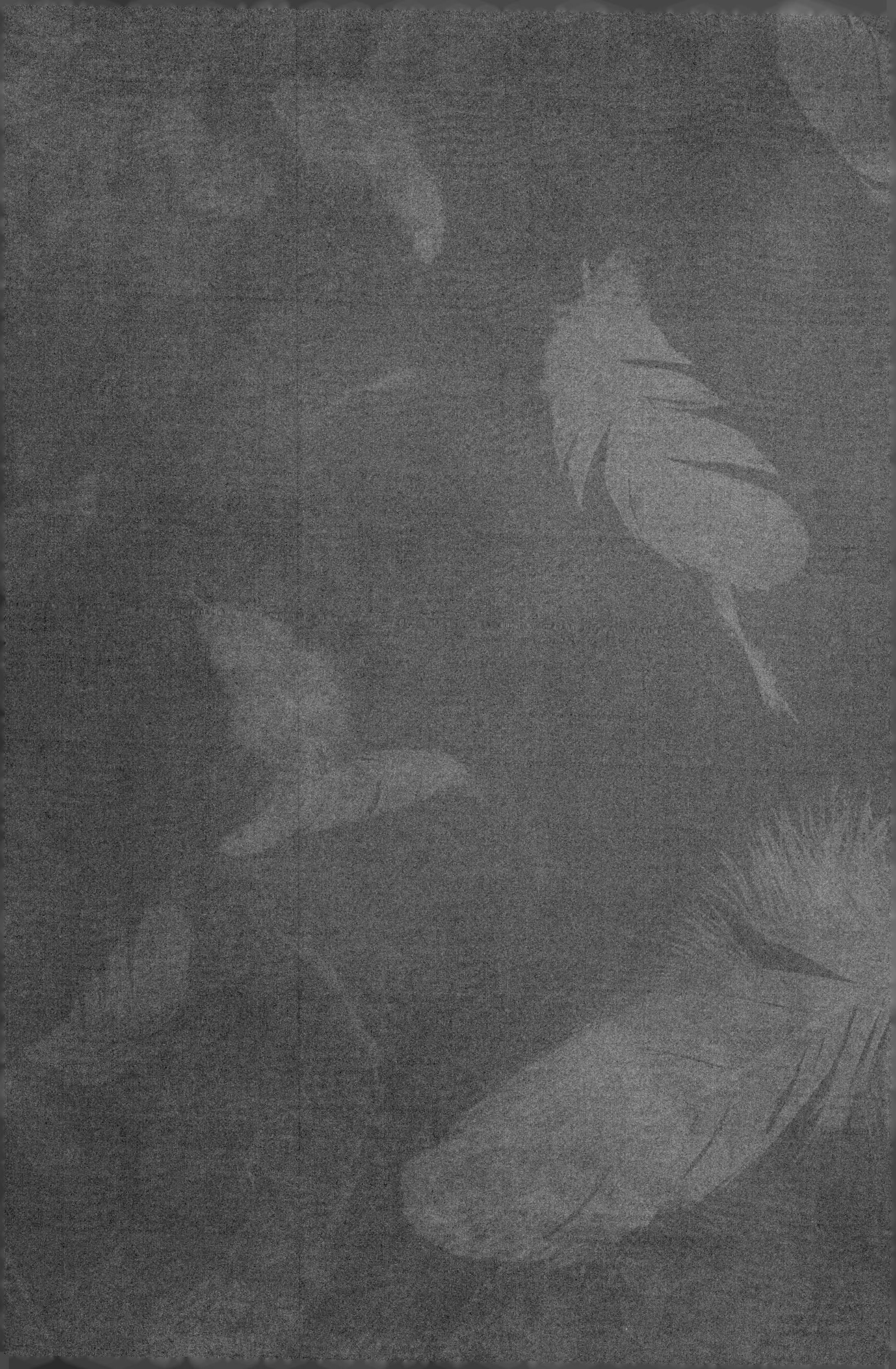

ACKNOWLEDGEMENTS

Every time I come to write my acknowledgements, I can never figure out exactly what to say. So this page usually ends up being rambling of the people who have helped me along the journey of this story. But even for those who aren't listed, I need you to know you have an impact on my life. You have an impact on each story that I write, plot, put together. You are there. I remember those who interact, and reach out, and care about me.

The journey for writing this book was bumpy. I struggled both mentally and emotionally to get words on paper because sometimes life is… life. But I persevered, and I made it through, and I couldn't have done that without each and every person in my life. So, thank you.

Thank you to my husband, Preston, and my two daughters, Arianna and Eliza. You are there through it all and allow me to follow my dreams. You love me at the end of the day, and I couldn't ask for anything more.

Hailey, I love you. You're first because let's get it, you're first. Thank you for the countless Facetime calls and cheering me up through this rocky road. I miss you across the country but you're forever my best friend until the end.

Rachel, I'm counting down the days until I see you in June. You're going to get the biggest hug. Thank you for always being an ear when I need to verbalize my thoughts. I wouldn't be here without you.

To the rest of my team, thank you. You are all such a major crutch in my life that I couldn't function without. So thank you for always being there, I love you all!

To my author friends, thank you for being there for me. Helping me write and being there for me is unlike anything. I've made some wonderful friends in this community.

To all my readers, ARC readers, bloggers, and followers, thank you! I write for you. You guys motivate me and inspire me to write dark, deep stories from deep in my soul. Every story has a part of me in it, and for you

guys to take the plunge on me means everything.
Thank you, I love you.

BOOKS BY A.R. BRECK

Grove High Series
Reapers and Roses
Thorn in the Dark

The Grove Series
The Mute and the Menace
Lost in the Silence

The Seven MC Series
Chaotic Wrath
Reckless Envy

Standalones
BLISS
Where the Mountains Meet the Sea
Wicked Little Sins

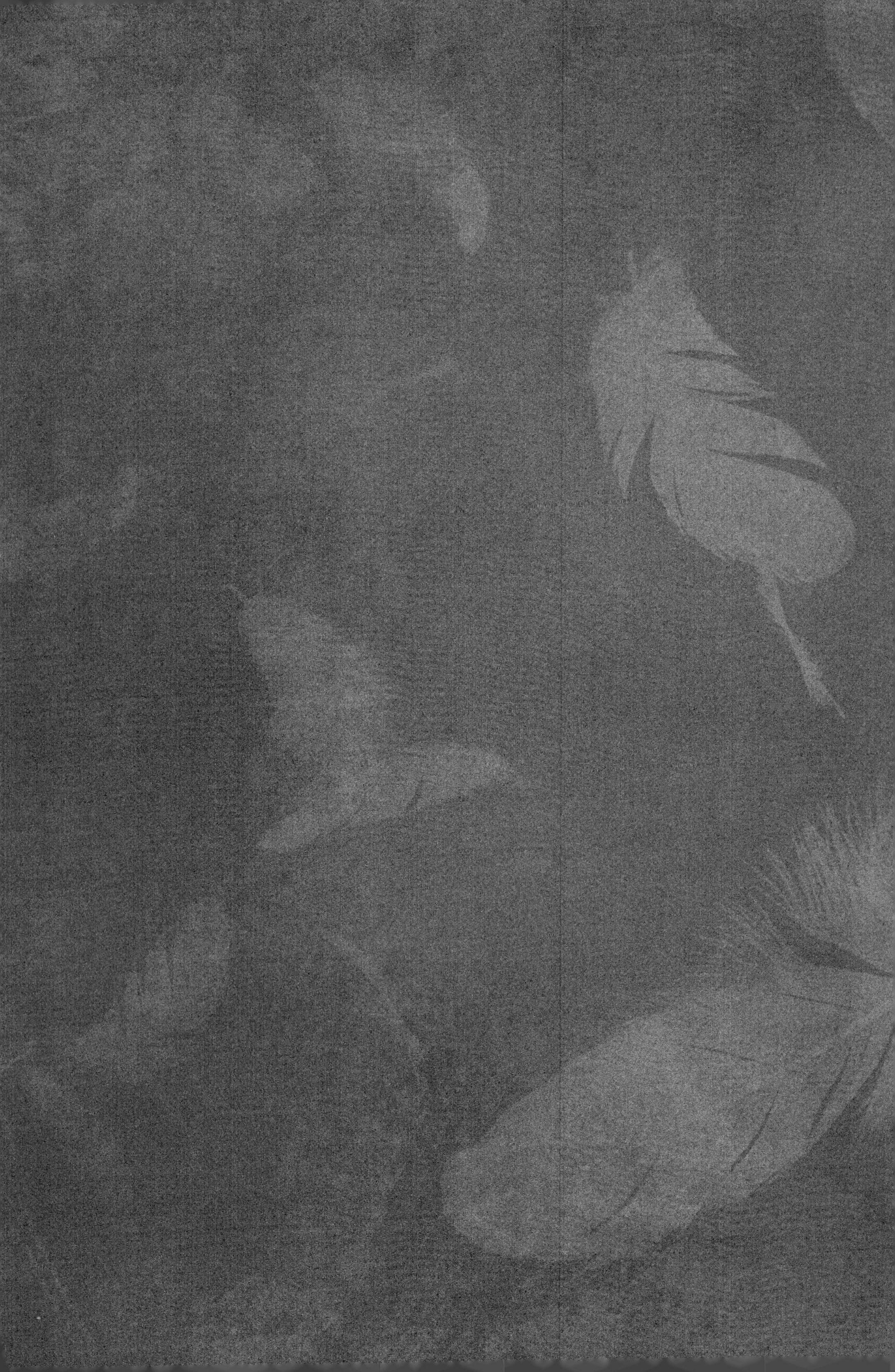

ABOUT THE AUTHOR

A.R. Breck lives in Minnesota with her husband, two children and two dogs. Socially introverted and slightly sarcastic, she enjoys watching horror movies and reading romance novels. When she isn't writing, she enjoys road tripping with her husband, two kids, and fur babies around the country. She writes primarily dark and edgy romance books with a touch of suspense. Follow her on social media to stay up to date on new and upcoming releases!

Printed in Great Britain
by Amazon

CW01215219

商務印書館壹佰貳拾年紀念

SINCE 1897

生肖日历

2017

锦鸡吉祥

薛晓源 主编

胡运彪 审校

周　硕 编译

商务印书馆
The Commercial Press

2016年·北京

前 言

鸡，德禽也，寓意吉祥，其来有自。汉代人韩婴《韩诗外传》："头戴冠者，文也；足搏距者，武也；敌在前敢斗者，勇也；见食相呼者，仁也；守夜不失时者，信也。"鸡被赋予"文、武、勇、仁、信"五种德行，"鸡生五德，食则相呼"，因此有德禽之美誉。在我国的十二生肖中，鸡是唯一的鸟类，能够被先人选作生肖之一，更说明鸡在日常生活与传统文化中的重要意义。

本年历收集整理了西方博物学家绘制的 365 张鸡的图片，其中包括各种珍稀的家鸡品种，也包括在分类上与家鸡同属鸟纲鸡形目的野生"鸡"，例如羽色华丽的波兰鸡、披着华服的孔雀以及色彩斑斓的红腹锦鸡。这些图片生动悦目，全部采自博物画家精心手绘，有水彩画、石版画、木刻画，用多元的艺术形式栩栩如生地展示了各种家鸡和它们的"族亲"——野生"鸡"类绚丽多姿的形象，其中许多品种和种类乃国人所未见。可以说本年历丰富了关于鸡及其相关文化的想象与认知，是一部具体而微的以鸡为主角的百科全书。

本年历的文字介绍主要采撷自 19 世纪博物学大师如约翰·古尔德、奥格尔维·格兰特、乔治·弗格森等人的著作篇什，并邀请相关动物学专家结合现代文献资料精心编译，力求简洁清晰传递博物学旨趣。也因为本年历的图片与文字取自不同博物学家的作品，不同学者的命名难免有所不同，为了尽可能降低这些因素带来的混淆，年历中进行了相应的处理，家鸡部分仅保留了某些大类的英文名，野生鸡形目鸟类则是中文名配以现今学名（斜体拉丁文）呈现。

2017 年是中国传统生肖的鸡年，集锦西方博物学之德禽彩绘，为中国新年报晓，这是一次有意义的中外文化交流与碰撞，旨在以西方图像讲好中国故事，传播中国吉祥。以日历形式，百字篇幅，图文并茂，寓知识于审美，祝愿读者诸君吉祥如意相随日常。

本年历主编　薛晓源

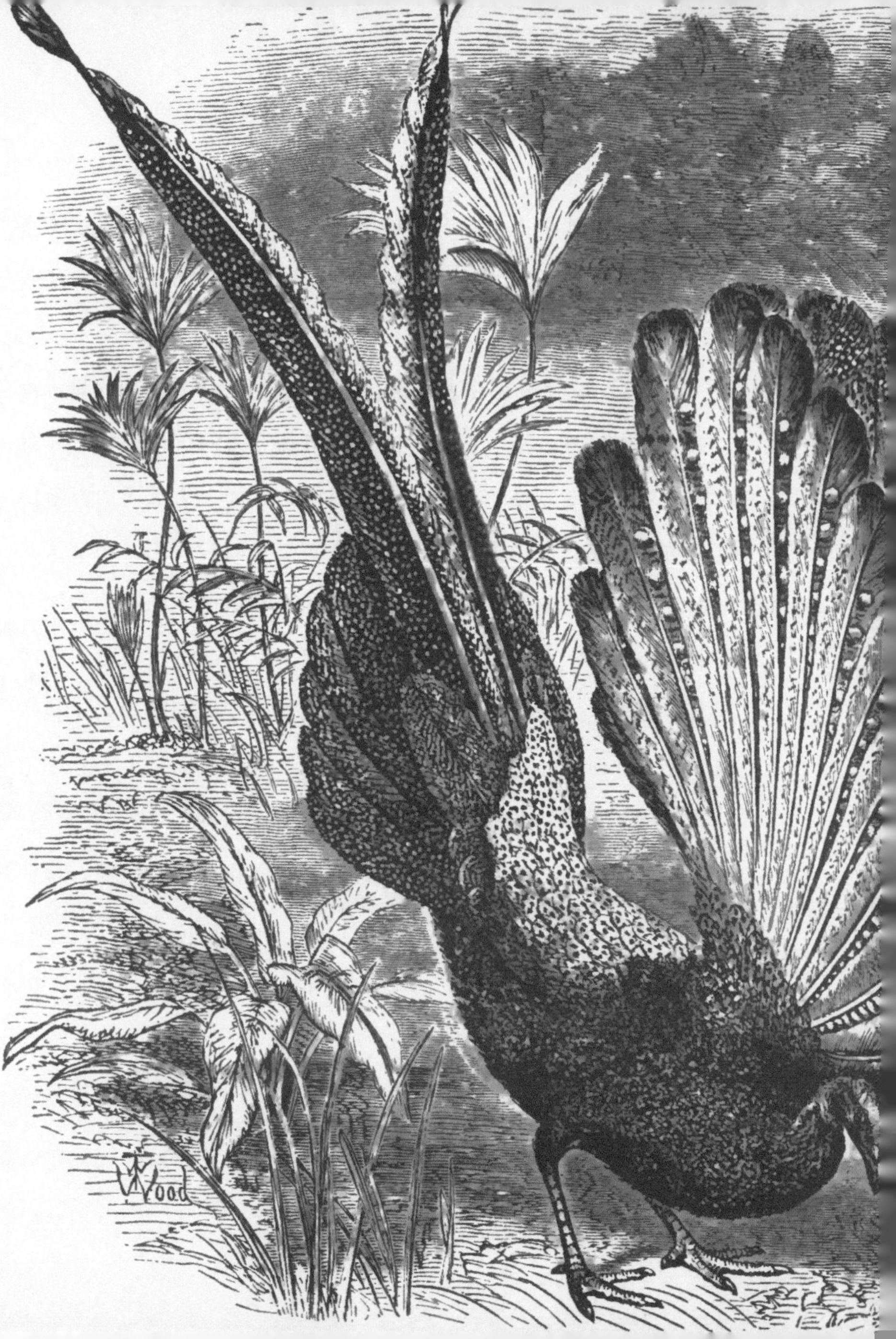

1 月

January

白交趾鸡和米色交趾鸡、雄性马来鸡、浅婆罗西摩鸡和深婆罗西摩鸡

一月

Sunday, 1
January
2017

1

农历丙申年 十二月初四

星期日（元旦）

婆罗西摩鸡（Brahma）

  这种鸡或许是马来鸡和交趾鸡杂交的品种，或者说它更可能就是交趾鸡。

一月

2

Monday, 2
January
2017

农历丙申年　十二月初五

星期一

交趾鸡、深婆罗西摩鸡、马来鸡

  没有其他家禽比交趾鸡更受人瞩目，它的引进很大程度上引发了当时著名的"家禽狂热"。

  从外观看，婆罗西摩鸡的鸡冠最为奇特，好像把三个鸡冠压到一起。除了一两个同样来自印度或印度群岛的品种外，这种鸡冠独一无二。

  马来鸡是最早引进到英国的大型亚洲品种，除长腿的狼山鸡以外，它的身材超过其他任何品种。

一月

3

Tuesday, 3 January 2017

农历丙申年　十二月初六

星期二

英国女王陛下的交趾鸡（Cochin）

　　大名鼎鼎的交趾鸡来到英国，或许可以追溯到 1843 年第一次鸦片战争后，在那次战争中，包括上海在内的中国若干港口被迫对欧洲船只开放，交趾鸡由此引进至英国。

一月

Wednesday, 4
January
2017

4

农历丙申年　十二月初七

星期三

雄性暗黄交趾鸡

　　公鸡的仪态和体型精致、高贵,并且气宇轩昂;翅膀奇短,紧贴身体;与身体其他部位相比,腿、胫、腰大得不成比例。

一月

5

Thursday, 5
January
2017

农历丙申年　十二月初八

星期四（小寒）

雌性暗黄交趾鸡

母鸡的体态大致与公鸡相同,只是头要低得多。对于优中选优的个体而言,面容小巧雅致、俏丽秀美,可谓赏心悦目。

一月 6

Friday, 6
January
2017

农历丙申年　十二月初九

星期五

雌性黄棕色交趾鸡

母鸡全身为黄棕色，而公鸡的颈部和背部为浓重的深红褐色。

一月

7

Saturday, 7
January
2017

农历丙申年　十二月初十

星期六

山鹑交趾鸡

　　山鹑交趾鸡是交趾鸡中颜色偏暗的品种，公鸡的胸部是黑色的，母鸡的胸上部则为清晰明朗的条纹。

一月

8

Sunday, 8
January
2017

农历丙申年　十二月十一

星期日

白交趾鸡

  白交趾鸡拥有交趾鸡中最美丽的形体和纯白的羽毛,羽毛中没有任何杂色。它们应该算是交趾鸡中最易培育的品种。

一月

9

Monday, 9
January
2017

农历丙申年　十二月十二

星期一

雄性白交趾鸡

　　白交趾鸡脾性友善，容易饲养——一码高的围墙就能让它们安安稳稳。

一月

10

Tuesday, 10 January 2017

农历丙申年　十二月十三

星期二

白交趾鸡（左雌右雄）

  它们粉色的蛋个头儿很大，是其他交趾鸡蛋的两倍。白色交趾鸡饲养起来成本较低，因为它们的食量比米色品种小得多。

一月　　　11　　Wednesday, 11
January
2017

农历丙申年　十二月十四

星期三

雌性交趾鸡

　　交趾鸡庞大的体格，古怪的啼鸣，退化的尾部以及腿部和身体下部异常蓬松的绒毛，都为人们熟知。图中的母鸡把这些特征展现得淋漓尽致。

一月

12

Thursday, 12
January
2017

农历丙申年　十二月十五

星期四

米色交趾鸡

  各式交趾鸡都起源于中国。来自中国的米色交趾鸡,不仅是所有交趾鸡的先驱,而且是所有米黄色家鸡的鼻祖。再没有比它更引人注目的品种了,当毛色和体格适中时,它的美丽首屈一指。它体格魁梧,羽毛丰满,身体浑圆,有着优雅的曲线。身体的每一个部位都或多或少呈现出球状。

一月

13

Friday, 13
January
2017

农历丙申年　十二月十六

星期五

雄性米色交趾鸡

　　这种鸡最标准的个体应该是全身呈均匀的浅黄褐色，胫上的羽毛也是同样的色彩，颈羽不掺杂其他线条或黑斑，在所有交趾鸡中最受人们青睐。

一月

14

农历丙申年　十二月十七

Saturday, 14
January
2017

星期六

雌性米色交趾鸡

图中这只母鸡的颜色有些深,和最标准的个体相差较远。

一月

15

Sunday, 15
January
2017

农历丙申年　十二月十八

星期日

黑交趾鸡

  从体格、体型和羽毛看,它是名副其实的交趾鸡,它与其他交趾鸡的区别在于毛色。它周身闪亮着黑色,公鸡的黑色羽毛上笼罩着一层浓郁的金龟子绿色;母鸡则没有那么明显。

一月

16

Monday, 16
January
2017

农历丙申年　十二月十九

星 期 一

山鹑交趾鸡

  再没有比这种山鹑交趾鸡更难培育出的完美品种了。它不仅要在体型和羽毛上达到交趾鸡的标准，色度、色调和条纹也必须呈现出完美的状态。它的价值在于选美。它的生长特征和其他交趾鸡相同，颜色差异显著。胸前和身体上的黑色越深、越有光泽，就越美丽。

一月

17

Tuesday, 17
January
2017

农历丙申年　十二月二十

星期二

山鹑交趾鸡

一月

18

Wednesday, 18
January
2017

农历丙申年　十二月廿一

星期三

马来鸡(Malay)

　　和其他被人类驯养的动物一样，马来鸡的准确起源已无迹可寻。不过普遍认为它们应该是原鸡的后代且驯养的历史应该不是很长。

一月

19

Thursday, 19
January
2017

农历丙申年　十二月廿二

星期四

雄性马来鸡

公鸡的头宽且长,浓重垂悬的眉毛使面部表情看起来异常凶狠。它们奇怪的冠独一无二,既不是单冠,也不是玫瑰冠,更不是三叶冠,倒是更像半块儿非常小的胡桃——圆形的隆起,上面布满小小的凸起。

一月

20

*Friday, 20
January
2017*

农历丙申年　十二月廿三

星期五（大寒）

黑胸暗红马来鸡

　　这一品种的马来鸡看起来有些奇怪,尤其是它们有着与身体极不相称的奇怪尾羽,类似于马来鸡和小种斗鸡的杂交体。

一月

21

Saturday, 21
January
2017

农历丙申年　十二月廿四

星 期 六

白马来鸡

一月

22

*Sunday, 22
January
2017*

农历丙申年　十二月廿五

星期日

黑狼山鸡（Langshan）

　　狼山鸡来自中国一个叫作狼山的地方，1862年英国陆军官员发现了这一品种，十年后，人们将它带到英国。今天的黑狼山鸡由美英家禽饲养员繁育而成，它们有着美丽的外形，丰满却又不失高挑。

一月

23

Monday, 23
January
2017

农历丙申年　十二月廿六

星 期 一

白狼山鸡

　　白狼山鸡最初是黑狼山鸡的变种。1885 年，人们在英国注意到这一品种的出现。尽管它们的毛色在今天有所改进，却依旧不够洁白。

一月

24

Tuesday, 24 January 2017

农历丙申年　十二月廿七

星期二

贵妇鸡

  许多印度鸡都可以归为马来种。以突出的身高、长有短毛的蛇形长颈、稀疏的覆尾羽、紧致坚硬的羽毛和细长结实的胫为特征。1865 年 4 月,《伦敦新闻画报》刊登了这幅图,时称贵妇鸡。

一月

25

Wednesday, 25 January 2017

农历丙申年 十二月廿八

星期三

斗鸡和杜金鸡

  自古以来，人们为了竞技培育出斗鸡这一知名品种。它们过关斩将，永不屈服。今天，用来参展的斗鸡和过去用于打斗的品种已经差别迥异。

  杜金是一种优质的英国鸡，深受女士们喜爱。其原因显而易见，它们不仅艳丽迷人，而且是质量最好的肉禽，后一特点更容易让女士们产生浓厚的兴趣。

一月

26

Thursday, 26
January
2017

农历丙申年　十二月廿九

星期四

雄性白杜金鸡、彩色杜金鸡和粗翼黑胸红斗鸡

一月 27

Friday, 27
January
2017

农历丙申年　十二月三十

星期五（除夕）

彩色杜金鸡
（Dorking）

　　体积对杜金鸡至关重要，彩色杜金鸡尤为如此。它们的体积不分性别，都非常庞大，外形格外厚重、丰满。公鸡从侧面看应呈方形，且宽胸阔背。

一月

28

Saturday, 28
January
2017

农历丁酉年　正月初一

星期六（春节）

雄性白杜金鸡

　　白杜金鸡比彩色杜金鸡小得多，有着独特的外形和体态。白杜金鸡很可能是最早的品种，彩色杜金鸡由白色品种和大型萨里（Surrey）或萨塞克斯（Sussex）鸡杂交而成。

一月

29

农历丁酉年　正月初二

Sunday, 29
January
2017

星期日

雄性杜金鸡

　　杜金鸡主要分为两种——白色和彩色。此外，还有一些特征各异的变种。

一月

Monday, 30
January
2017

30

农历丁酉年　正月初三

星 期 一

雌性杜金鸡

一月 31

Tuesday, 31
January
2017

农历丁酉年　正月初四

星 期 二

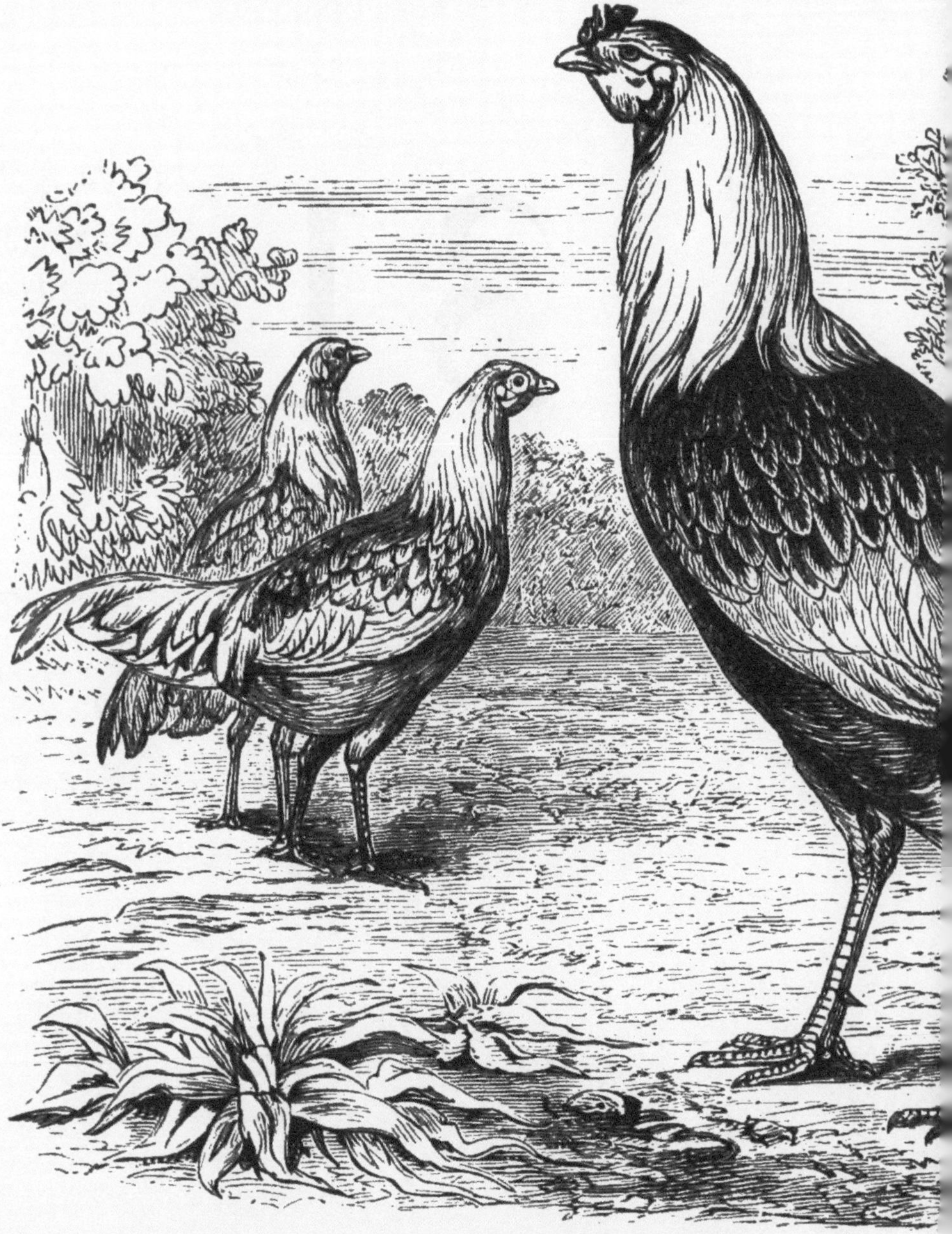

二 月

February

白杜金鸡

二月

Wednesday, 1
February
2017

1

农历丁酉年　正月初五

星期三

灰杜金鸡

二月

Thursday, 2
February
2017

2

农历丁酉年　正月初六

星期四

银灰杜金鸡

  有证据表明，杜金鸡最初由英国萨塞克斯和萨里的农民培育而成。银灰杜金是最美的展禽之一，在所有杜金鸡中最受家禽爱好者青睐。

二月

3

Friday, 3
February
2017

农历丁酉年　正月初七

星期五（立春）

白杜金鸡

  它全身雪白纯净,不掺一丁点杂质。喙、胫、趾为白色,眼、冠、面、肉垂、耳叶呈红色。英国人形容它们的眼睛长着亮红或黄色的虹膜,前者被他们偏爱。

二月

4

Saturday, 4
February
2017

农历丁酉年　正月初八

星期六

斑点杜金鸡

　　杜金鸡体色差别迥异。有人认为，无论从外观还是成活率看，毛色偏深的品种都最适合养殖。一只身形魁梧、胸肌宽阔、羽毛黝深的公鸡和一只身材结实、胫部短小的母鸡，堪称家禽中的绝配。

二月

5

Sunday, 5
February
2017

农历丁酉年　正月初九

星 期 日

鸣笛雄鸡(Le Coq Hupé)

　　这种鸡应该是法国高卢鸡和波兰鸡杂交的后代,它既遗传了高卢鸡雄赳赳的体态,同时又承袭了波兰鸡独特的冠羽。

二月

6

Monday, 6
February
2017

农历丁酉年　正月初十

星 期 一

安科纳鸡（Ancona）

　　玫瑰冠安科纳鸡发源于英国。玫瑰冠和单冠的唯一区别在于前者的玫瑰冠大小适中，前端矮而方，后端逐渐变细变尖，冠随头顶倾斜。

二月

7

Tuesday, 7
February
2017

农历丁酉年　正月十一

星期二

黑奥尔平顿鸡（Orpinton）

公鸡和母鸡的羽毛都非常紧凑，一点也不蓬松。

二月

8

Wednesday, 8 February 2017

农历丁酉年　正月十二

星期三

暗黄奥尔平顿鸡

  人们最初用了将近十年时间才培育出一只能够参加英国牧业博览会的暗黄奥尔平顿鸡。这一品种与黑色和白色的奥尔平顿鸡相比，羽毛更显致密。

二月

9

Thursday, 9
February
2017

农历丁酉年　正月十三

星期四

白奥尔平顿鸡

　　白奥尔平顿鸡分为两种：玫瑰冠和单冠，据说都是由雄性白莱克亨鸡和雌性黑色汉堡鸡杂交培育而成。

二月

10

Friday, 10
February
2017

农历丁酉年　正月十四

星期五

金线汉堡鸡、银亮汉堡鸡和黑西班牙鸡

二月

11

Saturday, 11
February
2017

农历丁酉年　正月十五

星期六（元宵节）（商务印书馆馆庆）

金亮波兰鸡、西班牙鸡和白冠黑波兰鸡

"白脸"是西班牙鸡的关键特征。整个白色的表面就像"白色小山羊皮"(white kid)一样。

所有波兰鸡都长着同样奇怪的冠,即所谓的"双角"(two-horned)特质。对狭义的波兰鸡而言,尽管它们的冠微乎其微,在构成上仍然显现出分叉的特质。

二月

12

Sunday, 12
February
2017

农历丁酉年　正月十六

星期日

西班牙鸡（Spanish）

  我们已知的大部分家禽被冠以的地理名称无疑都是张冠李戴：直到英国人把交趾鸡从上海带到交趾支那，那里的人才得知这一品种；波兰人根本就不知道所谓波兰鸡；亮汉堡鸡无疑是英国鸡；布拉马普特拉河岸的人们也从来没见过婆罗西摩鸡。话说回来，西班牙鸡这个名字却有些例外。辽阔的地中海沿岸，从直布罗陀到叙利亚，众多海岛密布的国家盛产各种与西班牙鸡大同小异的禽类，或许可以证明我们将其归为一大类的合理性。有些鸡的名字若隐若现地揭示了它们共同的发源地：安达卢西亚鸡、安科纳鸡和米诺卡鸡，这些名称都指向地中海沿岸。

二月

13

Monday, 13
February
2017

农历丁酉年　正月十七

星 期 一

黑西班牙鸡与白西班牙鸡

　　纯种黑西班牙鸡在所有鸡中个性最为鲜明。羽毛与面部的肉垂形成强烈的颜色对比,加之体型的完美对称和体态的威严,使它们成为鸡舍中当之无愧的贵族。白西班牙鸡则缺少黑色品种身上鲜明的颜色对比,外观的艳丽相形见绌,因而并不太受人喜爱。

二月

14

Tuesday, 14
February
2017

农历丁酉年　正月十八

星期二

黑西班牙鸡

　　黑西班牙鸡华丽高贵，通体黢黑，羽毛上闪耀着鲜艳夺目的绿斑。冠和肉垂高度发达，面部白得出奇，不掺杂任何其他颜色。作为经济家禽，它们的产蛋量高，蛋也非常大。

二月

15

Wednesday, 15
February
2017

农历丁酉年　正月十九

星 期 三

雄性黑西班牙鸡

　　真正的黑西班牙鸡标新立异、光彩夺目。我们可以毫不犹豫地将其列为一个独立品种，只有几种家禽能具备如此醒目的个体特性。它的与众不同在于那身闪亮的黑礼服，以及雪白的面部和耳叶，发育到极致的冠和腮部（gills）给整个面部增添了许多生机。

　　母鸡的羽毛近似，只是没有公鸡那般华丽。面部和耳叶，尤其是后者，呈珍珠白色。

二月

16

Thursday, 16 February 2017

农历丁酉年　正月二十

星期四

黑西班牙鸡

二月

17

Friday, 17
February
2017

农历丁酉年　正月廿一

星期五

雌性黑西班牙鸡

二月

18

Saturday, 18 February 2017

农历丁酉年　正月廿二

星期六（雨水）

白脸黑西班牙鸡

　　它们从诞生之始就被人们描述成身材挺拔靓丽的大型鸡。它们长着修长的腿,揭示了与马来鸡的亲缘关系。这种鸡雄性和雌性的体色相同。

二月

19

Sunday, 19
February
2017

农历丁酉年　正月廿三

星期日

金线汉堡鸡(Hamburgh)

　　金线汉堡鸡属于小型鸡,体格结实匀称,体态轻盈活泼。

二月

Monday, 20
February
2017

20

农历丁酉年　正月廿四

星期一

金线汉堡鸡

二月

21

农历丁酉年　正月廿五

Tuesday, 21
February
2017

星 期 二

银线汉堡鸡

二月

22

Wednesday, 22 February 2017

农历丁酉年　正月廿六

星期三

银亮汉堡鸡

　　银亮汉堡鸡包括两个品种：兰开夏银色牡尼鸡(Silver Mooney)，在兰开夏郡培育和展出；以及约克郡银雉鸡（Yorkshire Silver-pheasant Fowl）。前者的母鸡比后者的母鸡大得多，然而公鸡相比之下体积却更小、腿更短。

二月

23

农历丁酉年　正月廿七

Thursday, 23
February
2017

星期四

汉堡鸡（金线 / 黑 / 银亮）

  汉堡鸡有几个不同的品种，它们的共性在于体格较小，长着华美的玫瑰冠，向后延伸成上翘的长钉状，蓝色的胫，以及华丽的羽毛。

二月

24

农历丁酉年　正月廿八

Friday, 24
February
2017

星期五

金线汉堡鸡

  雄性金线汉堡鸡的颈羽和胸部为亮褐色或赤褐色,身体为赤褐色;雌性的身体为赤褐色,每片羽毛都镶嵌着黑色的横纹。

二月

25

农历丁酉年　正月廿九

Saturday, 25
February
2017

星期六

银线汉堡鸡

  白色的身体，黑色的横纹，带有金属绿光泽的黑尾巴，浅蓝色的胫，这些特征印证了它们土耳其鸡的血统。它们已经由最初粗糙的形态被培育成今天美丽的外观。

二月

26

Sunday, 26
February
2017

农历丁酉年　二月初一

星期日

银亮汉堡鸡

雄性和雌性的颈部羽毛都是银白色的,每一片羽毛的末梢都点缀有一小块匕首状的黑色。

二月

27

Monday, 27
February
2017

农历丁酉年　二月初二

星期一

博尔顿湾汉堡鸡

　　图中的母鸡完全代表了人们对这一品种羽毛底色的要求。公鸡则比严格意义上的标准偏红。不过,我们不能单以颜色论输赢,因为这种鸡的体色千差万别,通常又都呈现出浓重而华丽的色彩。

二月

28

Tuesday, 28 February 2017

农历丁酉年　二月初三

星期二

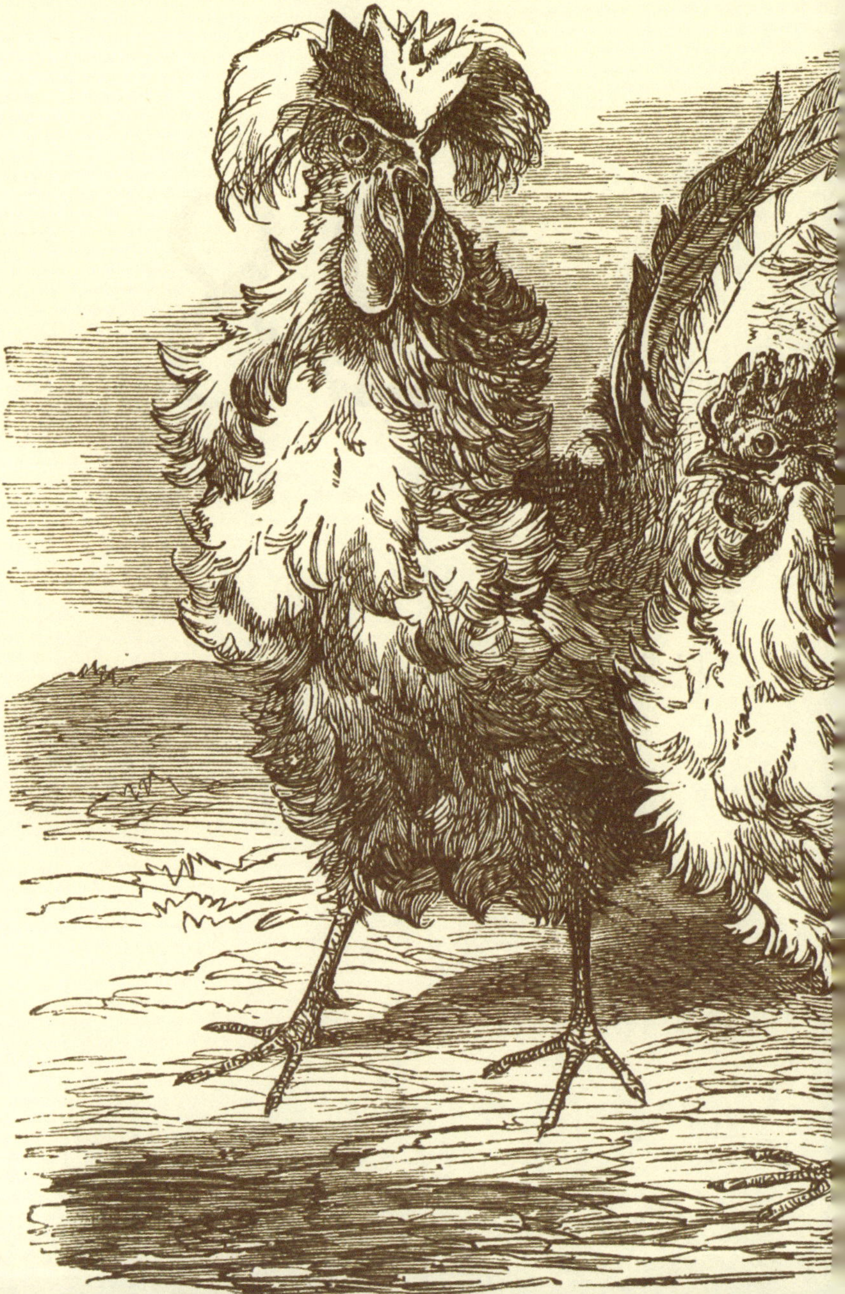

三月

March

银汉堡鸡

　　它们纯白的底色上点缀着精致的黑色条纹，这些条纹在公鸡身上却很少见：颈羽均为白色，不夹杂其他条纹；胸部与颈羽相同；羽翼缀满黑条。它们长着黑尾，但大翘羽则镶嵌着一圈粉白的花边。它们有珊瑚色的双冠，耳叶为白色，肉垂大而圆，光滑的蓝色胫部灵巧美丽。

三月

Wednesday, 1
March
2017

1

农历丁酉年 二月初四

星期三

帕多瓦鸡（Paduan）

  公鸡美丽出众，身披五彩羽衣，即黑、白、绿、红和赭石。毋庸置疑，它们是今天波兰鸡的祖先。

三月

2

Thursday, 2
March
2017

农历丁酉年　二月初五

星期四

白冠黑波兰鸡（Polish）

  它们既不强壮，也不多产，除非地点、温度、阳光都非常适宜；潮湿低洼的地方会阻碍它们的生长。就外形而言，它们的美丽不容忽视。

三月

3

Friday, 3
March
2017

农历丁酉年　二月初六

星期五

白冠黑波兰鸡

三月

4

*Saturday, 4
March
2017*

农历丁酉年　二月初七

星期六

白冠黑波兰鸡和金亮波兰鸡

三月

5

Sunday, 5
March
2017

农历丁酉年　二月初八

星期日（惊蛰）

金亮波兰鸡

三月

6

Monday, 6
March
2017

农历丁酉年　二月初九

星 期 一

银亮波兰鸡

三月

7

Tuesday, 7
March
2017

农历丁酉年　二月初十

星期二

银亮波兰鸡

恐怕再难有其他鸡比这种鸡的选美标准更具争议了。有人认为它们应该是银亮色的；有人却认为它们最初是羽毛带花边的。有人认为它们应当长着颔毛；其他人却正好相反，并且认为它们就该有白冠黑波兰鸡一样的肉垂。

三月

8

Wednesday, 8
March
2017

农历丁酉年　二月十一

星期三（妇女节）

金亮波兰鸡

　　就仪态而言，它们几乎和矮脚鸡一样自命不凡；胸部高高隆起，尾部非常饱满垂坠，背部呈标准的拱形。

三月

9

农历丁酉年　二月十二

Thursday, 9
March
2017

星期四

白冠黑波兰鸡

波兰鸡的羽冠和颌毛最引人注目——呈大而丰满的球状。不同波兰鸡的区别主要取决于羽冠和颌毛的大小。对于那些不长颌毛的品种，羽冠的大小决定了它们的差异。

三月

10

Friday, 10 March 2017

农历丁酉年　二月十三

星期五

白冠黑波兰鸡

羽冠和身体其他羽毛的颜色对比醒目又不失和谐,身材玲珑紧致,生性温顺、轻信人类——它是我们已知最美丽的家禽之一。

三月 11

Saturday, 11
March
2017

农历丁酉年　二月十四

星 期 六

银色须波兰鸡

金色和银色须波兰鸡的区别在于底色,前者是金栗色,后者是白色或银白色。

三月

12

Sunday, 12
March
2017

农历丁酉年　二月十五

星期日（植树节）

银亮波兰鸡

羽冠是所有波兰鸡的看点。细长的羽毛组成的羽冠，以饱满为佳。外形至关重要，前方应高高挑起，向两侧和后侧倾斜，中间不能分叉，应当整齐匀称。许多鸡的羽冠耷拉到脸前，这是一大缺陷。因为在汲水时，沾湿的羽冠使它们看上去垂头丧气。在形状完好的前提下，羽冠以大为美。母鸡的羽冠应当呈饱满的球状，满足形状要求的前提下，也是越大越好。羽冠应当是个球体，不能分叉或分缝。

三月

13

Monday, 13
March
2017

农历丁酉年　二月十六

星期一

金亮波兰鸡

 这种鸡和银亮型的羽毛的条纹完全吻合,只是底色不同。

三月

14

Tuesday, 14
March
2017

农历丁酉年　二月十七

星期二

雄性白亮波兰鸡

关于波兰鸡起源的说法并不能让人十分满意。它们最早或许是从波兰引进的,但更可能来自荷兰,前者只是中转国。之所以叫作"波兰"鸡,似乎是因为它们花哨的羽冠和波兰士兵的头盔近似。

三月 15 *Wednesday, 15*
March
2017

农历丁酉年　二月十八

星期三

雌性白亮波兰鸡

三月

16

Thursday, 16
March
2017

农历丁酉年　二月十九

星期四

君主鸡（Sultan）

　　君主鸡的肘关节像秃鹫一样，羽毛一直分布至脚趾。它们生性活泼快乐，是很好的产蛋鸡；鸡蛋又大又白；它们不伏窝，食量也小。随意撒些吃的，它们很快就能满足地吃饱并散开。

三月

17

Friday, 17
March
2017

农历丁酉年　二月二十

星期五

卷毛鸡（Frizzled）

　　阿尔德罗万迪在 1645 年曾经描述过卷毛鸡。它们是驯养品种，来自南亚、爪哇、苏门答腊和菲律宾群岛。这种鸡多为白色，胫部光滑，但也有许多个体带有各式各样的黑色和棕色，有些胫上也会长有羽毛。

三月

18

Saturday, 18
March
2017

农历丁酉年　二月廿一

星期六

黑卷毛鸡

它的羽毛最为奇特：每一根都向相反的方向卷曲生长，好像被人草草拨弄了一番，外表相当怪异。当然，尾部的羽毛并不后弯，但羽瓣却松散杂乱。其中最常见的品种是白色的，也有非常漂亮的棕色或鹧鸪色，还有黑色。我们认为最后一种颜色是最华美的。

三月

19

农历丁酉年　二月廿二

Sunday, 19
March
2017

星期日

安达卢西亚鸡（Andalusian）

　　安达卢西亚鸡是地中海区域家鸡中最古老的品种之一。它出现于人们对家禽最早的分类里。除西班牙鸡和米诺卡鸡外，它的体格超越任何地中海同类。

三月   **20**   *Monday, 20*
March
2017

农历丁酉年　二月廿三

星期一（春分）

米诺卡鸡和莱克亨鸡

  地中海沿岸——至少是欧洲大陆这边的沿岸——所有的家养鸡类，尽管或多或少略有不同，都显然属于一个大类。它们长着高耸的单冠，巨大的肉垂和耳叶（后者一般呈白色），光滑的跗跖和紧致的羽毛。它们都不抱窝，白色的鸡蛋相对偏大。

三月 21 *Tuesday, 21 March 2017*

农历丁酉年　二月廿四

星期二

棕色莱克亨鸡（Leghorn）

　　意大利无疑是莱克亨鸡的老家。玫瑰冠棕色莱克亨鸡必须长有如汉堡鸡般漂亮的玫瑰冠。

三月

22

Wednesday, 22
March
2017

农历丁酉年　二月廿五

星 期 三

玫瑰冠米色莱克亨鸡

　　米色莱克亨鸡产于意大利，随后被引进丹麦。这种鸡分为单冠和玫瑰冠两种，它们唯一的区别就是冠的差异。米色莱克亨鸡的特征在于黄色的胫与喙，以及完美的羽毛。图片展示的是最理想的体型和颜色。

三月

23

农历丁酉年　二月廿六

Thursday, 23
March
2017

星期四

单冠白莱克亨鸡

　　这种鸡在美国、英国和澳大利亚的繁殖特征差别迥异。美国人关注它的参展价值和经济价值；英国人提升了它的体积，降低了产蛋量；澳大利亚人则采取了美英在体型和体积方面折中的标准。纯白色的耳叶是参展必不可少的条件。

三月

24

Friday, 24 March 2017

农历丁酉年　二月廿七

星期五

单冠黑米诺卡鸡（Minorca）

　　大号的冠、肉垂和耳叶与体格最大的雄性最般配，雌性按比例也同样适用这一标准。

三月

25

Saturday, 25 March 2017

农历丁酉年　二月廿八

星期六

玫瑰冠白米诺卡鸡

　　这种鸡在培育时只能选用那些肤色为白色、跖跗为粉白色、羽毛为纯白色的鸡作为母体。它们的冠最引人注目。

三月

26

Sunday, 26
March
2017

农历丁酉年　二月廿九

星期日

银康宾鸡（Campine）

  康宾鸡很可能是散布在比利时及周边国家人口聚集区的意大利鸡的后裔。它的美在于优雅的体型和纯净的体色。银康宾鸡的颈羽，不分性别，必须是不含任何黑、棕或其他杂色的纯白色。

三月

27

Monday, 27
March
2017

农历丁酉年　二月三十

星期一

哥伦比亚鸡（Columbian）

　　这种叫法并不恰当，无论是我们今天常见的家禽，还是那些原鸡属中密不可分的品种，都不是美洲大陆土生土长的。所谓的哥伦比亚鸡显然是西班牙鸡和马来鸡杂交的产物。它继承了前者丰满的冠和肉垂，以及黑色的羽毛；又袭得了后者庞大的体格、茁实的分量和旺盛的生命力。

三月

28

Tuesday, 28 March 2017

农历丁酉年　三月初一

星期二

法国鸡：乌当鸡、雄性拉弗莱什鸡、雌性克莱维科尔鸡

三月

29

农历丁酉年　三月初二

Wednesday, 29
March
2017

星期三

法国鸡：克莱维科尔鸡、乌当鸡、拉弗莱什鸡

　　大多数法国品种多多少少都长有羽冠。另一个不同寻常之处在于，它们大多都不抱窝，或者说极少孵蛋。

三月

30

Thursday, 30
March
2017

农历丁酉年　三月初三

星期四

克莱维科尔鸡
（Crèvecaeur）

　　1855年，第一届巴黎农业展览会（Agricultural Exhibition in Paris）隆重举行，主办方为参展家禽设置了两组平行的奖项：第一组专为克莱维科尔鸡设立，第二组为其余所有品种设立。

三月

31

Friday, 31 March 2017

农历丁酉年　三月初四

星期五

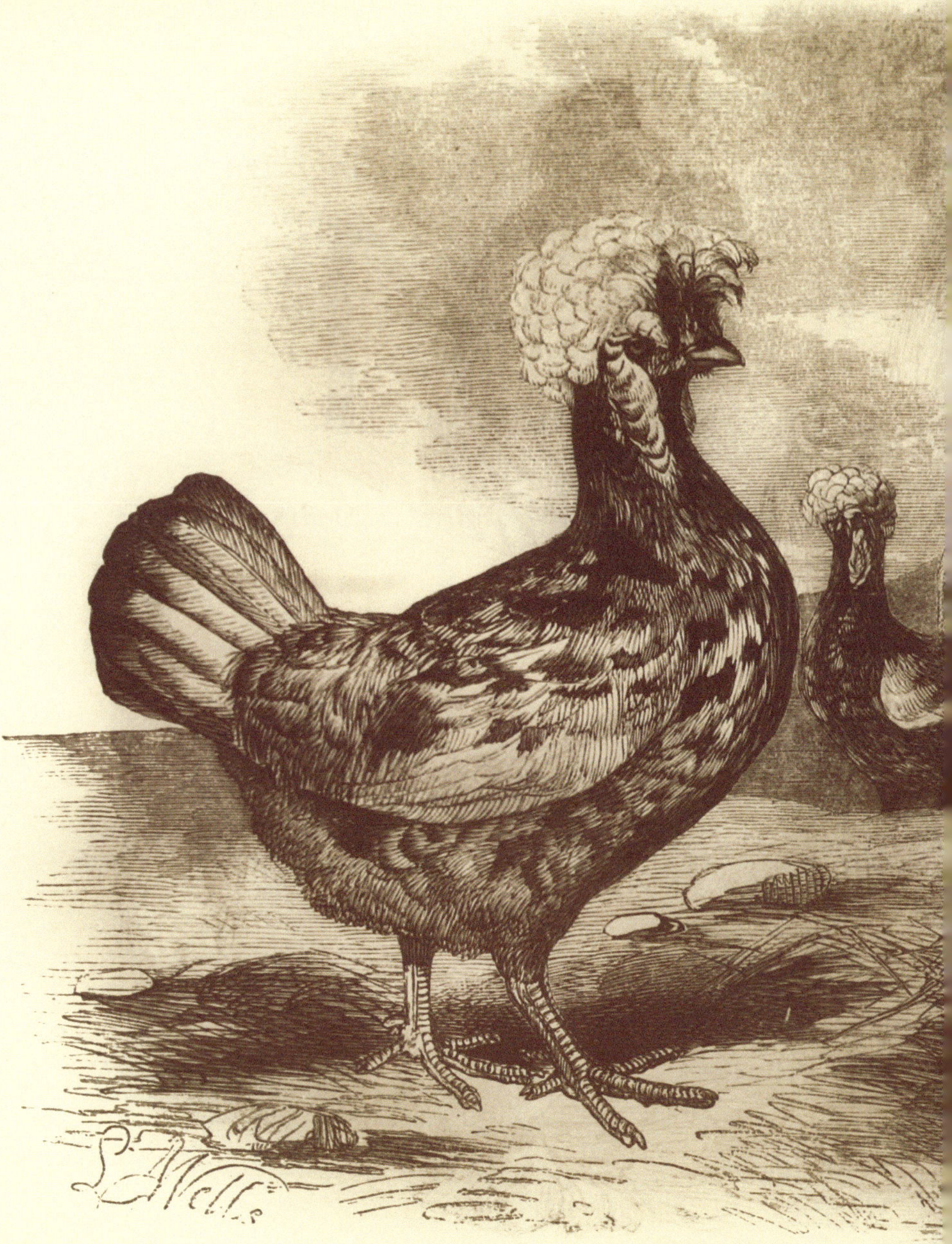

HOU

四月

April

克莱维科尔鸡与交趾鸡

  克莱维科尔母鸡脖子下方裹着一条厚重的羽毛围巾，看上去庄重安详。公鸡也系着浓密的羽毛围巾，佩戴着俊美悬垂的肉垂。

四月

Saturday, 1
April
2017

1

农历丁酉年 三月初五

星期六

克莱维科尔鸡

  它们和其他法国鸡共同的怪异之处在于具有鹿角状或 V 字形的冠。它们腿短、结实,长着椭圆形的庞大羽冠和丰满的颌毛,除了冠、喙和肉垂,整个头部都遮盖其中。

四月

2

Sunday, 2
April
2017

农历丁酉年　三月初六

星期日

乌当鸡（Houdan）

　　作为肉禽它们品质卓越。没有任何纯种鸡比它们，或者说像它们一样早熟。它们羽毛生成得早，生命力异常强大，因而很好养殖。成年鸡精力充沛，不计其数的鸡蛋几乎都能成活。它们的经济价值，尤其是食用价值，不容小觑。

四月

Monday, 3
April
2017

3

农历丁酉年　三月初七

星期一

乌当鸡

  图中的乌当鸡于 1865 年在巴黎获得一等奖，随后归国家家禽公司（National Poultry Company）所有。它们展示了这一品种的特性：外形异常笨重，长有三层冠，外侧像两页书一样摊开，中央好像一颗畸形的长草莓。公鸡长着巨大的冠，母鸡的冠则几乎是隐形的。

四月

4

Tuesday, 4
April
2017

农历丁酉年　三月初八

星期二（清明节）

乌当鸡

　　乌当鸡发源于法国,并以它们赖以生息一个多世纪的地名命名。早期的家禽权威称其为法国杜金鸡(Dorking)。英美标准最大的差异在于对其冠和毛色的界定:英式标准认为它们应该长有单冠,形似蝴蝶,在头顶正中,倚着羽冠,外形整齐,大小适中;美式标准认为冠应为V字形。

四月

5

Wednesday, 5
April
2017

农历丁酉年　三月初九

星期三

浅婆罗西摩小公鸡

四月

6

Thursday, 6
April
2017

农历丁酉年　三月初十

星期四

浅婆罗西摩小母鸡

四月

7

Friday, 7
April
2017

农历丁酉年　三月十一

星期五

拉弗莱什鸡
（La Flèche）

拉弗莱什鸡高大俊美，坚硬的羽毛排列紧密，使它们的实际体重比看上去要沉得多。作为蛋禽，它们产大型的蛋；作为肉禽，它们肉质丰厚。它们的外表与西班牙鸡近似。

四月

8

Saturday, 8 April 2017

农历丁酉年　三月十二

星期六

拉弗莱什鸡

　　现代学者认为它起源于法国拉弗莱什地区,由黑西班牙鸡和波兰鸡杂交培育而成。它们头顶 V 字形冠,庄严高贵。

四月

9

Sunday, 9
April
2017

农历丁酉年　三月十三

星期日

法沃罗勒鸡（Faverolle）

　　法沃罗勒鸡起源于法国北部，临近法沃罗勒地区。这种鸡的与众不同在于：当浅色婆罗血统占主导时，它的毛色与浅色婆罗品系一致；当杜金血统占主导时，羽毛又偏向杜金品系的颜色。

四月　　　　　10　　　*Monday, 10*
　　　　　　　　　　　April
　　　　　　　　　　　2017

农历丁酉年　三月十四

星 期 一

马来斗鸡和矮脚鸡

　　马来斗鸡身形直立，它们头颅的形状是亚洲鸡中的特例。矮脚鸡这一品种诞生于 1796 年，其后衍生出不同的品种，最早的品种是金带和银带西布赖特矮脚鸡。

四月

11

Tuesday, 11
April
2017

农历丁酉年　三月十五

星期二

黑红斗鸡(Game)

公鸡羽毛颜色的关键在于头部应为偏橘色的暗红色；颈部羽毛直到尖部都是亮橘红色；背、肩、肩覆羽为深紫红色，蓑羽橘红色，胸和尾深黑色，不掺杂任何白斑。

四月

12

Wednesday, 12
April
2017

农历丁酉年　三月十六

星期三

血翅绒羽鸡、黑胸红鸡

四月　　　　　　　　　　　　　　　　　　*Thursday, 13*
April
13
2017

农历丁酉年　三月十七

星期四

红褐色鸡

四月 14

Friday, 14
April
2017

农历丁酉年　三月十八

星期五

黑胸白翅鸡 (Duckwings)

四月

15

农历丁酉年　三月十九

Saturday, 15
April
2017

星 期 六

金翅斗鸡

　　公鸡的颈羽应当接近亮白色，略呈浅黄色调，不带任何明显的黄色调或黑色条纹。蓑羽应尽量接近颈羽的颜色；背部呈栗黄色；肩覆羽为黄铜或铜栗色；胸、尾为纯黑色。

四月

16

Sunday, 16
April
2017

农历丁酉年　三月二十

星期日

金翅斗鸡

  公鸡的颈部应为交织着黑色条纹的亮银色，银色一直延伸到冠，在眼上方略暗；背部及肩覆羽为蓝灰色，几乎与其他羽毛的颜色相同；胸部为橙红色，色度浓郁而美丽。

四月 | **17** | *Monday, 17*
April
2017

农历丁酉年　三月廿一

星期一

黑胸斗鸡

  高贵的斗鸡与马来鸡和马来雉（Pheasant Malay）有关，尽管那已经是很久以前的故事。在欧洲人饲养斗鸡之前，马来半岛，以及东方各地的居民，就已经开始繁育这些品种，并将它们主要作为斗鸡竞技之用。

四月

18

Tuesday, 18
April
2017

农历丁酉年　三月廿二

星 期 二

黑胸红斗鸡

斗鸡头部狭长,长着强劲有力的喙和直立的单冠。胸部丰满突起,体格健壮发达,姿态勇武挺拔,羽毛格外紧实。斗鸡的体色大相径庭,黑胸红斗鸡是最著名的品系之一。

四月

19

Wednesday, 19
April
2017

农历丁酉年　三月廿三

星 期 三

黑胸红斗鸡

人们普遍认为斗鸡是所有家鸡的祖先。它们好战的天性为其赢得了斗鸡的称号。对于一只达到参展水平的黑胸红斗鸡而言,当它直立时,从眼睛中部沿翅膀和小腿再到地面,几乎可以画一条直线。图中展示了最受欢迎的斗鸡身姿。

四月　　　　　　　　20　　　*Thursday, 20*
　　　　　　　　　　　　　　　　April
　　　　　　　　　　　　　　　　2017

农历丁酉年　三月廿四

星期四（谷雨）

雄性黑胸红斗鸡

作为家禽，一只优质的黑胸红斗鸡应满足以下标准：强有力的喙，略弯曲，基部结实；头部偏长，不能呈圆形，而呈弹壳形；眼部最好没有凹陷，能使人联想到蛇的神态。

四月 21

Friday, 21 April 2017

农历丁酉年　三月廿五

星期五

雌性黑胸红斗鸡

图中的母鸡算得上一流个体，羽毛纯净无瑕，没有其他母鸡身上常见的难看线条。

四月

22

Saturday, 22
April
2017

农历丁酉年　三月廿六

星期六

棕胸红斗鸡

　　公鸡的头部和颈部通体橘红，羽毛不掺任何杂质；肩羽是比条状胸纹的绯红色略浅的颜色；脊部或与颈羽相同，或呈暗柠檬黄色；背部是稻草栗色的；胸部覆盖几乎全黑的底色，每一片羽毛都精美地点缀着浅枣红色——这些点缀丝毫没有掺杂进羽毛的颜色里，而只是给羽毛的边缘镶嵌了淡淡的花丝。跟公鸡相比，母鸡则呈现出华丽的黑色，颈羽披挂着艳丽的金色条纹。

四月 23 *Sunday, 23 April 2017*

农历丁酉年　三月廿七

星期日

金翅斗鸡

四月

Monday, 24
April
2017

24

农历丁酉年　三月廿八

星期一

银灰白翅斗鸡

　　白翅斗鸡分为两种：银色和金色。银色与金色唯一的不同在于羽毛的颜色和条纹：雄性的羽毛包括颈羽都长有白色条纹，雌性则为浅灰色。

四月 25

Tuesday, 25 April 2017

农历丁酉年　三月廿九

星期二

阿希尔和康尼希斗鸡

早在 1820 年,康尼希斗鸡在英国德文郡和康沃尔诞生。它们纯为战斗而生,由当地皮特斗鸡与马来鸡和阿希尔鸡杂交而成。

四月

26

Wednesday, 26 April 2017

农历丁酉年　四月初一

星期三

绒羽斗鸡

这一品种一直深受人们喜爱。它的几个分支仅仅在特定羽毛的颜色上有所不同,像伍斯特绒羽鸡和柴郡绒羽鸡,身体和尾巴上掺杂了一些黑色羽毛;而兰开夏绒羽鸡则为纯色。

四月

27

Thursday, 27
April
2017

农历丁酉年　四月初二

星期四

红褐斗鸡

　　这种斗鸡比其他任何斗鸡都更加顽强倔强。可以作为证据的是，早在1873年1月底，就曾有一篇关于斗鸡的报道使《纽约先驱报》专栏颜面扫地。

四月

28

Friday, 28 April 2017

农历丁酉年　四月初三

星期五

雄性马来斗鸡

　　图中展示了品种最好的马来斗鸡（"马来"仅表示地域，并非我们通称的"马来"品种）。最好的鸡一般长有高耸的单冠。距的外观各异，有直有弯，还有波浪形，但都长有锋利的边缘，好像佩戴了折叠小刀的刀片一样，因而决斗总能迅速定胜负。

四月

29

Saturday, 29
April
2017

农历丁酉年　四月初四

星期六

洛克鸡和温多特鸡

  洛克鸡的羽毛被称为"杜鹃色",美英关于颜色的标准不同。美国人将它描述成带有"蓝黑色"条纹的"灰白色";英国人认可的底色更暗,更接近石板色,条纹则更深、更大,轮廓不那么明显。

  人们认为俊美的温多特鸡是深婆罗西摩鸡、银亮汉堡鸡和波兰鸡杂交的产物。第一种鸡赋予它身形,第二种鸡成就了它的冠,第三种鸡为它装点了花边。

四月

30

Sunday, 30
April
2017

农历丁酉年　四月初五

星 期 日

A.F.Lydon.

五 月

May

英国女王陛下的婆罗西摩鸡，引进于 1852 年

　　1853 年 1 月 22 日的《伦敦新闻画报》曾记载如下信息："新近从美国驶来的一艘轮船为维多利亚女王陛下呈送了一笼上等家鸡，这是一份来自马萨诸塞州波士顿乔治·P. 伯翰的礼物。乘船而来的是九只美丽的鸟儿——两只公鸡和七只小母鸡，由伯翰先生从中国引进的家鸡培育而成。"

五月

Monday, 1
May
2017

1

农历丁酉年 四月初六

星期一（劳动节）

深婆罗西摩鸡，引进于 1853 年

伯翰先生说，它们由灰吉大港鸡和交趾鸡杂交而成，色彩上与浅色品种差别迥异。

五月

2

Tuesday, 2
May
2017

农历丁酉年　四月初七

星期二

深婆罗西摩鸡

　　硕大的体格、沉甸甸的体重、顽强的生命力、多产的繁殖力以及对狭小空间的耐受力使它们受到公众的普遍青睐。与此同时，它们外表的高贵以及羽毛特征遗传的稳定性还引来了一大批家禽选美狂热者的追捧。

五月

3

农历丁酉年　四月初八

Wednesday, 3
May
2017

星期三

浅色婆罗西摩鸡

　　它诞生于 1845 年至 1860 年间,由美国家禽饲养员从来自印度希姆普尔(Lakhimpur)的禽类培育而成。人们最初用一条河的名字为它命名,据说它最早就起源于附近。它的外形与众不同,尽管高大,却匀称优美。

五月

4

Thursday, 4
May
2017

农历丁酉年　四月初九

星期四（青年节）

深婆罗西摩鸡

 它被认为是最难培育出完美品质的家禽之一。尽管与浅婆罗西摩鸡同属一种,二者除体型外却大相径庭。除了那些长有同样体色和条纹的品种,羽毛黑白相间的比例以及个体间的差异使它们独树一帜。

五月

5

Friday, 5
May
2017

农历丁酉年　四月初十

星期五（立夏）

横斑洛克鸡（Plymouth Rock）

优雅是洛克鸡的标签，横斑洛克鸡的体色和条纹尤其受到选美爱好者的追捧。细长的条纹横贯羽毛，从头顶覆盖至尾梢，在身体的末端逐渐加粗。如果颜色深浅交织得当，雌性看上去甚至比雄性更具魅力。在选美比赛中，横纹以窄为佳。

五月

6

Saturday, 6
May
2017

农历丁酉年　四月十一

星期六

横斑洛克鸡

用于繁殖母鸡的雄性（左）。

用于繁殖公鸡的雌性（右）。

图中雄性的羽毛浅于雌性，这种偏淡的体色和斑纹最有利于繁殖参加选美的雌性。图中雌性的体色则恰恰展现了用于繁殖雄性选美选手的标准。

五月

7

Sunday, 7
May
2017

农历丁酉年　四月十二

星期日

米色洛克鸡

　　它通体金褐色,不掺杂色,体格和体色都达到最佳。喙、胫、趾为金黄色,眼睛为红色。

五月

8

Monday, 8
May
2017

农历丁酉年　四月十三

星期一

山鹁洛克鸡

最早可以考证的山鹁洛克鸡来自美国新泽西州韦斯顿。

五月

9

Tuesday, 9
May
2017

农历丁酉年　四月十四

星 期 二

白洛克鸡

  在洛克鸡的众多品种中,只有白色和黑色的品种是它们祖先的直系后裔。白洛克鸡是第一种从横斑洛克鸡直接繁育的品种。

五月

10

Wednesday, 10
May
2017

农历丁酉年　四月十五

星期三

银边温多特鸡（Wyandotte）

  温多特鸡最显著的特征是它的玫瑰冠，顶部为椭圆或月牙形，紧贴头顶。冠的末梢朝下，不应呈水平或上扬状。其美丽在于完美的形状，折中的大小和表面规律的缺口。

五月   **11**   *Thursday, 11*
May
2017

农历丁酉年　四月十六

星期四

哥伦比亚温多特鸡

人们最初用横斑洛克鸡与浅婆罗西摩鸡、横斑洛克鸡与白温多特鸡,以及白温多特鸡与浅婆罗西摩鸡杂交繁殖出哥伦比亚温多特鸡。所有的哥伦比亚温多特鸡体内都流淌着浅婆罗西摩鸡的血液。

五月

12

农历丁酉年　四月十七

Friday, 12
May
2017

星期五

银线温多特鸡

　　雄性上部的羽毛为纯银白色,颈羽和蓑羽点缀着黑色条纹。雌性通体银灰,羽毛上镶嵌着随形的深色线条。

五月　　　13　　　*Saturday, 13*
　　　　　　　　　　　May
　　　　　　　　　　　2017

农历丁酉年　四月十八

星期六

罗德岛红鸡（Rhode Island Red）

它诞生于美国罗德岛农区。五花八门的禽类随航船而至，散落到当地的农场，并与当地家禽杂交。其中许多外来的亚洲禽类身披黑红色的羽毛，被人们引进所有的农场，直至黑红色成为当地家禽羽毛的主体颜色。随后，它们很快遍布罗德岛及马萨诸塞州毗邻地区。

五月

14

Sunday, 14
May
2017

农历丁酉年　四月十九

星期日（母亲节）

多米尼克鸡（Dominique）

　　人们认为它是美国最早确立的一个品种，也是美国最早的条纹鸡。它们一般被称为美国多米尼克鸡。

五月 　　　　　　　　　　　　　　　　　*Monday, 15*

May

15

2017

农历丁酉年　四月二十

星期一

白矮脚鸡和黑矮脚鸡、西布赖特矮脚鸡、小种斗鸡

五月

16

Tuesday, 16
May
2017

农历丁酉年　四月廿一

星期二

矮脚鸡（金线，黑，银线）（Bantam）

五月

17

*Wednesday, 17
May
2017*

农历丁酉年　四月廿二

星期三

白矮脚鸡和小种斗鸡

　　白矮脚鸡的主要特征在于尽可能小的体积，无瑕的白色羽毛，丰满的镰尾，整洁的玫瑰冠，红脸，白耳叶，以及匀称小巧的腿和足。参展公鸡的体重不能超过20盎司，母鸡不能超过18盎司。

　　小种斗鸡，不分性别，都是普通斗鸡完完全全的缩小版。

五月

18

农历丁酉年　四月廿三

Thursday, 18
May
2017

星期四

矮脚鸡（丝羽、英国斗鸡、卷毛、毛脚、君主）

  丝羽矮脚鸡由体格最小的乌骨鸡繁育而成，以缩小体积。在体积和品种特性上劣于其他矮脚鸡。英国矮脚斗鸡由大型英国斗鸡繁殖而成。在众多品种中，银亮色和黑红色在英国最受欢迎。卷毛矮脚鸡颜色各异——黑、赭黄、红、白，其中以纯白为最美。君主矮脚鸡外表新奇，但从未被大规模繁育。

五月

19

Friday, 19
May
2017

农历丁酉年　四月廿四

星期五

矮脚鸡（银色西布赖特、金色西布赖特、日本、黑色、黑红小种、白色）

  毫无疑问，这种叫作矮脚鸡的小型鸡绝非某种野生禽类的自然后裔。它们很多都与普通家禽一一对应，经人类精细培育，演化出矮小的身材和更趋完美的特质。即便有时并非人工培育，它们诞生的过程也偶有记载。可以说，它们比任何鸡都更具"人造"色彩。它们的迷人之处在于美丽，而非任何经济价值。

五月

20

农历丁酉年　四月廿五

Saturday, 20
May
2017

星期六

黑矮脚鸡、北京矮脚鸡、日本矮脚鸡

矮脚鸡的命名完全基于错误的推测,因为它们并不起源于班坦(Bantam)。这种鸡一直深受家禽饲养者喜爱,在一流展会中,它们的鸡栏总被围得水泄不通。它们有一个突出的优点——可以在小笼子里圈养,甚至连鸣叫都不会激起其他公鸡的共鸣。

五月 21 Sunday, 21
May
2017

农历丁酉年　四月廿六

星期日（小满）

白翅、派尔和白色矮脚斗鸡

　　白翅矮脚斗鸡必须具备白翅斗鸡的特性、矮脚鸡的体积,如果可能的话,其颜色和条纹也应该比大型鸡精致。红色派尔矮脚斗鸡的体型和颜色非常靓丽,雄性美丽的白衣上点缀着红色条纹,在小种斗鸡中算得上漂亮的颜色搭配。白色矮脚斗鸡诞生于1900年,由派尔和其他小种斗鸡培育而成。

五月

22

农历丁酉年　四月廿七

Monday, 22
May
2017

星期一

黑胸红色和绒矮脚斗鸡

矮脚斗鸡的诞生是禽类繁育艺术的登峰造极之作，它们既有矮脚鸡的小型身材，又兼具斗鸡完美无瑕的优雅体型和靓丽羽毛。它们体格虽小，却肉质鲜美，并且成熟得非常早。它们无疑是英国品种，由英国斗鸡和矮脚鸡杂交而成。

五月

23

Tuesday, 23
May
2017

农历丁酉年　四月廿八

星期二

深、浅婆罗西摩矮脚鸡

婆罗西摩矮脚鸡产于英国,由婆罗西摩鸡(Brahma)、灰阿希尔鸡(Gray Aseel)、交趾矮脚鸡(Cochin Bantam)以及一些黑尾日本矮脚鸡(Japanese Bantam)杂交而成。婆罗西摩矮脚鸡分为两种:浅色和深色。

五月

24

Wednesday, 24
May
2017

农历丁酉年　四月廿九

星期三

交趾矮脚鸡

　　交趾矮脚鸡是最受欢迎的矮脚鸡,它们散布在世界的各个角落。最早的交趾矮脚鸡来自中国,呈深棕黄色。它们又被称为北京矮脚鸡,很多都长有绿色的胫和五个趾。

五月

25

Thursday, 25
May
2017

农历丁酉年　四月三十

星期四

小种斗鸡

　　小种斗鸡是所有矮脚鸡中最常见的。它们由最专业的人士培育而成，除去英国信鸽和冠金丝雀外，它们比其他任何驯养鸟类都更彰显人工雕琢的精致。

五月

26

Friday, 26
May
2017

农历丁酉年　五月初一

星 期 五

日本长尾鸡和日本矮脚鸡

　　大约在 1860 年，日本矮脚鸡从日本来到英国。它们颜色混杂，最引人注目的要数黑白两色。它们最早被称为"爬行鸡"（creeper），据说腿短到好像用羽翼在地上滑行一样。这种说法某种程度上适用于雌性，有些走起路来确实像趴在地上。

五月   # 27   *Saturday, 27*
May
2017

农历丁酉年　五月初二

星期六

日本长尾鸡 (Yokohama)

德国进口商从日本将这种古里古怪的鸡引入英国。它的奇特之处在于公鸡巨大的颈羽和旗形尾。在日本东京,据说有的羽毛竟长达 27 英尺。显然,这一品种只具备观赏价值,人们必须精心护理它的羽毛。优质羽毛的长度也就自然而然成为主要的选美标准。

五月

28

Sunday, 28
May
2017

农历丁酉年　五月初三

星期日

波兰矮脚鸡

  小型波兰矮脚鸡总是能推陈出新。有些已经大到不能称为矮脚鸡了,然而它们优美的体型、靓丽的颜色依然能够博得公众的盛赞。这种鸡由雄性波兰鸡和雌性矮脚鸡交配而成。

五月

29

Monday, 29
May
2017

农历丁酉年　五月初四

星期一

金、银条纹矮脚鸡

美丽的金、银条纹矮脚鸡,也就是人们熟知的西布赖特矮脚鸡,或许极好地印证了精细人工培育取得的卓越成就。它们是彻头彻尾的艺术杰作。它们是由羽毛的底色命名的,前者是金棕色,后者是亮白色。对完美的品种而言,每根羽毛,包括颈羽(或者说是羽毛,因为公鸡并不长有真正意义上的颈羽)、副翼羽、尾羽,除了外观不可见的羽颈或镖尾,无一例外都镶嵌了一层黑色花边。

五月

30

农历丁酉年　五月初五

Tuesday, 30
May
2017

星期二（端午节）

黑色与荷兰矮脚鸡

　　这些黑色的品种非常勇猛，为了争虫争米可以奋战到底，即使遇到更魁梧的同类也不会退缩。这样看来和斗鸡倒是有几分亲缘。

五月

31

Wednesday, 31
May
2017

农历丁酉年　五月初六

星期三

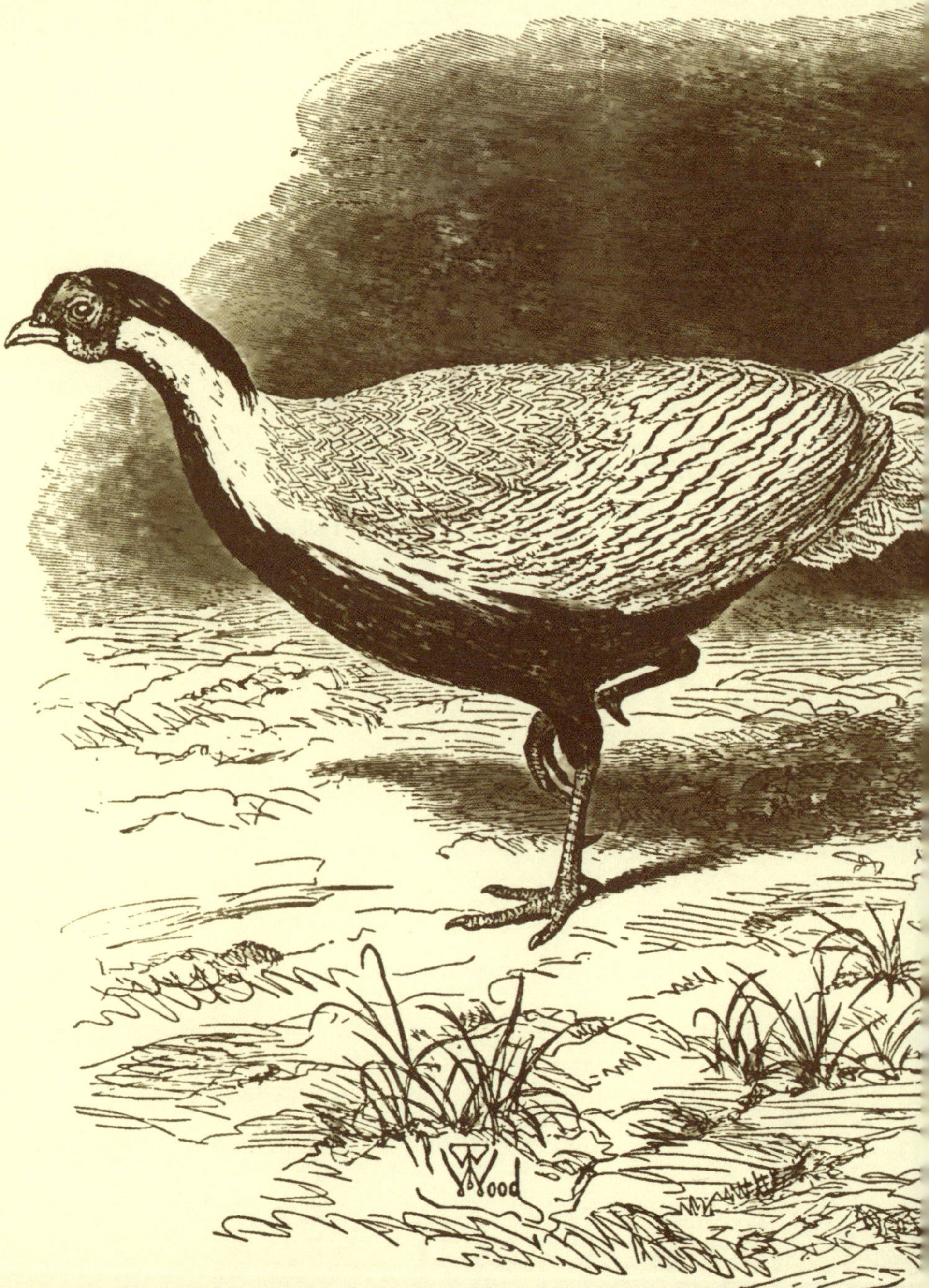
Wood

六月

June

山鹑矮脚鸡

　　它们的雏鸡很像山鹑，因而不难猜出它们得名的原因。它们也被用于孵化和养育山鹑。

六月

Thursday, 1
June
2017

1

农历丁酉年 五月初七

星期四（儿童节）

火鸡和珍珠鸡

　　现代的驯养火鸡最早在墨西哥驯化，目前已经成为很常见的驯养家禽。其体型比家鸡大 3~4 倍，体长超过 1 米，最重可达 10 千克。

六月

2

农历丁酉年　五月初八

Friday, 2
June
2017

星期五

火鸡 (Turkey)

六月

3

Saturday, 3
June
2017

农历丁酉年　五月初九

星 期 六

火鸡

六月

4

Sunday, 4
June
2017

农历丁酉年　五月初十

星期日

青铜火鸡

　　青铜火鸡由野生北美火鸡与黑火鸡杂交而成。它长长的头部构造奇特,雄性整个颈部毫发不生,长满疙疙瘩瘩的肿块,叫作肉垂。雌性有相似结构,只是没有那么明显。

六月

5

Monday, 5
June
2017

农历丁酉年　五月十一

星期一（芒种）

拿刚塞火鸡和黑火鸡

　　拿刚塞火鸡原先在爱尔兰、德国和法国部分地区数量众多。和体格偏大、身形偏长的青铜火鸡比,它们更显紧致。图中展示了参展的最佳品种。黑火鸡是最早的家养火鸡,它随早期移民来到美国,自此作为一个独立品种被人们饲养。

六月

6

Tuesday, 6
June
2017

农历丁酉年　五月十二

星期二

白火鸡

早期学者认为白火鸡来自荷兰,并因此得名白荷兰火鸡。白羽毛的火鸡可能是黑羽毛品种的变种。

六月

Wednesday, 7
June
2017

7

农历丁酉年　五月十三

星期三

野生火鸡
(*Meleagris gallopawo*)

　　母火鸡一般在北美大草原丛林边缘200到300码的地方筑巢,永远靠近水源。因为嗜水,它每天要光顾河边三次——分别在早、中、晚。一旦公鸡发现巢,会将其捣毁,并且杀掉所有小鸡,毫不手软。

六月

Thursday, 8 June 2017

8

农历丁酉年　五月十四

星期四

野生火鸡

  野生火鸡是北美的原住民。它们的领地从加拿大延伸至墨西哥,沿密西西比河和密苏里河流域的茫茫林海,拓展至西北部,直至落基山脉。这些华贵的鸟类成为猎人们稳定的食物来源和娱乐对象。然而,随着文明的入侵和人口的激增,野生火鸡步步撤退、数量缩减,并且在不久的将来即将走向灭绝。

六月

9

Friday, 9
June
2017

农历丁酉年　五月十五

星期五

野生火鸡

家养与野生火鸡的唯一区别在于尾上覆羽和尾羽上的白色。再没人比奥杜邦对野生火鸡的习性描述更到位了,他不会错误地认为野生火鸡不可驯养;他肯定了正好相反的事实,甚至提到自己亲自驯服过的一只野生火鸡。

六月

Saturday, 10
June
2017

10

农历丁酉年　五月十六

星期六

眼斑火鸡（*Meleagris ocellata*）

眼斑火鸡，也叫眼斑吐绶鸡，来自中美洲地区的洪都拉斯和危地马拉等地，目前也已经被成功驯养繁殖，作为一种观赏和肉用家禽。其体型比火鸡要略小，体长近1米，重4~6千克。这种火鸡最独特的当属羽毛，其底色是一种异常美丽的青铜色，上面的条纹呈现出金铜色和亮黑色，沿背部而下的是浓重的蓝色和红色，好似闪亮的丝绸。和孔雀一样，在接近尾部的位置，这些条纹变得如此醒目，以致看上去像长了"眼斑"或眼睛，眼斑火鸡也由此得名。

六月

11

Sunday, 11
June
2017

农历丁酉年　五月十七

星期日

眼斑火鸡

六月

12

农历丁酉年　五月十八

Monday, 12
June
2017

星期一

眼斑火鸡

六月

13

Tuesday, 13
June
2017

农历丁酉年　五月十九

星期二

珍珠鸡 (*Numida meleagris*)

  珍珠鸡来自非洲，来自西非的野生珠鸡被普遍视为今天家养品种的祖先。野生珠鸡主要分布在撒哈拉沙漠以南的非洲地区，主要生活于稀树草原和农田生境中。珍珠鸡有着较长的驯养历史，在罗马帝国时期曾盛极一时，是许多宴会上的重要菜品，现多当作观赏用，也作肉用。体长近 60 厘米，重 1.3 千克左右。

六月

14

Wednesday, 14
June
2017

农历丁酉年　五月二十

星期三

珍珠鸡

六月

15

Thursday, 15
June
2017

农历丁酉年　五月廿一

星期四

珍珠鸡

六月　　　　　　　　　　　　　　　　　　　　*Friday, 16*
June
2017

16

农历丁酉年　五月廿二

星期五

珍珠鸡

六月

17

Saturday, 17
June
2017

农历丁酉年　五月廿三

星期六

珍珠鸡

六月

18

Sunday, 18
June
2017

农历丁酉年　五月廿四

星期日（父亲节）

黑翅型的蓝孔雀

(*Pavo cristatus*)

蓝孔雀体长90~230厘米，重2.5~6千克。野生蓝孔雀分布于南亚地区的各个国家，作为一个重要的观赏鸟种，已经有很久的驯养繁殖历史。图中这只就属于人工驯养所培育出的色型。

六月

19

Monday, 19
June
2017

农历丁酉年　五月廿五

星期一

蓝孔雀

六月

20

Tuesday, 20
June
2017

农历丁酉年　五月廿六

星期二

白孔雀

　　白孔雀是蓝孔雀在人工繁育条件下产生的变异品种,数量稀少,是比较名贵的观赏鸟。

六月

Wednesday, 21
June
2017

21

农历丁酉年　五月廿七

星期三（夏至）

庭院中的蓝孔雀

蓝孔雀被引入欧洲后，就成为许多贵族和上层人士喜爱的宠物。

六月

22

农历丁酉年　五月廿八

Thursday, 22
June
2017

星期四

散养在一起的蓝孔雀和珍珠鸡

六月

23

农历丁酉年　五月廿九

Friday, 23
June
2017

星期五

蓝孔雀（左雄右雌）

  蓝孔雀华美的羽毛在鸟类中无可匹敌。在它的富丽堂皇面前，任何鸟都会败下阵来。它简直无与伦比，大自然赋予这种生灵无疆的美丽，我们或许可以尝试将其称为造物主的"代表作"，千姿百态的美的集合，辉煌壮丽的顶点。它的华服集万千鸟类艳丽于一身，如彩虹般靓丽，如宝石般熠熠生辉，闪烁着天宇的蔚蓝，荡漾着大地的青葱。

六月

24

*Saturday, 24
June
2017*

农历丁酉年　六月初一

星 期 六

蓝孔雀

蓝孔雀是印度的国鸟,非常受人尊敬,在大多数的印度教寺庙中均有圈养的蓝孔雀。

六月

25

Sunday, 25 June 2017

农历丁酉年　六月初二

星期日

印度捕猎孔雀

作为印度的国鸟,蓝孔雀数量众多,目前还属于无危级别。在19世纪,印度一些地区允许狩猎孔雀。在森林里并不容易击中猎物,且孔雀喜欢成群逃命,40到50只同时飞奔,猎人命中率极低。而且奇怪的是,孔雀避难的地方,老虎总是近在咫尺。可以说,狩猎孔雀危机四伏。

六月 26

Monday, 26
June
2017

农历丁酉年　六月初三

星期一

绿孔雀

(*Pavo muticus*)

绿孔雀体长180~230厘米,头部的冠羽和蓝孔雀迥异,与身体方向垂直,而蓝孔雀的冠羽顺着身体方向。野生绿孔雀现主要分布于中国的云南地区以及东南亚的部分地区,数量稀少。在中国被列为国家一级保护动物,在《世界自然保护联盟濒危物种红色名录》中被列为濒危。

六月

27

Tuesday, 27
June
2017

农历丁酉年　六月初四

星期二

灰孔雀雉（*Polyplectron bicalcaratum*）

  灰孔雀雉体长 33~67 厘米，雄鸟比雌鸟大一些，头部有蓬松的发状冠羽。目前灰孔雀雉主要分布在不丹、印度北部、缅甸、泰国、老挝以及越南等地，中国的云南西部亦有分布。主要栖息于热带雨林和季雨林中，目前数量稀少，在中国被列为国家一级保护动物。

六月

28

Wednesday, 28
June
2017

农历丁酉年　六月初五

星期三

灰孔雀雉

六月

29

Thursday, 29
June
2017

农历丁酉年　六月初六

星期四

灰孔雀雉

六月

30

Friday, 30
June
2017

农历丁酉年　六月初七

星期五

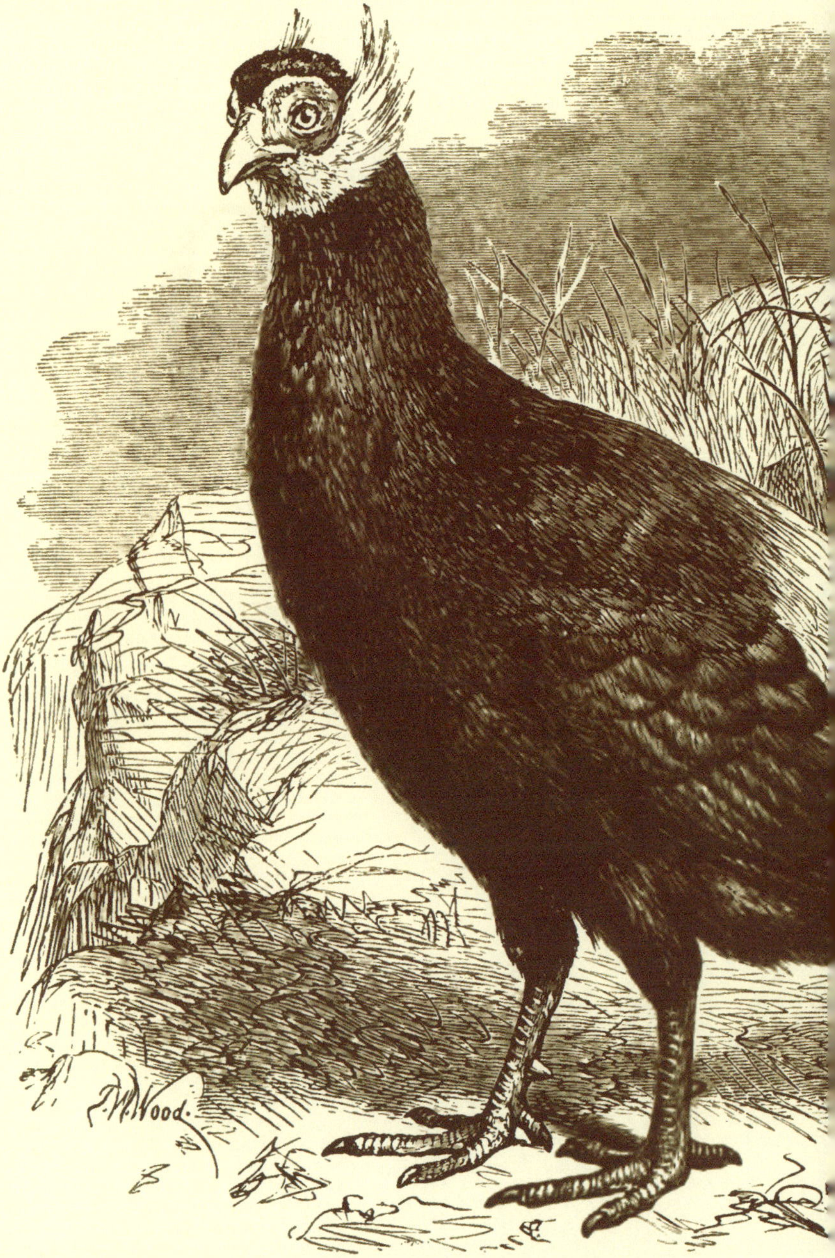
T.W. Wood

七月

July

巴拉望孔雀雉
(*Polyplectron napoleonis*)

七月

Saturday, 1
July
2017

1

农历丁酉年 六月初八

星期六（建党节）

大眼斑雉(*Argusianus argus*)

　　大眼斑雉尾羽非常长,部分雄性个体的体长可达 2 米。主要分布在马来西亚、苏门答腊岛以及加里曼丹岛的热带雨林中。由于栖息地的丧失和过度捕猎,大眼斑雉目前被列为易危物种。

七月

2

农历丁酉年　六月初九

Sunday, 2
July
2017

星期日

大眼斑雉求偶

七月

3

Monday, 3
July
2017

农历丁酉年　六月初十

星期一

大眼斑雉

七月

4

农历丁酉年　六月十一

Tuesday, 4
July
2017

星期二

瓦努阿图塚雉
(*Megapodius layardi*)

瓦努阿图塚雉体长30厘米左右,仅分布在瓦努阿图。主要栖息在低山地区的森林中,在近海岸处筑巢产卵,人为捡蛋是其面临的最大威胁,目前被列为易危物种。

七月

5

Wednesday, 5
July
2017

农历丁酉年　六月十二

星期三

摩鹿加塚雉

(*Eulipoa wallacei*)

体长31厘米左右，雌雄羽色相似，分布在华莱士线以东、巴布亚新几内亚以西的区域。主要生活在山区的热带雨林中，由于栖息地丧失、分布区狭窄以及过度捕猎，目前已被列为易危物种。

七月

6

Thursday, 6
July
2017

农历丁酉年　六月十三

星期四

塚雉（*Macrocephalon maleo*）

体长近60厘米，属于塚雉中体型较大的种类。塚雉是印度尼西亚苏拉威西岛的特有鸟种，生活在岛上的热带雨林中。产卵场所则位于开阔的沙地、火山灰以及海滩上。由于栖息地的丧失，目前塚雉被列为濒危物种。

七月

7

Friday, 7
July
2017

农历丁酉年　六月十四

星期五（小暑）

大凤冠雉

（*Crax rubra*）

体长90厘米左右，雌雄羽色差异显著。主要分布在自墨西哥东部至厄瓜多尔北部的中美洲地区，多栖息于常绿阔叶林和红树林中。目前被列为易危物种。

七月

8

Saturday, 8
July
2017

农历丁酉年　六月十五

星期六

栗腹冠雉

(*Penelope ochrogaster*)

体长 70 厘米左右，雌雄羽色相近。主要分布在巴西，也有可能见于玻利维亚。主要栖息于沼泽林地，也出现在稀树草原生境中。目前被列为易危物种。

七月

9

农历丁酉年　六月十六

Sunday, 9
July
2017

星期日

山冠雉

(*Penelopina nigra*)

体长 60 厘米左右，具有典型的性二型，雄性要小于雌性。主要分布在中美洲地区（墨西哥南部、洪都拉斯、尼加拉瓜中北部以及萨尔瓦多）。栖息在潮湿、茂密的森林中。目前被列为易危物种。

七月

10

Monday, 10
July
2017

农历丁酉年　六月十七

星 期 一

彩冠雉（*Penelope pileata*）

体长 80 厘米左右。分布在巴西亚马孙河流域的低地热带雨林中。目前被列为易危物种。

七月

11

Tuesday, 11
July
2017

农历丁酉年　六月十八

星　期　二

古铜冠雉

(*Penelope ortoni*)

体长 60 厘米左右。分布在南美洲的哥伦比亚和厄瓜多尔西部,主要栖息在较高海拔的热带雨林中,最高可达 1500 米。目前被列为濒危物种。

七月

12

Wednesday, 12
July
2017

农历丁酉年　六月十九

星期三

褐镰翅冠雉

(*Chamaepetes goudotii*)

体长60厘米左右。分布在南美洲的哥伦比亚、厄瓜多尔以及玻利维亚等地,主要栖息于湿润的森林及森林边缘地带。

七月   **13**   *Thursday, 13*
July
2017

农历丁酉年　六月二十

星期四

乌腿冠雉

（*Penelope obscura*）

体长 70 厘米左右。分布在南美洲的巴西、阿根廷、玻利维亚、巴拉圭和乌拉圭等地，多栖息在高大的森林、河谷林地以及小的河中岛屿等生境。

七月

14

Friday, 14
July
2017

农历丁酉年　六月廿一

星期五

紫冠雉（*Penelope purpurascens*）

体长 70~90 厘米。主要分布在中美洲的走廊地带，北部可达墨西哥，往南延伸到委内瑞拉，多栖息于潮湿的森林和林缘地带。

七月

15

Saturday, 15
July
2017

农历丁酉年　六月廿二

星期六

棕腹小冠雉

(*Ortalis wagleri*)

体长 65 厘米左右。分布在墨西哥，是墨西哥的特有种。多栖息于较为干旱的落叶林和半落叶林中。

七月

16

农历丁酉年　六月廿三

Sunday, 16
July
2017

星期日

棕腹小冠雉（上）和棕头小冠雉
(*Ortalis erythroptera*)

棕头小冠雉体长60厘米左右。主要分布在哥伦比亚、厄瓜多尔以及秘鲁，与棕腹小冠雉的分布区并不重叠。生境比较多样，干旱的落叶林、季雨林、潮湿的雨林、林缘地带、退化了的森林以及农田等都有它们的身影。

七月

17

Monday, 17
July
2017

农历丁酉年　六月廿四

星 期 一

披肩榛鸡（*Bonasa umbellus*）

  体长 45 厘米左右，雄鸟在求偶展示时颈部的环状羽毛会张开，类似披肩，因此而得名。披肩榛鸡分布在北美洲，主要在美国北部地区以及加拿大的大部分地区，生境多样，从内陆到海岸附近的林地生境中均有它们的踪迹。

七月

18

Tuesday, 18
July
2017

农历丁酉年　六月廿五

星期二

花尾榛鸡（*Tetrastes bonasia*）

体长35厘米左右，雌雄羽色有差异，雌鸟羽色暗淡，雄鸟喉部为黑色，在野外比较容易区分。花尾榛鸡分布广泛，欧亚大陆北部的针叶林生境中均有分布，中国境内主要见于东北地区的森林中。花尾榛鸡在中国东北地区被叫作"飞龙"，早期曾是重要的野味之一，数量下降明显，目前已经被列为国家二级保护动物。

七月

19

Wednesday, 19
July
2017

农历丁酉年　六月廿六

星 期 三

黑琴鸡（*Lyrurus tetrix*）

体长近 60 厘米，雄鸟略大，雌雄差异显著，雄鸟几乎全黑，而雌鸟以棕色为主。黑琴鸡分布广泛，在欧亚大陆北部的针叶林和针阔混交林中均有分布，在中国见于东北地区和新疆北部的天山、阿勒泰地区，属于国家二级保护动物。

七月

20

农历丁酉年　六月廿七

Thursday, 20
July
2017

星期四

黑琴鸡

七月　　　　　　21　　　*Friday, 21*
July
2017

农历丁酉年　六月廿八

星期五

黑琴鸡雌鸟

七月

22

Saturday, 22
July
2017

农历丁酉年　六月廿九

星期六（大暑）

黑琴鸡的求偶场

　　黑琴鸡的婚配制度为一雄多雌制，在繁殖季节雄鸟们会聚在一起互相展示，雌鸟则在四周观望，并最终选择自己的如意郎君。一般来说，位于中间地带的雄鸟更容易受到雌鸟的青睐。

七月

23

Sunday, 23
July
2017

农历丁酉年　闰六月初一

星期日

高加索黑琴鸡

(*Lyrurus mlokosiewiczi*)

体长38~53厘米,同黑琴鸡一样,雌雄差异显著,整体和黑琴鸡比较相似,但羽毛颜色偏绿,翅膀的白色翼斑位于翼角处。高加索黑琴鸡主要分布在欧洲东南部的高加索山及周边地区,生活在森林及林缘灌丛生境中。

七月

24

Monday, 24
July
2017

农历丁酉年　闰六月初二

星期一

西方松鸡（*Tetrao urogallus*）

　　西方松鸡是体型最大的松鸡类，雄鸟体长可达115厘米，雌鸟则只有60厘米左右。西方松鸡分布广泛，自西伯利亚中部往西一直到欧洲都有分布，往南可见于西班牙。主要栖息在针叶林和针阔混交林生境中。中国境内的新疆北部地区也有西方松鸡分布，属于国家二级保护动物。

七月

25

Tuesday, 25
July
2017

农历丁酉年　闰六月初三

星期二

西方松鸡

　　西方松鸡的白色型个体,这种色型比较少见,仅在某些亚种中出现。

七月

26

Wednesday, 26
July
2017

农历丁酉年　闰六月初四

星期三

西方松鸡

七月

27

Thursday, 27
July
2017

农历丁酉年　闰六月初五

星 期 四

西方松鸡

七月

28

农历丁酉年　闰六月初六

Friday, 28
July
2017

星期五

西方松鸡

七月

29

Saturday, 29
July
2017

农历丁酉年　闰六月初七

星期六

西方松鸡

七月

30

农历丁酉年　闰六月初八

Sunday, 30
July
2017

星期日

西方松鸡求偶

　　西方松鸡和黑琴鸡一样，属于一雄多雌制，在繁殖季节雄鸟会进行炫耀展示，吸引雌鸟。

七月

31

Monday, 31
July
2017

农历丁酉年　闰六月初九

星 期 一

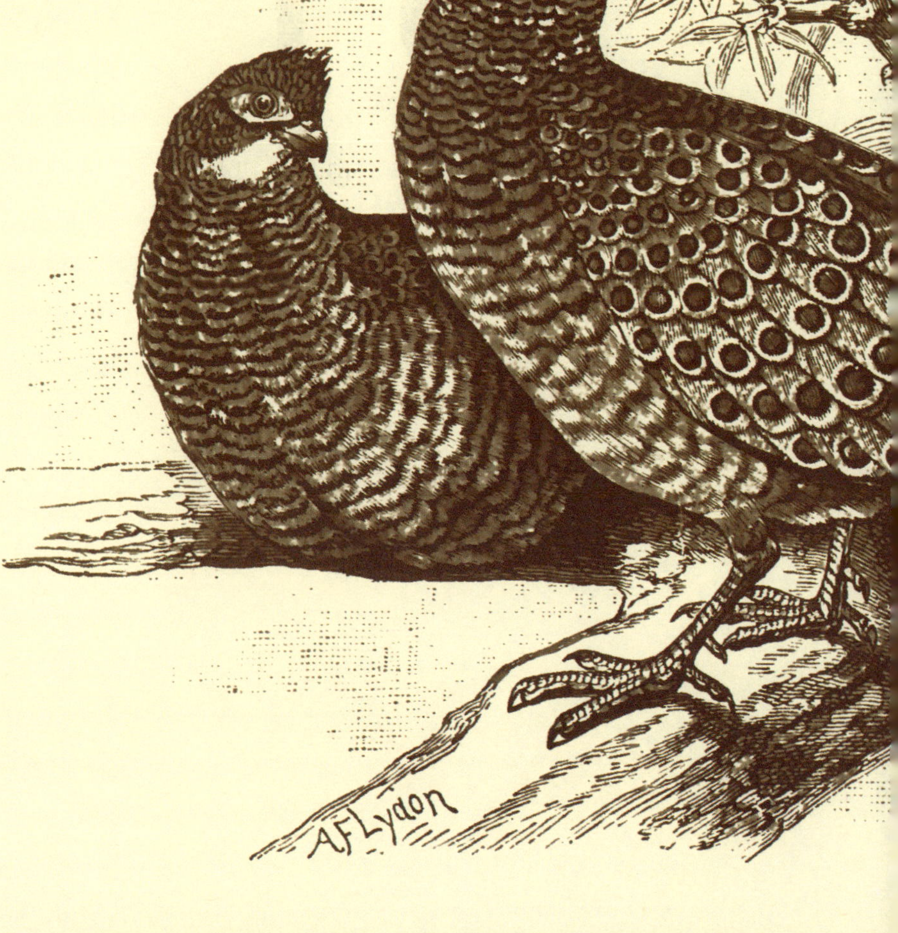
A.F. Lydon

八月

August

西方松鸡求偶场

八月

Tuesday, 1
August
2017

1

农历丁酉年 闰六月初十

星期二（建军节）

西方松鸡和人

  西方松鸡雄鸟的攻击力非常强,一般不惧人,会激烈地攻击入侵领域的人类。

八月

2

Wednesday, 2
August
2017

农历丁酉年　闰六月十一

星期三

西方松鸡冬猎

在欧洲,西方松鸡是一种重要的狩猎鸟类。

八月

3

Thursday, 3
August
2017

农历丁酉年　闰六月十二

星期四

草原松鸡（*Tympanuchus cupido*）

  体长 45 厘米左右，分布在美国中部地区，栖息于美国中部的平原，生境中多散布着橡树林地。目前被列为易危物种。

八月

4

Friday, 4
August
2017

农历丁酉年　闰六月十三

星期五

艾草松鸡（*Centrocercus urophasianus*）

体长 48~76 厘米，雄性大于雌性。雄鸟的尾羽长而尖，颈部有两个气囊，繁殖季节会充气膨大以吸引配偶。艾草松鸡分布在美国西部以及邻近的加拿大的部分省份，多生活在山区有灌丛的草地生境中。它们曾是北美地区的一种重要狩猎鸟类，现在由于栖息地丧失等原因，数量明显下降，已被列为近危物种。

八月

5

Saturday, 5
August
2017

农历丁酉年　闰六月十四

星期六

尖尾松鸡（*Tympanuchus phasianellus*）

  体长38~48厘米，雄性略大于雌性，雌雄羽色差异不显著。主要分布在加拿大以及美国北部的部分地区，草原、灌丛草原、灌木丛以及混交林等生境都是它们喜爱的生存环境。数量众多，也是北美地区的一种重要狩猎鸟类。

八月

6

Sunday, 6
August
2017

农历丁酉年　闰六月十五

星 期 日

柳雷鸟夏羽（*Lagopus lagopus*）

  体长40厘米左右，柳雷鸟冬季和夏季的羽色差异显著。夏季雌雄羽色相近，但雄鸟羽色略深，腹部白色，而到了冬季，雌雄的羽毛均变为全白色。柳雷鸟的分布广泛，整个北半球环北极圈一带的苔原、灌丛、森林以及草甸生境中均有分布，有20个亚种。中国境内的东北地区以及新疆北部地区亦有分布，属于国家二级保护动物。

八月

7

Monday, 7
August
2017

农历丁酉年　闰六月十六

星期一（立秋）

柳雷鸟冬羽

八月

8

Tuesday, 8
August
2017

农历丁酉年　闰六月十七

星期二

柳雷鸟冬羽

八月

9

Wednesday, 9
August
2017

农历丁酉年　闰六月十八

星期三

黑琴鸡和柳雷鸟杂交个体

  杂交个体在野外并不多见。

八月

10

Thursday, 10
August
2017

农历丁酉年　闰六月十九

星期四

岩雷鸟（*Lagopus muta*）

  体长 33~40 厘米，和柳雷鸟羽色类似，主要依靠头部以及翅膀的特征来区分。冬羽时岩雷鸟的喙基部至眼部有黑色贯眼纹，很容易和柳雷鸟区分。岩雷鸟的分布范围基本和柳雷鸟类似，见于北半球北部的许多地区。中国境内见于黑龙江西北部以及新疆北部，属于国家二级保护动物。

八月

11

农历丁酉年　闰六月二十

Friday, 11
August
2017

星期五

岩雷鸟夏羽

八月

12

Saturday, 12
August
2017

农历丁酉年　闰六月廿一

星期六

岩雷鸟冬羽

八月

13

农历丁酉年　闰六月廿二

Sunday, 13
August
2017

星期日

雉鹑（*Tetraophasis obscurus*）

  体长 48 厘米左右，雌雄羽色相近。雉鹑为中国特有鸟类，主要分布在四川、甘肃、西藏和青海的部分地区，多生活在海拔 3000 米以上的针叶林、灌丛以及多岩地带。属于国家一级保护动物。

八月

14

Monday, 14
August
2017

农历丁酉年　闰六月廿三

星 期 一

里海雪鸡（*Tetraogallus caspius*）

  体长 60 厘米左右，分布在里海南部和西部的高山生境中，多见于林缘、灌丛以及多岩地带。

八月

15

Tuesday, 15 August 2017

农历丁酉年　闰六月廿四

星期二

阿尔泰雪鸡
(*Tetraogallus altaicus*)

体长近60厘米,分布在中国新疆阿勒泰地区以及阿尔泰山脉,多见于高山草甸以及苔原等生境中,属于国家二级保护动物。

八月

16

Wednesday, 16
August
2017

农历丁酉年　闰六月廿五

星期三

阿尔泰雪鸡

八月

17

Thursday, 17
August
2017

农历丁酉年　闰六月廿六

星期四

暗腹雪鸡（*Tetraogallus himalayensis*）

体长 60 厘米左右，分布在阿富汗、土耳其至尼泊尔以及中国的西北部地区，非常罕见，主要生活在高山的多岩石草甸以及碎石滩生境中，属于国家二级保护动物。

八月

18

农历丁酉年　闰六月廿七

Friday, 18
August
2017

星期五

藏雪鸡（*Tetraogallus tibetanus*）

　　体长 50 厘米左右，分布在喜马拉雅山脉、从帕米尔高原至整个青藏高原，栖息于多岩石的高山草甸以及流石滩，在中国属于国家二级保护动物。

八月

19

Saturday, 19
August
2017

农历丁酉年　闰六月廿八

星期六

石鸡（*Alectoris chukar*）

  体长 38 厘米左右，分布范围广泛，欧亚大陆北方地区均有分布，广泛分布于中国境内的北方地区，多栖息于开阔的山区、高原、草原以及干旱草地。

八月

20

农历丁酉年　闰六月廿九

Sunday, 20
August
2017

星期日

红腿石鸡

(*Alectoris rufa*)

体长35厘米左右，分布在法国、意大利以及伊比利亚半岛地区，主要生活在农田以及开阔多岩的生境中。

八月

21

Monday, 21
August
2017

农历丁酉年　闰六月三十

星 期 一

漠鹑（*Ammoperdix griseogularis*）

　　体长 25 厘米左右，分布在土耳其以东至里海东南部的阿拉伯地区，多栖息于干旱多岩的戈壁生境。

八月

22

Tuesday, 22
August
2017

农历丁酉年　七月初一

星期二

沙鹑（*Ammoperdix heyi*）

  体长 25 厘米左右，分布在阿拉伯半岛及红海沿岸的非洲地区，多栖息于有岩石的荒漠和半荒漠生境中。

八月

23

Wednesday, 23 August 2017

农历丁酉年　七月初二

星期三（处暑）

黑鹧鸪（*Francolinus francolinus*）

体长35厘米左右，分布在欧亚大陆南部地区，自塞浦路斯和土耳其东部一直延伸到巴基斯坦和印度东部地区，多栖息于有水的生境中，如河岸和有湖泊的草原等。

八月

24

Thursday, 24
August
2017

农历丁酉年　七月初三

星期四

栗顶鹧鸪

(*Peliperdix coqui*)

体长 25 厘米，分布在非洲南部的广大地区，多栖息于各种各样的多草生境，如稀树草原以及稀疏的林地生境。

八月

25

农历丁酉年　七月初四

Friday, 25
August
2017

星 期 五

彩鹧鸪

(*Pternistis rufopictus*)

体长40厘米左右，分布在非洲的坦桑尼亚，多栖息于开阔平原和稀树草原。

八月

26

Saturday, 26
August
2017

农历丁酉年　七月初五

星期六

灰山鹑（*Perdix perdix*）

  体长 30 厘米左右，主要分布在欧亚大陆北部，中国见于新疆西北部的准噶尔盆地及阿尔泰山，多栖息于有矮草的开阔原野。

八月

27

农历丁酉年　七月初六

Sunday, 27
August
2017

星期日

灰山鹑

八月

28

Monday, 28
August
2017

农历丁酉年　七月初七

星期一（七夕节）

斑翅山鹑（*Perdix dauuricae*）

  体长 28 厘米左右，主要分布在中亚、西伯利亚、蒙古以及中国的北部地区，喜欢开阔的原野生境。

八月

29

Tuesday, 29
August
2017

农历丁酉年　七月初八

星期二

高原山鹑（*Perdix hodgsoniae*）

  体长 28 厘米左右，主要分布在喜马拉雅山脉和青藏高原，多见于海拔 2800~5200 米之间的多岩山坡生境。

八月

30

Wednesday, 30
August
2017

农历丁酉年　七月初九

星期三

马岛鹑

(*Margaroperdix madagarensis*)

体长30厘米左右,仅分布于马达加斯加岛,栖息于次生林地和灌丛,偶见于草地。

八月

31

Thursday, 31
August
2017

农历丁酉年　七月初十

星期四

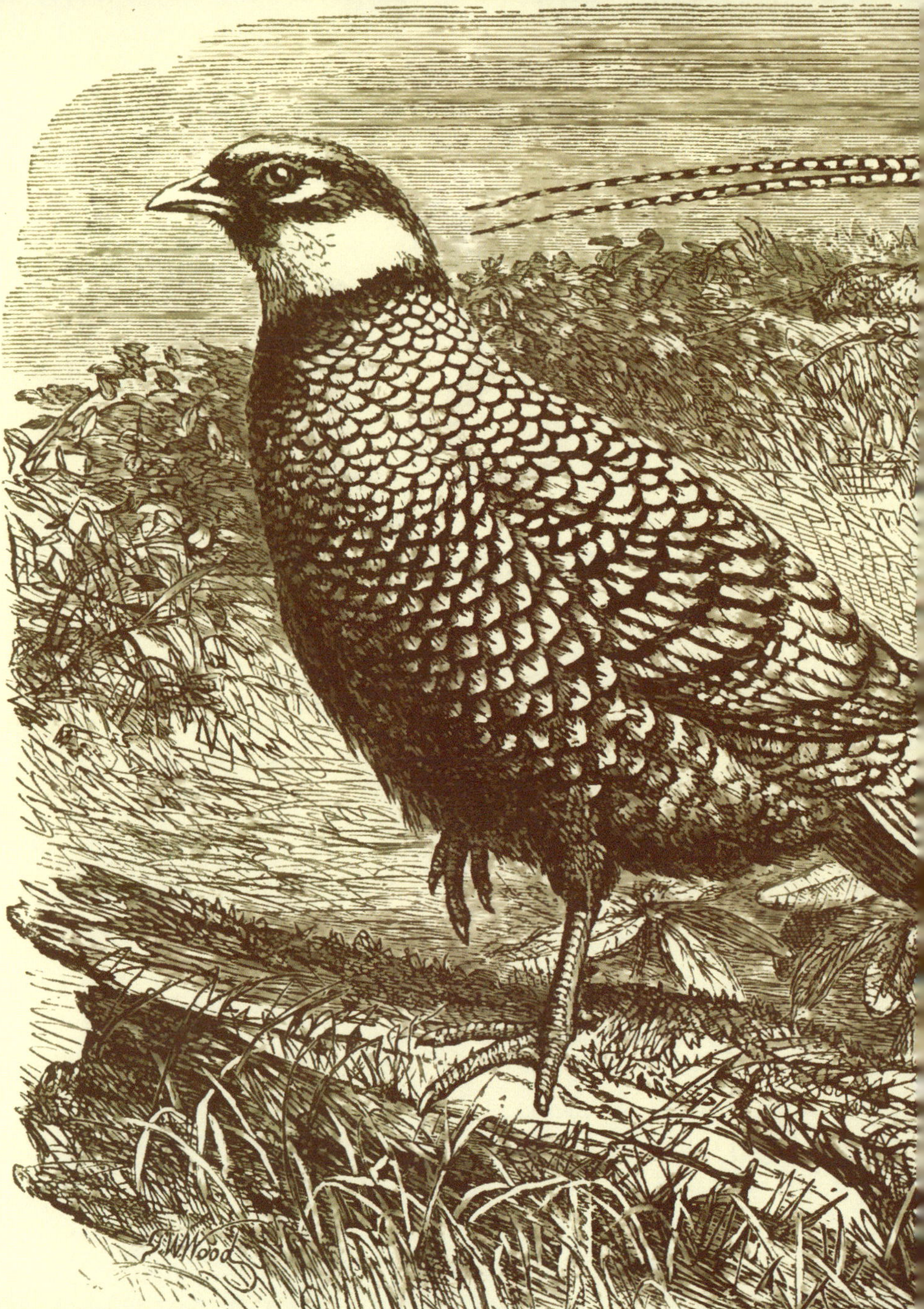

九月

September

霍氏长嘴山鹑
(*Rhizothera dulitensis*)

体长37厘米左右，仅零散分布在马来西亚的部分地区，生活在低山原始森林中，数量较少，被列为易危物种。

九月

Friday, 1
September
2017

1

农历丁酉年 七月十一

星期五

鹌鹑（*Coturnix coturnix*）

体长 18 厘米左右，分布在非洲、欧洲、亚洲西部和南亚等地。中国主要见于新疆西部以及西藏东南部地区，喜欢农耕区和草地等生境。

九月

2

Saturday, 2
September
2017

农历丁酉年　七月十二

星期六

日本鹌鹑

(*Coturnix japonica*)

体长 20 厘米左右，分布在亚洲东部、南亚东北部及东南亚。中国的大部分地区均有分布。栖息于矮草地和农田生境。现代人工饲养的鹌鹑多由日本鹌鹑培育而来。

九月

3

Sunday, 3
September
2017

农历丁酉年　七月十三

星期日

黑胸鹌鹑（*Coturnix coromandelica*）

　　体长约 18 厘米，主要分布在印度半岛以及中南半岛的部分地区，多栖息于草地和农田生境。

九月

4

Monday, 4 September 2017

农历丁酉年　七月十四

星期一

蓝胸鹑(*Excalfactoria chinensis*)

体长约14厘米,主要见于印度、中国南部、东南亚以及澳大利亚等地,栖息于草地、灌丛以及农田生境。

九月

5

Tuesday, 5
September
2017

农历丁酉年　七月十五

星期二（中元节）

蓝胸鹑

九月

6

Wednesday, 6
September
2017

农历丁酉年　七月十六

星期三

丛林鹑（*Perdicula asiatica*）

体长约 18 厘米，主要分布于印度，见于干旱灌丛以及多岩多草低矮灌丛生境中。

九月

7

Thursday, 7
September
2017

农历丁酉年　七月十七

星期四（白露）

岩林鹑(*Perdicula argoondah*)

体长约 18 厘米,主要分布于印度的西部地区,见于半干旱的具稀疏灌丛的荒漠生境。

九月

8

农历丁酉年　七月十八

Friday, 8 September 2017

星期五

阿萨姆林鹑（*Perdicula manipurensis*）

  体长约 20 厘米，主要分布于印度的阿萨姆邦，只生活在又高又密的草地生境。目前已被列为濒危物种。

九月

9

Saturday, 9 September 2017

农历丁酉年　七月十九

星期六

喜马拉雅鹌鹑（*Ophrysia superciliosa*）

  体长 25 厘米左右，仅分布在印度北部的喜马拉雅地带，见于南向的陡峭山麓的草地生境中。目前被列为极危物种。

九月

10

Sunday, 10
September
2017

农历丁酉年　七月二十

星期日（教师节）

雪鹑（*Lerwa lerwa*）

　　体长 35 厘米左右，分布于喜马拉雅山脉至中国的青藏高原和中西部地区。常见于高海拔的高山草甸及碎石地带，属于国家二级保护动物。

九月

11

Monday, 11
September
2017

农历丁酉年　七月廿一

星期一

白喉林鹑

(*Odontophorus leucolaemus*)

体长 25 厘米左右,分布于哥斯达黎加和巴拿马,见于热带和亚热带雨林中。

九月

12

Tuesday, 12 September 2017

农历丁酉年　七月廿二

星期二

黑额林鹑

(*Odontophorus atrifrons*)

体长 24~30 厘米，分布于哥伦比亚和委内瑞拉的部分区域，见于中海拔的山区热带雨林，被列为易危物种。

九月

13

Wednesday, 13 September 2017

农历丁酉年　七月廿三

星期三

赤胸山鹧鸪（*Arborophila hyperythra*）

体长27厘米左右，分布于加里曼丹岛中部地区，多栖息于各种山地森林中。

九月 14 *Thursday, 14 September 2017*

农历丁酉年　七月廿四

星期四

红头林鹧鸪(*Haematortyx sanguiniceps*)

体长 25 厘米左右,分布区基本和赤胸山鹧鸪重叠,见于加里曼丹岛中部的山区,多栖息于低海拔的山地森林,尤其是沙地和冲积平原上的森林。

九月

15

农历丁酉年　七月廿五

Friday, 15 September 2017

星期五

红胸山鹧鸪
(*Arborophila mandellii*)

　　体长30厘米左右,仅分布在印度东北部、不丹以及中国的西藏东南部等地,见于潮湿多竹子的常绿阔叶林中。目前被列为易危物种。

九月

16

Saturday, 16
September
2017

农历丁酉年　七月廿六

星期六

红嘴山鹧鸪(*Arborophila rubrirostris*)

体长29厘米,分布在印度尼西亚的西苏门答腊西海岸的山脉附近,见于中高海拔的山区森林以及灌丛中。

九月 17

Sunday, 17
September
2017

农历丁酉年　七月廿七

星期日

冕鹧鸪

(*Rollulus rouloul*)

体长约26厘米,分布于马来西亚和印度尼西亚等地,栖息于低山地区的常绿森林中。被列为近危物种。

九月

Monday, 18 September 2017

18

农历丁酉年　七月廿八

星期一

灰胸竹鸡（*Bambusicola thoracicus*）

  体长 30 厘米左右，中国的特有种，分布在四川东部至浙江南部以及广东北部的广大区域，生活在竹林、灌丛和多草生境中。目前已被引种至日本和美国夏威夷。

九月

19

Tuesday, 19 September 2017

农历丁酉年　七月廿九

星期二

彩鸡鹑（*Galloperdix lunulata*）

体长30厘米左右，主要分布于印度，见于多刺的灌丛生境。

九月

Wednesday, 20 September 2017

20

农历丁酉年　八月初一

星期三

赤鸡鹑（*Galloperdix spadicea*）

　　体长 38 厘米左右，主要分布于印度，栖息地类型多样，干旱、潮湿的山地灌丛均适合它们生存。

九月

21

Thursday, 21 September 2017

农历丁酉年　八月初二

星期四

斯里兰卡鸡鹑（*Galloperdix bicalcarata*）

体长 35 厘米左右，仅分布于斯里兰卡，栖息于潮湿的没有干扰的高大森林中，偶见于干旱一些的林地。

九月

22

Friday, 22 September 2017

农历丁酉年　八月初三

星期五

茶脸鹑

(*Rhynchortyx cinctus*)

体长20厘米左右,分布于中美洲地区的哥斯达黎加、洪都拉斯、尼加拉瓜、巴拿马以及哥伦比亚和厄瓜多尔的西海岸,栖息于海拔1500米以下的低山热带雨林中。

九月

23

Saturday, 23 September 2017

农历丁酉年　八月初四

星期六（秋分）

山齿鹑

(*Colinus virginianus*)

体长 25 厘米左右，分布于北美洲的中东部、中美洲以及加勒比海的部分岛国上，栖息地类型多样，因亚种而异，针叶林、林缘、灌丛以及农田等生境中均有它们的身影。

九月

24

Sunday, 24 September 2017

农历丁酉年　八月初五

星期日

血雉（*Ithaginis cruentus*）

　　体长约46厘米，分布在喜马拉雅山脉、中国中部和青藏高原地区，多栖息于高海拔的针叶林和灌丛生境。属于国家二级保护动物。血雉亚种众多，不同亚种之间羽色差异显著，后面几幅图分别为不同的亚种。

九月

25

Monday, 25 September 2017

农历丁酉年　八月初六

星 期 一

血雉

九月

26

Tuesday, 26 September 2017

农历丁酉年　八月初七

星期二

血雉

九月

27

Wednesday, 27
September
2017

农历丁酉年　八月初八

星期三

血雉

九月

28

Thursday, 28 September 2017

农历丁酉年　八月初九

星期四

红腹角雉(*Tragopan temminckii*)

  体长 68 厘米左右,主要分布在中国境内,以及喜马拉雅山脉东部、缅甸和越南的部分地区。主要生活在亚高山森林中。红腹角雉雄鸟炫耀时喉部会膨胀吹起,非常漂亮。属于国家二级保护动物。

九 月

29

Friday, 29 September 2017

农历丁酉年　八月初十

星 期 五

红胸角雉

(*Tragopan satyra*)

体长 70 厘米左右，主要分布在喜马拉雅山脉中段，中国仅见于西藏东南部。生活在高山灌丛生境中，属于国家一级保护动物，被列为近危物种。

九月

30

Saturday, 30 September 2017

农历丁酉年　八月十一

星期六

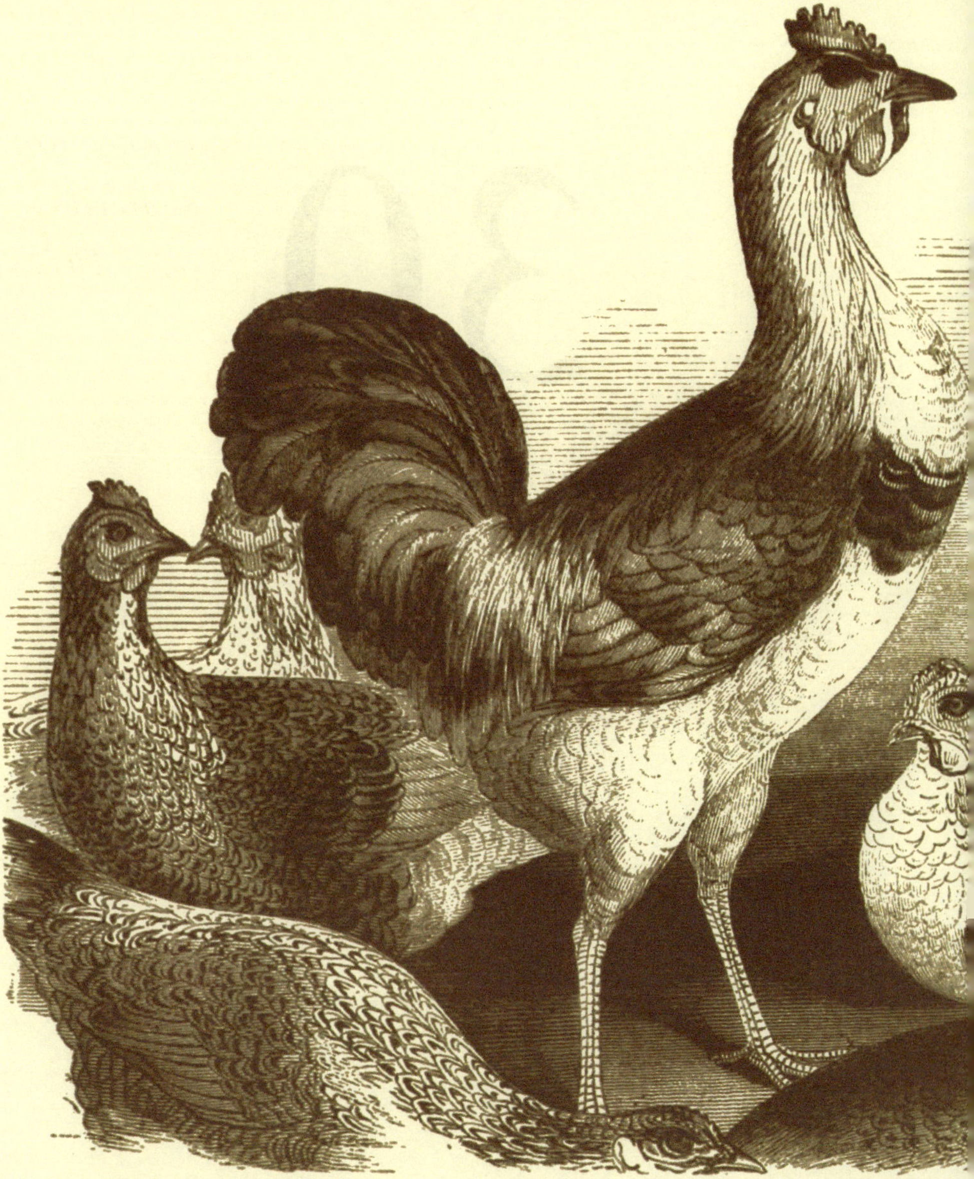

十月

October

红胸角雉

十月

Sunday, 1
October
2017

1

农历丁酉年 八月十二

星期日（国庆节）

黄腹角雉（*Tragopan caboti*）

  体长 61 厘米左右，中国特有鸟类，仅分布在福建、江西、浙江、广东和广西的局部地区，栖息于亚高山森林中，属于国家一级保护动物，被列为易危物种。

十月

2

Monday, 2
October
2017

农历丁酉年　八月十三

星期一

黄腹角雉

十月

3

Tuesday, 3 October 2017

农历丁酉年　八月十四

星期二

灰腹角雉（*Tragopan blythii*）

  体长68厘米左右，分布于喜马拉雅山脉东段的部分地区，中国见于西藏东南部和云南西北部。栖息于亚高山针叶林和杜鹃灌丛。属于国家一级保护动物，被列为易危物种，其中一个亚种受威胁等级接近濒危。

十月

4

Wednesday, 4
October
2017

农历丁酉年　八月十五

星期三（中秋节）

黑头角雉
(*Tragopan melanocephalus*)

体长 71 厘米左右，分布于喜马拉雅山脉的西段，中国仅见于西藏西部的局部地区。栖息于高山针叶林和灌丛生境中，属于国家一级保护动物，被列为易危物种。

十月

5

Thursday, 5
October
2017

农历丁酉年　八月十六

星期四

黑头角雉

十月

6

Friday, 6
October
2017

农历丁酉年　八月十七

星期五

黑头角雉

十月

7

Saturday, 7
October
2017

农历丁酉年　八月十八

星期六

黑头角雉雌鸟

十月

8

Sunday, 8
October
2017

农历丁酉年　八月十九

星期日（寒露）

勺鸡（*Pucrasia macrolopha*）

　　体长 61 厘米左右，主要分布在中国境内，还见于喜马拉雅山脉中段。中国国内分布范围广泛，见于华北山地、太行山、秦岭、横断山脉以及东南部的山地地区，栖息于多岩的开阔林地。亚种众多，各亚种羽色差异较大。属于国家二级保护动物。

十月

9

Monday, 9
October
2017

农历丁酉年　八月二十

星期一

勺鸡

十月

10

农历丁酉年　八月廿一

Tuesday, 10
October
2017

星期二

勺鸡

十月

11

Wednesday, 11
October
2017

农历丁酉年　八月廿二

星期三

勺鸡

十月

12

农历丁酉年　八月廿三

Thursday, 12
October
2017

星期四

勺鸡

十月

13

Friday, 13
October
2017

农历丁酉年　八月廿四

星期五

勺鸡

十月

14

农历丁酉年　八月廿五

Saturday, 14
October
2017

星期六

勺鸡

十月

15

Sunday, 15
October
2017

农历丁酉年　八月廿六

星 期 日

勺鸡雌鸟

十月

16

农历丁酉年　八月廿七

Monday, 16
October
2017

星期一

绿尾虹雉（*Lophophorus lhuysii*）

体长 76 厘米左右，为中国中部地区的特有鸟类。主要栖息在亚高山针叶林的林缘及高山灌丛生境中。属于国家一级保护动物，被列为易危物种。

十月

17

Tuesday, 17
October
2017

农历丁酉年　八月廿八

星期二

绿尾虹雉

十月 18 *Wednesday, 18 October 2017*

农历丁酉年　八月廿九

星期三

棕尾虹雉

(*Lophophorus impejanus*)

体长70厘米左右,主要分布于喜马拉雅山脉中段,中国见于西藏南部和东南部高海拔的林缘和高山草甸中。属于国家一级保护动物,被列为易危物种。

十月

19

Thursday, 19
October
2017

农历丁酉年　八月三十

星期四

棕尾虹雉

十月

20

农历丁酉年　九月初一

Friday, 20 October 2017

星期五

棕尾虹雉

十月   21   *Saturday, 21 October 2017*

农历丁酉年　九月初二

星期六

棕尾虹雉雌鸟

十月

22

农历丁酉年　九月初三

Sunday, 22
October
2017

星 期 日

棕尾虹雉

十月

23

Monday, 23
October
2017

农历丁酉年　九月初四

星期一（霜降）

棕尾虹雉

十月　　24　　*Tuesday, 24 October 2017*

农历丁酉年　九月初五

星期二

白尾梢虹雉（*Lophophorus sclateri*）

体长 70 厘米左右，主要分布于喜马拉雅山脉东段，中国见于西藏东南部和云南西北部，栖息于高海拔的林缘地带。属于国家一级保护动物，被列为易危物种。

十月

25

Wednesday, 25
October
2017

农历丁酉年　九月初六

星期三

黑鹇（*Lophura leucomelanos*）

  体长 70 厘米左右，羽毛具有金属光泽，分布于喜马拉雅山脉、印度东北部、缅甸北部和西部。中国国内比较罕见，仅见于西藏南部和东南部以及云南西部的部分地区，栖息于海拔较高的亚热带森林中，属于国家二级保护动物。

十月

26

Thursday, 26
October
2017

农历丁酉年　九月初七

星期四

黑鹇

十月

Friday, 27
October
2017

27

农历丁酉年　九月初八

星期五

黑鹇雌鸟

十月

28

Saturday, 28 October 2017

农历丁酉年　九月初九

星期六（重阳节）

白鹇

(*Lophura nycthemera*)

比黑鹇略大，体长94~110厘米，分布在中国南部至海南岛，国外分布于东南亚等地，主要栖息于开阔林地及次生常绿林中，和黑鹇在部分地区有重叠分布，二者似乎可以杂交。属于国家二级保护动物。

十月

29

Sunday, 29
October
2017

农历丁酉年　九月初十

星期日

白鹇

十月

30

Monday, 30
October
2017

农历丁酉年　九月十一

星期一

白鹇

十月 # 31

Tuesday, 31
October
2017

农历丁酉年　九月十二

星期二

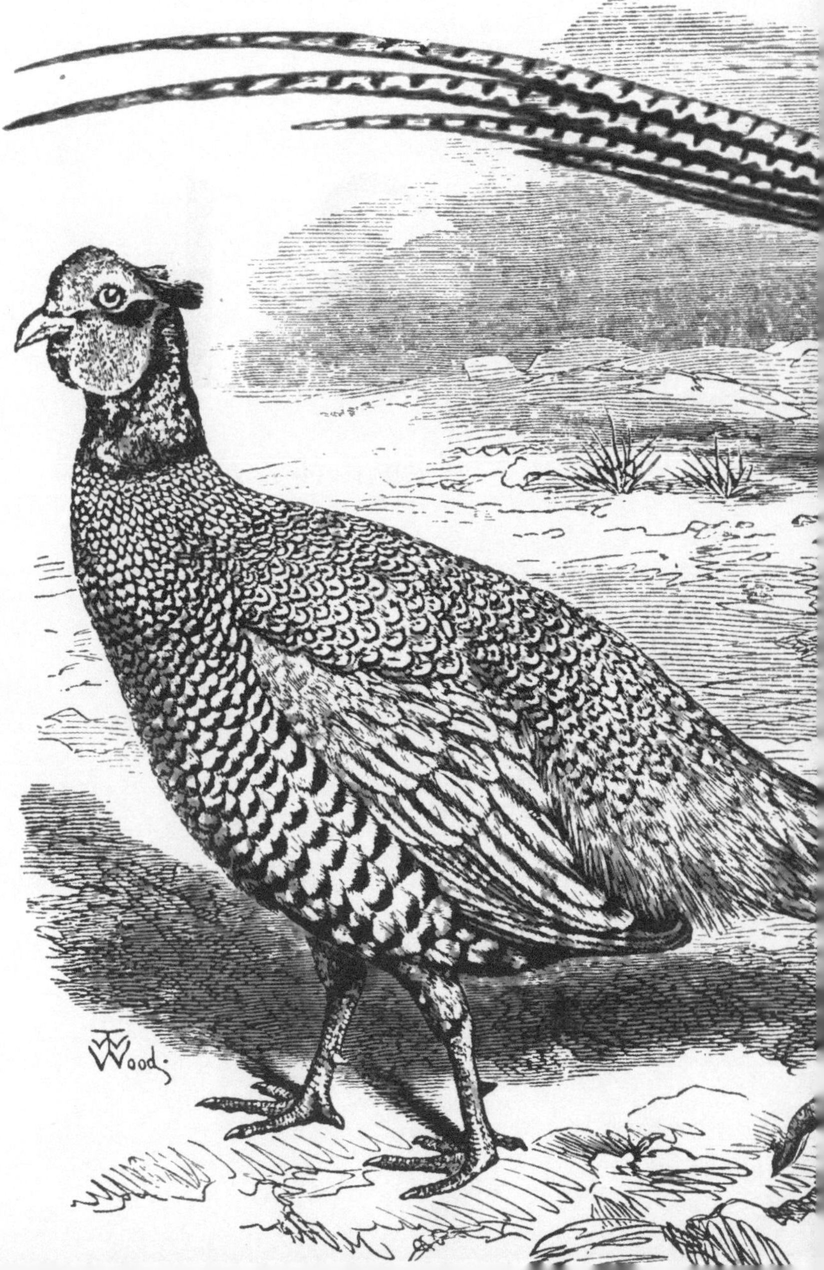
Wood

十一月

November

蓝鹇

(*Lophura swinhoii*)

体长 72 厘米左右，中国台湾地区的特有鸟类，栖息于中高海拔的潮湿林地中。属于国家一级保护动物，被列为近危物种。

十一月

Wednesday, 1
November
2017

1

农历丁酉年　九月十三

星期三

蓝鹇

十一月

2

Thursday, 2
November
2017

农历丁酉年　九月十四

星期四

蓝鹇

十一月

3

Friday, 3 November 2017

农历丁酉年　九月十五

星期五

鳞背鹇

(*Lophura bulweri*)

体长80厘米左右,仅分布在加里曼丹岛,栖息于亚高山的林地以及竹林生境中。被列为易危物种。

十一月

4

Saturday, 4
November
2017

农历丁酉年　九月十六

星期六

鳞背鹇

十一月

5

Sunday, 5 November 2017

农历丁酉年　九月十七

星期日

戴氏火背鹇(*Lophura diardi*)

体长 80 厘米左右，分布于中南半岛的泰国、缅甸、老挝、柬埔寨以及越南等地，主要栖息于低山的林地。

十一月

6

*Monday, 6
November
2017*

农历丁酉年　九月十八

星期一

凤冠火背鹇（*Lophura ignita*）

  体长65厘米左右，分布在加里曼丹岛以及邦加岛，主要生活在低山的林地生境中。由于栖息地比较专一，目前被列为近危物种。

十一月

7

Tuesday, 7 November 2017

农历丁酉年　九月十九

星期二（立冬）

凤冠火背鹇

十一月

Wednesday, 8
November
2017

8

农历丁酉年　九月二十

星期三

棕尾火背鹇（*Lophura erythrophthalma*）

  体长50厘米左右，分布在马来西亚半岛和西苏门答腊岛，仅生活在发育完好或者原始的低山森林中。目前被列为易危物种。

十一月

9

Thursday, 9 November 2017

农历丁酉年　九月廿一

星 期 四

褐马鸡

(*Crossoptilon mantchuricum*)

体长近1米，中国北方地区的特有鸟类，仅分布于山西、北京以及河北西北部的山区，且呈零散分布。栖息于山地森林以及灌丛林中，偶尔到草甸活动。属于国家一级保护动物，目前被列为易危物种，但实际情况可能接近濒危。

十一月

10

Friday, 10
November
2017

农历丁酉年　九月廿二

星期五

褐马鸡

十一月

11

Saturday, 11
November
2017

农历丁酉年　九月廿三

星期六

白冠长尾雉（*Syrmaticus reevesii*）

体长 180 厘米左右，部分个体超过 2 米。雄鸟的尾羽非常有特点，曾是戏剧表演中雉鸡翎的主要来源。白冠长尾雉是中国的特有鸟类，分布在中国中部和东部的部分地区，栖息于中低海拔的多林山地中。属于国家二级保护动物，被列为易危物种。

十一月

12

农历丁酉年　九月廿四

Sunday, 12
November
2017

星期日

白冠长尾雉

十一月

13

Monday, 13 November 2017

农历丁酉年　九月廿五

星 期 一

白冠长尾雉

十一月

14

Tuesday, 14 November 2017

农历丁酉年　九月廿六

星期二

白冠长尾雉

十一月

15

Wednesday, 15
November
2017

农历丁酉年　九月廿七

星期三

白冠长尾雉

十一月

Thursday, 16
November
2017

16

农历丁酉年　九月廿八

星期四

白颈长尾雉(*Syrmaticus ellioti*)

　　体长 81 厘米左右,是中国的特有鸟类,仅分布于东南部地区。栖息于针阔混交林中的灌丛和竹林生境。属于国家一级保护动物,被列为易危物种。

十一月

17

Friday, 17 November 2017

农历丁酉年　九月廿九

星期五

白颈长尾雉

十一月　　　　　　　　　　　　*Saturday, 18*
　　　　　　18　　　　　　　*November*
　　　　　　　　　　　　　　　　2017

农历丁酉年　十月初一

星期六（寒衣节）

白颈长尾雉

十一月

19

Sunday, 19 November 2017

农历丁酉年　十月初二

星期日

彩雉(*Catreus wallichii*)

  体长 1 米左右，分布在喜马拉雅山脉西部，自巴基斯坦东北部至尼泊尔西部。栖息于高山草甸和灌丛生境。被列为易危物种。

十一月

20

Monday, 20
November
2017

农历丁酉年　十月初三

星 期 一

彩雉

十一月

21

Tuesday, 21 November 2017

农历丁酉年　十月初四

星期二

彩雉

十一月

22

Wednesday, 22 November 2017

农历丁酉年　十月初五

星期三（小雪）

彩雉

十一月

23

Thursday, 23 November 2017

农历丁酉年　十月初六

星期四

彩雉

十一月

24

Friday, 24
November
2017

农历丁酉年　十月初七

星期五

铜长尾雉(*Syrmaticus soemmerringii*)

体长1米左右,分布于日本,属于日本特有鸟类。栖息于针叶林以及针阔混交林中。被列为近危物种。

十一月

25

Saturday, 25
November
2017

农历丁酉年　十月初八

星期六

铜长尾雉

十一月

26

农历丁酉年　十月初九

Sunday, 26
November
2017

星　期　日

绿雉（*Phasianus versicolor*）

  体长 80 厘米左右，是日本特有鸟类，也是日本的国鸟。属于日本的常见鸟类，栖息地多样，见于灌丛、茶园、河岸林地、农田以及城市公园等生境。

十一月

27

Monday, 27 November 2017

农历丁酉年　十月初十

星 期 一

绿雉

十一月

28

Tuesday, 28
November
2017

农历丁酉年　十月十一

星 期 二

雉鸡

(*Phasianus colchicus*)

体长 80 厘米左右，原先分布于东亚、中亚、西伯利亚东南部以及朝鲜半岛等地，现已被引入到欧洲、澳大利亚、新西兰、夏威夷以及北美洲等地。属于常见鸟类，见于各种生境，从低海拔到高海拔均有分布，也是平时人们最常说的野鸡。亚种多样，多达 30 个，各亚种之间羽色差异明显。

十一月

29

Wednesday, 29 November 2017

农历丁酉年　十月十二

星期三

雉鸡

十一月

30

Thursday, 30 November 2017

农历丁酉年　十月十三

星期四

A.F.Lydon

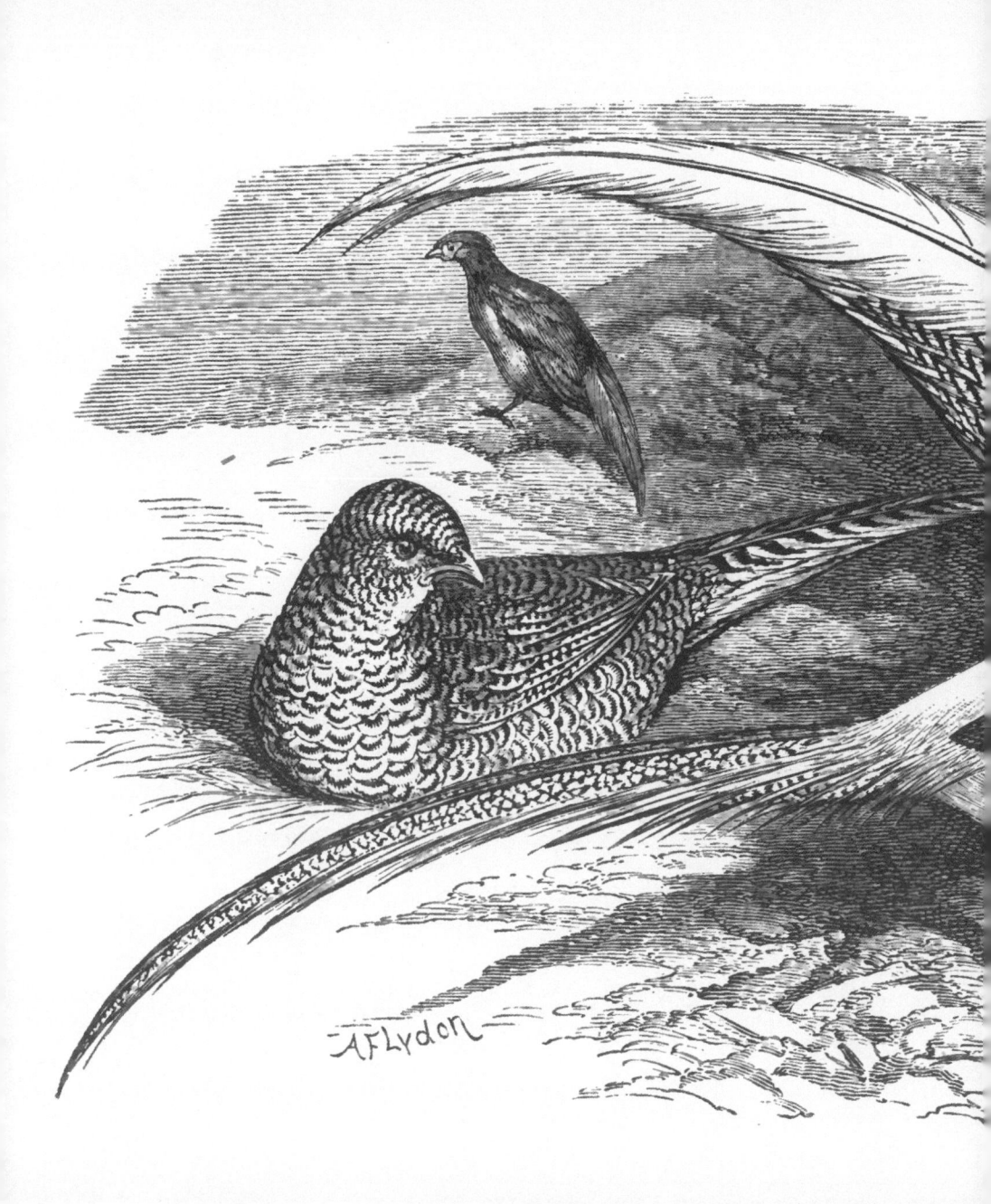

十二月

December

雉鸡

十二月

Friday, 1
December
2017

1

农历丁酉年 十月十四

星期五

雉鸡

十二月

2

Saturday, 2
December
2017

农历丁酉年　十月十五

星期六

雉鸡

十二月

3

农历丁酉年　十月十六

Sunday, 3
December
2017

星期日

雉鸡

十二月

4

Monday, 4 December 2017

农历丁酉年　十月十七

星期一

雉鸡

十二月

5

Tuesday, 5 December 2017

农历丁酉年　十月十八

星期二

雉鸡

十二月

6

Wednesday, 6
December
2017

农历丁酉年　十月十九

星期三

雉鸡

十二月

7

Thursday, 7 December 2017

农历丁酉年　十月二十

星期四（大雪）

雉鸡

十二月

8

Friday, 8 December 2017

农历丁酉年　十月廿一

星期五

雉鸡

十二月

9

Saturday, 9 December 2017

农历丁酉年　十月廿二

星期六

雉鸡

十二月

10

Sunday, 10
December
2017

农历丁酉年　十月廿三

星期日

雉鸡（下）以及雉鸡和白冠长尾雉的杂交个体（上）

十二月　　　　　11　　　*Monday, 11 December 2017*

农历丁酉年　十月廿四

星期一

红原鸡（*Gallus gallus*）

  体长 70 厘米左右，典型的性二型鸟类，雌雄差异巨大。分布于印度半岛、中南半岛、中国西南部以及东南亚的岛屿上，现已被引入北美洲和澳大利亚等地。中国国内见于云南、贵州、广西以及海南等地。红原鸡主要栖息于开阔林地以及次生常绿阔叶林中，在中国属于国家二级保护动物。一般认为，现代的家养鸡是从红原鸡驯养繁殖而来。

十二月

12

Tuesday, 12 December 2017

农历丁酉年　十月廿五

星期二

灰原鸡（*Gallus sonneratii*）

　　体长 70 厘米左右，没有红原鸡那样红亮。分布于印度中部和南部地区，主要栖息于常绿阔叶林和混交林中的竹林和灌丛中。

十二月

13

Wednesday, 13
December
2017

农历丁酉年　十月廿六

星期三

灰原鸡

十二月

14

Thursday, 14 December 2017

农历丁酉年　十月廿七

星期四

灰原鸡

十二月

15

Friday, 15
December
2017

农历丁酉年　十月廿八

星期五

灰原鸡

十二月

16

Saturday, 16
December
2017

农历丁酉年　十月廿九

星期六

蓝喉原鸡(*Gallus lafayettii*)

体长 70 厘米左右,相比于红原鸡,鸡冠没有那么发达。仅分布在斯里兰卡,自海岸至山地的灌丛和森林生境中均有分布。

十二月

17

Sunday, 17
December
2017

农历丁酉年　十月三十

星期日

蓝喉原鸡

十二月

18

Monday, 18
December
2017

农历丁酉年　十一月初一

星 期 一

绿原鸡（*Gallus varius*）

体长约70厘米，分布在爪哇岛、巴厘岛及其附近的岛屿上，栖息于海岸和山区河谷的林地中。

十二月

19

Tuesday, 19 December 2017

农历丁酉年　十一月初二

星 期 二

绿原鸡

十二月

20

Wednesday, 20
December
2017

农历丁酉年　十一月初三

星 期 三

白腹锦鸡（*Chrysolophus amherstiae*）

　　雄鸟体长接近 150 厘米，典型的性二型鸟类，雌雄差异巨大。白腹锦鸡主要分布在缅甸北部和中国境内，中国分布于西藏东南部、云南、四川南部、贵州西部以及广西西部等地，部分地区和红腹锦鸡的分布区重叠。多栖息于山坡林地和次生林中。属于国家二级保护动物。

十二月

21

Thursday, 21 December 2017

农历丁酉年　十一月初四

星期四

白腹锦鸡

十二月

22

Friday, 22
December
2017

农历丁酉年　十一一月初五

星期五（冬至）

白腹锦鸡

十二月

23

Saturday, 23
December
2017

农历丁酉年　十一月初六

星期六

白腹锦鸡

十二月

24

Sunday, 24
December
2017

农历丁酉年　十一月初七

星期日（平安夜）

红腹锦鸡(*Chrysolophus pictus*)

也叫金鸡,雄鸟体长接近1米,具有典型的性二型,雌雄差异巨大。红腹锦鸡为中国的特有鸟类,分布在青海东南部、甘肃南部、四川、陕西南部、湖北西部、贵州、广西北部以及湖南西部等地,主要栖息在有矮树的山坡以及次生林中。红腹锦鸡色彩艳丽,深受人们喜爱,陕西省宝鸡市的名称即由其而来。属于国家二级保护动物。

十二月　　　　　　　25　　　　　　*Monday, 25*
December
2017

农历丁酉年　十一月初八

星期一（圣诞节）

红腹锦鸡

十二月

26

Tuesday, 26 December 2017

农历丁酉年　十一月初九

星期二

白腹锦鸡（上）和红腹锦鸡（下）

十二月

27

Wednesday, 27 December 2017

农历丁酉年　十一月初十

星期三

红腹锦鸡

十二月

28

农历丁酉年　十一月十一

Thursday, 28 December 2017

星期四

红腹锦鸡

十二月

29

农历丁酉年　十一月十二

Friday, 29
December
2017

星期五

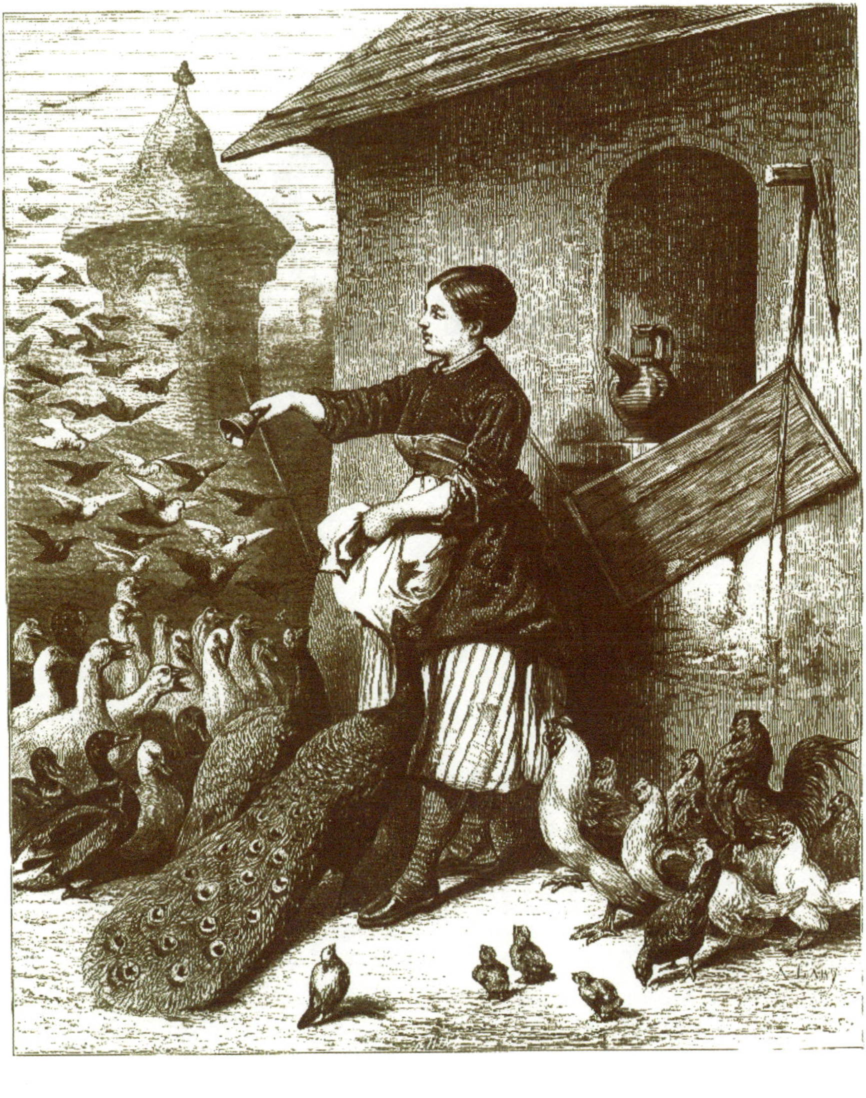

十二月

30

Saturday, 30 December 2017

农历丁酉年　十一月十三

星期六

THE POULTRY OF THE WORLD
Portraits of all known valuable breeds of fowls

十二月

31

Sunday, 31 December 2017

农历丁酉年　十一月十四

星期日

图书在版编目(CIP)数据

生肖日历:2017锦鸡吉祥/薛晓源主编;周硕编译.—北京:商务印书馆,2016
ISBN 978-7-100-12559-8

Ⅰ.①生… Ⅱ.①薛…②周… Ⅲ.①鸡—世界—通俗读物 ②十二生肖—文化—通俗读物 Ⅳ.①Q959.7-49 ②K892.21-49

中国版本图书馆 CIP 数据核字(2016)第 219842 号

所有权利保留。
未经许可,不得以任何方式使用。

生肖日历:2017锦鸡吉祥

薛晓源 主编

胡运彪 审校 周硕 编译

商 务 印 书 馆 出 版
(北京王府井大街36号 邮政编码100710)
商 务 印 书 馆 发 行
南京爱德印刷有限公司印刷
ISBN 978-7-100-12559-8

2016 年 10 月第 1 版   开本 780×1260 1/32
2016 年 10 月第 1 次印刷   印张 23¾
定价:98.00 元